Recent Titles by Margaret Pemberton from Severn House

THE FORGET-ME-NOT BRIDE

THE GIRL WHO KNEW TOO MUCH

THE LAST LETTER

MOONFLOWER MADNESS

TAPESTRY OF FEAR

VILLA D'ESTE

YORKSHIRE ROSE

THE FAR MORNING

THE FAR MORNING

Margaret Pemberton

This title first published in Great Britain 1998 by
SEVERN HOUSE PUBLISHERS LTD of
9–15 High Street, Sutton, Surrey SM1 1DF.
Originally published 1981 under the title *Harlot*.
This title first published in the USA 1998 by
SEVERN HOUSE PUBLISHERS INC., of
595 Madison Avenue, New York, NY 10022.

British Library Cataloguing in Publication Data

Pemberton, Margaret
   The far morning
   I.   Title
   823.9'14 [F]

   ISBN 0 7278 2246 2

Printed and bound in Great Britain by
MPG Books Ltd, Bodmin, Cornwall.

For Mamba,
with love.

Chapter 1

The two children ran breathlessly up the steeply winding road, their bare feet hardened to the rough cobbles. On either side back-to-back cottages pressed in on them, open doors giving brief glimpses of dark, crowded interiors. A few women stood in the doorways, coarse pinafores tied tightly around their thick waists, seeking a brief breath of air before returning to the ceaseless round of washing and scrubbing, baking and mending. A group of roughly clad children squatted by a gas lamp, playing jacks with handfuls of stones. They paused as the two ran past them, gazing after them with a mixture of resentment and curiosity.

"If he thinks he's coming back to us when *she's* gone, he's got another think comin'," their self-styled leader said disgustedly. "Bloody namby-pamby!"

"Why's he want to play with a girl anyhow?" his young admirer asked. "And a *gypsy* girl at that."

Another flurry of stones was sent flying into the air and was deftly caught on the back of a grimy hand.

"My mam says gypsies are mucky."

Their gang leader grinned at the dirt-streaked face before him and the tattered pants held up with a piece of string.

"God 'elp 'em if they're muckier than you, Tom Leach."

The girl was yards ahead of the boy, black hair

1

blowing untidily around her face as she pushed herself to the limit. Another fifty yards and they'd be in the cemetery and she would have won.

Josh Lucas swore. He was two years older, and to be beaten by a nine-year-old, and a girl at that . . . He closed his eyes, exerting every ounce of strength. He sensed her in front of him, her breath coming in harsh gasps, and then he passed her, through the broken down walls of the cemetery entrance, throwing himself over the nearest tombstone and struggling not to be sick.

She collapsed beside him, eyes dancing, holding her side as a stitch convulsed her thin body.

"You all right?" he managed at last, his chest hammering painfully, pushing a lank lock of hair back off his forehead.

She grinned. "Course I am." The stitch was easing now. She began to giggle. "Only let you win so you wouldn't be cross!"

"You did 'ell as like," Josh said grimly, wishing he had the strength to sit up and box her ears.

She didn't persist. Perhaps next time she would beat him, but primitive feminine intuition told her that it might be best not to. Boys were funny about things like that. Even boys like Josh. A silent truce being made, they simultaneously flopped over on their bellies and lay across a moss-covered mound that bore no stone or cross, and gazed across the weed-filled cemetery to the view of the city below them. Tier after tier of soot-blackened cottages led down to the glitter and bustle of the docks. A heat haze began to creep in from the sea, misting a fleet of working barges that were entering the wide estuary of the Mersey, their tall topmasts and tanned sails shimmering against the skyline. Christina half closed her eyes against the sun, trying to pick out the barge that was her own home from among the hundreds of boats that crammed the wharves, but the *Lucky Star* was indistinguishable among the trawlers and trading ketches.

"When do you sail?" Josh asked, not looking at her, his chin propped on his clenched hands.

"Tomorra." Josh did not speak but she saw the muscles in his shoulders sag and felt instantly repentant.

"Won't be long before we're back. Two weeks. Three if daddy sails on up to Rotterdam."

"Doesn't matter," Josh said indifferently, determined not to let her see that it did.

The sun beat down on their backs, striking through their thin clothes. Josh felt its heat on his buttocks and the backs of his legs. He sucked his bottom lip hopefully.

"Will you do it again?" he asked with apparent indifference.

Christina rolled onto her side, looking at him as he kept his gaze determinedly seaward.

"Do what? Race up that bloody hill? Not bloomin' likely."

"Not that," Josh said exasperatedly. "The other."

Christina sighed. The *Lucky Star* had been docking regularly in Liverpool for the last six years and in all that time the only friend she had made in dock was Josh. Now, for some reason that Christina didn't understand, he seemed far more interested in her taking her knickers down and looking at her than he did in playing hop-scotch or hide and seek, or pirates or cowboys and Indians.

"No," she said. "It's silly."

"Give you a bag of sweets," Josh said hopefully.

Unlike most of his companions he had no sisters and the sight of Christina's slim brown body aroused his curiosity. It had been done as a dare the first time and now all he wanted was another look. It wasn't much to ask after all.

"Go on," he nudged her with his elbow. "Got a bag of sherbet here."

He dug into his pocket, discarding bits of string, a piece of wire that served as a fishing hook and a broken bit of pencil, finally producing the treasured sherbet.

Christina eyed it longingly. Josh saw the look and knew he had won. The anticipation rising within him was far better than that of playing hide and seek.

"Go on," he urged. "Let's 'ave a look."

Christina sighed and pushed her tangle of black curls away from her face.

"If you really want to, but what the fuss is about I don't know. Can we play pirates after?"

"Yes. You can even be Black Jack," Josh said generously as Christina sprang to her feet.

A tattered skirt was lifted waist high with one hand while the other dragged down a pair of serviceable drawers that had seen better days. They hung round her ankles as Josh gazed wonderingly, wanting to touch the soft place that held so many mysteries, but not daring to ask. Christina had already hitched her drawers back up and grabbed the sherbet.

"Come on then. I'm Black Jack so *I'm* the one to win the treasure and *you're* my prisoner this time."

For close on two hours they shrieked and shouted as they ran between the tombstones, swinging from the giant oak trees that grew in the corner of the cemetery until Christina noticed with a pang that the sun was sliding down to the west and that the shadows were lengthening in the tall grass.

"I'll have to be getting back, Josh. Daddy will be worrying."

Josh shrugged. His dad never worried. But then Captain Haworth was an alien being to Josh, as indeed he was to the rest of Liverpool.

Glumly he dug his hands in his pockets. "Can I come back with you?"

"To the boat?"

"Course you can. That's if you remember to be quiet and not ask such a lot of stupid questions when daddy's reading."

Josh grunted noncommittally. If she'd said no he

would have had to sit on the pub step waiting for his dad and mum until closing time and that was hours away and it would be freezing cold by then. The warmth of the cabin aboard the *Lucky Star* was preferable, even if it did mean listening to the eccentric Captain reading to Christina. He couldn't see what she saw in it himself, sitting there night after night listening to her father read, but then it was well known in Liverpool that Captain Haworth wasn't quite right in the head so no doubt that accounted for it. He had a few special cronies he drank with on shore but not many. He didn't fit in and made no attempt to try. Josh supposed it was because his wife had been a gypsy. That was the name his friends yelled at Christina whenever they saw her.

"Gypsy—dirty little gypsy!"

Josh didn't understand it. For one thing Christina was cleaner than any of them. Leastways she never had lice in her hair and the cabin on board the *Lucky Star* was like nothing else Josh had ever seen. There was a big sturdy table, shelves filled with books, two comfortable chairs, a gaily colored tab rug that Christina had made herself.

His friendship with Christina had cost him dear in other ways. For one thing, the *Lucky Star* only docked every few weeks and when she did it was only for two or three days. For the rest of the time Josh had to fall back on his mates at school and in the streets, and they did not take kindly to being dropped whenever Christina appeared. If it weren't for the fact that he was tall and well built for his age and always came off the best in a fight, it was a foregone conclusion he would have had no one to play with during Christina's absences. As it was, his knuckles saw to it that he was grudgingly accepted by his street gang.

The epithet "dirty little gypsy" wasn't heard so much since Josh had given the last boy foolish enough to utter it not only a black eye and split lip but a broken nose into the bargain. His father had taken his belt to him for that, buckle-end as well, but though it had taken weeks for the welts to heal, Josh had not regretted it. It made him feel proud to be able to protect Christina. She was so good at everything else: at running, jumping, swimming, climbing, she was as daring as any of his mates. Yet in this one thing she was vulnerable and he, Josh, could enjoy the feeling of superiority.

"Hello, young fella." Captain Haworth held a hand out to the filthy urchin, climbing aboard the *Lucky Star* with his daughter.

Josh, feeling every kind of a fool, took it awkwardly.

Captain Haworth threw his arm around his shoulders.

"Nice to have the pleasure of your company. What'll it be? Cocoa or hot milk?"

"Cocoa, please," Josh said, wondering if the captain knew that his visits on board the *Lucky Star* were the only time he drank anything other than tap water, strong tea or the dregs of his father's beer.

John Haworth led Josh down into the cabin while Christina bustled happily in the galley, making three steaming mugs of cocoa and sliding a few biscuits onto a plate.

Two chairs thick with home-made cushions were pulled up to the table and Christina set the tray down, seeing with feminine pleasure the expression on Josh's face when he saw the biscuits. Then she pulled up a low stool and sat at her father's feet. It was not yet dark, but Captain Haworth pulled red plush curtains across the porthole and lit the oil lamp that swung low over the bleached and scrubbed table, creating the atmosphere he and his daughter loved best.

"I think we'd better put *Pride and Prejudice* to one side this evening, my love," her father said fondly, rumpling the riotous curls. "I doubt whether Elizabeth and her silly sisters will be of interest to Josh."

"Not bloomin' likely," Josh said fervently. "Sounds soppy."

"Oh, but it isn't!" Christina's dark eyes glowed as she hugged her arms around her knees. "You see, Elizabeth's mother wants her to marry Mr. Collins but Elizabeth thinks she is in love with Mr. Wickham, though of course she is *really* in love with Mr. Darcy but she won't admit it and neither will he. That he *loves* her I mean. And he is terribly rich and owns a fine house and park and there are balls and parties . . ."

"Sounds a lot of rubbish to me," Josh said.

"Then we will continue with the story we were reading when you were last with us," Captain Haworth said, suppressing a smile. *"Robinson Crusoe."*

Josh brightened. "Is that the one about the geezer that gets shipwrecked?"

"The very one," Captain Haworth replied solemnly.

"Then that's all right. Just so long as it ain't soppy. You know, *girls!"*

"I assure you, *Robinson Crusoe* is a book any man can be proud to have read," Captain Haworth said gently, selecting the green-bound volume. "Now where were we? Yes. Here we are. I marked it specially."

Christina leaned her head lovingly on her father's lap. Josh leaned back well-content, the sounds of the docks fading and the world narrowing into a charmed and timeless circle as Captain Haworth held the volume in his massive hands and began to read.

" 'I, poor miserable Robinson Crusoe, being shipwrecked, during a dreadful storm in the offing, came on shore in this dismal, unfortunate island, which I called "The Island of Despair," all the rest of the ship's company being drowned, myself almost dead.' "

"Don't envy him," Josh said with a laugh. "Even Black Jack couldn't get out of that one!"

"Oh do be quiet," Christina said crossly, "and let daddy get on with his story."

Josh subsided. She was a queer one and no mistake.

He wanted to know what happened to the geezer as
well, but it was only a story after all. To look at Christina's face you'd think every blinkin' word was true.
And *Daddy*. Dad. Me pa. Me father. But *Daddy!* He
supposed she'd picked that up from that other book
about the dandy and the big house.

It was going on for eleven before Captain Haworth
indicated that Josh should be returning home. By now
the sounds of the pubs emptying carried even into the
sacrosanct cabin of the *Lucky Star*. Josh's parents
would be weaving their way homewards. The boy
would have been spared a long wait for one night at
least.

"Go to bed, lass. I'll take a stroll with Josh and see
him home."

"I don't need no seeing 'ome!" Josh said indignantly.

A crowd of sailors fell out of the nearest pub, obscenities filling the air.

Captain Haworth re-lit his pipe, lying glibly. "Course
you don't lad, but I have a friend to see and you'll be
company."

Slightly mollified, Josh allowed himself to fall into
step beside the impressive figure of the captain. The
man was a giant. Six-foot-three at least. The sailors,
drunk as they were, gave him a wide berth. The dockside lights were left behind them as they entered the
warren of two up and two down cottages, the passageways between them sinister and dark.

Josh hadn't been afraid of going home by himself
through streets full of drunken seamen. He'd come a
cropper once or twice, but he knew how to steer clear
of trouble and though only eleven could fend well
enough for himself. Still, it was nice having someone
to walk with, someone who talked to him as an equal.

"So you don't like school, lad?"

"Not flippin' likely. Old Gawthorpe does nowt but
box our ears and as to old Porritt . . ." Josh shuddered
descriptively.

"What sort of a man is Porritt?" the captain asked.

"Isn't a man. It's a woman. Sort of makes it worse being hit by a woman."

"Does she box your ears as well?"

Josh shook his head. "No. She used to, but she brained little Willie Jones senseless and his big brother came down the school and there was all hell on. Thought he was going to choke the life out of her. Now the old cow just uses a cane but it don't 'alf hurt."

"And when does she do that? Whenever you are insolent?"

Josh laughed. "She does it all the time. Get a sum wrong and there's old Mother Porritt behind you, just waiting to swipe your backside. It's . . ." Josh struggled for words, ". . . it's *humiliating.*"

The captain nodded understandingly. "Can you do your sums, Josh?"

Josh grinned. "No, and neither would you if you knew you were going to get beaten 'alf to death when you tried to answer. Come to think of it, no one in our class can do sums and with old Porritt teaching us, I reckon they never will."

The captain sucked on his pipe thoughtfully. The school to which Josh was referring was the one the authorities said Christina should attend. Should have attended for the last four years. After listening to Josh, the captain decided he would take even stronger measures if anyone tried to force Christina to attend a school that taught by fear alone.

The trouble was, he was more than just an itinerant sailor. His cousin and wife and five children lived in Liverpool. He himself docked with clocklike regularity. His run was a simple one. Any cargo he could find was shipped from Liverpool to the ports of the Low Countries. Then he reloaded at Ostende or Rotterdam and returned. The only school it was practical to send her to was Josh's, but Captain Haworth had made his decision years ago and he'd never regretted

it. She'd learn more from him in a week than she
would learn in that mausoleum in a lifetime.

"Looks like me mam's in," Josh said, breaking in
on his thoughts as they stopped outside a smoke-be-
grimed cottage with a piece of rough calico hung on
a string to serve as a curtain.

"Goodnight Josh." The captain took his hand in his
giant paw. "I know you look after Christina and I
appreciate it." Then he swung on his heel, striding
back toward the docks.

Josh came as near to blushing as he had ever done.
The captain had thanked him for looking after Christina. Man-to-man it had been. He squared his shoulders and stepped into the small room lit only by an oil
lamp and with masses of damp clothes strung across
above the blackened range.

"Where the soddin' hell 'ave you been?" his mother
asked and then, not waiting for a reply, said "Get fire
laid for morning. I've 'ad one too many and your dad
still ain't 'ome."

After laying the fire, he scurried up to the room he
shared with his three younger brothers. They were
sleeping heavily and Josh slid in next to young Sam,
snuggling up to him for warmth. It would be a long
time till he saw Christina again. He remembered the
afternoon in the cemetery when she had let him look
at her, and felt suddenly hot, his hands going instinctively down between his legs. Jimmy Murdoch had
actually done it once. Just what doing it quite entailed
Josh wasn't too sure and he wasn't going to look a
fool in front of a fourteen-year-old like Jimmy Murdoch by asking. And whatever it was he couldn't do
it with Christina. She was only nine. Jimmy said he'd
done it with Kate Kennedy and that Kate had liked it.
She was only one form above him and whenever he
saw her he couldn't help wondering and imagining her
with Jimmy Murdoch. Kate had breasts too. He wondered how long it would be before Christina grew
breasts. Perhaps if he scrounged all he could this next

three weeks, he could earn enough money to buy Christina something really pretty and then perhaps she'd lie down for him like Jimmy Murdoch said Kate had done and then he would touch her and have a proper look. Why the hell, he thought unreasonably, his hand working feverishly, couldn't Christina be *older*.

The captain strode quietly back toward his boat. He didn't like leaving Christina alone even for a short while, but neither did he like the thought of young Josh walking home through streets crowded with drunks and prostitutes.

She was asleep when he opened the cabin door, her hands folded beneath her cheek, her knees drawn up to her chin.

Captain Haworth smiled tenderly down at her. Gently he lifted a stray curl away from her mouth and tucked the knitted blanket more securely around her shoulders. The very idea of her being caned by some sadistic old woman by the name of Porritt made him feel physically sick. She was his. All his. And no one, not even the Lord Mayor of Liverpool himself, would do anything to prevent John Haworth educating his daughter the way he saw fit.

He went back into the main cabin and put the book back on the shelf with the others. He refilled his pipe, sitting in the darkness thoughtfully. It had been a long time since his own schooldays. Close on forty years. His thick eyebrows flew up in surprise. Was it possible he was nearly fifty? He sighed. Life, which seemed to drag by so interminably slow at times, did finally slip away. Fifty years old and nothing to show for it but a battered hulk of a boat and an unbelievably beautiful daughter. And this for a man who had had the best education his father could find. Latin. Greek. A whole world away from the schools that greeted young Josh every day. He had entered the Royal Navy at eighteen, made officer rank by the time he was twenty-one, married respectably to a girl his family had approved of. Even after all those years he shivered. God! What a life she'd led him. She was fair-haired and dainty and he was envied by every man he met. And if they had known her in the bedroom he would have evoked equal amounts of pity. Physical intimacy, his young bride had confidently told him on their wedding night, was unnecessary. Her mother had told her all about it and she had no desire to behave in such an unladylike way. She was sure John would understand. John had not, but he had waited patiently, confident that love and affection would wear down her resistance. It did not. Mary Goodman even hated to be touched. If he held her hand she would remove hers fastidiously, wiping it on her cambric handkerchief as if he had soiled it. For over a year he had exerted patience, cajoled, been as tender as it was possible for any man to be, all to no avail. Then with surprise and relief he realized he no longer wanted this porcelain piece of delicate finery in his bed. He desired her as little as she desired him. He'd bought her a house, settled an annual amount out of his income on her and never saw her again. For the next ten years he had drunk and whored his way round the ports of the world. Then, in a gaudy tavern on a Spanish waterfront, he had seen a woman dance, her black hair swinging round her like a glossy curtain, her dark eyes flashing, her skirt swirling around long slender legs as she whirled on a table top surrounded by a crowd of clapping, cheering sailors.

Carlotta. He never knew her second name because she never knew it herself. From the night he first set eyes on her he was never parted from her. That she was a bastard, a whore, a foreigner, all was of no account. It had been like the coming together of two great tides. No force on earth could have parted them. His family disowned him. The Navy no longer required his services and for five blissful years John and Carlotta had sailed the seas together, needing no one but each other. His throat constricted and he rose to his feet. Memories. He was a fool to have given in to them. He tried to close them from his tired brain but they assailed him on all sides.

Carlotta giving birth to Christina miles out in the Mediterranean and with no one to help her but himself. Two happy months shored up in Mahon while Carlotta regained her strength and they'd strolled hand in hand up the steep grassy hillside to the red and white mansion that had housed two other lovers. Lord Nelson and Lady Hamilton. Christina running as a two year old into Carlotta's outstretched arms. The sound of Carlotta singing her babe to sleep. Whispering her caresses to him in the darkness of the night. Carlotta . . . To live without her was a physical pain. One that never eased.

She had caught fever off the coast of Italy and died within three days. John Haworth remembered all too vividly his uncomprehending numbness. She had to be buried, his beautiful, vivacious Carlotta, but where? How? He had been brought up a Protestant but hadn't been inside a church for years. He had no idea what faith Carlotta was. To hand her over to the ministrations of strangers was unthinkable. The afternoon that she died John Haworth docked at a small village in America. Taking his little daughter by the hand he had led her up into the fields and they had gathered armfuls of summer flowers, jasmine and mimosa and sweet-smelling bougainvillaea. Then, while the little girl watched, wondering why mummy didn't move any more, John Haworth clumsily made garlands of the flowers, placing them round her neck and wrists, laying a perfect red rose on her breast. Tears coursing down his cheeks, he had laid her on a lovingly made boat of wood and sailed out through the Straits of Gibraltar and into the Atlantic. Finally, in the pale light of dawn he had slipped the raft afloat, Carlotta's black hair trailing behind her like that of a sea nymph. He had stood at the helm watching as the frail bier and its precious cargo disappeared from view, knowing it would be only a matter of time before it sank beneath the heavy swell of the grey-green waves.

That night Christina had been frightened and bewildered as her big, laughing father had wept. Not understanding, she had toddled into his cabin, pushing her chubby little hand into his.

John Haworth saw her clearly for the first time in twenty-four hours. The mop of unruly dark curls, the near black eyes, the curve of the lips. He hadn't lost Carlotta completely. He still had Christina and while he still had her, Carlotta would live on. He had sat her on his knee, hugging her so tight that it felt as if the breath was being squeezed from her tiny body. From that day on nothing separated John Haworth from his daughter, and from that day on he never sought comfort in the arms of another woman. To do so would have been sacrilege.

Chapter 2

When Christina awoke the *Lucky Star* was far out in the heavy swell of the Irish Sea, her great mass of brown canvas carrying her along at a brisk pace, her blunt bows creaming the water. She was a sturdy ship. Flat-bottomed and made of fine English oak with pitched pine decks, she was designed to carry anything from coal to the Continent to china clay from Cornwall to the Thames. Her father was at the helm, his thick-knit blue jumper protection against the cold breeze.

Christina knew her mother had knitted him the jumper. She had to darn it many times but he would never let her throw it away, and she wondered if he would let her knit him a new one. A few gulls flew desultorily landwards and the sea and sky were blank and grey, but Christina breathed in a deep breath of pure joy. Here she was free. Away from the rows and rows of crowded cottages, the oppressive bustle of the docks. This was what she liked best. Standing next to her father, the fresh clean wind on her face and the sea stretching endlessly around them.

Josh had no inclination to be a seaman, and Christina could not understand it. Once, many months ago, she had managed to wheedle him aboard the *Lucky Star* for a day's voyage and he had been violently ill and swore he would never put to sea again.

Ned Carter, so old no one else would employ him, grinned across from the stern. "Tell the captain the wind's backed an' come on to blow. They'll be no chance of a bit of fishing this trip. 'Tis beginning to blow hard. You'd best get below and into something warmer. I told Captain twasn't bitty when we shoved off."

The cream-capped waves were beginning to rise. Christina watched in anticipation. The rougher the weather the more exhilarating she found it. Then, as the wind began to blow through her thin frock, she did as Ned suggested and went below for warmer clothes.

By the time they reached the Channel the storm had blown itself out. Her father leaned against the mainmast, a preoccupied expression on his face, and Christina watched him, openly admiring the strong muscular body, noting that the blue of his jumper matched the blue of his eyes; then, as he became aware of her gaze, she saw how the web of tiny lines in the weather-beaten face creased round the corners of his eyes as he smiled across at her.

Captain Haworth was in no hurry to reach Ostende. Today was the tenth of April. Six years to the day since he had gently slipped Carlotta into the hungry waves of the Atlantic. He had an overwhelming urge to change direction, to cross the Bay of Biscay and out to the spot where he had committed her to the sea. Common sense got the better of him.

Christina, able to sense every shift in her father's mood, drew close to him.

"What is it, daddy? You look sad."

He tucked her arm in his, staring seawards, seeing things she could not possibly see.

"It's the tenth," he said explanatively.

Christina squeezed his hand, mortified that she had forgotten the anniversary of her mother's death. She tried to remember her but it was hard. Genuine memories inextricably mixed with the stories her father had told her of Carlotta. She could remember a laughing face and a feeling of warmth and the thick black hair that swung waist-length. Not curly like hers but straight and glossy as a raven's wing. Father and daughter remained in understanding silence with their own thoughts as the *Lucky Star* loped lazily along the southern coast of England.

They were sailing so close to land now that Christina could make out little towns and villages with heather-clad hills rising behind them. There was no sign of the soot-filled air that clung around Liverpool and Christina wondered idly if perhaps life in a small village, with cloud-capped hills behind, might not be quite pleasant. But not for good. Only as a port. Perhaps they could begin to use the southern coast of England as a port, and then she remembered Josh and knew how much she would miss him. No. Liverpool it would have to be. Surely two days out of twenty-one wasn't asking too much.

To Josh, the waiting for the *Lucky Star* seemed endless. Tom Leach had snitched to Jimmy Murdoch about Josh's preference for a girl's company—a gypsy brat at that, and no more than a kid into the bargain. Jimmy Murdoch had taunted him in front of the other boys, asking Josh if Christina was as good in the grass as her mother had been. Josh, not knowing exactly what the older boy meant but knowing it was an insult to both Christina and her mother, had hit out with all the force of a clenched fist. The other boys had scattered in a wide circle. Josh Lucas was known for his prowess with his fists, but Jimmy Murdoch was fourteen and big with it. To Josh's humiliation he had been left in the dust of the street, a bloodied nose streaming down over his torn shirt and pants. That had been the occasion for another belting from his father and Josh, determined to salvage his pride, had immediately gone out and taken on three of his contemporaries, leaving them battered and bruised and pleading for a truce.

Having regained some of his self-esteem, Josh presented himself at school the next day, arrogantly ignoring Jimmy Murdoch's presence. Kate Kennedy, having heard of the fight from the boastful victor, looked at him with interest. Of course he was still only a kid, but a good-looking one. She wondered what he'd be like in four years' time, then turned her attention back to Jimmy Murdoch who was suggesting that they go up to the brook together after school.

Finally in the golden light of early morning the *Lucky Star* slipped into port. Josh, deciding that school could go to hell for the day, ran down to meet her. Christina grinned, waving at him from the top of a pile of rope ends.

"Comin' up the hill?" he yelled, as she jumped nimbly across onto the dockside.

She shook her head regretfully. "Have to go and visit Uncle Miller first. You know that, Josh."

"After then? Up in the cemetery?"

"After," Christina agreed, for once her dark eyes not sparkling. "Oh, I do so *hate* visiting Uncle Miller. Aunt Miller is all right, but she hardly ever speaks and I can't bear to think that those snotty-nosed kids are my cousins!"

"They aren't," Josh said reassuringly. "They'd

only be your cousins if your Uncle Miller was your dad's brother and as they're only cousins, those kids must be second cousins or something.''

Christina's face showed relief and Josh felt quite proud of himself.

"Ready Christina?'' her father asked, giving Josh a friendly pat on the back. He hated the visits to Ernest Miller as much as Christina but had the discretion not to admit to it. His father's side of the family had been professional people, his own father a chemist and druggist of great renown. His mother's younger sister had married in haste and repented at leisure, and the result had been Ernest Miller. Ernest was now John Haworth's only living relation apart from Christina and as the family lived in Liverpool, John Haworth felt it his obligation to keep up the family ties. Especially as Ernest Miller showed as little inclination for work as his father had done and so condemned his wife and children to a life of unbelievable squalor. Captain Haworth's visits were the highlights of the Miller childrens' lives. He never came empty handed. A packet of tea, biscuits, fresh fruit, luxuries that never appeared at any other time.

With her hand firmly clasped in her father's, Christina prepared to face the ordeal ahead. The Millers lived in a cottage only two streets away from Josh. On the way John Haworth stopped at a little shop and bought several loaves of bread, eight ounces of boiled ham, six penny tins of condensed milk, six pennyworth of sugar, butter and tea. Finally he filled his pockets with a selection of cheap sweets and continued on his way, ducking his head beneath the lines of washing that were strung across the width of the street. As they neared the open door of the cottage that housed his cousin, John Haworth imperceptibly squared his shoulders and tightened his grip comfortingly on Christina's hand.

The children were round him first in a shrieking swarm as he scattered the sweets and they dived joyously after them. Captain Haworth turned his back on them and stepped into the dark, evil-smelling room. It was no better nor worse than any other of the scores that surrounded Liverpool's dockside, but that a blood relation of his should live in it, and live in it mainly through his own idleness, filled the captain with revulsion.

The room was dirty and dilapidated, the ceiling black with smoke, the walls shiny with grease. A large bedstead filled up one entire wall and as John Haworth saw the state of Liza Miller he understood why it had been brought downstairs. She looked so pale and thin he doubted she could stand, let alone climb the stone stairs to the bedroom. A baby sucked hopelessly at a shrunken breast and John Haworth cursed, saying angrily, "Where the hell is Ernest?"

"Out." The scrawny hand waved despairingly.

Captain Haworth's face was set in the grim lines that Christina rarely saw. He pushed money into Christina's hand, saying, "Go back to the shop and buy fresh milk, and buy more condensed milk and a bottle and a teat."

Then, as the children watched round-eyed in the doorway, he filled a big black kettle with water, put it on the range, and when it boiled he proceeded to scrub table, chairs, everything and anything in sight.

The woman on the bed made a mute protest that he ignored, just as he ignored the amazement on the children's faces. A man scrubbing! Why, he must be clean off his rocker!

Cursing heartily, John Haworth picked up all the debris that littered the floor, flinging it into an untidy pile on a sagging couch and then set to on the floor. He began scrubbing the filthy wooden boards and scraps of linoleum as if his life depended on it.

Christina came back with the milk, not daring to speak as her father took them from her in such a silent rage that even *she* quaked. He poured half a can of the condensed milk into the bottle, filled it with the cooled boiled water and took the whimpering baby from the woman's arms.

"Here," he said to Christina, handing her baby and bottle and leaving her to find the best way of pushing the rubber teat into the wailing mouth. The baby began to suck greedily and Christina felt a surge of pleasure. It was quite a bonny baby really and felt so nice in the crook of her arm.

Meanwhile, John Haworth was pushing a glass of warm milk into Liza Miller's trembling hand and then slicing large chunks of bread and buttering them liberally, filling them with the ham and handing them to the half-starved children at the door. Finally, as the children wolfed the sandwiches and the baby fell asleep, he turned back to the bed.

"When did you last eat, Liza?"

"I've not wanted food."

"If you don't eat, that babe will die."

He sat over her as she struggled with the ham.

"Is Ernest out of work again?"

She nodded, fighting a tide of nausea as the unaccustomed food settled in her stomach.

"Just in time for the feast, am I?" a slurred voice asked from the doorway, his bulk darkening the already dim room.

John Haworth spun round, fists clenched.

"Out!" he said to Christina, his blazing eyes locking with those of his cousin.

Christina didn't need to be told twice. She scurried from the room as fast as her nimble legs would carry her.

The activity in the Miller cottage had not gone unnoticed among the Millers' neighbors. Several women, children on their hips, were gathering interestedly within hearing distance.

"There's no bloody feast for you Ernest Miller!" John Haworth seethed. "To leave your wife and children half starved while you go up the pub! Look at her! She's dying in front of your eyes and all for the lack of nourishment."

"There's no money," Ernest began sulkily.

"There's money enough for the beer! I'm leaving instructions at the shop that a daily amount of food is delivered to this house. Food for Liza and the children. I'm going to do what I've wanted to do for years now. Beat the living daylights out of you and if I find you've been eating food I bought for the others I won't beat you! I'll bloody kill you!"

Ernest's eyes shifted uneasily. "There's no work."

"*I* offered you work!" As he spoke he was rolling his sleeves up, the huge muscles rippling. Ernest Miller was a big man but didn't have a body hardened by physical work. He stepped back into the street.

"It won't happen again, John. I swear. I'll get a job. I'll see the kids are fed."

John Haworth moved slowly forward like a panther after its prey. Ernest cowered against the wall and there was a concerted intake of breath as John Haworth pressed him against it by the throat.

"God man, you don't even have the stomach for a fight! You make me sick to my belly!"

John Haworth let go of him. "Just remember what I said, Ernest. I'll be back in three weeks time, and if I find you've been cheating Liza of the rations I'm leaving her I'll nail your puking skin to the house wall!" and with his fists still clenching and unclenching he strode off, wide-eyed women hastily making way for him. It was a long time before Christina dared to speak. When she did, she said, "I don't want to go back there, daddy. Not ever again."

"No more shall you, my little love. But I will. My God, to think that a man related to me by blood . . ." Sickness rose in him like a tide. "You go off and find Josh," he said, and made his way back to the *Lucky Star*.

With a little less than her usual sparkle Christina

made her way up the hill to the cemetery. Josh, peering down the narrow street from his vantage point, watched her, puzzled. Christina almost *ran* usually; it wasn't like her to walk with such a dragging step or to have such a serious expression on her pretty face.

"What's up?" he asked as she flopped down beside him in the long grass.

"Nowt." She'd no desire to tell anyone, even Josh, about the disgraceful way her father's cousin treated his family.

"Trouble at Millers'?" Josh asked perceptively.

She sighed, rolling over onto her back. "Daddy says I need never go there again. He says if Uncle Ernest doesn't treat them better he's going to beat him."

"Did he?" Josh's face lit up. "That'd be summat to look forward to." To see the usually hearty captain in a scrap would be a rare sight.

"No it wouldn't. Fighting's silly."

Josh, who fancied himself in this particular field, was affronted. "No it's not. Who said it was?"

"Daddy."

"But he was still going to fight Ernest Miller and he's *family!*" Josh's voice was triumphant.

"Oh, *men!*" Christina dismissed the whole episode from her mind.

Josh had a bead bracelet in his pocket that had taken him three weeks of hard work to buy. He'd sold papers, cut up chaff for Old Riley's horse, helped serve behind the counter in the grocery shop, helped the cabbies unload at the station. The bracelet clicked tantalizingly in the depths of his pocket but looking at Christina's woe-begone face, Josh knew he'd be wasting his time asking her. Instead he said, "I'm leaving school Friday."

She looked at him, and he noticed how thick and long her eyelashes were and how soft they lay against her cheek.

"You can't. You're only eleven."

"I'm not. I'm twelve now and I'm jolly well not

going any longer. Jimmy Murdoch's already left and got a job aboard a rigger."

"Jimmy Murdoch's fourteen. Besides, you couldn't get a job at sea. You'd be sick."

He cuffed her in mock severity. *"I'm* going to be a boilermaker."

"But they won't let you, Josh. Not till you're fourteen."

"I'm big enough for fourteen and dad says he'll tell them I am. He says the money will come in and it's daft keeping me at school. *He* started work when he was eight."

"Well I'm very glad I didn't," Christina said vehemently. "Ladies don't work at all."

"Who the 'ell is talking about ladies?" Josh asked exasperatedly, pulling on a blade of grass and wondering, if he asked her now . . .

"I am." Christina sprang to her feet, her hands on her unformed hips. "I think you're daft wanting to be a boilermaker. *I'm* going to be a *lady!"*

Josh guffawed with laughter, holding his stomach as he rolled helplessly on the ground. Christina stamped her foot angrily.

"And just what are you laughing at, Josh Lucas? You wouldn't recognize a lady if you fell over one!"

"Mebbe not, never 'avin' seen one. But I know one thing for sure. To be a lady you have to be born a lady!" He wiped the tears of laughter from his eyes and grinned up at her.

Christina's head went imperiously high. "Then that's just where you're wrong, Josh Lucas. *Anybody* can become a lady if they marry a man with enough money!"

Josh went off into fresh hoots. "And where the 'ell are you goin' to be finding a man with money in Liverpool?"

Christina folded her arms stubbornly. "There's more places in the world than Liverpool. Becky Sharp wasn't born a lady but she become one."

"Who the 'ell's she?" Josh asked, still gurgling with amusement. "She don't go to our school."

"Oh, Josh, sometimes I think you're stupid beyond belief."

Exerting all her patience, of which she had very little, Christina knelt down in the grass beside him. "Becky Sharp's in a book called *Vanity Fair*. Becky's friend Amelia was a lady, and Becky sort of towed along. Like your little brother does sometimes."

"Then she must have been a perishin' nuisance," Josh said feelingly.

"She wasn't. They were friends. Though *why* Becky Sharp put up with such a whey-faced creature as Amelia I can't imagine. She was like me really."

"You're not whey-faced!" Josh interrupted roundly.

"I mean I'm like Becky!"

Christina clumped him with a sod of earth and after an amicable tussle continued. "You see, Becky's father was a great artist only no one recognized his genius. He came from a *very* noble family, only no one believed him, and when he died she was sent to teach French at a posh school so she'd have somewhere to live."

"Well how does that make you like her?" Josh asked bewildered. "Your father ain't dead and you couldn't talk Frenchified if you wanted to."

"No, but my mother was *Spanish*," Christina said triumphantly. "And if she'd lived I would be able to speak Spanish, and she was famous just like Becky Sharp's father only not recognized if you know what I mean."

Josh didn't.

"*My* mother was a famous dancer. The best flamenco dancer in the whole of Spain!"

"Then why'd she leave?"

"Because she fell passionately in love with daddy of course, silly."

Josh felt embarrassed. Fancy talking about mums and dads being passionately in love. A turn down Gorman Street would open Christina's eyes to a thing or two!

"Becky Sharp was never a lady like *you* mean. But she *did* get called one *and* wore fine clothes and enjoyed life enormously. Just like I'm going to do!"

Seeing the set look on her face, the determined thrust of the little pointed chin, Josh sobered, putting his arm around her.

"Nay, lass. That's only in books, balls and jewels and carriages and fine clothes. They're not for the likes of us. You'll marry here and have kids like your Aunt Miller and me mam. . . .

She pushed him away so violently he fell backward, his mouth wide open.

"You're stupid! Stupid! Stupid!" she stormed, her black curls tumbling down over flashing eyes as she stamped her foot repeatedly. "I'll *never* be like Aunt Miller. *Never!* I'd rather be dead, just you see if I wouldn't!" And she disregarded his efforts to placate her and rushed from the cemetery, running non-stop down the cobbled street, tears streaming down her face.

Josh stared after her and then shrugged. The bracelet tinkled against his fishing hook. Since Jimmy Murdoch had left for sea, he'd caught Kate Kennedy giving him speculative glances, and had noticed that when her hair was washed it was quite a pretty color, pale gold like buttercups. She'd put a bit of ribbon in it yesterday and the look she'd given him had made him hot and uncomfortable.

It was just after eleven. If he hung around the school gates he'd see her when the bell rang. His fingers closed on the bracelet in a sudden fit of bravery. Resolutely he began to walk in the direction of the slate-roofed schoolhouse.

By the time Christina had reached the docks her tears had dried but she was still in a furious temper. It wasn't mollified by seeing a stranger aboard the *Lucky Star*. From the rear he looked to be in his late teens and broadly built with a shock of the reddest hair Christina had ever seen.

"Damn and blast," she thought bad temperedly. "Just when I want to have daddy to myself he's to be engaging another deck-hand."

She stormed up the rough gangplank, pushing rudely past the offending sailor.

John Haworth, facing her, raised his eyebrows slightly, seeing in the glittering eyes and the heightened flush of her cheeks an uncanny resemblance to Carlotta whenever she got into a temper. Many a plate had cracked against his head to be forgotten in frenzied love-making only two minutes later.

"My daughter, Christina," he said, introducing her.

Christina turned, looking at the new deckhand insolently, intending to resume her defiant stride to her cabin. But she hesitated at what she saw, losing her composure.

His face was deeply tanned, his eyes the bluest she had ever seen, his strong nose and firm jaw line softened by a beautifully molded mouth. He was like one of the Greek gods in the stories her father had told her, yet they didn't have hair the color of the setting sun. If he was aware that she was staring at him he didn't show it, merely nodded at her briefly and continued his conversation with her father. It was interrupted by Ned calling for Captain Haworth from the stern of the ship. Excusing himself, the Captain strode away toward him. It was no use shouting back. Ned was as deaf as a post. The Greek god turned his attention to the still admiring Christina.

"So you're the Captain's brat?" he asked lazily, leaning nonchalantly against the mainmast as if the boat was his own.

Christina's admiration vanished in a flash of fury. "I'm no brat!" she hissed. "I'm a princess! A *gypsy* princess!" and she rushed back to her cabin, his laughter ringing in her ears.

Hours later when her father came in to read to her,

she was still lying woodenly, fists clenched. She *was* a princess. She knew it. It was in her blood and her bones. Her mother had been a Spanish princess who had forsaken everything for her father and, like Becky Sharp's father, no one recognized her birthright.

"Have you had a row with Josh?" her father asked gently.

"No." The new deckhand had put all thoughts of her anger with Josh from her mind. "When does the new man start?"

"What new man?"

"The one you were talking to when I came on board."

John Haworth rumpled her curls. "He isn't a deckhand, my love. He's setting off for the Gold Coast soon and someone had told him I'd sailed that stretch of coast regularly in my youth."

Christina felt a curious sense of disappointment.

"What story tonight, my pet? *Vanity Fair* is at an end. What about *East Lynne?*"

She shook her head. "No. I don't want love stories tonight. I want—" Little fists clenched determinedly. "I want adventure. I want to hear about people who fight for what they want!"

Captain Haworth chewed his bottom lip, wondering what had happened between Christina and Josh to put her in such a defiant mood. He decided it was best not to pursue the matter and walked thoughtfully over to the bookshelves.

"Then we'll have *The Three Musketeers*. There should be enough adventure in there to satisfy even a heart as wild as yours, my love."

Chapter 3

Christina grew increasingly lonely over the next few years. No longer could she see Josh every time the *Lucky Star* docked. There was no playing truant from his job like there had been from school, and their reunions were cut down to one every three or four months. Also Josh had changed, and not only physically. He was sixteen now with arms and shoulders bulgingly developed through hard work. They had both outgrown the games they used to play but the cemetery was still their favorite meeting place. It was just that they didn't have that much to *say* to each other any more. But when the familiar figure began to stride up the winding street she felt her spirits lift.

"Been here long?" he asked, flopping down beside her as he had when they were children.

" 'Bout an hour."

"Sorry I made you wait, but it takes me mam ages to fill the tub. You wouldn't have wanted me here all filthy and greasy."

He smelled strongly of tar soap and his dark hair was still wet.

She grinned. "I wouldn't have minded, honestly."

She rolled over on to her back, enjoying the heat of the sun on her face. As she did so Josh noticed (not for the first time) the tantalizing thrust of her budding breasts and that her hips were softly curving—she was no longer skinny as a boy. Not since he had given the bead bracelet—intended for Christina—to Kate Kennedy had Josh made any overtures to her. His curiosity had been sated, and though Kate generously shared herself freely around the neighborhood, she spent far more time with Josh than with the other boys. Thanks to Kate there wasn't much Josh did not know now, and he reckoned Christina was old enough to learn too.

He leaned across to her, stroking a rebellious curl away from her face, noticing with sudden shock how much it had altered. Gone was the chubby prettiness of childhood. In its place was a beauty that was bone deep. High cheekbones set in a heart-shaped face. Honey-gold skin and sloe-black eyes inherited from her mother. And full, generous lips, that curved with innocent sensuousness as she smiled up at him.

Josh felt suddenly shy. Tentatively he lowered his hand, tracing the line of cheek and chin and then slowly letting it travel over her shoulders till it cupped the breast. Her eyes widened but she did not move. Josh felt his heart hammering painfully within his chest.

"Christina?" He could hardly force the words out. "Christina, will you let me love you?"

His eyes were full of pain and longing. She raised her hand, running it through the still damp hair.

"Does it mean so much to you, Josh?"

"Yes." His voice was husky, thick with desire. "I won't hurt you, Christina. I promise."

His hand felt warm over the thin cotton of her blouse and she had no wish to move it away. She was fourteen now and knew very well what Josh wanted to do. While she struggled to come to a decision Josh seized his advantage, unbuttoning her blouse and cupping her breasts reverently in his big hands, stroking the nipples gently with trembling thumbs.

Christina lay passive. It was a strangely pleasant sensation. Josh had done so much for her over the years. Fighting her battles for her; seeing that no one

called after her in the street without receiving just re-
taliation. It was such a little thing he was asking of
her and it meant so much to him.

"All right," she said obligingly.

Josh felt sick with excitement and suddenly nervous. This was Christina. Not Kate Kennedy or any
of the other willing girls he had taken in back alleys
and by brooks.

He bent his head to hers, kissing her awkwardly at
first and then with increasing confidence. Christina
wondered why Josh put his tongue in her mouth when
he kissed her. Her father never did. She sensed him
fumbling with his trousers, then at her drawers.

Helpfully she lifted her bottom off the grass and
pulled the offending articles down. Josh's weight was
on top of her now and he had parted her legs with his
knee. She waited curiously. Something strange and
alien tried to force itself up between her legs and there
wasn't enough room for it. She screamed, arching her
back, and Josh immediately rolled off her, his face a
mixture of frustrated desire and consternation.

"I don't want to hurt you, Christina. I don't want
to hurt. I want to *love* you."

She gritted her teeth. "It's all right. Try again."

Josh did, but to no avail.

"Perhaps I'm not made right," Christina suggested.

"Course you are," Josh said stoutly, wondering if
she was. It never hurt Kate.

His eyes were full of such thwarted longing that
Christina felt sorry for him.

"Then just touch me, Josh. I like that."

Josh felt a flood of relief. Clumsily his fingers
reached out for her, stroking and seeking. Christina
sighed pleasurably. This was a much nicer way of
being loved. Josh felt her soften and relax against him
and he grew increasingly bolder, wanting to show her
how much more experienced he was than she, and also
curious to know if his daring would have the same
effect on Christina as it did on Kate.

He heard her quick intake of breath as his head moved lower on her belly, her momentary protest as he began to kiss the mat of tightly curling hair, his tongue searching for that secret place, small as a cherry, that sent Kate into paroxysms of ecstasy.

For a few seconds he thought she was going to wriggle free, and then she was clutching his shoulders, pulling him closer, tighter. Josh raised his head, sliding her down beneath him, feeling like a king as he kissed her willing mouth.

"Don't be scared, Christina," he whispered. "Don't be scared," knowing that this time would be all right. This time the pain would not matter.

Later, their bodies spent, they lay arms around each other beneath the blazing sun, and Josh raised his head and looked at her with a grin.

"Like it?" he asked.

She smiled shyly, stroking his hair back off his forehead. "Yes. I didn't know it was like that. And Josh . . ."

Josh waited, his heart slamming.

"I'm so glad it was you."

"So am I," Josh said fervently. After this, his intimacies with the Liverpool girls faded into insignificance. He cupped her chin in his hand and kissed her again.

John Haworth was no fool. He knew the moment he saw the two of them walking hand in hand back to the boat, the glazed look about Josh's eyes, the heightened color on Christina's cheeks. He grinned to himself. Better Josh Lucas than anybody else. He only hoped that eventually she would find a man she would belong to body and soul. That man was not Josh Lucas. John Haworth knew that instinctively and felt a momentary pang of pity for him. Christina would soon outgrow Josh and his narrow world of work, pub and bed. But what world would she enter? He frowned, wondering for the first time in ten years if he hadn't perhaps acted rashly. He'd counted Ernest Miller his only living blood relations, but there was in fact an elder sister, lording it over a vast house and park in North Yorkshire. A house to which he was the rightful heir. In that environment Christina might meet a man more suitable. Then he shrugged. That environment had brought him only misery with Mary Goodman. The love of his life had been found dancing for pennies in a Spanish tavern. Christina would be all right. She was like Carlotta, a born survivor. And, like Carlotta, she loved the sea.

John Haworth smiled down at his daughter. The little bird would soon want to stretch her wings beyond the *Lucky Star*, and then what? He felt a chill around his heart.

"How about some mugs of cocoa?" he asked, pushing the unpleasant prospect away from him. "And biscuits as well."

Off Southampton the *Lucky Star* began to splutter like an old lady, and Ned and John Haworth struggled against an unfriendly sea for two hours to bring her into port.

"Leave her till tomorrow," John Haworth had said to his aged deckhand, wiping perspiration from his forehead with a red-spotted handkerchief. "I've had enough for one day."

Heaving his bulky jersey over his head, he sluiced his face, shoulders and chest with ice-cold water, slipped on a crisp, white shirt that went oddly with his weather-beaten trousers, and with Christina's hand in his, went ashore for rest and refreshment.

To Christina, Southampton's dockside was very little different from Liverpool's. Bars, crowds of sailors and cheaply-dressed young women jostled them. Despite Christina's presence, more than one of the women approached the giant-sized John Haworth and whispered intriguingly in his ear, only to be ignored as her father strode on.

"What did she want, Daddy?" Christina asked. A

little redhead's face changed from anticipation to sulky displeasure and she swore after them loudly.

"They're prostitutes, my love," Captain Haworth said, never having seen the reason to be less than totally honest with his daughter. "They go with men for money."

Christina looked after the red-haired woman. "Then she mustn't do it very well," Christina said with innocent frankness. "She's got holes in her stockings."

John Haworth laughed and pulled open the door of the Red Lion.

"A pint of ale and a ginger beer," he said, having shouldered his way with little ado to the front of the crowded counter.

"Big John Haworth," a voice boomed out, and a man her father's age forced his way through the throng and wrung his hand. "By hell and holy angels I never thought I'd see you again!"

"Dan Gilroy." Captain Haworth shook the proffered hand vigorously. "It's good to see you, Dan. What are doing, working the steamers?"

"Nah, got myself a number as trimmer on board the *Mauretania.*"

He grinned, satisfied at the rise of John Haworth's bushy brows.

"The *Mauretania* is it? You're flying high, Dan. Let's find a corner and talk. You've met Christina haven't you?"

Dan had, but then she'd been a red-faced baby. He looked at the young beauty and whistled through his teeth.

"By hell, if she ain't like her mother and no mistake. Thought I was seeing a ghost for a moment . . ."

John Haworth had no desire to discuss Carlotta with Dan Gilroy or anyone else. He turned the subject back to the *Mauretania* as they squeezed themselves into a corner of the crowded pub, and Christina tried not to notice as a man standing nearby spat onto the sawdust floor.

"You've never seen a ship like her," Dan Gilroy said, downing the contents of his glass at one swallow. "Thirty-one thousand tons and four raked funnels. There's never been a ship built like her before."

"Apart from the *Lusitania*," John Haworth said with a grin.

"Aye, sister ships they are and both as grand. By God, I wish you could see on board, John. You'd never believe it. I've been aboard now ever since her maiden voyage and I swear I've never loved a ship more."

"How long does she take to cross?" John Haworth asked.

"Five days."

Christina drew in her breath. Five days to cross the Atlantic. It didn't seem possible.

"Does she hold steady?" Joan Haworth was asking with professional interest.

Dan Gilroy wiped his lips with the back of his hand. "Well, the Atlantic's no pond and that's for sure. She has a roll with her and it'd be a lie to say otherwise. It's oilskins and seaboots for the crew the minute we leave Southampton. Course, as I'm a trimmer I'm below decks most of the time, but I try to sneak on board when we sail in the Bay."

"The Bay?"

"New York. When we leave it's like a party. We only sail at midnight and there's paper streamers and the dandies drinking champagne and the horns blowing."

Christina listened wide-eyed. "Do people have to be very rich to sail aboard the *Mauretania?*"

Dan Gilroy laughed. "Rich? God love us. They have to have more money than we could ever imagine. Yon's not a ship, child. It's a floating palace. I tell you, she's so big a man and wife could board at Southampton and never meet again until they docked in New York! We'll never see sailing ships on the Atlantic again. Steamships from now on, John."

John Haworth was intrigued. He'd sailed his fair share of sailing ships across the cruel waters of the Atlantic and had heard plenty about the two new luxury liners built by Cunard. In the old days it had been anything up to thirty-eight days of rough weather for the westward crossing and here was Dan Gilroy saying the *Mauretania* did it in five days.

"You must come and have a look at her before you leave port," Dan was saying. "She's half as long again as any vessel ever built and has three-quarters more power."

Beneath the stubble on his chin and the dirt encrusted in the lines of his face he looked enraptured. "Them engines are steam turbine, better than them old pistons we used to have. There's twenty-five boilers aboard. Can you imagine it? Twenty-five boilers on one ship!"

John Haworth swore appreciatively. "She'll have to be carrying a hell of a lot of coal."

"A mountain of it," Dan agreed enthusiastically.

"Is the *Mauretania* the name of a woman?" Christina asked dreamily, thinking how romantic it would be to have a ship named after her. Dan looked a bit non-plussed. He knew about the engines down to the last nut and bolt but as to *why* the ship was called *Mauretania* he hadn't the faintest idea.

"It was a Roman province," John Haworth said, smiling across at her.

"In Italy?" Christina's eyes shone. The hot Mediterranean countries drew her imagination like a magnet.

Her father shook his head. "Roman Morocco and Algeria."

The two men continued to talk, discussing the merits of steam over sail while Christina dreamed of the glories aboard the *Mauretania*. A floating palace inhabited only by the rich. She wondered what it would be like. If it would be as grand as Mr. Darcy's home or even rival the Courts of England and France. Of late she had preferred to read for herself, enjoying the stories of the great courtesans. Women like Diane du Poitiers and Lady Castlemaine. They had become rich and powerful because rich men and kings had fallen in love with them. Christina was sure she could make a rich man fall in love with her if only she had the chance.

"Come on." Dan staggered to his feet and John Haworth shook his daughter's shoulder gently, waking her from her reverie as he led her toward the door and the darkness, relieved only by a handful of stars.

"There she is," Dan hiccoughed, pointing in the distance to where a giant shadow stretched into infinity. "Come closer and have a better look."

Fifteen minutes later Christina gazed upwards in awe at the decks of the massive liner towering like a cliff hundreds of feet above her. The *Mauretania*. The greatest ship in the world. Impulsively she grasped Dan's hand. "Please take me on board, Dan. *Please!*"

"I can't do that! It'd be more than my job's worth!"

"Oh please, *please!* Just for a *tiny* look!"

Dan Gilroy had always been a pushover for a pretty face, and this one wasn't just pretty, it was ravishing. There were no passengers aboard and most of the deck crew were still ashore.

Only the firemen and trimmers were hard at work. For eighteen hours before she sailed they were busy in the bowels of the ship, raising steam. He should have been back aboard himself a good hour ago. Despite his eulogizing to John Haworth, Dan's job as trimmer was grueling work. At sea there was no rest— and no drink either. They worked two four-hour spells in every twenty-four, lifting five tons of coal each a day. Little wonder they sought the pub and a bottle whenever they had the chance! Dan Gilroy's days were spent being choked by coal-dust and gases, while the passengers drank champagne, nibbled their way through seven-course banquets and danced to the lilting strains of waltzes from Vienna. Nevertheless, he felt as proud of the ship he sailed as did her captain.

Buoyed up by the beer and the sensation of being able to show off and be admired, Dan Gilroy gripped her hand and said to her father: "Fifteen minutes and we'll be back."

"Good God man, you can't take her aboard!" John Haworth protested.

Half drunk, Dan Gilroy wagged his finger. "A little peep. Let her see for herself." And before her father could stop her Christina was half running, dragging a staggering Dan behind her. For the rest of her life Christina never forgot the next few minutes. She was transported to a world that exceeded all her imaginings.

Keeping a sharp look-out for any officers that were still aboard Dan led her from the sun deck all the way down to the main deck.

"They sit out here covered in rugs," he said to Christina as they left the upper deck. "Stewardesses bring 'em hot toast and soup and anything else their hearts desire, and here"—he indicated the wide expanse of the upper promenade deck—"nannies wheel babies around in perambulators just as if they were in Kensington Gardens!"

They hurried silently down to the lower deck, and Christina gazed incredulously at the vast splendor of the *Mauretania*'s first-class lounge and music room. Never in her life had she imagined a room to be so large. A pale turquoise ceiling with a gilt-encrusted dome was supported by what seemed to Christina to be golden pillars. Acres of deep, soft carpeting to match the ceiling sank softly and richly beneath her bare feet. Beautifully carved and upholstered chairs and sofas were grouped in intimate clusters around polished tables crowned with lush plants.

"Ooh," Christina gasped wonderingly. "Ooh Dan. It's like a fairytale palace!"

Dan grinned with satisfaction and hurried her down the grand staircase, modeled in the style of fifteenth-century Italy. The width and sweep of it took Christina's breath away.

The dining room was paneled in straw-colored oak, the carvings so delicate and fine that Christina lovingly ran her' fingers over the satin-smooth surface. It was a paradise of cream and gold, and Dan had to drag her away physically as she gazed in awestruck wonder.

Down on the main deck they dodged a whistling steward and Dan let her peep into the magnificent staterooms. Some in the style of Sheraton, some Chippendale, some Adams. Even if she had been told, the names would have meant nothing to Christina, but the luxurious bathrooms *en suite* with their silver plated fittings did. This was what being rich meant. Traveling the seas like a queen. There was even a magical box called an electric lift that Dan adamantly refused to work despite all her pleading, but he told her that when a person stood inside it and the grille was closed, the person was carried up in the air as if he were flying.

"Best be getting back now," Dan said, the effects of the liquor beginning to wear off.

"Oh not yet!" Impulsively she ran away from him, racing through the public rooms, determined not to miss anything. The first-class lounge had been copied from the Petit Trianon at Versailles and it was here, as she gasped in sheer joy, rooted to the spot, that Dan pantingly caught up with her. They'd get caught in a minute and he didn't want to lose his job for a moment's foolishness.

"Come on, girl. That's enough." His grip on her wrist was firm.

Reverently Christina ran her hand over the wood veneer paneling as Dan dragged her reluctantly back up on deck.

Everything was beyond belief. An Aladdin's cave of gold and silver, satin and velvet, marble and brass.

"Do people really *live* amongst all this?" she asked, awe-struck.

"That they do. Some come twice a year regular. Bring their maids and valets and little dogs with 'em."

Dazedly she followed him through the maze of rooms and back to the dark wharf and her anxiously waiting father.

"Well love, was it as grand as Dan said?"

"It was . . ." Christina searched for words. "It was magnificent, daddy. Another world."

Dan laughed, relieved that he had got away with his foolish escapade.

"You'll never see the likes of that again," he said to her as she stared wonderingly up at the dark hulk of the *Mauretania*'s side.

"Oh, but I will," Christina whispered. "And next time I'm not just going to see it. I'm going to live amongst it, just like those fine ladies with their maids and little dogs. I'm going to have one of those rooms with the golden beds and silken sheets and I'm going to be a lady like I always said I would be. A lady at sea!"

"You *what*, my love?" her father asked, barely catching her last words.

"I said I'm going to be a lady one day and live on a ship like the *Mauretania*."

Dan Gilroy laughed fit to bursting, but John Haworth didn't. There was such steel-like determination in the voice of his daughter that he stopped walking and looked down at her earnestly.

She peeped up at him, her hand in his, their eyes meeting in the darkness.

"I am, daddy. Truly."

"I believe you will. But I doubt I'll be around to see it," he said, and with his arm around her shoulder he continued walking, wondering how much longer it would be before he got another violent pain in his chest and arm and wondering if it wouldn't be wisest to write to North Yorkshire without wasting any more time.

Chapter 4

Christina snuggled happily beneath the knitted blankets, the oil lamp casting a rosy glow in the small cabin as her father read, his voice slurred from his evening of drinking but keeping up the nightly ritual as some people did their prayers.

For once the adventures of D'Artagnan, Aramis and Porthos left her completely unmoved. She was reliving every precious moment she had spent aboard the *Mauretania*, imagining the sumptuous room filled with ladies in low-cut evening dresses with feathers in their hair. With handsome men in lace-frilled shirts and evening dress and diamonds sparkling on their little fingers. Of the music and the dancing. She wondered what champagne tasted like or how it felt to be held in strong arms and waltzed round and round golden ballrooms with musicians playing and herself in a satin dress with flowers in her hair and emeralds at her throat, smelling of lavender or perhaps rose water. She sighed blissfully. It would happen one day. She knew it would.

With the supreme confidence of youth she closed her eyes and slept, sure of the attainment of her goal. Her father dropped the book to his lap. It was too late to write to his sister now. It had waited fifteen years. It could wait a little longer.

The next morning he felt fitter than he had for months. He dismissed his premature fears of the pre-

vious night and when Christina ran up on deck, the
Lucky Star's engine was again running smoothly and
Ned and her father were ready to cast off and continue
their journey.

"I've been thinking, little love," he said, as they
cleared the congested water lanes and reached open
sea. "We're wasting our lives on this milk run. How
about us taking off for a year, maybe two. And sailing
the Mediterranean and letting me show you all the
places I sailed to with your mother."

"Oh daddy!" she said, clasping her arms around his
neck in ecstasy, and then suddenly went on, "But the
Lucky Star isn't built for the high seas!"

"Neither she is, but the Mediterranean is like a
pond. If we take it easy across Biscay and hug the
Portuguese shore we'll come to no harm."

"Can we go to Italy and to Greece and oh, to Spain!
Can we go to Spain, daddy!"

"Aye lass, that we can."

It had taken him nigh on fourteen years to face the
painful memories Spain and the ports of the Mediterranean held for him. But now he wanted to go, wanted
to show Christina her mother's country. Show her
Menorca where he and Carlotta spent their blissful
two months after Christina's birth.

Old Ned shrugged philosophically when the captain
told him his plans. He would still be needed as deckhand. If the captain wanted to waste time jaunting
around the Mediterranean instead of earning honest
brass it was none of his affair.

Josh had been far less understanding.

"But you could be gone years!" he said aghast. "If
your father's got the traveling bug again it won't stop
at the Mediterranean. It'll be the Indian Ocean next!"

"Oh, I hope so!" Christina said blissfully.

They were lying deep in a tangle of grass thick with
poppies and buttercups. Twice she had tried to tell
him about the *Mauretania* and twice she had failed.
Josh just wouldn't understand. She was too busy with

her inner thoughts to be aware of Josh's sudden discomfiture. He fidgeted edgily. "I thought that in a couple of years, when you were sixteen, that we could, you know—"

With an effort she drew her attention back to him. "Could what?"

Josh swore inwardly. Why did girls always have to make things so difficult? He cleared his throat, saying with studied casualness, "Could get wed."

"*Wed!*" Christina's sleek brows flew up, her eyes opening wide with shock. Then she began to laugh.

"And where would we live? In one of those cottages down Gorman Street? You are a fool, Josh. I told you I'm going to be a lady." She clasped her hands behind her head. "I'm going to have fine dresses and jewelry and a maid . . ."

"*You're the one who's a fool!*" Josh sprang to his feet, his face mottled. "*You and your fancy ideas! Who the hell do you think you are? You're a bastard, Christina. A gypsy's bastard. There's as much chance of you becoming a lady as there is me sitting on the throne of England!*" And to Christina's dismay he swung on his heel, disregarding all her shouts after him to slow down and wait for her. He broke into a run and she raced pantingly after him. At the rusty cemetery gates she paused, gasping for breath. He was too far away for her ever to catch up with him. Tears sprang to her eyes. Josh had never been angry with her before and he had to choose today of all days to spoil everything. Today when it would be their last meeting for ages. She wiped the tears away and sniffed. She would miss him but he should have had more sense than to imagine she would marry and live like Aunt Miller in a crowded two-up, two-down cottage producing babies every year.

Josh, blind with anger, had only one intention, to find Kate Kennedy and vent all his pent-up violence and fury in a bout of lovemaking that would leave her bruised and delighted for weeks.

John Haworth discharged the last of his cargo at Liverpool, and Christina joined him in a happy week of stocking the *Lucky Star* and preparing her for their great adventure.

Every day she went up to the cemetery in the vain hope that Josh would be there and they would be able to part friends but he never came, and on the last day before they sailed as she sat on the *Lucky Star*'s deck, she saw him strolling along the dockside.

Instinctively she rose to her feet and waved, but then her hand faltered and fell.

His arm was around a fair-haired girl with a sharp, narrow face and full, thrusting breasts. Her blouse was cut as low as those of the prostitutes who paraded the docksides at dusk.

Christina knew who she was. She'd known Kate Kennedy as long as she'd known Josh and never a civil word had passed between them. Kate had been a ringleader, in those far-off days, at calling names after Christina that she had not then understood. To Christina, Kate was coarse and common, and that Josh should walk in public with her, his arm around her waist—

It was early dawn as the *Lucky Star* made her familiar way down the crowded Mersey and into the Irish Sea. Christina could only believe they were really going south instead of making their usual run of German and Belgian ports, when they left Land's End (in southwest England) behind them and began crossing the English Channel to Brest.

The *Lucky Star* was really a sailing barge, the largest type of craft in the world capable of being handled by only two men. Her sail area was impressive and Christina loved it when all six sails were filled with wind as the ship skimmed over the waves. The Channel crossing grew rough, and Christina helped Ned gather in the mainsail to the mast, leaving only the topsail and headsail to see them into the French harbor.

They stayed in Brest, where her father was well known, for over two weeks. In between reunions with old friends, John Haworth sailed the *Lucky Star* idly along the rugged coastline, calling in at tiny fishing villages where he and Christina gorged on oysters, mackerel, prawns, lobster, shrimp and sardines. Truly, Christina thought happily, her father did have the most wonderful ideas of how to enjoy life.

Soon they were enjoying the warmth of the Gulf Stream, and Christina saw her first palm tree and gathered armfuls of mimosa and magnolias to fill the *Lucky Star*'s cabins.

On the last day before setting sail across the Bay of Biscay, Christina and her father went on horseback to Morlaix some miles to the north. She was not used to riding, and found it a much more uncomfortable method of traveling than that of sailing, but the little town at the end of their journey made her discomfort worthwhile. It was an old Roman town, built on steep valley walls and clinging round a busy port. Captain Haworth told his daughter of how, during the twelfth century, it was one of the residences of the counts of Brittany and of how, in the sixteenth century, the English fleet had sailed up the estuary and, as the nobles were away enjoying a distant fair, had made free with the town; they got so drunk they didn't have the good sense to leave with their booty and were caught red-handed by the returning revelers. Since then the town's motto had been *"S'ils te mordent, mord les,"* which her father translated as "If they bite you, bite back." Christina thought it an eminently sensible motto and filed it in the back of her mind for future use, adopting it as her own.

Then began the most exhilarating sea voyage of Christina's life as they crossed the Bay of Biscay, with no more crew than an old man, a girl and one zestful and ruddy-faced Captain. Christina felt her first taste of fear as the *Lucky Star* pitched and rolled in the heavy seas, and she felt the flow of adrenalin through her veins and threw back her head and laughed joyously as she was drenched by yet another crashing wave. There was excitement in danger and she felt growing in herself a heady recklessness that was never to leave her. Only old Ned was thankful when they finally pulled into port at Bilbao.

They spent the autumn traveling leisurely along the northern coast of Spain and down the pine-clad shores of Portugal, but it was the Mediterranean coast of Spain that Christina ached for, as they spent a couple of weeks in the pleasant city of Viana do Castello, and then, some fifty miles further south, anchored the boat on a deserted beach of flawless sand and slept on shore for several days, the scent of miles and miles of pine woods filling the air with a heady fragrance.

On Christina's fifteenth birthday the *Lucky Star* sailed through the Straits of Gibraltar. Christina felt she had come home. The hot sun, the blue sky, the coastline of Spain with its high, parched, brown mountains. She saw for herself the flamenco dancers, gasping in pleasure and admiration, awe-struck as her father said matter-of-factly that they danced like laborers in clogs compared to the way Carlotta had danced.

The spring was a golden one. They rode on horseback into the mountains, lingered in every little fishing village that took their fancy; then, as spring turned to summer, John Haworth set sail for Menorca.

Christina knew all about the two months her parents had spent there and of what the little white-washed town of Mahon meant to her father. He had described it to her over the years, down to the last street. As they entered the glittering water of the narrow, incredibly deep harbor, she recognized, without being told, the rose-pink stucco house high on a hillside that had been the home of Lord Nelson and Lady Hamilton, and like a twin on the opposite side of the harbor, set high above it, the identical mansion that had been the residence of General Collingswood. Mahon did not disappoint her, and if her father was quieter than usual and his face wore a more abstracted expression, Christina knew why and understood. Sympathetically she left him to his memories, running barefoot up and down the narrow sun-filled streets, making friends with astonishing ease despite all the language difficulties. By the time they finally set sail for Italy, Christina felt she knew enough Spanish to have made her mother proud of her.

Even after Italy, Captain Haworth showed no desire to return to northern waters. It was as if he had a presentiment that these golden days were the last he was to spend with his daughter. Arm-in-arm or hand-in-hand they strolled the streets of Naples and Brindisi looking more like lovers than father and daughter, and attracting many strange glances from the local population.

Six months were spent sailing from Greek Island to Greek Island, staying in small tavernas, Christina drinking the local wines and retsina with as much relish as her father.

She was sixteen now and had lost any last vestige of childishness. She held herself like a princess, walking with a graceful, swaying walk that sent the men of the Latin countries mad with desire. The dark eyes, alive with vitality, were wide-spaced and fringed with heavy, silken lashes. Captain Haworth never tired of looking at the lovely line of cheek and the warm, generous curve of her lips. She was beautiful beyond belief.

Troy was twenty kilometers away from the nearest port so they hired horses, Christina having grown more expert at riding over the last few months. The track wound through the dusty foothills of Mount Ida, scented pine forests pressing in on either side. Down below the Aegean shimmered a startling blue, and her father recited Tennyson to her as they reached the ruins of what had once been Troy.

It was the last day of perfect undiluted happiness that Christina was to know for many a long year and it was as if she sensed it, for even when she was an old lady she could remember with crystal-clear clarity the feel of the breeze on her face, the fragrance of the air, her father's boisterous laughter as they scrambled among thistles and weeds, locating Priam's palace and looking down at the still waters of the sea, imagining the Greek ships that had lain there and of how tired they must have got of waiting; Christina found the remains of a battlement and walked it, just as Helen must have done.

The next day John Haworth felt less than well but shrugged it off as mere fatigue after the previous day's outing. He set sail for the Sea of Marmara, sailing between the Dardanelles shores, and Christina could scarcely believe that there, within sight, was Asia on the right and Europe on the left. The Hellespont lipped slumberously green and Christina, knowing all about Lord Byron, would have liked to try the swim herself, but her father's face had a strained expression on it, and instead of asking she helped him bring the *Lucky Star* not into Istanbul as they had planned, but into the nearest fishing village.

John Haworth was relieved. If they'd gone to Istanbul it would have taken till late evening and he was tired beyond belief.

The next morning he said hesitantly to Christina, "Would it disappoint you too much, lass, if we turned homewards now?"

Christina suppressed the disappointment she felt and hugged him. "Of course not. We've been gone two years. It will be lovely to go back to England."

She was a neat little liar, her father thought affectionately. But there was business he had to attend to in England. A sister to see in North Yorkshire. A sister who had given him up for dead years ago. He smiled grimly. Well, she'd have a shock coming to her when he stepped over the doorstep, but decent provision had to be made for Christina. His days were numbered and he knew it.

This time there was no lingering. They stopped for provisions and nothing else.

Just out of Malaga, he visited the village and tavern where he had seen his beloved Carlotta dance like a wild thing, hands clapping high in the air, proud head flung arrogantly back. He remembered every slender line and curve of the body he had loved so much. It was as though she were there with him as he walked back through the silent streets and boarded the *Lucky Star* for the last time.

"Christina!" It was little more than a gasp but it had her running immediately into the cabin, and taking one look at the white, distorted face, she shouted at the top of her lungs for Ned.

Then she was on her knees, clutching his hand, asking desperately: "What is it? What's wrong? Is it fever?"

With a great effort he shook his head. "Heart," he whispered. "Done for, lass."

"No! Ned—quick! The brandy!"

Her father smiled and she felt the pressure of his hand increase ever so slightly on hers.

"Pen and paper," he said with difficulty.

Stumbling in her haste, Christina ran to the captain's bureau, rushed back and pushed the pen into his hand. He pointed it over the paper weakly.

"Dear Sister," he began, the letters sloping down off the page. The pen fell from his fingers.

"Oh Daddy!" She took his face between her hands, willing him to live.

He smiled at her. "Carlotta," he said, opening his eyes fully, oblivious of his pain. "She's waiting. She's been waiting a long time." And as the last spasm contorted his strong features he closed his eyes and died.

Christina knelt at the side of the bunk, her father's

hand still in hers, sobbing with a grief that was unendurable. She was unaware of Ned and his pathetic attempts to help her to her feet or to get her to drink a glass of spirits.

At last, her body spent with weeping, she said without moving, "Set sail for the Straits, Ned."

"God love thee, Christina. The two of us'll never sail the *Lucky Star* across to Portugal."

"The Straits of Gibraltar, Ned," Christina said again, and hearing the steel in her voice even Ned did not try to persuade her otherwise.

She knew the manner of her mother's burial. Although she could make no funeral bier for her father as he had Carlotta, she was determined to bury him in the same manner and near enough the same place.

She left her father's body only to help Ned sail the *Lucky Star* through the Straits of Gibraltar and far enough into the Atlantic to be out of sight of land. Then, the young girl and the old man laid John Haworth reverently on a strong piece of sheeting and carried his heavy body with great difficulty onto the deck.

They laid the body carefully facing the sea, the feet just inches over the deck. Ned said the Lord's Prayer, blew his nose and wiped the tears away with the back of his hand. Christina stood for several minutes, the wild waters of that most dangerous of seas surging and swelling around the tiny boat. Silently she said her own private prayer, and then she and Ned lifted the sheeting on which John Haworth's head lay and tipped it until the giant body that had housed John Haworth's spirit slipped down into the grey-green depths.

Her mission accomplished, Christina ordered Ned to turn for shore and began the long, lonely journey home, hugging the Portuguese coastline and avoiding the Bay of Biscay by following the coastline of France until they reached Brest. After a difficult Channel crossing Christina saw the white cliffs of England again. They evoked no response in her. Her only reason in returning to Liverpool was that she knew she had to tell her Uncle Miller that her father had died; and it was Ned's home and he wanted to return to it.

As to what would happen to her, or the *Lucky Star*, Christina did not think. Her father was dead. There was nothing else to think about.

It took all Christina's willpower to walk back again into the fetid squalor of her Uncle Miller's cottage, but it was a task that had to be done. Eyes turned and tongues wagged as Christina walked with unconscious arrogance and grace up the cobbled streets.

Nothing much had changed in the Miller household. The atmosphere was dank, fetid; misery reigned. Christina was still too numbed by grief to see the speculative look that suddenly lighted Ernest Miller's bloodshot eyes as he offered the usual words of condolence and insisted she drink tea with them.

His wife was genuinely distressed at the death of the only man who had ever showed her a shred of human kindness and Christina, sensing it, stayed to comfort her, unaware of Ernest Miller's departure as soon as it seemed respectable, and of his breaking into a run as he made for the docks.

The room was a hovel and Christina, glad of the absence of her father's cousin, began to clean it as her father had done years before. Hard physical work was the only antidote to her pain.

It was dark several hours later when she returned to the *Lucky Star*.

Ned was standing helplessly on the dockside, his few belongings packed at his feet.

Christina stared. "Are you leaving me so soon, Ned?"

Ned shifted from one foot to another uncomfortably. "Looks like I'll have to under the circumstances."

"What circumstances?" She caught sight of movement on board and recognized the ox-like figure of Ernest Miller. Never, as long as Christina could remember, had he set foot on board the *Lucky Star*. It was *her* boat. Hers and her father's and not to be defiled by the likes of the Millers. She was seized with fury and, seeing the flash of her eyes and heightened color and her clear intention of boarding the gang-plank, Ned lay a restraining hand on her arm.

"Won't do no good, lass. I'm a man too old and tired to be of any help. Accept what God sends—'tis the only way," and he picked up his canvas bag and walked dispiritedly out of her life.

Furiously Christina rushed on board and seized one of her father's precious books out of Ernest Miller's filthy hands.

"What the devil do you think you're doing on board my ship? Get off! Get off this minute!"

Ernest Miller's big build had run to fat and his belly lay over the broad leather of his belt. Piggy eyes in rolls of red-veined flesh gleamed.

"Not so fast. Who says it's your ship?"

"Of course it's my ship!"

He began to laugh and reached for the cut glass decanter of brandy. Christina's hand shot out, knock-ing the decanter out of his grasping hand; the brandy soaked his greasy shirt and trousers. The expression on his face changed. He moved toward her menac-ingly, and Christina saw the cruelty that lay in the tiny eyes.

"Where's your father's will then? I've looked for it and I can't find one."

The bureau had been ransacked, papers scattering the floor.

"As next of kin the *Lucky Star* is mine, and you, little niece, being under age, are in my care."

Christina backed away. "No—no—I'm not your niece."

She'd never thought to look for a will and she knew with instant clarity that if there had been one Ernest Miller would by now have destroyed it.

Is that what her father had been trying to do when

he had asked for pen and paper with his dying breath? And who was the sister he had tried to write to?

"My father's sister will deal with you," she said, bluffing as if her life depended on it, as indeed it did.

For a second Ernest Miller frowned and then he laughed. "What sister? Do you know her name? Where she lives?"

Christina's face was his answer.

"From now on the *Lucky Star* is mine and so are you."

Christina felt her head swimming, the walls of the cabin closing in on her.

"I'm sixteen. I can look after myself."

"Fourteen," Ernest Miller lied, knowing the battle was won. "Big for your age I shall tell the authorities, but then that's the foreign blood has that effect. They'll be only too pleased to have a relative accept responsibility for you."

A flabby hand engrained with dirt, nails bitten to the quick, seized her wrist. "And you're going to be nice to your Uncle Ernest, aren't you, Christina? *Very* nice." And as she kicked and clawed at his face with her free hand, he pinned her back against the wall of the cabin; Dumas, Thackeray, Dickens and Jane Austen fell incongruously around them as he forced his thick lips on hers.

Chapter 5

Christina fought like a wild thing, kicking, gouging, twisting her head in a vain effort to rid herself of the wet, slobbering tongue forcing its way into her mouth. He wrenched her trapped arm so violently that she swung off balance, taking him with her. Her knee came up hard and high and Ernest Miller screamed in agony, doubling up as he cradled his battered testicles.

She made a vain dash for the door but though still crippled with pain he had recovered sufficiently to grab the long mane of hair, twisting it cruelly in his hands as he dragged her back.

"You'll pay for this, you little whore!" he gasped. The lust rising in him had been temporarily quenched. He drew in huge lungfuls of air and then, with an iron-like grip on Christina's right arm and his hand still yanking her head back by the roots of her hair, he pushed her roughly before him off the decks of the *Lucky Star* and onto the dockside.

Christina was no match for a man of Ernest Miller's build. By the time they reached the dingy cottage she was exhausted from her struggles, her face was streaked with tears of rage. Ernest Miller heaved her bodily over the doorstep, slammed the door shut behind him and began to unbuckle his broad leather belt.

"No!" Liza Miller rushed forward, seizing hold of Christina's arm, knowing full well her husband's intent. She and the children bore enough marks on their backs to know what his action signified.

"The little cow kicked me in the balls and fought and cursed me every inch of the way!" he said savagely, pushing his wife roughly out of the way, moving menacingly toward Christina.

"She's under my roof and she'll do as I bid her!" Ernest Miller said thickly, rounding the corner of the table as Christina dodged round the far side.

The children had long since scattered, cowering on the stone stiarway, watching round-eyed.

"Mucky little bitch!" The belt was raised high, catching Christina across the back and shoulders, searing through her flesh like a knife. She cried out in agony, and Ernest Miller's fat lips parted in a gloating smile as the belt swished through the air yet again. Christina steeled herself for the pain but it never came. Liza Miller flung herself between them; the belt caught her full across the face, sending her reeling against the fire range where a large kettle of boiling water was knocked over, pouring over her hands and arms.

Even Ernest Miller blanched as his wife screamed and the neighbors, hardened to Liza Miller's cries of pain, recognized in them a new note, worse than ever before.

Christina was the first to react. She rushed forward, dragging the demented woman away from the still hissing water running with her into the lean-to that served as kitchen and plunging her hand and arm deep into a bucket of ice-cold water that had been waiting to heat for one of the children's rare baths. Liza Miller sobbed and moaned and Ernest Miller, frightened, did what he had always done when afraid. He ran away. Running hell for leather to the Duke of Wellington, where he stayed until closing time.

By then Christina had bound the scalded hand and arm with the only clean linen available, her petticoat, and had put the terrified children to bed. Liza was still groaning, bands of sweat on her forehead. The door was open. Ernest Miller had gone. There were four hours in which Christina could have made her escape but to do so would have meant leaving Liza Miller to the wrath of her husband, and in her present condition Christina was certain that any more ill-treatment would kill her.

So she stayed. She had missed her chance but there would be others. Liza Miller leaned white-faced over the kitchen range and Christina made her sit down; she made the appallingly thin gruel that was the children's breakfast and unwrapped the home-made bandage carefully as Liza Miller winced in stoical silence. Christina stared at the scalded arm, appalled. She had no idea how to treat it. Very gently she sponged it with cold water and rebound it.

"I'm sorry, Aunt Liza. I don't know what else to do."

"There nowt else you can do lass. Just keep out of his way. He doesn't like to be crossed. No cheek, like."

"I'm leaving. *Now.*"

Liza Miller's pinched face blanched. "You can't, lass. Not now."

"I can," Christina said firmly, grateful for Ernest Miller's absence. "Goodbye, Aunt Liza. I'm sorry about your arm and everything. But I can't stay. I'm going back to the *Lucky Star*. I'm leaving." And she stepped out into the sunlit street, breathing in the fresh air gratefully, turning her face toward the sea.

Liza Miller shook her head despairingly. Ernest had been gone three hours now. It was long enough.

With wings on her heels Christina ran down to the bustling activity of the dockside and then stopped abruptly. The *Lucky Star*'s mooring was empty. She stared unbelievingly and began to run further along, searching with increasing anxiety for the familiar sight of her home.

There were steamers and tugboats, ketches and schooners, but an hour's fruitless search revealed no sign of the gaily painted *Lucky Star*.

"No—oh no!" She was crying now, running frantically up and down the dockside, oblivious of the attention she was drawing to herself. At last she saw a seaman she knew, an acquaintance of her father's. She rushed across to him, seizing him by the arm.

"The *Lucky Star*—Have you seen her?"

"Aye, lass. They sailed her out nigh on two hours ago."

"Who did?" Christina's nails dug deep into his arm. He looked down at her in surprise.

"Why, the Alton Brothers. That's who Ernest sold her to, lock stock and barrel."

Foam frothed at the corner of Christina's mouth and the seaman stepped away from her. The girl was deranged. Her eyes glazed like those of a mad woman.

How long she stood there Christina never knew, but when she finally walked away childhood had been left behind forever.

"If they bite you—bite back." Christina would bite back. No Ernest Miller was going to quench *her* spirit.

She made instinctively for the pubs. Josh. She must find Josh. Josh would help her.

"The Mucky Duck's his pub, love," the landlady of the Anchor said, and then, to her customers, "There'll be some fur flyin' now I reckon!"

"The Mucky Duck was crammed to capacity even though it was only early lunchtime. Christina ignored the ribald comments as she squeezed through the drunken sailors and laborers to the tap room at the back. The loud flow of blasphemies and friendly insults died as she was recognized and her intentions realized. Unknown to herself Christina had the attention of every man in the pub.

The men made way for her as she stepped into the smoke-filled tap room. In the far corner, round a beer-stained table, four men laughed and drank, their sleeves rolled up to their elbows, their flesh glistening with sweat and streaked with dirt.

Josh had his back to her and at the sight of the

familiar broad shoulders and shock of dark hair, Christina nearly burst into tears with relief.

"Josh! Oh Josh!" Her voice broke and she ran toward him, clinging to his arm.

He stared at her as if she was a ghost, setting his pint of ale slowly down on the table. For a minute she saw such unalloyed pleasure at the sight of her that her heart missed a beat, then the expression changed to one of consternation.

"Christina!" His voice held wonder and something else that Christina could not define.

"Oh Josh! Daddy's dead and Uncle Miller's sold the *Lucky Star* and I don't know what to do! He says I have to live with them Josh, and it's awful!"

The welt where the belt had fallen ran from her neck across her shoulders, speaking for itself.

She felt as if a weight had been taken from her. Josh would look after her as he had always done. She had nothing more to fear. Josh was here. Josh with his broad shoulders and strong arms would take care of her. Only her realization that they had an interested audience prevented her from breaking down in tears.

Josh cleared his throat uncomfortably. "Eh, lass, I'm right sorry to hear about tha father. And about the boat."

"But you can get it back for us! He'll be afraid of you!"

Josh wiped the back of his neck with a grubby handkerchief.

"If he's sold it, lass, there's nowt I can do."

"But at least I won't have to go back to him! Not now. Oh Josh, you've no idea how awful it was. What he tried to do to me. He . . ." She broke off, conscious of the listening men.

She pulled on his arm. "Let's go outside to talk, Josh. To the cemetery. Like the old days."

She felt almost carefree again. She had lost her father and the *Lucky Star* but one thing remained firm.

"I, er, I don't think I can do that, Christina."

She stared, suddenly aware of his blatant discomfort.

"But what's the matter? Come on Josh. We can't talk here." She indicated their audience.

"It's not that easy . . ."

She gazed at him uncomprehendingly, slowly sitting down and facing him across the table. This wasn't the old Josh. The Josh she had loved two years ago. Why, he would have taken one look at the welts on her neck and rushed out of the pub to knock Ernest Miller's brains out. Slowly, like drops of ice, there gathered in the pit of her stomach a cold foreboding.

Josh took another swill of his ale, wiped his neck again and, avoiding Christina's eyes, said with difficulty, "You see, after you left, well, I thought you weren't coming back. Leastways not after a year had gone by. It . . . I . . . got lonely like."

"Yes . . . ?" Christina's voice was distant.

Josh struggled vainly, saying with a rush, "I got Nellie Proctor into trouble and I married her."

The silence stretched from seconds into minutes. Through the small window shafts of sunlight fell on his familiar dark head; motes of dust caught in the shining bars.

"It wasn't like, you know, like it was with us, Christina. I swear to God it wasn't." He held his head in his hands and though she couldn't see she knew he was near to tears. "I loved thee, Christina—I did truly. You should have wed me when I asked!"

"And will you help me?" Christina said quietly.

He shook his head despairingly. "I can't! She knows all about you. God, there's never been a day since I wed her that I haven't had your name flung in my face. She can be a cruel cat, that one. If she knew that you were back—that I'd seen you . . ." He shuddered.

Christina stared at him, feeling suddenly calm and composed.

"Then I made the right decision in not wedding you, Josh Lucas. A man who's built like a bull and is too afraid of a woman's tongue to help a friend isn't worth my time of day. Goodbye."

"*Christina!*" He looked up at her, their eyes meeting—his agonized, hers only sad.

"Goodbye, Josh," she said again and with her head held high she walked out of the suddenly silent pub and back into the street.

So now she had no one to take care of her. Only herself. It would suffice. She turned as she knew she must toward the Miller's cottage.

Bessie Mulholland leaned out of her living room window at the Gaiety and gazed out at the dark-haired, olive-skinned girl who had run in such distress away from the dockside. She also noticed that every man's head turned as she passed them by and that even the busiest stopped what they were doing to watch the well-shaped bare feet and long slender legs, their eyes roving speculatively over the thin dress that barely disguised a body young, firm and with an unconscious grace and sensuousness that none of the Liverpool girls possessed.

"Who's that?" she asked one of the girls in the room behind her.

Kate Kennedy stopped admiring her reflection in the glass and looked out of the window, saying contemptuously, "Captain Haworth's brat. A gypsy bastard. She's never fit in here. I thought we'd seen the last of her. Josh Lucas used to be sweet on her."

"So, it seems, is every other thing in pants," Bessie said drily. "A pity she's only calling in."

"Oh, she's here for good this time," Kate said with cruel satisfaction. "Her old man died and his cousin, Ernest Miller, had the boat sold this morning before you could say Jack Robinson. So she'll have to live with the Millers now. Serve her right, stuck-up little bitch."

Bessie Mulholland leaned her head on her arms

thoughtfully. She hadn't seen a girl with so much promise since she'd left London. She made a mental note to find out where the Millers lived and have a private word with Christina.

"You knew, didn't you?" Christina quietly asked Liza.

Numbly, Liza nodded. In the silence Christina filled the kettle with water and put it on the range. If she had to live among wailing children and with hunger as a constant companion, at least she could live cleanly.

Where the money from the *Lucky Star* went Christina never knew. It certainly showed no appearance in the Miller household. A week of tolerating an empty stomach and Ernest Miller's constant presence and foul pawing of her at every opportunity was enough to turn Christina looking for work, any kind of work.

She found it in an ill-lit basement, sewing from eight in the morning to eight at night for sixpence a day

The overseer, a smooth-faced, middle-aged man referred to as "Groper" by the girls, seemed unaccountably patient at Christina's first disastrous attempts to keep pace with the other girls. His patience was explained when he asked her to stay behind on the Wednesday night as he had something to say to her.

When he grinned across at her and asked her if she'd like a drop of gin after a hard day's work, she stared uncomprehendingly. The gin was poured and Christina drank it, expecting it to be like the spirits her father had often given her. The rough alcohol nearly choked her. It was like drinking turpentine. As she tried to regain her breath, the overseer was round his makeshift desk, one hand up her skirt, the other pulling down the top of her blouse.

Using the same method that had proved so successful with Ernest Miller aboard the *Lucky Star*, she drew her knee up hard and high and left him groaning and gasping for breath.

It was summer, and though it was nearly nine o'clock at night the streets were still warm, the setting sun somehow managing to squeeze its way between the crowded streets of cottages and on to the cobbled stones.

Bessie Mulholland stepped forward, smiling and falling into step beside her. Christina looked at her suspiciously and then relaxed. She was becoming something of an expert at judging faces and the jolly, powdered and rouged face held no ill-intent or guile. The friendly eyes were sympathetic and Christina noticed that the dress she wore was of such fine material it hung softly and silkily, a necklace of pearls lying on her ample chest as though on a comfortable shelf. Her feet too were shod and she was wearing stockings, *silk* stockings.

"Bessie Mulholland," the woman said, holding out her hand in a friendly gesture. "Not much fun in there, is it?" She nodded over her shoulder to the grimy, small basement windows of the factory.

"Not much," Christina agreed fervently, noting that the hand that had taken hers had been soft and plump, the nails well shaped.

"Of course they do it because they have no choice, or not much." She indicated two of Christina's scruffy workmates loitering hopefully near a group of uninterested sailors. Their attention was all on Christina's swaying hips.

"Do you think *I'd* do it if I had a choice?" Christina asked wryly.

"Oh, you have," Bessie Mulholland said comfortably. "You could be in feathers and finery if you wanted to."

Christina stared at her. Life with the Millers had temporarily quenched her usual fire. "And just where is the fairy godmother who's going to wave her magic wand and take me out of *this*"—she indicated her sole dress with distaste—"for feathers and finery?"

"Right here," Bessie Mulholland said confidently. "Do you want to listen?"

Christina stopped walking and faced the older

woman. The eyes that met hers were a warm gray, their expression sincere.

"I'm listening," Christina said and Bessie Mulholland, Madam of the finest brothel ever to grace a provincial town, smiled and took her arm into hers.

"How would you like to work for me instead of in that sweatshop?"

"Doing what?" Christina asked, intrigued.

"Making yourself accommodating," Bessie said matter-of-factly. "There's always lots of sailors lonely for company, and I supply them with the company. Or rather my girls do."

Christina's eyes opened wide. "You mean be a prostitute? Go with men for money?"

"Well you might as well get paid for it, love, as do it for free," Bessie said practically.

"*No!*" Christina held her head high. "I'm going to be a lady one day. Not walk round the dockside with holes in my stockings."

Bessie chuckled. "Bless you love, them sort don't work for me. They're independents. They get what they can. When they can. They're at the bottom of the ladder. A girl has to be special to work for Bessie Mulholland at the Gaiety."

"I'm no prostitute," Christina repeated firmly.

"It's not a word I like myself," Bessie confided engagingly. "But there's many a lady has been a harlot and would never have become a lady if she hadn't been."

Christina continued to walk on in silence, remembering the stories she had read of the great courtesans. What Bessie said was true, only it seemed far removed from the girls she had seen loitering in the darkened Liverpool streets.

"There's independents, like the girls you've seen, And then there's brothels. Proper run and where the girls get paid a regular wage and commission on each customer and get fed and a place to sleep. However," she warmed to her theme, "there's brothels and *broth-*

els and the Gaiety is like nothing else you've seen
outside of London. That's because I'm a Londoner
and that's where I first set up business, and very successfully too. One, because I treat my girls well, and
two, because I understand men and cater to their
tastes. Some of them can be an eye-opener!'' She
laughed again. ''You will hear many a tale in Liverpool about Bessie Mulholland and why she had to
leave London. Each one more scandalous than the last
and not one of them true. Anyway, be that as it may,
leave I did and I opened the Gaiety here in Liverpool.
I don't take on just any girls and I don't take on just
any clients, and I don't know anywhere else where
that could be said. Come to me and I'll look after you
like a mother hen over her chick. You'll have good
food and a clean bed to sleep in. You'll have friends
because I don't put up with any unpleasantness in *my*
establishment. The girls all pull together. Share and
share alike. There'll be a lot you have to learn. How
old are you?''

''Seventeen last week.''

Bessie nodded. ''You'll have to do nothing that up-
sets you or go with anyone you take a dislike to. Now
I can't say fairer than that, can I?''

''No . . .''

They were at the end of Gorman Street. Bessie
patted her arm affectionately. ''I like you. We'd get
on well together. Think it over and when you've made
your decision, pack your bags and come to the Gaiety
and ask for Bessie Mulholland.''

''My uncle—he'd come and take me back.''

Bessie grinned. ''I'd like to see him try. I've two
chuckers out that'd make an army take to its heels, let
alone one pot-bellied creature like Ernest Miller. I'll
be seeing you.'' She walked off with a jaunty step, her
bright pink dress a vivid splash of color.

''You're bleedin' late.'' It was Wilf, the oldest of
the Miller boys, and nearly as free with his hands as
his father. There was no sign of Liza.

"Where's your mam?"

"Gone to see Florrie Bellingham. She's 'avin' a bad time with her sixth."

Wilf grinned, showing yellow teeth. He was eighteen, and only his mother's presence had prevented him from taking more liberties with their new lodger than he had. As it was he had pulled her blouse down a score of times but Christina's cries and struggles had always brought someone to her aid before he could do any more but look and lust. Those breasts. They tormented Wilf waking and sleeping. He wanted to get his hands on them, squeeze them till she cried out in agony and now with his mam out and his dad still at the pub he had his chance.

"Don't try it." The intention in the lustful eyes was nakedly apparent and Christina reached instinctively for the bread knife for protection.

Wilf laughed, springing across in one quick movement, the bread knife clattering to the floor as he grasped her wrists. Wilf had had too many tussles with Christina to be caught by having her knee hit hard into his groin. With one deft movement he knocked her legs from under her and fell on top of her, pushing her to the floor with a weight that would soon rival his father's. Christina cried and fought and Wilf laughed, transferring her right wrist to be imprisoned with her left, as his free hand wrenched her dress down to the waist. At long last Wilf felt the golden mound of flesh in his grasp, his nails digging in as he squeezed and twisted, biting her nipples so savagely that he tasted blood.

Christina had feared rape but this was worse. This was insane. She was screaming, and the more she screamed, the more Wilf's eyes gleamed and the more he hurt, tugging at her breasts like a wolf at the carcass of a dead animal. Christina had never thought it possible that she would be grateful for the sound of Ernest Miller's belt slicing through the air.

Wilf yelled, eyes dilated with pain, struggling to his

feet, his arms over his head to protect himself as his father's blows rained down on his head and shoulders. Chased by the strap and his father's obscenities Wilf fled into the street, Christina's blood still on his mouth.

She lay half senseless, knowing only that she must get up, must cover herself up. Ernest Miller's shadow fell across her and she tried to thank him but the words would not come.

Ernest Miller grinned. The lad had nearly done for her. Her eyes were rolling upward under the slumbrous lids in a way that indicated there was no fight left in her. She was as near unconscious as dammit. And Liza was at Florrie's.

He feasted his eyes on the bruised and bleeding breasts, at the careless way her legs were sprawled, her skirt high above her knees. And then, with pleasurable deliberation, Ernest Miller undid his pants and did to his cousin's daughter what he had wanted to do for years. He was no less gentle than his son, and even the anguished cries of his wife at the door was no deterrent to him until he had gained his satisfaction.

It was eons later and Liza was crying, sponging Christina clean with flannels wrung out in warm water. Clean. As if she could ever be clean again.

She was vaguely aware of Liza's incoherent apologies and of her covering her up decently; she watched like an impartial observer as Liza burned bloodstained rags on the fire. Christina gazed bemusedly at her abused breasts but the blood there had dried. The sodden rags Liza Miller was burning had been caused by the injuries inflicted on her by Ernest Miller and in quite a different part of her body. Christina felt herself sink into a sea of blackness. She didn't want to recover consciousness. Didn't want to face reality. If even his wife's presence was not enough to stop Ernest Miller from using her as he wished then there was no hope for her.

When her eyelids finally fluttered open, Liza was holding her hand, her face distraught.

"I'm sorry. He's an animal. There's no stopping him if he wants his way." She began to cry, covering her face with her coarse apron, unable to look at Christina for shame.

"It's all right, Aunt Liza." Christina's voice was weak. "Are they out?"

Liza nodded.

"Then help me get my things together."

This time Liza made no effort to stop her. Christina's pathetically few belongings were wrapped in a shawl.

"Where are you goin'?" she asked.

"To my fairy godmother," Christina said, still white with pain.

Walking was agonizing, but she gritted her teeth and stepped over the hated threshold for the last time. Nothing at the Gaiety could be as bad as life with Wilf and Ernest Miller.

It was nearly midnight when Christina reached the gaudily lit entrance of the brothel.

"Bessie Mulholland," she said to the giant of a man standing like a sentinel at the door, and then collapsed into a heap at his feet, her shawlful of belongings still clutched tightly in her hand.

Chapter 6

When she came to her senses she was in a large bed with clean sheets and the ceiling above her was a dusky pink, lavishly encrusted with golden cherubs. She closed her eyes again, content to continue her dreams, but Bessie, seeing the girl flutter her lashes weakly, said, "Sit up and have a sip of this. Put some warmth back into you."

Christina vaguely recognized the voice. It was cheerful and comforting. She made an immense effort and opened her eyes again. The cherubs were still there and so was a motherly figure in a pink velveteen wrapper edged with *marabou* feathers. She blinked and Bessie laughed, an ample arm helping her into a sitting position against the many pillows.

"Come on, have a sip of this first."

Christina, remembering Groper's gin, was hesitant, and then she smelled the familiar fragrance of the brandy her father had been partial to. She drank it gratefully, feeling the fiery warmth spread through her bruised limbs.

"Whoever he was, he gave you a bit of a rough time," Bessie said bluntly.

Christina's hand rose gingerly to her breasts. They were covered by a strange nightdress. A confection of lace and satin that scarcely covered her nipples. Her breasts were purple and mottled, the dried blood carefully washed away, Wilf's teeth marks carved into the soft skin so that it looked to Christina as though she would bear the marks for life. Reading her thoughts Betty said reassuringly, "A couple of weeks and there won't be a mark left. Mind you, you're going to be no good to me until then, but that's no bad thing. It will give you plenty of time to settle in."

The distant sound of music and the sound of male laughter floated upward.

Christina instinctively cringed, pulling the sheet to her chin.

"Thank you for looking after me, Bessie. But I couldn't—I don't ever want to see another man again . . ."

Bessie patted her hand. "You're forgetting what I told you. I look after my girls. You'll come to no harm here. Not harm like that." She nodded at Christina's maltreated body. "Close your eyes and rest. I'm thinking you're needing it. And don't worry about anything. You're not alone in the world any longer. You've got Bessie Mulholland behind you and that's worth more than His Majesty's fleet!" And she dimmed the gaslight and closed the door quietly behind her.

Christina lay in the darkness of Bessie Mulholland's bedroom; downstairs she could still hear the music and laughter and vibrations of people dancing. They no longer frightened her. Here, in the most notorious brothel outside of London, Christina felt safe at last.

Early the next morning a plain-looking girl in a drab brown dress came in with a tray of bacon and eggs and thick slices of bread and butter. Christina was too hungry to waste time questioning her, but surely, she thought (making short work of the bacon), she couldn't be one of Bessie's girls.

"Annie?" Bessie said with her deep chuckle when she came in later followed by an auburn-haired girl carrying a pile of clothes. "No. Annie hasn't got what it takes, but she's the best cook this side of the Mersey. Feeling better now?"

"Much."

"Good. Then let's get you into something decent. I burnt the dress you arrived in."

A galaxy of scarlet and emerald and brilliant yellow dresses were poured onto the bed.

"I'm Molly," the auburn-haired girl said as she and Bessie finally decided on the scarlet, and draped a black silk shawl over Christina's shoulders, to disguise the barbarity that had been perpetrated on her breasts. The Gaiety didn't possess a high-necked dress in its entire wardrobe.

"Right, that'll do. Now young lady, seeing as how this here is my bed I wonder if you'd mind moving yourself and your new clothes in with Molly and the girls!" Bessie's voice was thick with amusement.

Christina looked at her horrified. "You mean I forced you to sleep somewhere else last night?"

"Well, it wouldn't be the first time I hadn't slept in my own bed, that's for sure, so you didn't put me to any great inconvenience," she said as Molly gurgled with laughter. "Come on. Let's show you the ropes."

Clutching her new dresses, Christina followed Bessie and Molly into a wide corridor, the walls covered in a deep red plush, the carpets reminding her of the *Mauretania*.

"Here we are," Bessie said, opening the door of a small room that contained five beds, three of them occupied by sleeping girls and smelling of perfume and powder. Stockings, underclothes and shoes lay in untidy disarray and the dressing table was littered with pots and jars of creams and lotions, but Christina saw at a glance that the bed linen was as spotless as that in Bessie's own room and that the floor had been recently scrubbed, and beneath all the clutter was the cleanliness that Bessie had promised her she would find.

"You sleep in here," she said, dropping her voice to a whisper. "Put your things on the bed and we'll leave. Don't want to disturb them. It's only midday.

Day's night and night's day at the Gaiety. You'll soon get into the habit of sleeping through the day and working through the night. Now then,"—Bessie led the way into her living room overlooking the dock-side—"let's have a bit of a talk and see what you know and what you don't."

She patted the sofa next to her and Christina sat obediently as Molly curled up like a contented cat in the deep armchair opposite and gave her a conspiratorial wink. Annie came in with the tea tray and they discussed the profession of prostitution over bone-china cups and saucers as though they were ladies of leisure discussing the next hunt ball.

"Was last night your first time?" Bessie asked. The girl had been used so roughly and with such force and had bled so much that it could well have been.

Christina shook her head. "No. I'd done it before. With Josh Lucas."

"See," Molly interrupted triumphantly. "Kate told me Josh Lucas was sweet on her."

"And did you enjoy it?" Bessie asked disarmingly.

"With Josh, yes. But last night—" Her hand trembled and she had to put her cup and saucer down.

Molly and Bessie exchanged glances. "Thank God for Jenny," they both said together and collapsed into laughter. Christina, not understanding the joke, stared at them.

Bessie wiped her eyes and said, "One of the girls in your room, Jenny, would have been in seventh heaven if she'd had what you had last night. So she gets all the specials." Christina's eyes were uncomprehending.

Bessie put her cup and saucer down and said, "You said you enjoyed it with Josh. Well, that doesn't surprise me. You're a girl made for the enjoyment of the senses. I could tell that the minute I clapped eyes on you and that's why I want you to work for me, because so can every man that sees you and it excites them. But if Josh Lucas was sweet on you as Molly says, no doubt he made it nice for you."

Christina struggled to understand.

Bessie, seeing her difficulty, said: "I 'spect he touched you, kissed you, made you want him."

"Oh, yes." Unconsciously Christina's hand moved across her groin and Bessie laughed.

"Kiss you there, did he?"

Christina's face filled with sudden color and Bessie laughed.

"Well, you were a lucky one and no mistake. Specially if he was your first. Not many men bother about a woman's pleasure and that's what I'm trying to tell you. When you did it with Josh, the both of you were trying to please the other. That doesn't happen in a brothel—or very rarely." She chuckled again. "Anyhow, what happens is that men come to *be* pleasured, not to waste time putting themselves out getting *you* excited. Understand me?"

"Yes," Christina said cautiously.

"So *you* have to learn what to do to please them and that's what I'm going to teach you over the next couple of weeks."

"It can be a bit of a letdown," Molly said confidingly. "Sometimes you quite fancy it yourself, especially if he's young and strong, but they spend so much time drinking before they get upstairs that it's over and done with before you can say 'Bob's your uncle' and you're left high and dry as a kite."

"I don't think Kate was left high and dry as a kite last night," Bessie said slyly and Molly laughed.

"Lucky little bugger. Why's he always choose Kate?"

Bessie shrugged. He did and he came regular and if his preference was for the same girl each time he came to the Gaiety then it was her business to see that he was satisfied. Still, it caused a lot of dissatisfaction amongst the girls and Bessie could well understand why. Devlin O'Connor was a man to make any girl's heart miss a beat, and whenever his lithe body with rippling muscles and shock of red-gold hair came striding toward the Gaiety, every girl was on tenterhooks, hoping that just for once she would be given the chance of enjoying her work.

It never happened. Devlin spent most of the evening in Bessie's company, enjoying her salty conversation and when he did satisfy his bodily desires it was always with the big-breasted Kate Kennedy.

When asked what Devlin's performance was like in bed, Kate would laugh throatily and say: "Better than *you'll* ever experience," and return to beautifying her eyelids and lashes, or admiring another expensive trinket that Devlin had carelessly thrown to her as he left.

"So take my tip. Never expect to get anything out of it yourself, 'cos it's a waste of time and effort."

"But what did you mean about Jenny and the 'specials'?"

Bessie frowned slightly. "There's a lot of men like Wilf and Ernest Miller. They get more enjoyment out of hurting women than loving them. So they find they generally have to pay for their pleasures." She saw Christina's eyes darken and continued smoothly. "But strange though it may seem to you, some women actually enjoy being treated like that. Jenny does. So when we get anyone in who likes to hurt a girl, we give him Jenny."

"But doesn't she *mind?*" Christina's voice was unbelieving.

"Mind? God love you. I've had to get the boys in many a time to drag some sadistic beast off her or the silly girl would have let him kill her out of sheer pleasure."

"It's true," Molly said giggling. "And to look at her you'd think a breeze would knock her over."

"That's what I mean about you having a lot to learn. Laying on your back in the grass with a boy you fancy is no preparation for working here. You'd be surprised at some of the things our customers request, but what I'm trying to tell you is this: Girls have strange desires too, and I'm clever enough to always match them up. Any man wanting to give a girl a good beating, he gets Jenny and they're both happy. But it works the other way round too."

Christina stared at her, mesmerized.

Bessie laughed. "Forget the tea and let's all have a brandy, Molly. We've got a missionary on our hands."

"I'm not a missionary!" Christina said indignantly. "I've never even been to Sunday School!"

The two other women went off into such roars of laughter that Molly spilt most of the brandy on the tea tray.

"We call missionaries them that lie on their back and do nowt else," Molly gasped at last, handing her a generously full glass of golden liquid.

"Oh," Christina grinned. She never minded taking a joke against herself.

"I forgot what I was saying," Bessie said, wiping her eyes with a lace handkerchief. "Oh yes. The other way round. Then some men coming here will pay a fortune to *be* whipped."

"Blimey," Chirstina said expressively. "If you don't learn something new every day."

"Some girls don't mind doing it. Others do. I always respect their wishes. That's why I'm such a success. The Gaiety doesn't just cater for common seamen. It's well known as far as Europe. Dandies often come on the train and after they've registered in the best hotel in town they call a cab and ask for the Gaiety."

"Sheba Matthews enjoys that best," Molly said confidingly. "Giving them a good belt across their backsides I mean."

"And then," Bessie continued, "there's them that just like to watch."

Christina finished her brandy in a hurry and said,

knowing it would cause amusement, but wanting to know the answer, "Watch what?"

"Everythin' and anythin'," Molly said with a giggle.

"Then there's some who just like to watch you do it normal like, but with the sailors. They're usually the dandies. There's a special room with a peephole in. They have to pay double for that."

"And all they do is watch?" Christina asked in amazement.

Bessie nodded. "There's also some girls who like each other. Do you know what I mean? There's a lot of men like to watch that."

Christina didn't know what she meant but was beginning to get a good idea.

"So there's Letty and Sophie. They only like it with each other anyhow. Normal work drives them round the bend," Molly said dismissively.

"I usually find," Bessie said choosing her words with care, "that every girl has some *special* talent. Something that she personally likes and that we can put to good use. When you find out what yours is, don't be shy in letting me know. Just let them bruises die away first. As I said, there's some customers it would excite just to look at them, but I'll not make capital of you like that. I think we've told you enough for one day, any more and you'll be frightened off for good. I've the accounts to do now. Molly will show you over the Gaiety while it's still quiet." She dismissed them with a friendly wave of her hand.

"If everyone else is asleep, how come you're up?" Christina asked Molly as they left the room.

"Night off," Molly said explanatively. "We all have one every week. There's not many women like Bessie Mulholland and that's for sure. You'll be all right as long as you have her looking after you. The room where your bed is, that's your own bed. Not for work. There's four rooms like that and we all pig in and borrow each other's dresses and stockings. It's

all very friendly. *These* rooms,"—she touched the
brass knob of the first of a series of heavily carved
doors on the red plush corridor—"*these* are the *work*
rooms." She led the way into a series of intimate
rooms with red damask walls. "These are all numbered and you'll get your own number later on."

She opened the first door. The bed was huge, the
sheets black satin, the many lamps shaded by dark red
shades. Above the bed, in the ceiling, was the largest
mirror Christina had ever seen, and there were rugs
of animal skins on the floor.

The next room was all gold and red with mirrors
everywhere, velvet-covered divans and gas chandeliers vying for attention with a life size statue of Ve-
nus. Beside the enormous bed there was a long, low
stool and coils of thin, strong rope.

"What's that for?" she asked Molly.

"That's for one of the things we forgot to tell you
about downstairs," Molly said with a laugh. "Some
of 'em like to tie you up before they do it. I don't
mind that. Just lay there on me back and think of
something interesting while they get on with it. There's
one drawback about this profession," she said as she
led Christina out of the room, "it don't 'alf put you
off men!"

She showed her plainer rooms, and then the one
with the peephole and then a series of elaborate bathrooms.

"That's a house rule. Any gentleman wanting the
services of the upstairs has to have a bath first. Caused
uproar at first. Specially with the sailors. They never
heard the like of it, but Bessie was insistent. She'd
come up from London and had a lot of fancy ideas.
Now no one seems to mind, especially as they have
help scrubbing their backs." She laughed again. "Most
of the blokes are nice decent types. Just lonely for a
bit of company. Bessie only had that talk with you to
tell you straight the worst side of it. She's like that.
Always very straight with you. But you'll have no

problems. Anyone you take a dislike to, a nod in the direction of Bert—he's the chucker-out who carried you in yesterday—and someone else will replace you. It's a doddle of a job. Beats scouring floors any day!'' Like two old friends, Molly and Christina walked down the elaborate staircase to the bar downstairs.

It looked little different to the scores of other waterfront taverns and gave no hint of the gaudy splendor upstairs. The only difference was that it wasn't open for business. Seven o'clock was Bessie's opening time and not one minute before.

Bert, who, aided by an equally burly but more silent partner, kept order at the Gaiety, gave her a slow, friendly smile as he carried on re-arranging chairs and tables on the freshly swept floor.

"Feeling perkier now are you?"

"Yes, thank you, Bert.'' She felt suddenly shy, knowing that he had carried her into the Gaiety and upstairs and that he must know very well what the black shawl around her shoulders and negligently covering her from the throat down to the top of her dress concealed.

"Bastards, some of 'em,'' Bert said sympathetically. "Doesn't go on here. 'Cept for them that don't mind. Anyone try hurtin' you and you just yell at the top of your voice for me. *I'll* soon sort him out.'' He looked suddenly hopeful. "You wouldn't like to tell me who the bastard was that did that to you last night, would you?''

For a minute, Christina, remembering the ferocity of Wilf's attack and the appalling violence with which Ernest Miller had taken her in full view of his wife, was sorely tempted to tell him. But in the end it would be Liza Miller who would suffer.

"No,'' she said. "It doesn't matter now. It's all over with.''

"Bastards,'' Bert said again, moving a table and chair until it fell into line with the others.

"If Mrs. Mulholland wants us, tell her we've gone for a walk," Molly said, slipping a shawl around her slender shoulders.

Christina's eyes thanked her. She was grateful for Bessie and the Gaiety, but she needed fresh air like a flower needs the sun.

They strolled, arm in arm, Christina in her new scarlet dress and wearing her first pair of high heeled shoes that made her totter perilously every few yards.

"You'll soon get the hang of 'em," Molly said reassuringly. "I'd never worn nowt but clogs before I came here. Now I wouldn't be seen dead without my silk stockings and my high heeled shoes."

"That's something else you have to learn," Molly said confidingly. "How to take your clothes off. No use just scrambling out of them. Their girlfriends can do that. Have to make it a bit more exciting, see. Most of my clients like me to keep my stockings and garters on. Shoes as well sometimes." She sighed. "I had a boyfriend before I came here. Nice uncomplicated bloke he was. I thought he couldn't have been normal after I'd been in the Gaiety a few weeks, but you'll learn. I still see him sometimes. He doesn't like me doing any of my tricks for him. Nice and straight with him doing all the work. Lovely."

A little face, mischievous as a kitten's, smiled at Christina. "I'm glad you've come. I liked you straight away. I'd heard about you of course, but I didn't let that bother me."

"Heard about me?" Christina asked, frowning slightly. "Heard what?"

"That you were a reglar in Liverpool or used to be, and that you're a gypsy and that Liverpool folk didn't get on too well with either you or your father, but Bessie won't put up with bitchy gossip. Not if she knows about it. Course, there's plenty goes on she *doesn't* know about. Bound to be with twenty girls living together. Wouldn't be normal if there weren't."

"Who was it at the Gaiety knew so much about me?" Christina asked, enjoying the breeze on her face and the familiar cry of the gulls.

"Kate Kennedy."

Christina stopped walking, her face paling. "Does she work at the Gaiety?"

"Yes. She's been here a year. Why? Do you know her?"

Christina had recollected herself quickly but Molly had seen the reaction Kate's name had caused on her new-found friend.

Christina shrugged. The afternoon when she had seen Josh with his arm around Kate was light years away and no longer mattered. Silly to have felt such a sudden, painful reminder of the jealousy she had then felt.

"A little. We never liked each other very much."

"Then you're in good company. No one else does either, but we have to be careful because she's good with the customers and Bessie thinks highly of her. Kate thinks highly of herself too. That's the trouble. Always putting on airs and graces. Thinking herself better than the rest of us. *And* getting all the best customers." Molly remembered the swaggering Irishman with the sun-gold hair.

"It's not fair," Molly continued, "you should have seen my customers last night. A right pack of pale-faced ninnies and she has only the one for the night. It's not fair."

"But I thought you said Bessie was always fair?"

"So she is," Molly admitted grudgingly. "Devlin pays for the full night so he gets it. I only wish it was some bronchial, obese eighty-year-old that demanded her with such regularity. She'd still go with him, would Kate, because of the extras. Devlin always leaves a bracelet or pair of earrings. But to have both the pleasure *and* the profit. It isn't fair."

"Who is Devlin?" Christina asked.

"A sailor. Captain of the *Adventurer*. Been coming

every few months this last year. And only to Kate. It's the breasts that do it," Molly said looking down regretfully at her own small and beautifully shaped ones. "Kate's are huge. I think they make her look deformed myself. Her having such a tiny waist and hips. But there you are. The clients love it."

"And what's so special about this Devlin that it causes all the jealousy?" Christina asked idly, her eyes scanning the rows of boats, wondering where the *Lucky Star* was.

"You wait till you see him! *Then* you'll know." The mischief was back in her eyes. "I say, Christina. You know Bessie never makes a mistake. There *is* something special about you. There's not a head that hasn't turned since we left the Gaiety. Wouldn't it be a turn-up for the books if Devlin decided he preferred you next time he was in port? I wouldn't be jealous if it was you. It would be worth it just to see the expression on Kate's face." Her eyes gleamed with relish, and then she said more soberly, "But if he does, or if any of her special clients do, watch her. She's a hard-hearted little bitch and only Bessie's presence would prevent her from taking a knife to you and marking your face for life. I heard of how she did it to one girl before she came to the Gaiety. So be careful. She's not one to cross."

Chapter 7

Bert was sprawled out on two chairs, an empty pint glass by his side, his eyes closed, his mouth open as he snored peacefully.

Christina and Molly tip-toed round him and went upstairs. As they neared the door of the room she was to share with Molly and the three other girls, Christina could hear the sound of voices thick with sleep. She found herself hoping intensely that Kate Kennedy was not to be one of her roommates.

The disarray as Molly opened the door was even worse than before. A girl with a stunning head of bright red curls was surveying herself in the mirror through bleary eyes, a satin negligee trimmed with seed pearls half on and half off her shoulders.

"Is that the new girl?" she asked, still looking in the mirror, scrutinizing her skin with critical eyes.

The other two girls, one still in bed, the other pulling on a pair of black fishnet stockings, looked toward Christina with interest.

"Christina Haworth," Molly said, bouncing down on her bed. "Christina, this here is Nymphy." She indicated the tousled head and sleepy eyes emerging from a cocoon of blankets. "This is Belle." The dark haired girl pulling on her stockings smiled at her lazily. "And that's Sheba."

The red-head finished the examination of her face and stood up, stretching languorously. Christina's eyes widened. While she had been sitting down all that had been obvious had been the incredibly long legs. Now that she was standing she took on Junoesque proportions. She was easily six feet tall and her strong, firm body was that of a beautiful giantess.

"So you're Kate's infamous gypsy? She did you a disservice. With a face and a figure like that, Bessie would have been mad not to have taken you on."

"Kate doesn't like her," Molly said, "so take no notice of what *she* says."

"As if we would," Belle said, pulling on her other stocking and then straddling the low chair that faced the mirror, resting her arms on the back as she surveyed herself critically.

"Are you really a gypsy?" Nymphy asked, propping herself up against the pillows, a naked breast escaping from the sheets and bobbing plumply against her arm.

"Yes. My mother was Spanish."

"So it's not like being a tinker?"

"No." There was no malice in the question and Christina answered with a smile.

"Bessie says you've had a bad time and won't be working for a few days." Sheba's eyes were sympathetic.

"I'll say she did," Molly said, and before Christina could stop her had whisked the shawl from Christina's shoulders, exposing her purple and mottled breasts, the teeth marks standing out in ugly white relief.

"Jeez," Belle said expressively, "and you didn't even get paid for it!"

Molly giggled. "Don't you ever think of anything but money, Belle? I'd like to know what you do with it all. Those are *my* stockings again and you wore them last night as well."

Belle shrugged and burnt a match, carefully darkening her eyebrows with it.

"I shall probably set myself up in a nice little tea shop somewhere in another few years."

The other girls hooted with laughter.

"What! With a red light outside and fancies served upstairs!" Nymphy gasped at last.

Belle threw a pillow across at her, knocking her half out of bed. "It's all right for you," she said good-naturedly as Nymphy struggled into a sitting position again. "You'll still be on the game when you're fifty. Even if it means you're doing it for free!"

Nymphy returned the pillow with gusto, following it up by a salvo of others.

"Cheeky cow," she said with a grin as a pillow caught Belle full in the face.

"Help me with these, will you?" Sheba said to Christina, and threw a thigh-high black leather boot across to her.

Christina obediently held the sole and heel as Sheba forced her foot inside, standing up and pulling the boot high over her knee, repeating the operation with the other boot.

Christina stared in fascination. She looked like a female Gulliver. The negligee fell back into place and Sheba began manicuring her nails while Belle finished rouging her face and Molly helped her into a small black corset with suspenders for the fishnet stockings and then slipped on a scanty lilac satin dress that had more bead fringing than material.

"Ladies of fashion," Belle said knowingly, "wear hobble skirts but they're no use here. You've got to show a bit of leg and be accessible, if you know what I mean." The absence of undergarments indicated exactly what she meant.

Molly rouged her nipples and grinned at Christina. "One of my regulars likes me to put jam on 'em so he can lick it off. Keeps 'im 'appy but ain't 'alf a waste of good food!"

The door opened and a blonde-haired girl in a black taffeta dress entered. The dress was cut low at the bodice, revealing full, heavy breasts, but the material, the lack of cheap ornaments or a necklace, set her distinctly apart from the other girls.

The blonde hair lay straight and sleek, falling forward at both sides of her face in a style Christina had never seen before, helping to disguise the thinness of her face. Only when she spoke did Christina recognize Kate.

"So our new recruit is to be given special treatment and allowed a rest before she starts work." Kate leaned against the door, showing herself off to best advantage. There was no sign of the dirty street-girl that Christina had known. The girl who had always had lice in her hair and dirt engrained in her neck and hands. The girl who had initiated half the local boys into the pleasures of sex. The girl who had taken Josh from her when she had so childishly needed him. Only the eyes hadn't changed. They were still narrow and calculating and no amount of make-up could bring any warmth into them.

"You'd need a rest if you'd been through what she's been through," Molly said defensively.

"Would I?" Kate's voice was taunting. "I bet she enjoyed every minute of it, didn't you?"

Christina resisted the urge to slap Kate full across her smug face. The snakelike eyes were alight now, and Christina had the sense to know that Kate was goading her on purpose. Wanting her to react in such a way that Bessie would ask her to leave.

She said unemotionally, "No. I didn't."

Kate laughed huskily. "That's not what I heard. I heard you and Ernest Miller had a high old time in Gorman Street. Ernest says he's never had it so good, or in so many ways. And it didn't stop there, did it? Father and son both together. Not many can lay claim to that," she began to laugh and Christina's good intentions went to the wind.

Before Kate realized what was happening or before the other girls could stop her, she flew at Kate, clutching fistfuls of carefully groomed blonde hair and tugging viciously as she yanked Kate Kennedy's head from side to side.

"You lying little whore!" Christina spat and Kate screamed, squirming vainly.

"You take it back, every last word!"

"I won't! I won't! You even did it in front of his wife! And he was your uncle, mucky little cat!"

A hand hit Kate full across the face. *"He's not my uncle!"* Christina was panting, her nails clawed. *"You take it back. Every last word!"*

Sheba and the other girls ringed them, showing no inclination to go to Kate's aid.

"You've ruined my hair and you've hurt my face!" Kate was crying.

"I'll do to your face what you did to some other girl's face if you don't take back every lying word you have just said," Christina said grimly, yanking on Kate's hair again for good measure.

"All right! I take it back! But you'll pay for this, just you see if you don't!"

"None of it was true?" Christina's voice would have struck terror into a grown man.

"None of it," Kate gasped unconvincingly.

Christina let her go and Kate backed hastily to the door. "I'll get my own back on you, Christina Haworth! I'll make you wish you'd never been born!" And with her cheeks stained ugly scarlet, her hair in tangled disarray, Kate banged the door shut after her.

"Well, well," Sheba said approvingly. "At least you can stick up for yourself. But you've made an enemy there and not one I envy you."

"Bessie will be furious," Nymphy said from the safety of her bed.

"Bessie won't hear about it," Belle said confidently. "There were too many witnesses to what Kate said to Christina."

Sheba nodded in agreement. "Maybe so, but I'd

keep out of her way if I were you. Come on, we're going to be late."

From downstairs came the sound of music and laughter.

. "What have I to do now?" Christina asked, feeling suddenly at a loss.

"Stay in here and get some sleep," Sheba advised. "If the customers catch a sight of you, you'll find yourself working whether Bessie thinks you should or not."

Belle gave her arm a friendly pat and said, "If you want to borrow any make-up, just help yourself to mine"—and Nymphy, whose dress was so revealing that Christina thought she might just as well be stark naked, said, "I've a spare bottle of perfume in my top drawer. Help yourself to it. And don't take any notice of that cat Kate. No one believes it's like she said."

Molly grinned at her as the others left the room. "I told you that they were a nice crowd. See you later."

Christina sat down on her bed. Perhaps now Kate would leave her alone. She hoped so. She wasn't vicious by nature and had gained no pleasure or satisfaction from the unpleasant scene with Kate. She rolled onto her back, overcome by fatigue. She would behave to Kate as if nothing had happened. If Kate wished to continue the quarrel it was entirely up to her. There was the sound of doors opening and closing and loud male laughter and then Molly's unmistakable giggle. Christina closed her eyes and smiled. It seemed as if Molly was enjoying her work

Christina was more tired than she had known She slept long and deep and was only awoken by Belle slamming the door open so violently that it trembled on its hinges.

"Bloody fool!" she was saying explosively as she crossed toward her bed, followed by a giggling Molly.

"I told him! I don't care what they do in the brothels at Shanghai! He can take his bloody bulldog somewhere else!"

Molly collapsed into laughter and Christina said bewilderedly, "Doesn't she like animals?"

"Yes, but not in the way her customer wanted her to," Molly said, between fresh paroxysms.

Before Christina could ask for an explanation, Sheba strode in, clad in nothing but her thigh-high black leather boots and with a riding crop swishing angrily against the leather.

"Trouble?" Molly asked.

"There will be in a minute," Sheba said between chattering teeth as she pulled a negligee around her shoulders, and Molly began to help her off with her boots.

The door opened and Bessie came in, her lips compressed in a firm line.

"Where is Mr. Pierce-Jones?" she asked Sheba tightly.

"Where I left him," Sheba answered furiously. "Bending stark naked over the stool in room seven and waiting for me to thrash him."

"Then why are you not doing so?"

Sheba threw one boot to the floor and began struggling with the other.

"For the simple reason that Mr. Pierce-Jones is completely off his rocker. He insists on having all the windows wide open so that he can freeze to death as part of his 'punishment.' I've stood in there for over an hour waiting until he's bloody cold enough and he still isn't ready. If he thinks I'm waiting till my tits are blue and I catch pneumonia he's got another think coming!"

"And is Mr. Pierce-Jones *still* in number seven?"

"Yes. He probably hasn't missed me yet. I shouldn't worry about him. It's an east wind and blowing straight up his arse. He's having a whale of a time."

Tight-lipped Bessie left the room and there was an audible sigh of relief from the rest of the girls.

"You'll be in for it in the morning," Belle said. "Fancy just walking out and leaving him."

"If you feel so sorry for him, take my riding crop and run along there yourself," Sheba said, climbing into bed and burying herself beneath the blankets. "I've never been so cold in all my life! I'm *freezing!*"

Christina was already drifting back to sleep.

"Champagne! Goody!"

There was a loud pop and Christina sat bolt upright, terrified. A laughing Bessie was holding a foaming bottle and an unknown girl had sat herself down on Christina's bed.

The room was packed with girls, some still in their working finery, others wrapped in nothing more than a scrap of lace or satin.

"Here's to Christina," Bessie said, pouring the fizzing liquid into outstretched glasses. "Welcome to the Gaiety, luv."

There was a chorus of welcomes and Christina, recognizing Kate on Bessie's right hand side, saw her raise her glass and smile. She smiled back, glad that the silly fight had apparently been forgotten. If she had been a little more wide-awake she would have seen the expression in Kate's eyes and realized that nothing could have been further from the truth.

Molly squeezed beside her on the bed, and another girl Christina had never seen before perched at the foot.

"Well, now for introductions," Bessie said genially, as Christina tasted her first sip of champagne. The bubbles tickled her nose but she liked it. It was a drink that she could easily become accustomed to.

"These four lay-abouts here you've already met. And I believe you know Kate from the old days. This here's Letty." She nodded in the direction of a tall, dark girl sitting on the edge of the dressing table. "And that's Sophie." A fair-haired girl with a gentle face was standing, one arm resting lightly around her friend's shoulders.

"The one crushing your feet to pulp is Cassie." Cassie shifted obligingly. "And the other one on your bed is Rosie." A broad-hipped girl in a mauve satin wrapper with a bead fringe smiled warmly. "Marigold." Bessie waved a hand at a remarkably pretty girl with delicate features who raised her glass to Christina. "Her real name is Constance but we felt it was a bit out of place at the Gaiety so she's Marigold. She shares with Maggie, Su-Su, Francine and Jenny."

Maggie's heavy make-up made her face difficult to discern, but Su-Su was oriental, with a beautiful oval face and slanting black eyes and a mane of heavy, jet-black hair. Francine looked unmistakably French, but it was Jenny who attracted Christina's attention. Jenny, who loved to be maltreated and whipped. She smiled sweetly at Christina, curling up on the end of Molly's bed wrapped in what was, for the Gaiety, a demure high-necked dressing-gown. She had already brushed and plaited her long brown hair, and she looked as frail and fragile as a little bird. Her large eyes were soft, her generous mouth gentle.

"Violetta," Bessie continued like a school mistress taking the register. "Her name is really Violet, but she thinks it sounds common so Violetta it is. Merry was born and brought up in Liverpool." She indicated a small girl with a smiling face. Merry helped herself to another glass of champagne and gave her a friendly nod. "Dimity and Lalage."

Christina hardly noticed the oddly-named Dimity, but couldn't take her eyes off Lalage. Her skin was shining ebony, her hair a short cap of crinkling curls. Gleaming white teeth flashed in a smile. Lalage was used to being stared at.

The next two weeks enabled Christina to make friends with nearly all of the girls. Kate kept her distance but her eyes, when she saw Christina, were malevolent, and only a sharp reprimand from Bessie had kept her from spreading her vile lies about Christina amongst her roommates.

It was impossible not to like Nymphy, who spent

her daytime leisure hours doing what she did at night for profit.

Although Molly was her closest friend, Christina found herself liking the Junoesque Sheba more and more. There was a directness and honesty about her that appealed to Christina's own guileless nature. But that was where any similarity ended. Sheba did not like men. Any men. She whipped them, took their money and despised them.

Christina soon took as natural the fact that Letty and Sophie preferred to share the same single bed, and preferred each other to any of the customers. Cassie kept herself a little apart from the other girls, and her speech and bearing indicated that she came from a very different background to the rest of them. The apple-cheeked Rosie, at sixteen, was the baby and was treated accordingly.

Marigold was the oldest of the Gaiety girls and gave Christina plenty of straightforward advice.

Christina never got to know Maggie properly. Mainly because she liked to spend her free time in solitude and preferably with a bottle. So far it hadn't affected her looks, but when it did she would, Marigold predicted, be on the bottom rung, soliciting on the dockside and with no Bessie Mulholland to protect her.

Jenny afforded Christina the most wonder. She was so quiet and gentle, never laughing out loud like the rest of them, simply smiling quietly, her hands folded in her lap in a serene pose that would have done credit to a Madonna.

Violetta was constantly sulky and bad-tempered and had not an ounce of humor in her. Christina instinctively gave her a wide berth.

Merry was as happy-go-lucky as her name and often joined Molly and Christina on their afternoon walks. Like Kate and Christina she came from Liverpool and knew Josh Lucas. She often tried to get Christina to talk about him but on that one subject Christina was silent. She had never quite come to terms with the man who was now Josh Lucas and the loss of Josh, the boy who had been her childhood friend. The hurt at his refusal to help her had gone deep and was still raw. Whenever Merry brought the subject up she turned it deftly, and in the end Merry stopped asking her and kept to herself the knowledge that Josh often hung about the open doors of the Gaiety, never crossing the threshold but spending night after night pacing up and down the dockside in abject misery.

When Christina had asked Molly why Dimity had been called Dimity, Molly laughed and said, "Something to do with the dress she was wearing when Bessie took her in and also because she's not very bright."

As Saturday night approached Christina felt the muscles of her stomach tighten with excitement. She knew what was expected of her, but as Lalage dressed her hair fiercely, trying to smooth out the waist-length tangles, she felt suddenly nervous.

Bessie came in and surveyed Lalage's effort with a shrewd eye.

"Here, give me that." She took the hairbrush from Lalage. "Stand up," she said to Christina.

With legs suddenly weak, Christina obeyed. Bessie looked at her critically for a few minutes.

"Take off those stockings and shoes. I've seen the light at last. Tarting you up like all the other girls is ridiculous. You're not *like* the other girls. That's why I wanted you in the first place."

She tossed the discarded stockings and shoes on to the bed. "Take that dress off as well, Lalage! There's a cotton top and a full skirt on my bed. Bring them here."

Taking the hairbrush she began to tease Christina's thick curly hair into its usual wild tangle. Finally she threw the hairbrush after the shoes and finished the job off with her fingers. Lalage came in with the clothes and Christina slipped obediently into an ankle-length skirt of vivid yellow cotton with a deep frill round the hem. The top was scarlet, the neckline elasticized, and Bessie expertly adjusted it low on her shoulders, leaving a pleasing amount of olive skinned flesh showing between breasts and waist.

Bessie surveyed her handiwork approvingly. Now for the earrings.

She clipped huge gold hoops onto Christina's ears and stood back well pleased.

"Can you dance?"

"Of course I can dance!" Christina was indignant. "My mother was the best flamenco dancer in the whole of Spain!"

Bessie chuckled. "Then get down them stairs and shake your tail feathers!"

Christina surveyed herself in the mirror and liked what she saw. Her hair hung waist-length in a smoke-black cloud. Her olive skin needed no powder or rouge. The light cotton of her blouse showed the full swell of her breasts and the gold of the earrings hung gleamingly against her neck. Her legs and feet were bare, comfortably free of stockings and shoes. She could hear the music and was filled with an overwhelming desire to dance as her mother had danced: High on a table surrounded by cheering men, her head thrown back, hands clapping, feet moving like lightning to the ever increasing rhythm.

"Blood," Bessie said to Lalage with a satisfied smile on her face as they followed Christina downstairs, "will out. I think we're going to see a sight to remember tonight!"

Chapter 8

The downstairs of the Gaiety was divided into two bars separated by a bead and bamboo curtain. The first, the one that opened onto the street, serving drink to men who wanted nothing more, as well as catering for potential clients. The rear bar was more luxuriously decorated, with carpets on the floor and large, circular tables around which eight or ten men could gather at a time. Only customers crossed the great divide between the two bars, paying Bessie as she sat behind a leather-topped desk resplendent in a tight peach satin dress, with diamonds at throat and ears. Some, the regulars, simply handed over the money and entered. Others took longer, often looking mildly uncomfortable as they explained their preferences. Some already knew the girl they wanted. Others sat playing cards, drinking brandy and surveying the range of the Gaiety girls before singling one out and making an approach. Now and then Bessie's eyebrows would lift slightly as some gentleman returned to her desk and Jenny or Sheba would quietly slip away and after a brief introduction lead her client up the ornate staircase for specialist treatment.

The girls all had keys to the different rooms, and as there was a generous commission paid by Bessie on top of the weekly wage for every customer they accommodated, Christina saw with amusement that there was quite a lot of vying among the girls to gain the eye of any gentleman still playing cards or drinking.

The lights from the gas-lit chandeliers were brilliant, there was music from an accordion, and the room was full of perfume and smoke and laughter. Christina felt herself relaxing, conscious of the attention she was getting and enjoying the approval in the many pairs of eyes centered on her.

Approach after approach was made but Marigold referred everyone to Bessie with such deftness that Christina was hardly aware of it. Each time Bessie shook her head and sent the disappointed customer elsewhere.

"Have a brandy," Marigold said, handing Christina a half-full tumbler.

"I thought we weren't supposed to drink unless it was the customers who were paying?"

"It's your first night. A couple of drinks will do no harm."

At a signal from Bessie the accordion began to play a vibrant piece of music that evoked in Christina memories of Mahon and of Malaga.

"Like to dance?" Marigold asked, removing a hand from beneath her skirt without even bothering to look at the offender.

The brandy had gone to Christina's head; the lights, the color, the music, enveloped her in a world so far removed from the squalor of Gorman Street that her nervousness vanished and she knew only the gay recklessness that was so integral a part of her character.

"Not 'alf," she said, her teeth flashing in a wide smile. Without any further prompting from Marigold she jumped onto a table top, the men hastily reaching for their glasses as her skirt began to swirl and she gave herself up in utter abandon to the ever-increasing rhythm of the music.

The bearded sailor escorting Violetta upstairs changed his mind and to Violetta's fury walked back down to join the crowd around Christina.

Maggie, who had been enjoying the attention of two young men at the bar, found herself suddenly deserted.

The well-dressed middle-aged gentleman known only as Mr. Smith deferred his pleasure of watching Letty and Sophie and watched with growing arousal Christina's long brown legs as the yellow skirt swung high and wide, her nipples showing dark against the thin cotton of her blouse. The music grew faster and Christina whirled, her bare feet moving like quicksilver over the polished surface of the table, her hair a black curtain that whisked across the faces of the watching men. Then the accordion changed rhythm, slowing down to a throbbing melody that Christina matched with a sensuous rotation of her hips, her neck and arms swaying gracefully.

Bessie watched, well satisfied. She had discovered Christina's talent and it was one that would draw many customers.

Marigold, catching her eye, squeezed through the clapping, cheering men and crossed to her desk.

"The young one with fair hair," Bessie said, pointing to a good-looking, well-built boy of about nineteen. "He's asked for Christina."

"So has every other man in the place," Marigold said with a grin. "If we're not careful it could cause trouble."

"Not while I'm in charge," Bessie said confidently. "When she's finished dancing see the boy is her first customer."

An army of hands and arms helped a panting Christina from the table as the music ended. She was aware of the warmth of hot palms on her waist and hips but she was laughing, knowing she had been a success. Bessie would keep her and not send her back to Gorman Street.

"Number three," Marigold said to her above the pandemonium, and thrust Christina's hand into that of the waiting boy.

Leaving the room was no easy task and Bessie had to send Bert across to keep order and allow Christina and her customer access to the stairs.

Maggie's companions quickly returned. Mr. Smith resumed his journey to Letty and Sophie's room, and Violetta continued to sulk. Kate Kennedy stood apart from both customers and girls. Up till now she had held a favored place at the Gaiety. After the spectacle she had just seen she knew she was about to be supplanted. Unless she did something about it. Her narrow eyes followed Christina's retreating back with malice.

Buoyed up by the intoxication of the brandy and the cheers that had been solely for her, Christina led the way confidently up the staircase and along the red-carpeted corridor to number three. From the next room she recognized Nymphy's voice crying out in pleasure and hoped her customer didn't have a wife to return to. Nymphy was notorious for clawing deep scratch-marks into the backs of her customers.

She turned the key in the lock and entered. A lamp with a big silk shade cast its rosy glow over the room. The bed stood large and vast. Christina heard her customer close the door behind him and her confidence vanished. She couldn't bring herself to look at him. What was she supposed to do? What did he expect? He made no move toward her and her anxiety rose. If he simply wanted to make love to her it would be simple. She had caught a glimpse of his face downstairs and had liked what she had seen. But he obviously expected *her* to make all the moves and Christina didn't know what moves to make. Frantically she tried to recall all the advice given her.

First of all she had to take her clothes off, and *not* struggle out of them. That was what Molly had said. With trembling fingers she lifted the cotton blouse over her head as slowly and provocatively as possible, keeping her face turned away from him, feeling her cheeks color. She knew she hadn't done it very well, but how did one take off a blouse provocatively? It wasn't as if it undid down the front. Cassie's specialty was stripping and she had watched her, mesmerized, during the previous two weeks, feeling herself grow hot at the way Cassie slowly and teasingly divested herself of her clothes. If it had that effect on her, and Christina knew herself well enough to know that she was no latent Letty or Sophia, then God alone knew what it did to the men!

But her removal of her blouse held none of the suggestiveness of Cassie's movements. She swallowed, her fingers fumbling nervously with the button on her skirt. She should move. Cassie always moved, driving her audience into a frenzy.

The silence seemed to stretch into eternity and still the young man made no move toward her. For a panic-stricken moment she wondered if her naked body did not please him, and she turned her head tentatively toward him.

His back was toward her; her efforts at titillating him in removing her clothes had all been in vain.

She waited hesitantly. He drew his shirt over his head and began to fumble with the buckle of his belt. She heard him swear beneath his breath and saw that his arm was trembling.

With a flood of relief she realized that he was as nervous as herself. She moved forward, stepping out of the circle of her skirt, touching him lightly on the shoulder.

He jumped nervously, the buckle still obstinately fastened.

Christina smiled engagingly. "I do hope you don't mind, but tonight is my first time. I've never worked in a place like this before."

He turned to her, a clean-cut face filled with relief that equaled hers.

"You haven't?"

She shook her head. "And I don't quite know what to do," she added disarmingly.

He grinned, his confidence returning. "Me neither. I mean, I've never been in a place like this before, but I know what to do!" and he picked her up in his arms and carried her across to the bed, proceeding to prove it with zest.

Over the next few weeks Christina's initial feeling of elation left her. As Molly had so prosaically told her, entertaining customers was a job and like any other job it became boring and monotonous.

Her joyful experience with her first client was not repeated, and Christina found herself wondering how long it would be before his ship docked once more in Liverpool.

The majority of the men made love to her so quickly and perfunctorily that Christina couldn't imagine why they went to the bother of paying for such a brief pleasure in the first place. Certainly it was no pleasure to her, though she had the sense never to let them know it. And why should they want to spend half of the time talking about their wives and girlfriends back home?

After two weeks it seemed to Christina that a good three quarters of her sex had no sense at all. Seaman after seaman confessed bitterly that their wives undressed under cover of voluminous flannel nightgowns and that the actions Christina found so easy and natural to perform were looked upon as a painful duty by their wives. And it wasn't only the seamen. The dandies who entered the Gaiety by a discreet back door and via Bessie's parlor had much the same trouble.

Christina rapidly came to the conclusion that the majority of women were fools. By exerting a little effort they could have kept their menfolk in their own beds where they rightly belonged, not filling up the bars of the Gaiety.

One of her regulars was an older man, and it became quite a joke at the Gaiety that the elderly dandies had such a preference for Christina. Kate and Violetta had plenty of obscene reasons for it, but the truth was simple: Christina had a kind heart.

"I used to feel a fool with the others," Naylor Ackroyd said as he left her the first time.

"Whatever for?"

"Not being able to do anything. Just wanting to talk. That girl with the purple satin dress laughed at me."

"Violetta," Christina said grimly. "She'd laugh at anyone. Take no notice of her."

"It's just that I get lonely. My wife's been dead these past thirty years and my son is in India and my daughter down South. I've two grandchildren but I never see them."

"There's no need to be lonely," Christina said, patting his hand. "I enjoy talking to you."

"You're a right kind lass," he said. "You shouldn't be in a place like this."

"It's better than the place I was in before," Christina said, a brief shadow darkening her face.

On the next visit he told her of how he had built his business up from nothing and of how he had a large and empty house in Birkenhead, and Christina told him about her father and the *Lucky Star*.

On the third visit he asked her to marry him.

"There's enough servants in the house to keep a palace going. You'd not need to work and I've money to buy you whatever you fancy. I wouldn't ask anything of you, lass. Only your company."

His eyes were so pleading that Christina felt near to tears as she declined his offer.

For the first time Bessie was cross with her. "Little fool. He's worth half a million at least. You must be off your head!"

"Half a million pounds?" Christina's eyes opened wide.

"That he is, and I don't mind letting you go, not under those circumstances, though how the hell I'd replace you goodness only knows."

Half a million pounds. Christina sought the quietness of the dormitory. Molly was sleeping heavily. The other girls were spending their wages on new finery.

Half a million pounds. She would be a lady, just like she had always dreamed of. She would have fine clothes and, if she wanted, she could be a passenger on the *Mauretania* with maids to help her dress and maids to do her hair.

Half a million pounds. It was a tempting thought, and if the *Adventurer* had not sailed into port on the evening tide captained by Devlin O'Conner then Christina would have probably become Mrs. Naylor Ackroyd, setting the whole of Birkenhead gossiping for years to come. She would have been the dutiful wife, giving Naylor all the company and kindness he sought, enjoying her new-found wealth and subduing the needs of her young body.

But Devlin O'Conner dropped anchor and strode with easy assurance toward the open doors of the Gaiety, and Naylor Ackroyd and his half a million pounds faded into insignificance.

Chapter 9

Christina lay high on the grassy hillside overlooking the docks. Perhaps, Christina thought dreamily, she should marry old Naylor Ackroyd. She would be more than respectable if she did. She would be a lady. But there wouldn't be any children for her. Or any love, or romance or passion. Why, Christina thought for the umpteenth time, was life so unfair? Why couldn't Naylor have been younger or more attractive or at least capable of making love to her? The thought of a life without physical love chilled her.

It was something she had never known but she had caught glimpses of what it could be like. With Josh. With her first customer. She knew instinctively that there was something deep within her waiting for fruition. Something that would wither away and die entirely if she married Naylor. For the wife of a man worth half a million pounds had to live a life above reproach. There would be no opportunity for brief liaisons or affairs. She sighed. She didn't *want* brief liaisons or affairs. She wanted to love and be loved.

She shielded her eyes against the sun as a four-masted bark made its way gracefully into port. Christina loved ships. All ships. But for her the square rigged sailing ships were the most beautiful of all. Her father had once captained one before the days of the *Lucky Star*. The graceful flowing curves of the hull were a joy to Christina's eyes as the ship made its way through the flotilla of smaller vessels, its rigging a delicate tracery against the blue of the sky. Christina felt a surge of longing to be at sea again. To be on a ship like the one she was now watching. To feel the salt spray on her face and to see tier upon tier of swollen canvas straining at rigging and spars, the sails swinging along in perfect harmony with the wind and the waves.

The sun was searing, and she had to screw up her eyes to make out the name of the ship as its unseen captain sailed into the harbor and into her life. The *Adventurer*. She caught no sight of the figures on board. No glimpse of a thatch of flame-red hair. She closed her eyes and tried to concentrate her thoughts on whether she should or should not marry old Naylor Ackroyd.

Devlin O'Conner's thoughts were far from marriage. The Atlantic crossing had been a rough one, and he had the grueling task of discharging his cargo of case oil before he could even begin to relax, and enjoy a tub of hot soapy water and a fresh steak. He planned to share a bottle of the best cognac in town with Bessie Mulholland and then to spend the night in a soft bed with the ample-breasted Kate Kennedy beside, above and beneath him.

Once he had done that, he wanted to think. The *Adventurer* was not his own ship. She belonged to the Anglo-American Oil Company, for whom he worked. At twenty-seven he was the youngest captain on any of their vessels, and they seemed to think Devlin should be grateful for the honor they had bestowed upon him.

Devlin was not grateful. He was the best captain the company had and as far as he was concerned they were lucky to have him. He'd seen the sort of money his cargo was making for the company, and was painfully aware that none of it was going into his own pocket. If he could borrow enough money to buy his own ship he could repay it easily within three years, maybe even two. Perhaps Bessie would help him. She was a sharp businesswoman and there was money to be made in shipping cargo to and from America.

The Atlantic was a devil of a sea to sail but Devlin knew her like the back of his hand. He had been sailing ever since he'd been a boy. He couldn't remember his parents. His mother had died when he was eight and no one even knew his father's name. He'd begged and scrounged and finally lied about his age and gone to sea as a cabin boy aboard a schooner bound for the Pacific. By the time he was twelve he had crossed the equator four times and was as familiar with the shark-infested waters around the Cocos Islands as he was the English Channel. Steamships and traders followed. If it sailed then Devlin sailed her. At fifteen he was as blasé about the notorious brothels of Bombay as a man twice his age.

For five years he'd had the sweet taste of being his

own master, sailing a battered hulk that was his and his alone up and down the Gold Coast, until she had literally sunk beneath him and he had been forced to sign on as a captain with Anglo-American.

Bessie surveyed him candidly. "I just haven't got it, Devlin. Not that sort of money."

He grinned ruefully and poured himself another three fingers of cognac.

"I'll get it somewhere. I'm damned if I'm going to spend the rest of my life lining someone else's pockets."

"My sentiments entirely," Bessie agreed, surveying the refined luxury of her parlor with satisfaction. "The only one of my girls who has that sort of sense is Belle. Her aims may not be high but at least she has them. What's more, I believe she'll achieve them."

"What are they?" Devlin look across at the grandfather clock ticking majestically in its mahogany case. He'd had his soak in a hot tub of water. His belly was full. His thirst was slaked, and Kate was waiting.

"A tea shop," Bessie said.

Devlin's grin widened as he rose to his feet.

"And Christina. She won't stay here for long."

"Christina?"

"A new girl. Old Naylor Ackroyd has asked her to marry him. Now there's a thought. Why don't you approach Naylor for the money? He's got so much he doesn't know what to do with it."

"And he's going to marry one of your girls?" Devlin's eyes were amused. "The old goat must be in his dotage. I can't see satin dresses and black silk stockings going down very well in the sort of circles *he* moves in."

"Christina doesn't wear satin *or* stockings," Bessie said composedly.

"Or drawers either!" Devlin said, laughing. "Come off it Bessie. A man like Ackroyd wouldn't marry one of your girls in a million years. Tell the poor kid he's been having her on and put her out of her misery."

"It's rather the other way round."

Devlin's eyebrows rose questioningly. Bessie picked up the cognac bottle and replaced it in her glass-fronted cabinet. "She's not sure whether to accept him or not."

"We are talking about the same Naylor Ackroyd, aren't we? The one who owns at least thirty mills between here and Yorkshire?"

Bessie's mountain of bleached curls nodded. "The very one."

"And your girl isn't sure of her answer! Are you sure it isn't Dimity you're talking about?"

Bessie smiled. "No. If I were you I'd think seriously about having a word with him about a loan. He's coming tomorrow night to see Christina and find out whether she's made up her mind to marry him or not. I'll introduce the two of you and you can discuss the matter here, in my parlor. I'll stand as a reference for you. Old Ackroyd trusts my judgment."

Devlin's blue eyes gleamed. "If he's senile enough to want to marry one of your girls then he's senile enough to lend me all I need. Thanks, Bess."

He opened the door and Kate's eager arms grasped hold of him. For once the mask-like face showed animation. Her hair was freshly-washed, falling from a center parting to her shoulders, the color of ripened corn.

"I thought you were never going to get back. Your ship was two weeks overdue." She pressed herself close to him, winding her arms around his neck.

"It was a rough crossing," Devlin said, his mind still on Naylor Ackroyd and the prospect of a nice fat loan.

"I've been frantic." She rubbed herself against him, straining to feel the familiar hardness of his body, her small eyes glazed with passion. His hand slid idly down over her buttocks and she kissed him hungrily.

From downstairs came the music of the accordion playing a pulsating rhythm that Devlin had last heard in the ports of Spain. He lifted his head from hers.

"Has the Gaiety got a new musician?"

"No . . ." The key was hot and sticky in Kate's clenched palm. "Come on. It's eleven o'clock already." She took his hand, urging him toward her room.

Devlin resisted as the sound of clapping and cheers threatened to lift the Gaiety's roof.

"What the hell's going on down there?"

"*Nothing!*" The glazed look had gone from Kate's eyes and she tugged at Devlin's hand desperately. She had lost too many customers to Christina and she had no desire for Devlin to see Christina dance.

"I'm going down for a look."

"*No!*" Kate's eyes were ferocious, her thin-lipped mouth set in an ugly line, destroying the prettiness that had been there only a minute ago.

Devlin turned and began to descend the stairs. She was good in bed but he didn't take orders from anybody, man or boy. Certainly not from a whore.

She ran after him, grabbing at his arm. He removed her hand as if it were a dead fish.

"Bad temper makes you ugly," he said cruelly. "If you want to use that key tonight, sweeten your disposition a little," and he continued downstairs into the main bar.

Kate's breath hissed savagely. Her nails dug deep into her palms, then, with tremendous effort, terrified of losing him, she forced herself to breathe naturally and ran after him, linking her arm with his and smiling up at him.

"I was only impatient for you." She squeezed his arm, saying softly, "You're such a good lover. The best. There's no one else like you. No one."

Devlin wasn't listening and if he had heard he wouldn't have taken any notice. After all, she was only telling him what he already knew. Devlin

O'Conner's ego needed no boost from any direction. His devil-may-care arrogance had caused many a ship owner to say it was an ego that needed deflating, though the words they used were not so refined.

"Who is she?" he asked as the crowd parted instinctively to let him through to the front.

"Christina Haworth, a gypsy brat Bessie picked up," Kate said contemptuously.

"John Haworth's daughter?"

Kate shrugged, tight lipped, but the sailor behind her said, "That's right. He used to sail the Gold Coast in his younger days."

The music grew faster and faster and Christina laughed as she swirled, her skirt flaring out over the heads of the men who still remained seated around the table, her slender arms clapping high above her head, golden bracelets tinkling. She was sure she had seen the fair-haired head of the young man who had been her first customer standing near the door. Life was for living and Christina was living it to the fullest. It showed in every movement of her body. In her flashing eyes and glowing cheeks.

The music ended and Christina jumped nimbly from the table to the floor, landing only inches away from Devlin.

She stood before him, tall and slender, beautiful beyond belief, her breasts rising and falling against him as she gasped for breath, her cheeks flushed, her eyes sparkling.

John Haworth's daughter, the captain's brat he had last seen as a scrawny, ferocious-tempered child. His hand shot out, enclosing her wrist in a viselike grip.

Thinking at first he was only attempting to steady her, she smiled; and then as the painful pressure increased she looked up at him, startled.

Ten years had not changed him much. He still looked like a Greek god straight from the slopes of Olympus. His hair was a fiery red, his eyes a vivid blue. He was broader than she remembered, and tall with the leanness of hard muscle. Seeing him brought back such a rush of memories that her eyes filled with tears. Her father patting her head affectionately, the smoke of his pipe filling the *Lucky Star*'s cabin. The dearly loved timbre of his voice as he had said, "He isn't a deckhand, my love. He's setting out for the Gold Coast. . . ."

The Gold Coast had done nothing to improve the temper of the man before her. He had infuriated her as a child, laughing at her and leaning against the mainmast of the *Lucky Star* as though she were his own. Now he looked so vicious that the men around them had instinctively backed away.

"What the hell," Devlin asked between clenched teech, "are you doing?"

She snatched her arm away from him angrily. "Minding my own business," she said, swinging around and marching defiantly toward the bar. This time Devlin caught her in a grasp there was no escaping from. Her key hung from a slender chain around her neck, the figure three prominently displayed. He ripped it off so savagely that she cried out in pain.

Bert rose to his feet and hesitated. Devlin was a personal friend of Bessie's. It wouldn't do to interfere without her say-so. The girls were watching wide eyed; the sailors were curious and interested.

"*Upstairs!*" he said to her, a muscle twitching convulsively in his jaw.

"I wouldn't go with you for a king's ransom!" Vainly her eyes searched the room for help.

Bessie swept across to them like a ship in full sail, her plump face flushed with anger beneath her powder and rouge,

"Kate is waiting for you," she said curtly to Devlin. "Christina already has a customer."

Kate was being physically restrained by Bert only yards away, her obscenities making even the hardened sailors wince. Devlin seemed oblivious of them.

"In five minutes he can have her. But not until I've

given her the beating of her life! Out of my way, Bessie.''

There was a concerted gasp of disbelief and the crowded bar fell suddenly silent. Even Kate ceased her cursing, her eyes flickering from Christina to Devlin to Bessie and back again. No one spoke to Bessie Mulholland like that. Not even the millionaire mill owners.

Bessie felt as if she was reeling beneath a physical blow. Ten minutes ago they had been laughing and talking in her parlor, now he was behaving like an outraged father.

"No one beats my girls," she hissed, wishing she had the strength of mind to have him forcibly thrown out. But the thought of losing one of her best customers and never enjoying his company and conversation again deterred her.

"Don't worry—I'm no sadist. I'm simply going to do to her what someone should have done years ago." And he swept Christina up in his arms and carried her, kicking and protesting up the broad sweep of stairs toward room number three.

Bessie's hand clenched on the bannister. She was being made to look a fool in front of all her girls and customers as well.

"Give him five minutes," she said to Bert. "If he's not downstairs by then I want him out of here even if it means breaking his neck to do it, and you . . ." she swung around to a blaspheming, half hysterical Kate, "shut your mouth or you'll be out on the streets with him. You heard what he said. He's giving her a good hiding, that's all. There's nothing for you to get so jealous about. He'll be back for you in a minute. Some men," she said, turning, still white-faced, to Marigold, "just can't accept that their daughters, or the daughters of their friends, are no different from any other women. Perhaps he thinks she should have entered a convent!"

"I thought you said Christina hadn't to be exposed

to the sadistic side of the business?'' Marigold asked tentatively, as Christina's voluble protests faded with the slam of a door.

Bessie poured herself a cognac. "O'Conner's no savage. He's simply going to give her an old-fashioned good hiding on behalf of his friend. There's not a whip or belt in number three.''

Nevertheless she kept a sharp eye on the time. Five minutes would be plenty long enough with Devlin in such a fury, and besides, she couldn't count on Bert restraining Kate for much longer than that.

Christina wriggled and writhed in the strong arms, all to no avail. No matter how hard she tugged at his thick mass of hair, beat her clenched fists against his ears or clawed at his face, he continued purposefully, and without faltering, to her room. The door was ajar. He swung it open with his shoulder and slammed it closed with his heel.

"Let go of me, you bastard!" Christina spat full in his face.

He obliged by throwing her heavily onto the floor. Even the soft carpeting didn't alleviate the discomfort of her landing.

The base of her spine jarred painfully and her skirts fell around her flailing legs.

"You're mad!" she panted, struggling back to her feet. *"You're clean off your rocker! You're a maniac! You should be locked up! You should . . ."*

His hand caught her full across the face, stunning her into momentary silence.

"Your father," he breathed harshly, "was one of the finest men I ever knew. And you have to repay him like this. Lying on your back for the scum and riff-raff of a hundred ports!''

He had hold of her again and was dragging her toward the bed.

"I'm not lying on my back for you!" Christina gasped, struggling wildly.

"Don't worry," he said grimly, "I wouldn't lower

myself," and while she screamed with tears of rage and mortification he forced her over his knee, raising her skirt waist high to expose her bare and squirming bottom.

After the fifth time the palm of his heavy hand had come down hard onto her flesh, Christina lost count. She was too overcome with humiliation to even care about the burning pain.

At last, breathless with the struggle, he pushed her unceremoniously off his knee and back onto the floor, and stood over her, legs astride.

"Harlot," he said contemptuously. "In the morning I'm taking you back to your father where you belong!"

The door slammed behind him as Christina yelled, *"I'm going nowhere with you! Not now! Not ever!"* and then she lay face down on the bed, venting her fury by pummeling the pillows till the feathers flew.

Kate was still being physically restrained by Bert when Devlin strolled back into the bar and toward her. She fell against him with relief. Bessie had been right. He had not preferred Christina to herself. He had beaten her, not made love to her. She hadn't lost him after all.

Hours later, finally sated by Devlin's violent lovemaking, she said: "I'm glad you gave that mucky little cat a good hiding. Bessie spoils her rotten. Says she feels sorry for her, stupid old cow."

"Why?" Devlin's hand reached down to the brandy bottle on the floor beside the bed.

Kate shrugged carelessly, snuggling up against his naked back. "Her old man dying and that sob story she told about her uncle raping her. Not that it was true. She couldn't get enough of it. You can see that at a glance."

Slowly Devlin replaced the brandy bottle. "Her uncle raped her?"

"So she says but it's a pack of lies. They both had her, Ernest Miller *and* his son. It's my guess Liza Miller threw her out. Hey, where are you going?"

"To see Bessie." His shirt was already over his head. She knelt on the bed, her heavy breasts swaying.

"But what *for?* You spent two hours talking to her when you came! Devlin! *Devlin!*"

The door rocked on its hinges and she was alone.

"What the hell do you want?" Bessie asked, as she struggled to her door in a thin, boa-trimmed negligee. "It's dawn."

"Why did Christina Haworth come here?"

"It's a bit late to be asking that question," Bessie said warily, not wanting another scene.

"Don't fool around with me, Bessie. Why did she come?"

"Her father died. That miserable bastard Ernest Miller said he was her uncle and that he was responsible for her. He sold the boat and then both he and his eldest son ill-treated her."

"What did he do?" Devlin's eyes glinted dangerously.

"Raped her," Bessie said, eyeing Devlin with interest. "And as nasty and brutal a rape as ever I've come across. I told her she'd be well looked after here and not have to go with anyone she didn't want to go with or do anything for the specials. She's a nice girl. I like her. Good for the customers too. You won't see dancing like that for a good few hundred miles."

"And where does Miller live?" Devlin asked harshly, his mouth white at the corners.

"Gorman Street," Bessie said, and then flinched at what she saw in Devlin's eyes. She shouldn't have told him. The thrashing he had given Christina was one thing. Murdering Ernest Miller another.

The inhabitants of Gorman Street said afterward that it was only contempt for his victim that prevented Devlin O'Conner beating him into an early grave. Cowering and cringing on the cobblestones, begging for mercy, Ernest Miller had been such a despicable sight that Devlin had kicked him over with his foot in disgust, unable to continue the one-sided fight any longer.

It was the local doctor's opinion that in those few minutes Devlin O'Conner had stood in the shadow of the gallows. Another blow from his clenched fist and Ernest Miller would have either choked on his own blood or died of heart failure. As it was he managed to crawl across his own doorstep, his eyes too swollen to see the gleam of satisfaction in his wife's eyes as she dutifully applied cold compresses and staunched the flow of blood from a broken nose and split lip.

His mission accomplished, Devlin turned his step toward the Gaiety and a meeting with Christina. He had some apologizing to do.

Chapter 10

If Christina had known who it was waiting for her in number three that evening she would never have gone, but Bessie had merely told her that it was a backstairs client and that her dancing would have to wait till later in the evening.

"*You!*" she exclaimed when she saw who her client was, turning immediately to make a speedy exit.

He was too quick for her. The door slammed shut and he leant against it while Christina felt the breath tight in her chest. If Bessie thought she was going to allow herself to be beaten black and blue whenever her favorite customer felt like it, she was very wrong.

Believing that attack was the best form of defense

she sprang at him—but not fast enough. He seized her wrists, but Christina was like a wild cat, determined not to suffer humiliation a second time. A well-placed kick made him wince as he fought to keep hold of her.

"Listen to me, damn you!"

He ducked as she swung a clenched fist toward his ear.

"I came to *apologize*, for God's sake!"

He was feeling angry again—and something else. The more she kicked and bit at him the further down her shoulders her blouse slipped, exposing satin smooth breasts.

"Apologize?" she panted warily, her wrists still imprisoned in his hands, her hair tumbling in a wild cascade.

"Yes. I thought your father was still alive."

"What difference would that have made?" She was still struggling, but was held so tight that she could feel the hardness of his chest and the heavy slam of his heartbeat.

"If he had been you wouldn't be here."

Her eyes flashed and she wrenched her wrists from his grasp.

"You assume too much, *Mr*. O'Conner!"

He grinned. "I'm giving you the benefit of the doubt."

"You don't have to give me anything. Not even the time of day."

"You were a sulky little bitch as a child and you haven't changed." He was beginning to enjoy himself. She would be easy to anger and easy to make laugh. He wondered if she looked as beautiful when she was in a good temper as she did when she was in a bad one.

"Bessie told me about Ernest Miller. I've just knocked hell out of him."

Christina found it hard to look at him and hold onto her rage. He was smiling now, his hair a fiery nebula in the warm glow of the lamps.

"Did you really beat Ernest Miller?"

"Black and blue. I doubt if he'll ever be able to carry out his marital duties again."

Her mouth widened in a sudden smile. "I wish I'd been there to see it."

"So do I. Have I to go back and do it again?"

Their eyes met and they laughed.

"I'm sorry about those." She indicated the livid scratch marks on his face. "I thought you were going to smack me again."

"So I gathered."

Their laughter faded and they were suddenly uncomfortable. Devlin because he was aware of an overwhelming urge to take her to bed, and Christina because for the first time in her life she felt suddenly shy.

A frown creased his forehead. "I'm sorry about your father. He was a fine man."

"Yes. He was."

"He wouldn't have liked . . . this." He was painfully aware of the big brass bed behind him and the ornate gilded mirrors.

"He would have understood."

She could feel the sweat breaking out on the palms of her hands, and her heart was racing painfully. She wanted him to touch her and yet was terrified that he would. Devlin knew it was time that he went. He had made his apology. Kate was waiting for him downstairs. There was nothing to keep him any longer in the softly lit room. Still he stayed.

"Did you go to the Gold Coast?" Christina asked, aware that her voice held a tremble and not understanding why.

His shirt was open to the waist, a broad leather belt and gleaming buckle slung low on lean hips. She wanted to reach out and touch the magnificent hardness of the sun-tanned flesh, feel his thick hair curling against the palm of her hand. She had been desired by many men. For the first time in her life she knew what it was like to desire in return. She feasted her eyes on him knowing that in a moment he would be gone. Back to Kate and out of her life. Back to the sea again. She felt an overwhelming longing for the feel of the wind in her hair and the salt spray on her face. To brace her bare feet against the creaking timbers of a deck and to hear the screams of the gulls as they wheeled above her head. The sea was in her bones and in her blood, and she had never missed it so much as she did now, facing Devlin O'Conner, sea captain.

Kate would never have him for longer than a few brief hours. The elements were his home as they were her own. Only Devlin would soon be returning to them and she would not.

"I sailed the Coast for three years until my ship sank beneath me."

She sighed, pushing a tangle of curls back off her forehead, her eyes wistful.

"Did you see flying fish and dolphins and sharks?"

He grinned, deep laugh lines creasing the corners of his mouth.

"The Pacific's the place for flying fish. After a storm I've seen hundreds of them lying dead on the deck. I've seen dolphins too, but not off the Gold Coast."

"Daddy loved Africa. He said the light was different there from any other country in the world."

"It's the most magical country on earth."

Devlin had never seen eyes so dark or thick-lashed. One minute they were flashing with anger as she screamed and kicked at him, the next full of mischief and laughter as he told her of his reckoning with Ernest Miller. Now they were dreamy with longing at the thought of Africa. What would they be like in the height of passion? He wanted to know. He wanted her body beneath his, the provocative breasts naked under his chest. He wanted to make her cry out for him, feel her arching hungrily against him, mindless at the pleasure he gave her. And afterward her eyes slumbrous with love. His thoughts showed on his face and he could read the answer on hers.

"You're very beautiful," he said, and his voice was husky, thick with an emotion he had never felt before. He had had hundreds of women. To desire a woman and have that desire satisfied was as natural to him as eating and sleeping. Yet he was twenty-eight and he had never before told a woman she was beautiful.

She stood, hardly daring to breathe, terrified of breaking the spell.

Danger bells were ringing in Devlin's head. If he knew what was good for him he would smile his good-bye and leave her. Turn his back on her as firmly as if she were a siren of the sea luring him to his death. For once he had touched her she would be like a drug. He would want more and more of her. He knew this instinctively. For the past thirteen years he had taken any woman he wanted and he had never felt like this.

The generous mouth was curved in a slight smile. It was as if she knew the thoughts going through his head. She was John Haworth's daughter and he had beaten her in an ungovernable temper for shaming her father and being a whore. Now he was about to do something far worse than she had done. He was about to treat her as a whore himself. He had paid Bessie. Any girl he wanted was his. She couldn't refuse him even if she wanted to and Devlin knew with a lurch of his heart that she didn't want to refuse. It only increased the burning in his loins. He had always been in control of every situation. He was damned if he was going to let a moment's lust make him behave in a way he would be ashamed of afterward.

He had to pass close to her to reach the door. Christina felt the room swim around her. He had told her she was beautiful. His eyes had told her he wanted her as much as she wanted him. Yet he was going.

She could no more have stopped herself than ceased to breathe. Her hand shot out, grasping his, restraining him. Instinctively the fingers closed tight between her own. He looked down at her, at the heart-shaped face and firm chin, the soft sensuous mouth and the deep depths of her eyes that a man could drown in. Her hair was a wild mass of curls, her blouse and skirt merely cotton, her legs and feet bare as they had been when he had first seen her. She bore not the slightest resemblance to a whore. It was impossible to believe she was one of Bessie's girls. Instead of the overpowering smell of cheap perfume there was a fresh cleanness about her. She was like no other woman he had ever met. He touched her hair tentatively, their eyes holding, still not speaking. Then with a groan he acknowledged defeat and swung her up in his arms, carrying her purposefully across to the bed.

She made no effort to resist. Her heart was racing so wildly that she felt weak, her body trembling against his.

"Christina, Christina," he whispered, slowly removing the blouse and skirt, his hand caressing the swell of her breasts, the softly rounded hips, the moisture of her body unashamedly ready for his.

"Give me your mouth," he said, and as she shivered with an emotion she had never felt before, he kissed her long and deeply, his tongue searching for hers as her hands tightened around him in a frenzy of longing.

Her legs parted and he was inside her, so deep he seemed to fill her whole being. Nothing had prepared her for being made love to by a man she loved.

And she loved him. She had loved him on sight. She cried out, unaware of her cries as they climbed toward a summit of unbearable ecstasy. She was no longer in command of herself. Her hips moved faster and faster, her nails digging deep into his shoulders.

"Devlin . . . Devlin . . ." Her voice was a gasping moan and then, as they reached a point of mindless fusion of body and spirit, she was only semi-conscious, her cheeks wet with tears, her body answering his. Never again would she be Christina Haworth, a person in her own right with a body to do with as she pleased. From now on she belonged to Devlin O'Conner. She was his and his alone.

He had come back to her. The Greek god who had so captivated her imagination as a child. It had only been a matter of waiting, and with radiant clarity Christina knew that this was what she had been waiting for. Ever since she had first seen him she had been waiting for him to come and claim her for his own.

"Christina." Devlin's voice was harsh. Now he knew why the sight of her dancing for the pleasure of so many men had driven him into such a rage. He had wanted her for himself and himself alone. He would always want her for himself. Their love-making had been so intense, reaching such a height of joy and abandonment that neither of them had heard the shouts and thudding feet outside their room. Nothing mattered but each other. They stayed together until the dawn, her arms and shoulders, her breasts, warm and naked against him as the first light pushed its way around the heavy velvet drapes. Her head rested against the warm strength of his chest, his fingers pulling gently at her mass of black curls. He had made love to her again, this time with a warmth and tenderness that he had never shown to a woman before.

A half smile touched the corners of her mouth as she brushed her lips gently over the sun-tanned flesh beneath them.

There could be no more clients. She would leave the Gaiety and Bessie would be angry with her. The thought did not disturb her. Where she would go, what she would do, were decisions she would make later. She had given herself totally and utterly and nothing else in life mattered.

Devlin lay on his back, Christina's weight pleasurably across him. Eyes that were a vibrant cornflower blue in the light of day gazed up at the plaster embossed ceiling darkly; he was still shaken by the intensity of his feelings. He felt a tenderness and protectiveness toward the girl in his arms that unnerved him, and Devlin O'Conner was not a man easily unnerved. His first instinct, when the initial frenzy of their love-making had been quenched and sanity had returned, had been to reach for his breeches and leave the room. Leave the brothel. Leave Liverpool. Leave England. Anything but stay and become more and more ensnared by her. Wonderingly he traced the lovely line of her cheek and chin with his forefinger. He had never before associated love-making with love. Love was something one felt for one's parents, if one was lucky enough to have any. Or a brother. Perhaps even for a friend. Life was complicated enough without becoming emotionally involved with a woman. A life of freedom, without obligations or ties, that was what he wanted and what he had. One part of his brain urged him to move, to reach for his clothes, dismiss her as easily as he did Kate. The other part marveled at the shattering experience of making love to a woman who had been a disheveled child with burning eyes saying defiantly, "I'm a *gypsy princess!*"

Devlin O'Conner, the swaggering buck who had broken more hearts than he could possibly count, who had faced storms and shipwrecks with equal equanimity, was a lost man. Instead of reaching for shirt and breeches, his hand slid caressingly over her back, and instead of his intended impersonal word of goodbye he heard himself murmuring her name against the softness of her lips. He was flooded with a desire so deep it clouded all reason.

Downstairs Kate Kennedy had been a woman possessed. White-faced, consumed by jealousy and hatred, she had pushed her way through the roistering customers and into the kitchen. Then, a meat cleaver held firmly in her hands, she had walked with cold deliberation up the back staircase and toward the corridor that led to the room occupied by Devlin and Christina.

Only Molly's sixth sense had spared the Gaiety from carnage. Molly knew Kate's feelings for Devlin O'Conner. It was not just a case of losing a good customer to another girl. Kate was losing the only man who had ever aroused any emotion in her and the look in her eyes had been that of a woman about to commit murder.

Molly excused herself from the company of her prospective customer and against his protests tried to see Bessie, but Bessie was nowhere to be found. Molly's sense of unease increased. She knew that Kate was capable of physical violence. Damage she had done to a previous rival's face was legendary, and that had been about something that mattered far less to her than Devlin O'Conner.

Frantically she forced herself through the crowd of sailors who were pushing and shoving for the best vantage point in the room as Cassie prepared to strip.

Bert turned as she grabbed his arm.

"I'm worried about Christina," she yelled in his ear, over the roar of applause as the music started.

Bert frowned against the noise, bending his head toward her.

"What did you say? Can't hear a bloody thing over this racket."

"It's Christina. Devlin O'Conner's upstairs with her. Kate's furious and now I can't see her anywhere and Marigold says that she isn't with a customer."

Bert shrugged. Kate's sulks were well known and he didn't like her. "Serve her right. Might bring her down a peg or two."

Molly pulled desperately on his arm, her fear so naked it finally communicated itself to him.

"Kate looked like she wanted to kill her! *Please* Bert. Check everything's all right. Just for me."

So Bert, because he had a soft spot for Molly, abandoned his post at the door and lumbered heavily upstairs and into the red carpeted corridor just in time to catch Kate entering it from the other end, the meat cleaver in her hand. His pounding footsteps and oaths went unheard by the occupants of number three as were Kate's cries as Bert wrenched the cleaver out of her hand and forced her back down the stairs, her arm caught up high between her shoulder blades so that her face was white with pain as well as hate.

Bessie, finally aroused to the seriousness of the situation, had locked a raging and weeping Kate into her room, and Bessie's face as she turned away from the door that Kate was trying to beat down was grimmer than anyone had ever seen it.

Christina lay in Devlin's arms, his mouth nuzzling her nipples; she felt him harden against her thighs and hated the sight of the early morning sun as it crept through the chinks of the curtains. Dawn. The night was nearly over.

"Bessie will be furious," she said softly, running her fingers over the smoothness of his back.

He raised his head, cupping her breast in his palm, kissing her long and lovingly. Minutes later he said, leaning on his elbow, drinking in the sight of her, "Why?"

"My not working last night."

He kissed her again, rolling on top of her.

"She's got her money." His hands were parting her legs.

Christina stiffened, her voice changing. "What do you mean, she's got her money?"

"For last night. I'd already paid her."

She pushed him away so violently he nearly fell out of the bed.

"You *paid* for me?" Her eyes were bright with rage. "Is that all last night was, a change? Perhaps you'd like Maggie tonight. Or Francine. Then you'd *really* have a change." She was out of the bed, scrambling into her skirt, her breasts heaving.

Devlin laughed, reaching out for her, dragging her protestingly back on to the bed.

"Stop it, you little wildcat. I'd paid Bessie for Kate *before* I came to apologize to you."

"How very convenient!" Christina said, struggling in vain, "And as I just happened to take your fancy you thought it might as well be me!"

"I certainly thought it might as well be you and I wish to God I knew what you were so angry about." He was laughing, and Christina hit him across the face with the palm of her hand.

"If you don't know I'm not telling you!" She was crying now, and Devlin seized hold of her wrist, pinning her back on the bed.

"I paid Bessie for Kate. Kate . . . Not you."

"It was me you made love to!"

He stared down at her, knowing this was the moment of truth. You bought a woman, enjoyed her and left her. Christina was telling him that she had no desire to be bought. That she had given herself to him freely and in love.

"Let Bessie keep the money and let Kate take the commission on it," he said. "And let me love you again."

She smiled radiantly through her tears. "Do you love me, Devlin? Do you?"

"Let me show you." And for the first time in his life Devlin O'Conner surrendered himself totally to the act of love.

Christina had no more doubts left. She leaned against the pillows watching him dress.

"When do you sail?"

Devlin paused. He should sail with the tide if he wanted to keep his schedule. He couldn't bear the thought of leaving her. His mind raced. The cargo was at Plymouth waiting to be loaded. It could wait. It would lose him his job but he didn't want the damn job anyway.

"Not for a few days," he said.

She relaxed visibly and he said, "But then it will be another two months before I am back."

"I'll leave word with Bessie where I am," she said, finally moving from the warmth of the bed and reaching for her skirt.

His hands stilled on his buckle. "What do you mean? Where you'll be?"

She looked across at him and laughed. "Well I shan't be here. I couldn't go with anybody else now."

"No." He felt a sensation so terrible it made him tremble. "No. You damn well won't go with anyone else. You're mine."

He took hold of her roughly, kissing her with possessive savagery. Then, as they clung together, he said: "Where will you go, Brat? What will you do?"

She shrugged. "I don't know. Anywhere. Just as long as it's somewhere you can find me."

"I'll find you," he said hoarsely. "I'll always find you. And when I've found you we'll never be parted again. Never. I swear it."

Bessie stared at him across the paraphernalia-filled clutter of her parlor, two bright spots of angry color high on her cheeks.

"You expect me to keep her *here* without her working?"

"I'll pay you. You tell me what Christina would earn in the next couple of months until I get back and I'll pay you every damn penny."

"You haven't enough," Bessie said confidently. "If you had that sort of money you wouldn't have needed to ask me for a loan yesterday."

Devlin clenched his fists. "If you don't do as I ask she'll leave and then God knows what will happen to her."

"Leave?" Bessie's voice was incredulous. Then she remembered Kate. Some fool, most likely Molly, had already told Christina of Kate's intended attack on her.

"There's no need for her to leave."

"Christina thinks there is. I'll give you seventy

pounds. That should cover the cost of her keep until I get back and when I do I'll have more than enough money and I'll take Christina away with me."

Bessie sat down suddenly in her chair, staring at him unbelievingly.

"*You,* take her *away* with you! You've never been interested in any woman longer than it takes to make love to her and get your breeches back on again."

"I'm taking her away," he said again, and for the first time in her life Bessie felt at a loss. No longer in control of events.

"What about Naylor Ackroyd? He won't lend you any money if he knows how it is with you and Christina."

"I'm not going to ask him for it," Devlin said brusquely. "I'm sailing for New York, and I'll find someone there to back me or die in the attempt."

"And then what are you going to do?" Bessie asked, staring at the six-foot-three giant with his hands on his hips and an unfathomable expression on his face. "Marry her?"

Devlin grinned. "Now that you've mentioned it Bessie, that's exactly what I am going to do!" and he strode from the room, leaving her gazing dazedly after him.

Christina never knew of the intended attack on her life by Kate.

Next morning, while Kate remained locked in her room, passive now through exhaustion, Devlin led Christina down to the wharves and aboard the *Adventurer*.

"We'll sail through the Menai Straits to Wales," he said as she went with him unquestioningly. "There'll be somewhere in Cardigan Bay I can berth her."

"But what about your cargo?" Christina asked tentatively. "Shouldn't you be reloading?"

"The cargo is at Plymouth," Devlin had said, "and Plymouth can wait for a week at least."

"You'll be behind schedule."

"It will be my last run. Anglo-American can go to hell. When I come back I'll have enough money for my own ship and the only schedules I'll have to keep will be mine." He had lifted her lightly aboard. Christina had felt the wind in her hair and the comfortable deck timbers beneath her feet again and had thought she would die of happiness.

"Will we sail together?" she asked as they slipped their moorings and Captain O'Conner's crew exchanged meaningful glances between themselves. They'd seen plenty of strange things in their time but never anything to equal this.

"Yes." He took the wheel with hands hardened by years of tough, physical work. "Everywhere and anywhere. We'll never be parted again Christina, I promise you."

She hugged his arm. "What will you do? Try and get a coal contract or a clay contract? They ship a lot of clay from Liverpool."

"I'll carry whatever it is America wants," he said, and grinned down at her. "America, Christina. That's where a man's fortune lies."

His confidence and enthusiasm were infectious. "America," Christina repeated breathlessly. "Oh, how I would love to see America!"

Devlin's grin widened. "And how America would love to see you! They'd be fighting over you in the streets!"

"Silly," she said, flushing with pleasure.

"I'm not. It's the truth. At least it is in the parts of America I've been to. Some of the men there haven't seen a woman in years. I've done some logging out there. Up in the far Northwest. Those logging camps are hundreds of miles deep in the wilderness. And I've panned for gold and not seen a woman for a year at a time."

"Is that why you gave it up?" she asked mischievously.

He shook his head as the wind blew through his

shock of hair. "No. A year away from the sea was enough for me. No gold strike can compensate for living ashore."

Christina understood his sentiments entirely. "I've never sailed the Atlantic, but I've crossed the Bay of Biscay and sailed as far East as the Dardanelles."

"Have you sailed the Indian Ocean?" she asked, her eyes dreamy with longing as she thought of that far distant sea.

"I've sailed everywhere," he said with a grin. "I've carried cargoes of hides from Valparaiso to Australia and bullion from the Cape to the Thames."

"Is there anywhere you haven't been?" Christina asked ingenuously, and Devlin's face softened and he kissed her long and deep.

"Yes," he said at last. "Wales." And with her arm linked through his, their faces to the wind, steered a course for the Bay, not giving a damn what his crew thought. He was happy in a way he had never thought possible.

For the rest of her life Christina regarded the days that followed as days plucked out of time, too blissful to ever have been reality. Devlin dropped anchor off the shore of a small Welsh village much to the excitement of the local boys and the dismay of his crew. A generous handout of silver went a little way to alleviate their displeasure and they disappeared into the nearest bar and did not reappear until Devlin hauled them out at the end of the week.

Their days were spent high in the Welsh hills. Their nights in the cabin of the *Adventurer*. Even as an old woman the memory of those nights was enough to make Christina's blood throb at her temples.

Their plans, insofar as they had any, were simple. Devlin was scheduled to return to New York to pick up a fresh cargo of oil from Anglo-American. While he was there he was going to try and get financial backing to buy an old vessel. With his own ship to command, Christina could accompany him, just as she had accompanied her father. It was a prospect that seemed too blissful to be true. Yet it was going to come true, for hadn't Devlin paid every penny he had to Bessie? To ensure she had a roof over her head until he came back?

When she realized his sacrifice she was filled with anguish, wishing she had never told him of her intention of leaving the Gaiety, saying that she would stay, continue to work.

He seized hold of her, pinning her down on the narrow bunk in the cabin, his grip on her wrists so tight that she cried out in pain as he made her promise that she would never go with another customer again.

Her face was streaked with tears as she gasped, "I only wanted to help you. To save you the seventy pounds . . ."

And looking down at her face, at the love in her eyes that bordered on worship, Devlin kissed her bruised wrists, telling her the money mattered not a damn. She was his, his and no one else's. And his lovemaking left her in no doubt of it.

"What will you call your ship?" she asked one night, safe and secure in the strength of his arms.

"The *Princess* of course," he said, and she looked up at those laughing blue eyes in the sun-tanned face, at the straight, strong nose and firm chin, at the full, mobile lips and wondered how it was possible for one person to love another so much.

They had five days of laughter and loving, and then Devlin weighed anchor and set sail for Liverpool again.

Neither of them were touched with sadness at the parting. It was going to be a passing, transient thing, a necessary prelude to a lifetime together. She had refused his offer to walk her back to the Gaiety. A cargo, a week late, was waiting to be picked up at Plymouth. Gulls wheeled above their heads as they kissed goodbye.

"I love you," she whispered. "I love you. I love you. I shall always love you."

And Devlin O'Conner, who had never spoken the word to another human being, cupped her chin in the palm of his hands and raised the perfect oval of her face to his and said truthfully, "I love you, Brat. Till the end of time."

And then he gave her one last lingering kiss, and she stood on the dockside, oblivious of the glances she was attracting, her eyes fixed on the billowing sails till the *Adventurer* was lost to sight.

Then and only then did she turn toward the Gaiety. Kate Kennedy, standing at the open window of Bessie's living room, watched her approach through narrow, calculating eyes.

Kate's insane fury had left her, but not her hatred. As Bessie had so brutally pointed out to her, if she had succeeded in killing Christina it would not have brought Devlin back to her bed. Sullenly she had promised Bessie that there would be no more scenes of violence when Christina returned and for once Kate meant what she said. There were more ways than one of killing a cat. She would destroy Christina without implicating herself. And when Christina was destroyed she would slide once more into Devlin's arms and nothing and no one would prevent her. For five days Kate had schemed and planned and now, as she watched the unsuspecting Christina walking with easy grace toward the Gaiety, there was a cruel smile on her face, and her pale eyes gleamed like those of a snake about to strike.

Chapter **11**

"He's done *what?*" Molly asked, sinking down onto the bed, her legs weak.

"He's given Bessie enough money for my keep and I'm not working with the customers any more. I'll help Annie with the cooking and cleaning instead."

"God love us," Molly said, round-eyed.

Christina sighed luxuriously, stretching her arms high above her head.

"I'm so happy, Molly. I never knew anyone could be so happy."

Christina's radiant face spoke for itself. Molly, far more aware of the realities of life in the Gaiety, said hesitantly, "He'll be gone a long time and the other girls won't take kindly to it. Nothing like this has ever happened before. We've never had any freeloaders."

"But I'll still work," Christina said reasonably, "only not with the customers."

"I can just imagine what Violetta and Maggie will say to that! And Cassie too. As for Kate . . ." Molly shuddered descriptively.

"I don't care what they think. I'll pull my weight, and my cooking is far better than Annie's. I've got Devlin and nothing else matters." She rolled over onto her stomach. "He's so handsome, Molly. And strong. And I love him so much. Have you ever noticed how his hair curls in the nape of his neck and of how it burns like fire when the sun is on it, and of how blue his eyes are? It's like looking into the depths of the ocean."

Molly, who had noticed all these things without having enjoyed them, agreed. But happy as she was for Christina, her disquiet deepened.

Kate would not give Devlin up without a fight. She had been prepared to murder when Christina had spent the night with him. What would she do when she knew Devlin intended taking Christina away with him?

"Lock your door at night," she said somberly to Christina. "I don't think Kate is quite sane."

Christina began to shrug the warning off, and then, seeing the expression on her friend's face said: "All right, if it makes you feel happier. But there was never anything between Devlin and Kate but a business relationship."

"That's not the way *she* sees it," Molly said truthfully. "And now I've listened to all your news don't you want to hear mine?"

"I'm sorry, Molly," Christina said, immediately repentant. "I've been selfish. What's happened to you while I've been away?"

Molly curled her legs beneath her and said smugly, "You know I skipped off to see my fella? Well, he's asked me to marry him."

"But that's wonderful, Molly. You love him, don't you?"

"Not 'arf," Molly said expressively, "and I'm getting fed up with this place."

"So what are you going to do?"

"I wasn't sure, but now you're leaving I've made up my mind. I'm going to marry him, of course."

Christina hugged her. "Oh, I'm so glad, Molly. Just think, you'll be respectable!"

Molly giggled. "He's told his mother I'm in service, which Bessie says I am in a way so it isn't a lie. *And* it'll be a church wedding."

"Better not tell Bessie when it is or she'll muster

the entire house and your respectability will go to the winds.''

"God 'elp us. I'd never see him again. I'd never pass that lot off as domestic servants! But I'd like you to be there, Christina. Will you come?"

"Course I'll come," Christina said staunchly.

Molly looked suddenly shy. "Would you be my bridesmaid? You see my fella's family have ever such fancy ideas. A real proper wedding they want. Just like the dandies do."

"I'd be honored to be your bridesmaid, Molly. Have you told Bessie yet?"

"I'm going down now. Keep your fingers crossed for me. She's not going to be too happy losing two of us in the same month."

Bessie surprised Molly. She congratulated her, poured cognac for a celebration drink and told her she was delighted.

Molly scuttled back to the bedroom, and soon after, Merry entered.

"What's the matter with you two? We're opening in fifteen minutes."

"Christina is helping Annie in future, not accommodating the clients, and I'm ready. 'Cept for my stockings."

Merry's eyebrows flew upwards. "What's the matter? Taken a turn against it?"

"Yes," Christina said truthfully. "But I'll be cooking and cleaning."

"Better you than me," Merry said cheerfully. "Come on, Molly. Marigold sent me up for you and she isn't in the best of moods."

Molly hooked black silk stockings onto her suspenders, gave her eyebrows a quick wipe over with oil and winked at Christina. "See you later and don't forget what I said about the door."

"The door?" Merry asked, mystified.

"It creaks," Molly said, and hurried her out of the room.

When the other bedroom doors had opened and closed and the chattering, giggling girls had all gone downstairs, Christina walked into the room Dimity shared, took the pile of stockings and petticoats waiting to be mended and carried them back to her own room to stitch. Her thoughts were far away. On the high seas with Devlin. Soon she would be with him.

The door handle turned and then, finding it locked, there came a gentle knock.

"Who is it?" Christina asked, pricking her finger as she was wakened from her reverie.

"Merry."

Christina crossed the room and opened the door, seeing with surprise that Merry's eyes were troubled and that there was no smile on her lips.

"What is it, Merry? Trouble downstairs?"

"No. Not really. It's someone for you."

"I'm not seeing any more clients. Bessie knows. It's all right. I won't get into trouble."

"It's not a client. Well, not *really*. It's Josh."

"Josh?" Christina stared.

"He's in the bar, insisting he sees you."

Slowly Christina put her sewing down and rose to her feet. "Then I'd better see him. Is he in the outer bar?"

"No. The inner." Merry's face was scarlet. "He's come as a client. Paid Bessie his money and insists on seeing you. She told him you weren't working tonight but he wouldn't take no for an answer. He's been drinking and if you don't come quick Bert will be throwing him out and there'll be a dreadful brawl."

Christina ran down the stairs and stared appalled at the scene in front of her.

Josh was swaying on his feet, one arm locked in a vicious grip by Bert, the other pounding Bessie's desk while the girls and sailors watched him curiously.

Seeing Christina, Josh's shoulders sagged and he became quiescent. Realizing the promised fight had been averted the sailors returned their attention to their drinks and the girls.

"Josh, what on earth are you doing here?" Christina asked, taking his hand in hers and leading him away from the still suspicious Bert into a relatively quiet corner of the room.

"Come to see you," Josh said sheepishly.

"But you can't. Not here. If you want to talk to me I'll meet you tomorrow somewhere. Up at the cemetery."

Josh shook his head stubbornly. "I've paid my money and I've come to see *you*."

Christina stared at him, horrified. "You mean you've paid Bessie to see me as a *client*? Not just because you wanted to talk to me?"

Avoiding her eyes he nodded.

Christina took a deep, steadying breath. "I'm not working here any more. And if I was, I couldn't . . . Not with you . . ."

His hand groped clumsily for hers. "I need you, Christina. I can't stand it any longer. Nellie's tongue is like a razor. She rants at me from morning till night. I've done everything I can. I work hard and I lay every penny on the kitchen table on a Friday night but it's never enough. She comes in the pubs after me and makes me a laughing stock. I've tried everything I can to please her but it's hopeless. I just want . . ." He struggled for words. "I want someone to love, Christina. Just for a little while. It'd make life bearable-like."

Christina stood up and crossed the few inches of floor that separated them, laying Josh's hand against her breasts.

"Poor Josh. Doesn't she love you at all?"

His hands were tight around her waist, his voice muffled. "No. She pretended to. Before we were wed. But she never lets me touch her now and I don't want to. The child died at birth and now there's nothing left."

Christina stared down at the giant-sized figure clinging to her like a baby and her eyes filled with tears.
She remembered the boy she had known in childhood.
So handy with his fists there hadn't been one of his
peers would dared to have crossed him. Now some
little slut by the name of Nellie Proctor had reduced
him to a mockery.

"So you will let me stay with you, won't you?" He
raised his head to hers, brown eyes pleading.

Gently Christina shook her head. "No, Josh. I'm
sorry. I'll be your friend. I'll see you tomorrow up at
the cemetery after you've finished work."

"Fat chance of that," he said bitterly. "Nellie's
waiting for me at the works entrance every night."

Across the smoke-filled room she saw Merry watching them. With sudden determination Merry slipped
off her high stool and weaved her way through the
crowded tables toward them.

There was no need for her to ask what the situation
was. Josh's dejected shoulders spoke for themselves.
Merry's frank blue eyes met Christina's and then she
tapped Josh on the shoulder.

"Josh, I haven't got any customers and I'll be getting into trouble with Bessie soon. I wonder . . ." She
blushed prettily. "I wonder if you'd mind, seeing as
how you've paid your money and Christina isn't working any more. Would you mind going with me instead?"

Josh gazed wonderingly up at her, then at Christina.
Christina smiled and gave a slight nod of the head and
then Josh grinned. Something of the old perkiness returning.

"Reckon I might at that," he said, taking her hand
and allowing her to lead him toward the stairs. Christina sat down again staring after them. She should
have guessed before. Merry had always been trying
to lead the conversation round to Josh. It had been a
blatant lie about her not having any customers. Merry
was one of the most popular girls at the Gaiety, and

as for Bessie being cross with her, that was ridiculous.

She grinned to herself. Merry had looked as shy as a sixteen-year-old. A pity, she thought, as she went back to her sewing, that Josh was already married. Merry would have made him an ideal wife.

Kate was standing at the open door of her room when she returned. Christina's footsteps faltered for a second and then she continued to walk toward her with a firm tread.

Kate smiled. "I hear you're not working any more."

"No. At least not with the customers. I shall be helping Annie instead."

"Wise girl. I never did think you were cut out for life downstairs. Bessie always sheltered you from the worst side but you were bound to discover it sooner or later."

Gone was all trace of unfriendliness and malice, and it occurred to Christina that perhaps the trouble had been jealousy all along. Kate had always held a favored position with Bessie and then she, Christina, had come along and supplanted her. Now that Kate was viewing her no longer as a rival it seemed that their relationship couldat least be cordial.

"I hear Josh Lucas was causing a bit of a fuss downstairs."

"He's all right now. He's gone off with Merry."

Kate smoothed her black taffeta skirt with long lacquered nails. "She always was sweet on him," she said confidingly. "Even as a child. Of course, he never had time for her then. It was always just the two of you, wasn't it?"

"Yes. I suppose it was."

Kate's smile was disarming. "Let's bury the hatchet, shall we? I didn't like it when you came here, I'll admit it. But there's no sense in continuing the feud. I'm ready to be friends if you are." She held out her hand.

Christina took it feeling a wave of relief. At least her last few weeks at the Gaiety would not be spent

in animosity with Kate. There was still no warmth
in Kate's green eyes, but Christina felt that they were
so opaque that they never would reflect any emotion.

"And don't believe anything you hear about me re-
senting you and Devlin." The slender shoulders, bordering on thinness, shrugged. "Easy come, easy go.
It's part of the game," and small pearly teeth parted
in a laugh as she let go of Christina's hand and continued on down the corridor.

The next afternoon Christina walked up the cobbled
streets to the cemetery and lay on the familiar hum-
mock of grass, her chin resting on her hands as she
gazed down over tier after tier of soot-blackened cottages to the bustling activity of the wharves.

"Been waiting long?" a familiar voice asked as Josh
flopped down beside her.

"A couple of hours. I've been watching the ships.
I thought you said you wouldn't be able to get away
from Nellie."

Josh grinned. "I told her either I was master of my
own house or she could leave it."

"About time, too. What did she say?"

Josh's grin widened even further. "Said that if that
was the line I was taking she was going back to her
ma till I apologized. She left this morning."

"And will you apologize?"

"Not bloody likely," Josh said cheerfully. "I feel
like a new man."

"And what finally gave you the courage to put her
in her place?" Christina asked curiously.

He plucked a long blade of grass and began to chew
it. "Reckon it was last night. She's a nice girl that
Merry."

"Very nice," Christina said, waiting expectantly.

"Do you know she used to fancy me when she was
a kid? Said I was the biggest and strongest lad in the
whole of Liverpool. She'd seen me hanging around
the Gaiety but didn't like to speak to me. Knowing it

was you I wanted to see an' all. Said she'd heard all
about Nellie and what a hard piece she was.''

"And?"

He laughed. "You'll never believe it, but she says
she still fancies me." He colored slightly. "Says she
loves me."

"Then you're a very lucky man. Merry never says
anything she doesn't mean.''

"So I thought right. I'd give Nellie one more
chance. But when she opted for her ma I wasn't 'alf
glad." He squared his shoulders determinedly.
"There's lots of good jobs for boilermakers down in
Southampton. I'm off down there. And taking Merry
with me.''

"Blimey," Christina said chuckling. "That's the
third in a month.''

"Third what?"

"Third girl that Bessie's lost. It seems like it's turning into an epidemic.''

"Merry told me about you and this O'Conner chap.
Sounds like a really decent fella," Josh said generously.

"He is. I'm so happy. For you, for Merry, for
Molly, for myself. Life is so wonderful I can hardly
believe it.''

Josh, remembering Merry soft and supple in his
arms, her laughing eyes and heart-shaped face making
him feel a giant of a man, fervently agreed.

Christina's thoughts were elsewhere as well. On
Devlin, and the color of his eyes and the slant of his
brows. The mouth that could be firm or astonishingly
tender. The texture of his skin and the red-gold of his
hair and the feel of it beneath her fingers.

"Devlin," she whispered beneath her breath.
"Devlin O'Conner, I love you. I love you so much
couldn't bear to live life without you!"

Chapter 12

A little over a month later Devlin O'Conner stood with barely concealed insolence before the raging president of Anglo-American Oil.

"Over a week late and no explanation!" he spluttered. "No storms, no fog . . ."

"We crossed in the usual amount of time," Devlin said easily. "If you look at the log you'll see we sailed on the fifteenth, not the eighth. That's the reason for the delay."

"And what's the reason for sailing seven days behind schedule? There was no sickness, no difficulty with the cargo." Feverishly he thumbed through the pages of the battered logbook. "There's nothing here. No explanation at all!"

"No," Devlin agreed pleasantly.

"No *sir* when you speak to me!" The president's eyes threatened to bulge out of their sockets. "Insolent young puppy! I want an explanation and I want it fast!"

Devlin smiled, a slow lazy smile that drove the president to the edge of apoplexy.

"I berthed the *Adventurer* in Cardigan Bay for a week. I had business there. Personal business."

The president wiped his mottled face and neck with a white silk handkerchief, reached for a glass of water with a trembling hand and stuttered, "P—P—Personal business! On Anglo-American's time! You're fired. You'll never set foot on another ship of mine again!"

"No," Devlin agreed smoothly, moving toward the polished mahogany desk and sitting on the corner, one leg swinging idly. "Those ships are a bit beneath me. Too much penny-pinching and not enough money spent aboard."

He reached for one of the president's fat cigars, trimmed it and blew a ring of fragrant smoke into the air. The president remembered his high blood pressure and hastily fumbled for his box of pills.

"And before you get your strength back and have me forcibly removed perhaps, just for your records of course, you'd better know just what my business was for that week in Wales."

The president was already recovering, stabbing violently at the bell for his underlings, but much as he wanted to see the back of the swaggering, muscled body sitting so arrogantly on his desk, he wanted to know what business had been so important it had been worth O'Conner losing his job with Anglo-American.

Devlin, reading the other man's thoughts like an open book, laughed and stubbed the barely-smoked cigar out in a glass ashtray.

"It was a woman," he said, his face only inches away from that of his former employer. "The most beautiful goddamned woman in the whole wide world!"

He turned, paused, gave the half-demented president of Anglo-American a mocking bow and closed the door behind him. Not till he reached the ground floor of the enormous building did the wrathful shouts and blasphemies of Anglo-American's president fade amongst the hustle and bustle of the noise of the streets.

Horse-drawn cabs vied with automobiles for the right of way. The sidewalks were crowded with earnest young men hurrying to their offices and pretty women window-shopping. New York. It was the financial center of America. Surely someone—somewhere—would lend him the money he needed? He reached into his back pocket for a slip of paper with two names on it. It wasn't much to go on but it was a start. Several eyes flirtatiously tried in vain to catch his as he sauntered down the crowded sidewalk, his sun-tanned face and casual dress setting him distinctly apart from the somber-suited businessmen around him. His shirt was open at the neck showing a tantalizing expanse of strong chest; the broad leather belt with its silver buckle slung low on lean hips drew the gaze of even the most respectable matron. Dainty heads turned, annoyed husbands grabbed angrily at their wives' arms, but the attention he was causing was lost on Devlin. He had more important things on his mind than the effect he was creating on New York's female population. He looked again at the first name on the paper. Elias Franklin.

The soaring offices of Wall Street would have intimidated a lesser man. Devlin merely asked for the great Mr. Franklin as though they were on intimate terms, and something in his manner prevented the doorman from refusing his request with the chilly contempt he normally used in turning away applicants seeking a few minutes of the great man's time.

The score of other minions who separated Elias Franklin from the annoyance of casual callers also faltered at Devlin's blatant confidence.

No, he had no appointment, but Mr. Franklin wanted to see him.

Gradually he progressed from the outer offices to the deeply carpeted inner sanctum. A youth in his early twenties with sharp bright eyes rose to meet him from behind a paper-strewn desk.

"Devlin O'Conner," Devlin said without preamble, "to see Mr. Franklin."

Guy Bishop wondered how on earth the powerful young man in front of him had managed to crash the barrier of personal assistants and secretaries.

"Is Mr. Franklin expecting you?"

"He wasn't, but he is now." The telephone could be heard ringing in the next room.

Guy Bishop grinned, instinctively liking his self-assured contemporary. He moved toward the heavily-carved door to announce to Mr. Franklin that there was a certain Mr. O'Conner to see him, but before he could do so the door was flung open and a stocky, bald-headed man with the obligatory cigar in his mouth barked, "What the hell do you mean by storming into my office this way? No one sees me without an appointment!"

"I figured if I'd asked for one I'd have been refused," Devlin said smoothly.

"Damn right you would have been," Elias Franklin agreed. "Now that you're here, what is it you want? I'm a busy man."

"Money," Devlin said, aware of a quick intake of breath from Guy Bishop. "A loan. I'll pay it back in three years. Possibly two. And at good interest."

"Half of the city is trying to borrow money from me. Why should I lend it to you? What do you want it for anyway?"

"I'm a sea captain. I've sailed every sea there is and I know the Atlantic like the back of my hand. I've been ferrying oil from New York to Liverpool for Anglo-American. There's money to be made in carrying cargo from America to Europe and I want a ship of my own to cash in on it." He warmed to his theme. "Think of it. The two greatest civilizations in the world, both desperately needing each other's goods and the only way to supply them is by ship."

Elias Franklin grinned. "There's plenty of cargo ships on the Atlantic run. Think up an original idea before you waste my time again," and he slammed back into his office, leaving Devlin clenching and unclenching his fists in frustration.

"Where are you staying in New York?" Guy Bishop asked, a curious light in his eyes.

Devlin snapped the address of his rooming house at him and marched frozen-faced back through the endless offices full of speculative eyes and down onto the sun-baked sidewalk again.

He'd blown it. He should have been more persuasive, less direct. Cursing himself for a fool he looked at the second name on his crumpled bit of paper and set off with fresh determination.

Austin Natsch was even more scornful than Elias Franklin. Every opportunist in the country was after his money. He told Devlin crudely what he could do with himself and went back to his stocks and shares.

Devlin wondered for the first time if he had been a little hasty in getting himself fired from Anglo-American. The money in his pocket wouldn't last long, and there was Christina to return to.

He felt an overpowering longing for her presence. The concept of a woman being a comfort to a man when life was treating him harshly was one entirely new to Devlin. Nevertheless he knew that if Christina was with him, her supreme belief in his abilities would renew his confidence. He bought himself a bottle of bourbon and made his way back to his sleazy rooming house to plan his next move.

Guy Bishop waited until Elias Franklin had departed for his customary three-hour lunch and then picked up the telephone and asked for a local number.

"Mr. Yates?"

Duane Yates eased his young companion off his lap and with his feet crossed nonchalantly on his massive desk said, "What is it, Guy?"

"I think I've found the man you're looking for. Devlin O'Conner. Aged between twenty-five and thirty. Irish, I think. Says he's sailed every sea there is. He's been working for Anglo-American "

"What makes you think he's the man I want?" Duane Yates asked, studying immaculately manicured nails.

"He managed to see Franklin this morning without an appointment and that's never happened before. He

was after a loan for a ship of his own. I imagine he'll
get it eventually, too. He's a determined man and in
my opinion could be a dangerous one. He's certainly
someone to be reckoned with.''

Guy Bishop was young, but Duane Yates knew
from past experience that he was an excellent judge
of character.

''Give me his address and we'll pay him a call. I'll
pick you up in an hour.''

''Mr. Franklin will be back at three,'' Guy said,
torn between two loyalties.

''Forget Franklin,'' Duane said pleasantly. ''If your
hunch is right you won't need him much longer.''

''Two gents to see you,'' Devlin's landlady said.
Mountains of fat could be seen escaping from around
her greasy apron.

Devlin put down his glass and concealed his surprise.

''Here you are,'' she said, ushering Devlin's guests
into the junk-filled room. ''But don't make a habit of
it. It's not a bleedin' hotel.''

''Drink?'' Devlin asked as Guy Bishop gingerly sat
down on a sagging chair.

''Thanks.'' With relief Guy thought that though the
room was indescribable the bourbon was of the best
quality.

''What can I do for you?'' Devlin asked, suppressing any inflection of interest. They wanted something
from him, that was for sure. Guy Bishop and his expensively dressed companion were not paying a courtesy call on Devlin O'Conner, sea captain with no
ship to command.

''I understand you're looking for a ship to captain,''
the blond-haired man asked in cultivated tones.

''Not unless it's my own.''

''We might be able to come to some sort of mutual
understanding. What experience have you had?''

Devlin eyed the slim, effeminate-looking man who
sat opposite him. He was no seaman. Those elegant

hands had never done a day's work. The hair was fine
and sleek, and a beautifully-groomed pencil moustache graced a well-formed mouth. Devlin judged him
to be somewhere in his late twenties. Slate-gray eyes
fringed by thick, almost girlish lashes met his and
Devlin revised his opinion. Despite his outward appearance there was nothing soft about Yates. He was
a man used to getting his own way. The gold pocket
watch and diamond signet ring were also not lost on
Devlin. Whoever he was, he had money. He decided
civility would cost him nothing and might well reward
him.

"I've been at sea all my life, except for a year logging in the Northwest and a short spell panning for
gold."

"What have you sailed?"

"Everything. Schooners. Three-masted barks. Brigs.
Trawlers. Cutters. Sloops. Steamships. Whalers."

"And you know the Atlantic well?"

"I've been sailing her on and off for ten years."

Duane Yates leaned forward. "Guy tells me you
went to Franklin for a loan. That you felt there was
money to be made ferrying cargo across to Europe."

Devlin nodded.

"Have you any particular cargo in mind?"

Devlin had, but he wasn't going to give any information away for free. "Anything and everything," he
said noncommittally.

Duane Yates grinned and helped himself unasked
to another glass of Devlin's bourbon.

"I'll tell you what cargo is at a premium. People."

Devlin, who had run across slave traffic in his days
on the Gold Coast, stared.

Yates laughed. "Tourists. Businessmen. Cunard
saw it years ago. Their two ships, the *Mauretania* and
the *Lusitania* are making them a fortune. The Atlantic
crossing is the voyage of voyages and anyone who's
anyone wants to make the trip. There's money in it,
O'Conner. Big money."

"And to earn it you need big ships," Devlin said drily.

Yates drained his glass. "I'm not a seafaring man myself, but I have money. Lots of it. I'd like to cash in on the Atlantic crossing but I need a man who knows ships and the sea. A man I can trust and a man who isn't afraid to take risks."

"You just might," Devlin said cautiously, "have found him. Providing you have the ship, of course."

Yates laughed. "That is a little problem, I agree. I have no ship. Yet. But I've seen one. A steamship of 14,000 tons. She's lying up at Halifax."

"How old is she?" Devlin asked cautiously.

Duane Yate's smile was disarming. "Fairly old, but I reckon if her structure is sound I can have her looking pretty as a picture within a matter of months. Comfort and luxury is what the passengers want. How long do you think it would take you to make the crossing?"

"The old Cunarders passage from England to Halifax was twelve days, give or take a few hours. I hear the *Mauretania* does it in five."

"Could we equal that?"

Devlin laughed. "With a refurbished hulk of a ship? No chance. Till I see it I don't even know if the idea is feasible."

"Then the sooner you see it, the better," Yates said decisively, rising to his feet. "We'll go tomorrow. Be at my office at nine." He handed Devlin an embossed card bearing his name in elegant script.

"Good day to you. I think our meeting is going to prove beneficial to both of us."

The long journey from New York to Halifax was made bearable by the help of Duane Yates's undoubted wealth. The first class carriage in the train had comfortably upholstered seats. Cold chicken and beef went down well with iced champagne and the best brandy. Whatever the state of the ship they were about to see, or however hare-brained Duane Yates's

scheme, Devlin was living well for a few days and he
had the sense to enjoy it. Besides, there was something about Duane that gave him the pleasurable feeling that his scheme wasn't the idle whim of a rich and
bored young man. He was deadly serious and if the
ship *was* structurally sound . . .

The monotonous rhythm of the wheels on the tracks
had lulled Devlin to sleep. If it *was* sound then he
could find himself being the captain of the biggest ship
of his career. He narrowed his eyes thoughtfully. And
working for Duane Yates instead of Anglo-American.
If Duane Yates wanted him, he'd have to offer him
a lot more than just a job. He'd have to offer him a
partnership.

The train chugged painfully into Halifax and Duane
shivered in the unaccustomed chill of the northern air.

"Bloody outback," he said to Devlin as they made
their way toward the shipyard.

Devlin, a veteran of Antarctic whalers, grinned and
said nothing. He was aware of a knot of excitement
growing in the pit of his stomach. Spreading through
him like the warmth of the brandy.

Her name was the *Ninevah*, and she lay like a
beached and rusted whale in the drydock. Devlin
stared at her, his hands deep in his trouser pockets.

"I take it I'm not the first sucker you've dragged a
few hundred miles to see this sight?"

Beneath his black-beavered coat Duane's narrow
shoulders shrugged.

"I thought not," Devlin said grimly.

Duane watched him closely. Devlin's piercing blue
eyes held a speculative gleam. He wasn't going to turn
without a closer look like the other faint-hearted prospective captains had done. He gave a sigh of relief
as Devlin walked away from him toward the apparently derelict ship.

Three hours later he was back, wiping grime and oil
off his hands with a rag.

"What do you think?" Duane asked nervously.

"I think you'll have to have a hell of a lot of cash," Devlin said bluntly.

"But she'll sail?"

"She'll sail all right. Sound as a rock under that rust and peeling paint. How long has she been beached?"

"Eight years."

Devlin flinched. "It isn't just the superstructure needs attention. You'll need skilled engineers on that engine."

"Do *you* know what needs doing?"

"*I* do. No one else would."

Duane accompanied him back to the waiting train in thoughtful silence.

As they settled themselves back in the warmth of the compartment he said, "And will you take her on? Supervise her restoration?"

Devlin's eyes met his. "I might, but not just for the pleasure of becoming her captain."

"What then?"

"I want a partnership. You provide the money for the venture. I'll provide the expertise. Without me you'll never get that ship afloat. Not on the Atlantic."

"And without me you'll be back to long-haul freight."

"Just so," Devlin agreed. "Is it a deal?"

Yates grinned. He'd known all along the red-haired Irishman would ask for more than just the pleasure of sailing the *Ninevah*. He held out his hand.

"Agreed. We'll get the papers signed up the minute we reach New York."

Devlin felt a surge of elation. Two days in New York and he was joint owner of a ship that could make him a fortune.

Duane poured champagne and the two men raised their glasses.

"To the Conyates Shipping Company," Duane said, almost as exultant as Devlin. "May the *Ninevah* be the first of a whole fleet of ships."

"To the Conyates Shipping Company," Devlin echoed as the train began to pick up speed, and then silently as he felt the familiar burning sensation in his loins, "And to Christina!"

Chapter 13

For the next two weeks Devlin hardly emerged from his rooming house. Duane Yates completed the purchase of the ship and they had agreed to retain its original name of *Ninevah*. Devlin spent twenty hours out of twenty-four drawing and discarding plan after plan for her refitting.

"We'll have to use Southampton as a port," Duane said. "Most American tourists are wanting to go on to France and the rest of Europe. Liverpool is out."

Devlin nodded. He'd been working on his schemes for the *Ninevah* with such single-mindedness that Christina had faded into the background of his thoughts. Now he realized that it would be several months before he would be able to return to England for her. And his partner didn't even know of her existence.

"I shall want to break a few rules when we finally get the *Ninevah* seaworthy."

Duane's face didn't flicker. "Such as?"

"I want to take someone with me when we sail."

"As partner and captain of the ship you're entitled to invite any guest you want on her maiden voyage," Duane said affably. "I shall invite as many of New

York's elite as I can and turn the whole affair into one magnificent party."

"That wasn't what I meant. I shall be taking someone with me every trip."

Duane smoothed his immaculate moustache and raised his eyebrows. "I take it you're referring to a woman?"

Devlin nodded.

Duane shrugged. "You're the seaman. If having your wife on board would cause no trouble and keep you happy I've no objections."

"She isn't my wife," Devlin said, thinking that she would be the minute she reached New York.

"Then all I can say is she must be one hell of a woman if you want to have her with you all the time!"

"She is."

They grinned at each other, and as the secretary hurried in with a pile of papers for Duane to sign, Devlin took his leave. For once he didn't return immediately to his dingy room and plans and calculations. He walked down to the wharves and lit one of Duane's cigars.

"I hear Anglo-American's fired you," a friendly voice said, and a man nearly as tall as himself and with a luxuriant beard clapped his hand on Devlin's shoulder.

"*I* fired them."

"That sounds more like it. What are you doing now? Going back to the South American run?"

Devlin shook his head. "I've finished working my guts out for other people."

Jemmy Cadogan eyed him with interest.

Devlin liked Jemmy Cadogan. They'd spent a hard ten months together on the whalers.

"You're looking at one half of the Conyates Shipping Company."

Jemmy laughed. "Congratulations. What are you going to do? Rival them?" He nodded in the direction of the Cunarder.

Devlin didn't laugh. "One day," he said through narrowed eyes. "One day I'll have Cunard, White Star and Collins all looking to their laurels."

Jemmy Cadogan shifted his kit more comfortably over his shoulder. "You probably will, you bugger. Never known a man like you for bloody single-mindedness. I'd stay and have a drink with you, but we sail in an hour's time."

"To Liverpool?" Devlin asked.

Jemmy nodded.

"Do me a favor will you? Call in at the Gaiety and give a message to one of the girls."

"I'll give her more than a message," Jemmy said with gusto.

"Not this one you won't," Devlin said grimly. "Ask for Christina Haworth and tell her I've got a ship but she needs re-fitting. Tell her it could be months before I can come back to Liverpool for her, but tell her I will be back. Tell her nothing has changed. And tell Bessie Mulholland to keep her promise to me. Tell her I've struck it lucky and that money is no problem."

"O.K., and all the best. If you want a good second mate you know where to find one. What cargo are you carrying?"

"Same as them." Devlin nodded in the direction of a pier where one of the great White Star liners was berthed. "People. Tourists. Businessmen. Immigrants."

Jemmy Cadogan whistled through his teeth. "Either you've taken leave of your senses or you're a bloody lucky bastard. I'll look you up next time I dock. I'm cheesed off with the run I'm on. A spell of entertaining bored young ladies at sea would be a welcome change!"

"You'd have to work bloody hard if you worked for me," Devlin said good-naturedly. "I'll keep a place for you. And bring me any messages there are back from the Gaiety, will you?"

"You bet." Jemmy Cadogan looked across at the

splendor of the White Star liner again. "Are you *really* going to captain a ship like that?"

"Not *quite* like that," Devlin admitted. "But she's half mine and when I've finished with her she'll be twice as grand. Don't forget to see Christina Haworth the minute you dock."

"I won't," Jemmy said, slightly dazed. "Devlin O'Conner, shipowner. Who the hell would have thought it?"

"I would," Devlin said with a grin. "I always did."

By the end of the month Devlin was settled in Halifax, backed by Duane's money, and with overall authority had an army of carpenters and mechanics slaving day and night. Duane was as eager as Devlin to get the ship seaworthy in the shortest possible time.

Duane's father had once owned river steamers, and the opulence that made them such a romantic method of travel Duane intended transferring to the *Ninevah* on a much larger scale.

Devlin had frowned when Duane had begun talking of fitted carpets in both first and second class.

"It's a bloody ship. Not a hotel!"

"You stick to the nuts and bolts. Let me deal with the decorations!"

The ship was now in two complete halves as hundreds of workmen sweated over red hot rivets, inserting a brand new section amidships to lengthen her.

Duane continued with his arrangements for steam heating and a music room and even a barber's shop, while Devlin redesigned the interior so that in addition to ample accommodation for first and second class passengers, there was room for nearly a thousand steerage passengers as well.

Hammermen, mechanics, master shipwrights, caulkers, blacksmiths, joiners and riggers worked round the clock, and as the rust and peeling paint disappeared Devlin saw with satisfaction that his original judgment as to the strength of the ship had been sound.

Duane booked himself a passage on one of the White Star liners, coming back and telling Devlin that the plans for the interior would have to be altered. First class passengers would be accommodated amidships in the new section of the *Ninevah* and he wanted the dining saloon to stretch the whole length of the ship in imitation of the much bigger White Star liners. Devlin let him have his way.

On one of his fleeting visits Duane pulled on his cigar and eyed the *Ninevah* with satisfaction.

"She's coming along, Devlin. We'll be able to start on the first class suites soon. I want hot running water *and* private baths and lavatories. I want this ship decorated with Yankee dash and none of your old English restraint!" And then he returned to the luxury of his chauffeur-driven Ford automobile.

A languorous redhead waited for him and Devlin felt himself grow hot and hard. Celibacy didn't suit him. There were plenty of bars and women in Halifax. Certainly enough to keep his workmen happy. After having bathed, Devlin toweled himself dry, pulled on a clean shirt and his best pair of breeches and set out for a night on the town.

A well-built brunette with bold eyes draped herself over his shoulder as he sat at the beer-stained bar and asked for a drink.

"I wondered when you'd come out of hiding," she said, rubbing her thumb along the back of his neck. "Seen you around, but the guys said you never did anything but think about that bloody ship. Ready to think about something else now?"

She raised her leg, resting her foot on the supporting bar of Devlin's stool, her skirt high over her knee. It was, Devlin noticed, an extremely shapely knee and the glimpse of thigh above it was equally inviting.

"Maybe."

She shrugged her shoulders carelessly so that the

thin strap of her dress slipped downward, showing even more of her full breasts.

Devlin pushed the money for his drink across the bar, put his arm around her waist and told her to lead the way.

The room was not much better than his rooming house in New York but Devlin had been in plenty of worse places in his life. The girl wound her arms around his neck, kissing him tongue deep, her body straining against his. Then she unhooked her dress and sprawled provocatively on the iron bedstead.

It was a scene Devlin had been through a hundred times. In another hour he would be back at the bar, the girl as forgotten as all those who had gone before her. Except for Christina.

The girl pouted carmine-red lips and rotated her hips on the sheets suggestively.

"Come on, big boy. We're wasting time."

Devlin's shirt lay on the end of the bed, and his hands were on his belt buckle. He stared at the full, tempting breasts, the inviting legs, and all he could think of was Christina. Slowly he reached for his shirt.

The girl sprang up, her eyes uncomprehending. "What the hell are you doing?"

"Going back to the shipyard," Devlin said impassively. He threw her a couple of dollar bills. "That's for wasting your time."

"What's the matter with you?" she asked indignantly. "Are you a man or aren't you? You had a big enough hard-on downstairs in the bar!"

"Maybe I had, but it wasn't for you." He grinned and walked back down the rickety stairs and the girl followed him to the door, screaming abuse after him.

There was nothing for it. He would have to return to Liverpool for Christina, and fast. The *Ninevah* wouldn't be ready for another six months. He couldn't wait that long for her. He would just have to delegate the work to his foreman and take time off. He could easily get a passage as crew on one of the steamers.

Duane was furious but Devlin was immovable. At last, forced to give in, Duane booked him a passage aboard one of the Cunarders.

"They cross in the shortest time and it will give you some idea of what I want for the *Ninevah*. This girl had better be worth it. She's costing me a fortune," he said as he forked out the cash for one return and one single ticket.

"She's worth it, all right," Devlin said with a grin as he pocketed the money. "And don't worry about the *Ninevah*. We'll have her on the Atlantic by the end of the year."

Almost simultaneously Jemmy Cadogan strolled into the inner bar of the Gaiety and asked Marigold if he could see Bessie.

"She's not available at the moment," Marigold said, taking his money.

"Can I see Christina Haworth then?"

Marigold shook her head. "She's no longer one of the girls."

"Know where I can get in touch with her? I've a message for her from Devlin O'Conner."

Some yards away from them Kate kept on her conversation with a prospective client without faltering.

"Best give it to Bessie then," Marigold said. "Rosie's your usual isn't she?"

Jemmy nodded and moved toward the bar. O'Conner's message could wait until he'd finished enjoying himself.

Kate slipped away from her customer and tapped Dimity on the shoulder. "I'm not feeling very well, Dimmy. Could you be an angel and take a customer off my hands for me? He's over there, the one with the heavy beard."

Dimmy agreed, wondering perhaps if the rest of the girls hadn't misjudged Kate. She could be quite pleasant when she wanted to be.

Kate made her way to the bar and Jemmy Cadogan. She smiled.

"Nice to see you back. Rosie's busy at the moment."

Jemmy eyed Kate's fall of straight blonde hair and magnificent breasts.

"Fancy a change?" Kate asked with a slight smile.

Jemmy remembered that Devlin had always patronized Kate—he wouldn't have done so if Kate hadn't been exceptionally talented.

"Why not?" he said, downing his brandy. "I've heard a lot about you. Going to show me if it's all true?"

Thirty-five minutes later Jemmy had to admit that it was.

"I heard you had a message for Christina?" Kate said with studied casualness as she climbed on top of him. "She's still here. I'll give her the message if you want."

"Thanks." Jemmy's manhood had never before been questioned, but he was beginning to think that the girl in his bed was insatiable, and that unless he made his exit quickly he was going to be humiliated. Three times in quick succession was too much for a man who had just crossed the Atlantic, yet Kate's enthusiasm showed no sign of abating.

"What was it then? Is he coming back soon?"

Jemmy wondered how she could move so frantically and talk so casually at the same time.

"Yes," he gasped valiantly. "He's got a ship but she needs re-fitting. He says to tell her not to worry. He's going to come back for her."

"Is it his own ship?" Kate asked and Jemmy mistakenly took the white teeth biting into his bottom lip as a sign of ecstasy.

"Half his." Sweat was breaking out on Jemmy's brow. "He's formed a company with an American. They're calling themselves the Conyates Shipping Company and they're re-fitting the ship as a passenger liner. Reckon he's going to marry this Christina. Never known O'Conner serious about a girl before."

"No," Kate agreed, and Jemmy cried out aloud as Kate's nails scored his back and she rode herself into a frenzy, trying to satisfy her never-ending desire for Devlin on Jemmy Cadogan and failing miserably. No matter how many men she had, it was never enough. Only Devlin was capable of quenching the voracious needs of her hungry body.

"Poaching on Rosie's regulars?" Sheba said to Kate as the Gaiety closed its doors and the girls began to make their way to their rooms.

Kate shrugged. "Giving him a bit of a change, that's all. He had news of Devlin. The bastard's got what he wanted at long last."

"What's that?"

"His own ship." Kate laughed mirthlessly. "But he's paid a high price for it. Seems like he met some old American with more money than sense and talked him into going into the passenger liner business. The old guy was agreeable on one condition. That Devlin marry his daughter. Some prim and proper virgin from Pennsylvania. Bloody bastard." Her eyes flashed angrily and Sheba went back to her own room, not seeing the expression on Kate's face change to a smile of malice. Christina was laughing as Nymphy recounted her experiences with her last client of the evening.

Sheba waited until Nymphy had gone and Belle and Molly were asleep and then she said, "Christina?"

"Mm." Christina roused herself from the warmth of drifting sleep.

"There was a sailor in tonight. Jemmy Cadogan. He comes here regularly. He used to sail the whalers with Devlin."

Christina was instantly wide-awake.

"He's just sailed in from New York and he has news of Devlin."

Christina sat up in bed, hugging her knees. "What

is it? Please don't keep me in suspense, Sheba. Has Devlin got his ship?"

"Yes, but . . ."

"Hooray!" Christina was uncaring of the sleeping girls. "Oh isn't that *wonderful!* I knew he would do it! There's nothing Devlin can't do if he puts his mind to it. When is he coming back? Is it soon? Oh please let it be soon or I shall die!"

Sheba said gently, "It isn't all good news, Christina. Jemmy Cadogan says Devlin has gone into partnership with an American, and that they are re-fitting a ship as a passenger liner."

"But that's *fabulous* news!"

"And that to get the old man's financial backing Devlin married his spinster daughter."

The silence stretched for so long that Sheba grew afraid. She got out of bed and slipped across to Christina, taking her hand in hers. It was ice-cold.

"I'm sorry, Christina. But I think it was better me telling you than you hearing it casually in the bar."

"Yes." Christina's voice was expressionless. "He always said he would do anything for a ship of his own. Obviously he meant it."

Christina lay prone, her hands clenched into tight fists, her eyes unseeing as they stared at the darkened ceiling.

He'd loved her but he'd married some prissy spinster to get his own ship. Well, the lady in question was welcome to him. He'd be back. Wanting her in his bed as his mistress. Expecting her to be grateful for his return. Full of sweet reason. Telling her that he still loved her and that his marriage meant nothing.

Scalding tears coursed their way down her cheeks. He would be in for a shock when he did return. Never again would she allow anyone to hurt her in this way. Devlin O'Conner could rot in hell. She never wanted to see him again. She closed her eyes against the memory of his lovemaking and laughter. She hated him. *Hated* him.

Christina turned over, burying her face in the pillow, sobbing as she never had since the death of her father. Both times love had been lost. But this time was far, far worse. If Devlin had died it would have been easier for her to bear than this betrayal of everything that had happened between them. She pressed her fist against her mouth, sobbing silently until the dawn.

Chapter 14

The next evening Christina took the unprecedented step of borrowing Molly's jars and pots of cream and disguising the dark circles beneath her eyes. Then, one hand on her hip, she descended the staircase into the crowded bar.

Bessie's eyebrows flew upward. "What on earth do you think you're doing?"

"Working," Christina said with a brittle smile, and continued to walk with swaying grace to the long length of the bar, hooking her arm boldly through that of the first sailor she came across.

"Cor blimey, you're luck's in!" his companion said appreciatively, eyeing Christina's waist-length black wavy hair and high thrusting breasts.

"Fancy a drink first?" he asked, letting his hand slide down over her shoulder so that it cupped her breast.

"Don't mind if I do. A brandy, please."

Across the smoke-filled room Merry stared at her

horrified. Christina rarely drank and she had never before seen her let a client take liberties with her in full view of everyone else.

The brandy was gone in one swallow. The sailor's hand closed tighter over Christina's bare breast, the nipple hard in his palm.

"What about taking a bottle up and making a party of it?"

Christina rubbed her long bare leg against his. "Why not?" she said throatily.

He thrust another handful of notes across the bar, picked up his brandy, and with the bulge in his trousers throbbing pleasurably took Christina hastily up the stairs and along the corridor to room number three.

The last time she had been in here had been with Devlin. A wave of pain, so intense she thought she would drown beneath it, swept over her and then bitterness took its place. She would never have slept with another man in her life if Devlin had wanted her. But he had preferred a respectable, straitlaced spinster. She poured herself another glass of brandy, laughed wildly and threw her clothes to the far side of the room, raising her arms high above her naked body as the sailor's hands moved over her breasts and between her thighs.

An hour later, half drunk and with her blouse so low her breasts showed at the slightest movement, Christina was taking her third customer upstairs, her head thrown back, as a bull of a man kissed her throat hungrily.

"What the hell," Marigold asked Bessie, "has come over her?"

"I don't know but come the morning and I'll damn well find out. She's had more customers in the hour than even Nymphy!"

"Hell's light if you aren't a goer," the massive sailor said as he rolled pantingly off her. "If I didn't have to be back on board the *Corinthia* to check the stores I'm damned if I wouldn't pay for the extra."

"She's a passenger liner isn't she?" Christina rocked unsteadily on her feet, dizzy from the effect of the alcohol, as she struggled back into her skirt and blouse.

"One of the best. Not the size of the *Mauretania* but pretty big. We sail in the morning."

He reached reluctantly for his pants.

"Going on board now?" Christina hiccoughed swayingly.

"Got to. The luggage needs checking off before the passengers board at eight A.M."

Christina pressed her mouth against his. "Tace me with you," she murmured, "just for a little look. No one will know."

"What the hell for?"

She shrugged. "Just like to have a see."

Deep down within her the pain was almost unendurable. The *Corinthia* would be like the ship Devlin had sold himself for, destroying all hope of their happiness.

"Go on. We can do it again if you take me on board. I haven't shown you anything yet."

The sailor, nearly as drunk as Christina, grabbed a satisfying handful of Christina's buttocks in his hand and grinned.

"O.K., but how do we get out? Bessie will never let you through the door."

"Don't worry about Bessie," Christina said as the room swam around her. "There's more exits than the one in the downstairs bar. Come on."

With his brawny arm around her waist for support, they crept along the corridor, through Bessie's parlor, and down the backstairs to the gas-lit street.

The *Corinthia* had many of the refinements of the *Mauretania*, but on a more modest scale. Christina's vision was too blurred to take any notice of them and anyway, her companion gave her no time. His main interest was getting her into his cabin in the shortest time possible. The rest of his shipmates were still drinking on shore and he wanted to enjoy the infinite variety of pleasure that Christina's body promised for as long as possible.

The twelve hammocks swung neat and tidy and empty.

"Ever done it in a hammock before?" he asked her, pulling his thick woolen jumper over his head.

"No." The words were strangled in her throat. If she had sailed with Devlin as he had promised would they have slept in hammocks or in bunks? A captain would have had a bunk. A big, double bunk. Christina fought down the sobs rising in her throat.

"Where the hell's that brandy bottle?" she asked, drinking greedily, wanting only oblivion.

Why, Christina thought heartbrokenly, could it mean so much with one man and so little with another? And then her need to be revenged on Devlin reasserted itself. There would be lots of other men. Lots. And Devlin O'Conner would be just one number among hundreds. In another few weeks she would have forgotten all about him. She wouldn't even be able to remember his face or the feel of his touch upon her skin. But even through her alcoholic haze she knew she was fooling herself. It would take longer than weeks for her to forget Devlin O'Conner. It would take months. Even years.

The burly sailor put Christina's promise to the test and by the time his satisfaction was complete he was too exhausted to struggle back into his clothes and deposit her on the dockside. A little sleep. Just a few minutes. The brandy had already taken its toll of Christina. She was asleep, her arms and breasts warm and naked against him. He rolled on his side, shielding her from view in case they should be unexpectedly disturbed, and was soon snoring soundly.

If his shipmates thought Victor Jackson's hammock hung heavier than usual they were all too drunk to notice. Christina, half waking in the middle of the night, her head throbbing and her ears ringing from the effects of the brandy, wriggled out from under the uncomfortable sweaty weight of her companion. Fumbling, she took one of his blankets and curled up in a corner on the floor, the coarse wool high over her head and shoulders.

Jackson woke at first light, filled with horror. He stared at the empty space beside him and relaxed. The girl had more sense than he had, he thought. She'd obviously left. By God, but it had been a night to remember. Fifteen minutes later he was fully dressed and with the rest of his shipmates on deck, preparing to sail as soon as the passengers had boarded.

Christina half woke once or twice, her throat parched and her tongue dry. The prospect of staggering to her feet and finding water was too daunting. In her sleep she felt the vibration of engines and it seemed to her that she was back on board the *Lucky Star* again, and that she and her father were about to take off for Brest and the golden ports of the Mediterranean. She hugged her knees beneath her chin as she had when a child and drifted into still deeper sleep.

The exhaustion of the previous day's grief and the unaccustomed effects of the brandy took their toll. By the time Christina finally regained consciousness and staggered to her feet, the *Corinthia* had discarded her pilot and was well out at sea. She stared uncomprehendingly at the sight of great waves splashing against the familiar roundness of a porthole, turning the thick glass a dark green and then a foaming white. Slowly, memory flooded back and she sat down suddenly, her legs weak. She had no idea of the time but from the look of the sunlight on the water it was well past midday. She was stranded aboard the *Corinthia* and land was receding further with every passing minute.

Panic stricken, she struggled to her feet, her one intention that of finding the captain and demanding that he return to Liverpool so that she could disembark.

"What the hell . . ." A broad, muscled body barred

her way. "Hey, Sam, come and see what I've found!"

At the expression in his eyes Christina instinctively backed away, pulling her blouse high over her shoulders. There came a clatter of feet down the companionway and another sailor swore softly beneath his breath.

"Now who'd have been fool enough to bring a woman on board and forget all about her? If he *did* forget all about her. Perhaps he was saving her for himself."

"Then he'll just have to share and share alike," the other said with a grin, moving toward her.

Christina stood her ground, her head high. "I came on board last night to have a look at the ship and I fell asleep. And now, if you'll please let me pass, I want to see the captain and explain . . ."

"Explain!" The first man who had ugly little red veins in his cheeks laughed heartily. "You'll never explain this to old Reed! The best thing for you to do is to keep quiet and be cooperative until we dock."

"And where will that be?" If it was Southampton that wouldn't be too bad. She'd be able to get back to Liverpool somehow.

"New York."

"*New York!*" Christina's eyes were horrified. "But surely you'll be calling for some more passengers at Southampton?"

He shook his head, his grin widening.

"Cherbourg?" she tried valiantly to think of the ports of call for the liners that crossed the Atlantic. He shook his head.

"There's nothing now but the wide blue sea until we reach America, so you just might as well make the best of it. What do you say, Sam?"

"Couldn't agree with you more, old mate," Sam said, moving closer still.

"I demand to see the captain. I . . . ."

"Come off it, luv. We know what you are. No sense in playing the outraged lady."

Christina's wildness of the previous night had completely vanished. She wanted the familiarity of her room at the Gaiety and Molly and Merry laughing and talking and the reassuring presence of Bessie in the background. At the Gaiety she had felt safe, knowing that nothing unpleasant could happen to her. Bert was protection against the most formidable customer. As the two men leered at her she felt suddenly afraid.

"You're making a mistake. I'm not what you think. I cook and clean for Bessie Mulholland. . . ."

"Bessie Mulholland is it? I was told she only took the best. Seems like they was right."

She struggled desperately as the two grinning sailors laid hands on her, one on each of her arms.

They dragged her, struggling and kicking, across to an old chest, one of them snatching at her blouse and pulling it down to her waist.

"Better shut her up, Sam, or there'll be all hell to pay!"

Christina's voice rose to a high-pitched scream and then a sweaty hand was pressed firmly across her mouth as they dragged her, face down, over the chest, pulling her skirt up high above her waist. Cruel fingers dug deep into her inner thighs as she fought, tasting blood on her lips as her teeth sank into the suffocating palm. It was all to no avail. Her strength was waning. She could feel one of them behind her . . .

"Let go of her this minute, you stupid bastards!"

With a sob of relief Christina recognized the voice of her companion of the previous night, humiliatingly aware that she was still exposed to the general gaze.

"Was it you who brought her on board, Jackson?" Her captor was panting, his mouth slack and wet with anticipation.

"It was and it's me that'll see she gets off. Now let go of her before I thump the living daylights out of you!"

The grasp on Christina's wrist eased as the men turned to face Victor Jackson.

"Now what makes you think you can carry out a

promise like that?" the sailor named Sam said with an unpleasant grin. "It won't just be us you have to reckon with. What do you think the rest of the lads are going to say when they realize there's a woman aboard? They'll have the same ideas as we have and there's not going to be much you can do about it."

Christina trembled. There were twelve hammocks in the cabin. The thought of being at the mercy of twelve men made her feel faint.

"No!" Christina forced herself to move, gripping hold of Victor Jackson's brawny hand. *"Please* tell the captain! *Don't* leave me with *them. Please don't!"*

"He hasn't any choice, luv," Sam said, reading the defeat on Victor Jackson's face. "And neither have you."

Christina gave a cry of alarm as Victor broke loose from her hold and walked quickly out of the cabin and up the companionway. There was a fresh clatter of feet on the iron rungs and then a boy burst in saying, "You're wanted up top and . . ." He gazed open-mouthed at Christina.

"Nice surprise, eh? That fool Jackson brought her aboard last night and fell asleep on her. Seems we've got her company for the next few days till we reach New York. Should be a memorable voyage." He gave the boy a knowing wink.

"You lay one hand on me and I'll scratch your eyes out!" Christina said viciously, her nails clawed in readiness.

"Didn't do you much good last time," Sam's friend said with a laugh.

"Let her alone," the boy said suddenly. "Can't you see she's scared to death?"

"Scared to death, my foot." Sam spat on the floor expressively. "She's one of Bessie Mulholland's girls. Used to anything her lot are."

"I'm not used to anything." Christina fought down rising hysteria. "You'd never have been allowed across the Gaiety's threshold. You're nothing but a pack of animals!"

"Oh, and do the dandies do it differently?" Sam asked, moving forward. "I've heard they get a lot of 'em in the Gaiety. Not just a common brothel for us poor seamen, is it? I suppose you think you're a cut above us?"

"I just want you to let me see the captain and explain," Christina said, her voice shaking.

"Perhaps she thinks she's only good enough for a man of rank," Sam's friend said with a grin. "Let's show her different lads, eh?"

Victor Jackson had two choices. He could remain quiet about the girl's presence and hope to God no word leaked to the captain, or he could tell Reed himself. If he told Reed the girl would be protected but he would lose his job. If he didn't she would be the plaything of every man in his cabin. And she *was* a whore. It would hardly be a fate worse than death for her. It was to Victor Jackson's credit that he only hesitated for a second before making his way to the bridge.

Captain Reed was a well-set man in his early sixties, with bushy white eyebrows, a white moustache waxed at the tips, and a luxuriant beard. He had been sailing for nigh on fifty years and was confident that nothing that happened aboard his well-run ship could shake his almost permanent affability. Victor Jackson succeeded.

"*A woman!*" Even the massively built Jackson quaked before the ferocity of his Captain's fury. "Evans, remove this man from duties and confine him immediately!"

First Officer Evans hurried to comply with his orders as Captain Reed marched seethingly below decks.

Christina had fought and struggled like a wild thing, and the men's faces were scratched and bleeding. The young cabin boy had watched with growing alarm, protesting vainly as Christina's blouse had been ripped to tatters and his two shipmates had finally succeeded in pinning her down before tossing up to see who was to be the first to enjoy her.

"Second Officer Carfax, put these two under arrest immediately!"

Christina was released so suddenly that she fell onto the floor.

Sam and his friend were white-faced and at attention. The young boy trembled with fright.

"This *instant*, Carfax!"

There were no protests. Mutely the men filed out after the Second Officer.

"As for you . . ." Captain Reed's blazing eyes transfixed the boy like a fox stalking a rabbit.

"He tried to stop them," Christina said, clutching the pathetic remnants of her blouse in a vain attempt at covering up her bare breasts.

"When I want to speak to you I will address you!" Captain Reed's voice cut through the air like a knife. "I'll see *you* in my cabin at 1200 hours," he said to the terrified cabin boy, "and Chief Officer Pegham," he turned to the man beside him who was trying gallantly to keep his gaze on Christina's face and not on her body, "take this—this *woman* to my cabin and cover her up. I don't want a scandal before we've scarcely left port!"

The cabin boy's jacket was unceremoniously requisitioned and the chief officer hung it across Christina's naked shoulders. She clutched at it gratefully, giving him a shaky thank-you.

Chief Officer Pegham regarded her with interest. She was obviously a slut, but no ordinary one. As he accompanied her up the companionway and across the saloon deck he noticed the unconscious grace with which she walked and the proud tilt of her head, as if she were dressed in furs and feathers instead of barefoot and in a grubby cotton skirt and borrowed jacket.

Chief Officer Pegham led the way into Captain

Reed's oak-lined cabin and withdrew. It would be interesting to see how the old man handled *this* situation. One thing was for sure: her virtue would be safe with Reed. His reputation as a devoted family man was known far and wide.

Minutes later Captain Reed stormed into the cabin and faced Christina across his enormous desk.

"We're bound for New York," he said tightly. "I hope that itinerary is acceptable to you?"

"I demand to be returned to Liverpool," Christina said, her composure fully regained, her eyes as angry as those of the man opposite her.

Captain Reed stifled a choke. "You demand nothing of me, you little whore! Nothing! You've lost. one good man his job and two others are confined to quarters."

"I'm sorry about Victor Jackson. It wasn't his fault. But I'm not sorry about the other two. They deserve all they get."

"And so do you!" Captain Reed's fist thumped down hard on his desk. "Do you know what sort of ship this is? It isn't some scrubby trading barge. It's a luxury liner. If word of your presence got out to the passengers . . ."

"If you're assuming I would lower the tone of your ship, Captain Reed," Christina said icily, "then you assume too much."

"Take her away," Captain Reed waved to Chief Officer Pegham who was standing in the doorway. "Lock her in a spare cabin until I can sort this mess out."

Christina's head went even higher as Chief Officer Pegham took her arm.

"As for the two men you confined to quarters, it's a good thing you did so, Captain, or I might have taken my own revenge. I have a motto in life: *'S'ils te mordent, mord les,'* " and leaving the captain open-mouthed, she swept out of the cabin after the chief officer.

Chapter 15

Captain Reed cursed again for good measure. He liked a neat, orderly ship. And having a stowaway on board, and a harlot at that, was not in his scheme of things. Not that the girl had intended to stow away.

"Drunken little slut," Reed said to himself as he made his way onto the main deck. Then, despite himself, he grinned. *'S'ils te mordent, mord les,'* indeed! She was obviously French, though her Northern accent would have fooled anybody. Not her looks, though. There was nothing Northern in the olive skin and flashing eyes or the arrogant tilt of the head. "Province I shouldn't wonder," Reed said to himself, acknowledging the smile of Mrs. Fitzgerald, who bore down on him, a fur stole around her throat as protection against the sea breeze, her fat beringed hand clasped inside her muff.

"*Dear* Captain Reed. I *do* hope we will have the pleasure of being able to dine with you at your table. As you know, my husband, Colonel Fitzgerald is Chairman of Hatton, Hatton and Hatton . . ."

Captain Reed waved the effusive Mrs. Fitzgerald aside with a charming smile and murmured an acknowledgment that meant nothing whatsoever. However, the lady retreated feeling she was the victor. Herbert would be *so* pleased with her.

It was Captain Reed's customary habit to make a

personal inspection of his ship every day, to greet new passengers, especially those with wealth and titles, and to make sure their every comfort was being seen to. Competition at sea was hard. The Cunarders were the *crème de la crème* of lines, and it was hard for smaller lines to attract the same glamorous passengers. And it was the glamor of life aboard a great ship that attracted them in the first place.

Captain Reed's progress took him from the main deck to the saloon deck. One thing was becoming increasingly obvious. Despite the luxury of the *Corinthia*'s fitments, the lushness of the glass enclosed promenade deck, the small orchestra playing pleasantly in the background, glamor was distinctly absent from the *Corinthia* on this voyage. And it had been absent on her last voyage, Captain Reed reflected, his hands clasped behind his back, his head down, deep in thought.

Young Van Hethlin, heir to more than a million, had complained bitterly to him over cigars before he had disembarked on the last trip.

"Hate to say it, Captain. But I guess the *Mauretania* will be having my custom next season."

The captain had expressed alarm, and inquired as to whether Mr. Van Hethlin's steward had been in any way lax.

"Not at all. It's just that the crossing's been a bit of a bore on the whole. I mean, look at them." Van Hethlin had pointed his cigar in the direction of the ladies around them. Not one was under forty. Rich and pampered, they drank their champagne, nibbled their way decorously through all seven courses of dinner, and then danced with restraint with their elderly but wealthy husbands.

"I hear Lana de Palmer, the nickleodeon star, is sailing on the *Mauretania* this trip. Now *that* would have livened this voyage up."

Captain Reed could only agree. Shipboard romance

was the main ingredient in his company's publicity material, encouraging tourists to sail on their line. On the *Corinthia* it was in very short supply.

On the upper deck he saw the usual crowd of immaculately dressed young American businessmen, already with drinks in their hands, and no wonder. There was certainly no other diversion on board. True, there were three young ladies under twenty-five on the first class passenger list. Captain Reed made a point of seeking them out and making their acquaintance, much to the delight of their fond mamas.

Miss Victoria Pucy was tall and gaunt, with a sallow skin that would only grow sallower the further they sailed into the Atlantic.

Miss Constance Fleery was a pleasant-faced girl with shy eyes who, her mother proudly told the captain, was about to take holy orders, on reaching New York, and become a nun.

Miss Ethel Goldman had braces on her teeth and spots on her chin.

There would be very little dallying on the sundeck after dinner on *this* trip. He sighed. The *Mauretania* and *Lusitania* were famed for their exotic shipboard life. Cunard conjured up luxury and beautiful women trailing chiffon scarves over the deck rails as they listened to sweet nothings from handsome, virile young men.

He doubted the young businessmen returning from Europe would find much romance in enticing Miss Goldman or Miss Pucy to a secluded corner on deck. And if they succeeded with Miss Fleery all they would get for their pains would be attempted conversion to the Roman Catholic church. The overall number of passengers was lower on this voyage, too. If it weren't for the steerage and cargo they would be practically traveling at a loss, and Theobald Goldenberg, President of the Goldenberg Shipping Company, was not a man to take a loss lightly. Responsibility would fall onto the captain's shoulders. If only they had *one* Lana de Palmer in first class, then the young bucks would brighten up considerably, vying for her attention. As it was it looked as though they would remain in the bar for most of the crossing and when the time came for them to sail back to Europe, like Mr. Van Hethlin, they would plump for the *Mauretania* and the prospect of a brief dalliance with a beautiful woman.

"That Frenchie's kicking hell out of the door and demanding to be let out," First Officer Pegham said when Captain Reed returned to his position on the bridge. "Says we have to turn the ship around and take her back to Liverpool!"

"Like hell we will," Captain Reed said grimly. "I'm not losing a day's sailing time for a common whore."

"Wouldn't have said she was that common myself," the first officer, who was also Captain Reed's nephew, said with a grin. "Though I must admit she knows words my grandmother never told me."

Captain Reed breathed in deeply, clasped his hands even tighter and made stately progress to the depths of the lower deck. From the deck above he could hear Christina's muffled shouts and the vibration as her foot kicked savagely on the door. He nodded dismissal to the steward on duty outside, took the key from him and entered.

Christina, born with innate respect for men with four rings of gold braid on their cuffs, said pantingly, "You can't take me to New York. How would I ever get back? You've *got* to get me home again!"

Captain Reed shook his head. Beneath his formidable exterior he was a kindly man and he saw that the girl was obviously seriously distressed by her plight.

"To turn back to Liverpool would cost me a day's sailing time. It's quite impossible."

The finality in his voice chilled her.

"But what will I do in New York? I haven't a penny on me. No clothes. Nothing!"

"Then you must earn your living as you did in Liverpool," Captain Reed said frankly.

Christina went cold, remembering her horrifying moments in the cabin with Sam and his friend.

"I can't. You don't understand. I'm not a whore. Not *that* sort of whore anyway."

Shapely fingers pushed back a mass of damp hair from her forehead. The lovely lines of her cheek and chin and the amber of her wide-set eyes with their heavy fringe of lashes was not lost on Captain Reed. There was no sign of hardness or debauchery on her face. Nothing of the usual look of dockside prostitutes. Even now, in utter despair, she sat tall and straight-backed, her head high and proud.

"I'm sorry," he said at last.

"But you can't keep me locked up in this little cabin! I need fresh air and the sun! I can't breathe in confined spaces!"

"There's no alternative. The crew know the circumstances of your arrival on board and would only take advantage of the fact."

Christina shuddered.

"I would ask for your cooperation Miss . . ."

"Haworth," Christina said dully. "Christina Haworth."

"The noise you were making could be heard on the deck above. It cannot continue."

Christina gazed desperately around at the walls of the stark cabin. It was well below the water line and there was not even a porthole.

"To think," she said bitterly, "I've yearned to be at sea again for months. And now I am I can't even see it or smell it!"

"The sea is not as romantic as you young girls think."

Christina exploded at him. "There's nothing you

can tell me about the sea, Captain Reed! I was born at sea. I lived all my life at sea, except for the last few months after my father's death."

There was a slight break in her voice and Captain Reed said gently: "I'm sorry. Is that why you were . . . ?"

"Working at the Gaiety? Yes. Bessie Mulholland took me on and looked after me. She's a good woman. More of a Christian than those who profess it and do damn little about it."

Captain Reed moved toward the door. Christina caught his arm pleadingly. 'Please don't leave me locked up in here. I'm a good worker. I'll work in the galley. I won't cause any trouble. I won't lead the men on or anything. I promise."

Captain Reed hesitated. The crew in the galley were a good lot of men.

"Please!"

Captain Reed was only human. "All right," he said at last, and was rewarded by radiant eyes and a beaming smile from the loveliest mouth he had ever seen.

"But you'll have to borrow some of my wife's clothes. She always leaves a small wardrobe of things on board. I'll send the steward for something suitable."

Christina was too happy at the prospect of leaving what had become to her a cell to worry about how she would look in Captain Reed's wife's clothes. No doubt the lady was forty around the hips if she was an inch. No matter. A safety pin would take care of all that.

She was in for a pleasant surprise. One of the reasons for Captain Reed's reputation as a family man was that his wife of twenty-five years had looked after herself with remarkable care. The green velour dress that the steward brought back to the cabin was only a few inches larger at waist and hips than Christina's own.

"And shoes."

Christina squeezed her feet into the unaccustomed articles with a pained expression on her face. Captain Reed saw to his relief that the shoes fit.

He had waited discreetly outside the door while Christina had changed. Now, with the shoes on her feet, the expensively cut green velour dress giving her respectability, Captain Reed stared.

The girl had been beautiful before, but now, apart from the riot of black hair, she was every inch a lady.

"Shall I take Miss Haworth to the galley, sir?" the steward asked, staring transfixed at the vision before him.

"Yes." Captain Reed's voice was distant and preoccupied.

As Christina disappeared eagerly in the direction of the galley he continued his duties, a vague idea taking shape in the back of his mind. It wasn't an idea that would normally have come to a man of such moral integrity as Captain Caleb Reed, but it was one that would have certainly occurred to his employer, Theobald Goldenberg. And it was Theobald Goldenberg that Reed had to please if he wanted to continue as the captain of the *Corinthia*.

"Young blood" was a cry often heard from the interior of Goldenberg's paneled office. "I'm sick of old fuddy-duddies. What I want is young blood and vigor. New ideas. Push and drive!"

Captain Reed knew very well that he came into the category of a fuddy-duddy. Only his unbeatable experience at sea had gained him the position of the *Corinthia*'s captain. Goldenberg, at fifty, was only five years younger than he, but he was twenty-five in outlook. This idea he had was one Goldenberg would approve of. He knew that instinctively. And it would serve to show the president of the line that Caleb Reed wasn't quite the old stick-in-the-mud that he sometimes appeared.

"How is the girl doing in the galley?" he asked his second officer some hours later.

"Working like a trooper. So are the men. She's given them fresh enthusiasm for the job, sir."

"Has she indeed. Send her along to me. I want to have a word with her."

The second officer, hoping his comments hadn't been misconstrued and got Christina into trouble, obeyed. Christina, equally apprehensive, knocked on the door of the captain's cabin and entered.

He remained silent, viewing her from head to foot in much the same way as Bessie had the evening before she had started work. That mass of black curls would have to be tamed, but apart from that everything else was perfect.

"Are you French or English?" he asked at last.

"English," Christina said surprised.

"Yet you quoted flawless French to me a little while ago."

"I can give you Spanish too if you want it. And Latin and a touch of Greek."

Captain Reed's bushy white eyebrows arched.

"My father was a scholar," Christina said proudly.

"So you can talk without that execrable accent you were using when you wanted to be let out of the cabin?"

"If you mean can I talk proper—properly—yes, if I want to. I don't normally. It causes too many problems. Sets you apart from the rest."

Captain Reed rested his chin on his hands and stared at her. "You really are quite a remarkable girl, Miss Haworth."

"I am, aren't I?" Christina agreed. "But not remarkable enough for you to turn this ship round and take me back home."

"No, but perhaps when I put this proposition to you, you won't want to go back to Liverpool. You say you've been at sea all your life. Do you know anything about ocean going passenger liners like the *Corinthia?*"

"Not much," Christina said. "But I've been aboard the *Mauretania.*"

"Then you know that passenger liners cater to luxury and comfort and romance."

"Yes." Christina wondered what the captain was getting at.

Captain Reed tapped the top of his pen thoughtfully against his teeth. "Miss Haworth, here is a publicity handout from my company. I have underlined the relevant passages. It encourages future passengers to anticipate a little romance on board."

He put the pen down. "Romance and glamor are in very short supply aboard the *Corinthia* and have been for some time. The moving picture artistes and debutantes all choose to travel by Cunard. Rich, single young men, either businessmen or playboys, travel likewise. All in search of those brief moments of flirtation that heighten the glamor of life on board ship."

He traced the pen down the passenger list. "On this voyage in first class we have twenty-seven young, single men and seven single ladies. Only three of the ladies are under twenty-five. The others are, to put it kindly, matrons. Regrettably the three younger ladies are unable to contribute anything either to romance or glamor on this ship or any other. You, Miss Haworth, could."

"I'm not sure that I understand you. You couldn't possibly want me to *accommodate* the gentlemen on board?"

"Not at all," Captain Reed said hurriedly. "The reputation of Goldenberg Shipping must remain above reproach. No. What I have in mind is for you to indulge in light flirtations. To bring to the first class deck that sparkle that it so badly lacks. Would you be agreeable to that suggestion, Miss Haworth?"

"Not 'alf."

"Not *half*," Captain Reed corrected. "I can hardly

pass you off as a first class passenger if you speak like that.''

"Of course not, Captain,'' Christina said with a plum in her mouth.

Captain Reed permitted himself a smile. ''My wife's wardrobe will be at your disposal and you will have the use of a spare first class cabin for the duration of the voyage. It would look too odd if you were to disappear every night to the depths of the lower deck. You will dine with me at my table this evening. There is just one more thing. Your hair. I'm not conversant with exactly what it is ladies do with their hair, but if you could pile it up on *top* of your head and not have it hanging down to your waist.''

"I'll plait it and wear it in a bun if it will make you happy,'' Christina said obligingly.

Captain Reed flinched. ''Such extremes will not be necessary. Miss Pucy wears her hair like that and the only effect it has is to make her more like a horse than ever.''

He picked up a silver-framed photograph on his desk. ''*That* is the effect I would like you to strive for.''

Mrs. Reed had a fine boned face and a gentle half smile on her lips. Thick, luxuriant hair was swept in deep waves away from either side of her face, knotted on the crown of her head with a single rose.

"She's a very beautiful woman.''

"Yes,'' Captain Reed said proudly. ''She is. And she's a lady. And from now on that's what you will have to be.''

"That's no problem,'' Christina said with a cheeky grin. ''I always knew I would be some day. It's just been a question of time, that's all!''

Chapter 16

Devlin looked as comfortable and natural in the expensive silk suit and beaver-collared coat with a dark-grey fedora pulled rakishly over one eyebrow as he did in his customary working clothes.

He stepped from Duane's limousine onto the wharf with the careless arrogance of one who had been used to wealth since birth. With other first class passengers he boarded the *Mauretania*, his valet carrying initialed leather suitcases behind him. Duane had been insistent that if Devlin was to know what was expected from the *Ninevah* he had to experience the creature comforts at first hand.

The fox-furred socialites and chorus girls eyed him speculatively as they were ushered on board.

Devlin had no time for them. Either then or in the remaining days of the voyage. He spent the whole time walking the great ship from end to end. With the captain's reluctant permission he disappeared for hours on end in the engine room, watching the firemen and trimmers as they sweated to raise steam.

He didn't spend the voyage in complete isolation. Once he had seen his fill of the engines and the set of the decks he purposefully put himself out to study the passengers who chose to travel at such expense to the Old World.

The vast majority were young, female, American,

rich and on the lookout for romance. The slight swagger of Devlin's lean hips had the same effects on the nicely brought up daughters of railroad barons and steel tycoons as it had on the dockside girls of a hundred ports.

His longing for Christina was growing unbearable. Every slender line and curve of her body was burned in his memory. He wanted to wind his fingers through the mass of tangled curls and kiss her until nothing else in life mattered. Kiss her eyes, her forehead, her temple, her cheeks. Kiss the lovely generous mouth that sent him mad with desire. He ached for the feel of her, warm and naked against him, soft and supple in his arms. Christina was his last thought on sleeping and his first on waking.

He grinned to himself in the privacy of his stateroom as he imagined the expression on her face when he arrived at the Gaiety dressed like a millionaire. Of the delight the dresses and silken lingerie in his suitcase would give her. Of the expression on her face when he gave her the ring that lay securely in his breast pocket. Every day brought him nearer to her and every day increased the knot of anticipation deep within him. On the third day at sea Devlin saw in the distance the white prow of another liner.

"Who is she?" he asked the New York banker by his side.

"Dunno, pretty big. Mebbe the *Lusitania*." He handed the binoculars that hung around his neck to Devlin.

Devlin focused them.

"The *Corinthia*," he said with no interest. "One of the Goldenberg Line."

The banker, who fancied himself as something of an authority on shipping, viewed the *Corinthia* with studied care.

"She sure is a pretty sleek ship but she hasn't the class of this one."

Devlin turned his back on the sight of the distant *Corinthia* and resumed his observation of his fellow passengers.

The bulk of the men were businessmen and they seemed to Devlin to be the customers the *Ninevah* should cultivate. They had money and they traveled often. There was a fair collection of women traveling on business too. Mostly to the great fashion houses of London and Paris for the latest collections. There were wool merchants and stockbrokers and other less desirable passengers. Professional gamblers and card sharps whose company Devlin found more entertaining than that of the more respectable businessmen.

As they neared Southampton the pilots came out to guide the liner into port. For the first time in his life Devlin left ship like a gentleman, walking hastily down the drafty platforms to a waiting cab and the nearest railway station.

He felt like a young boy as the train finally steamed into the soot and smoke of Liverpool. He sent his luggage on to the Station Hotel and strolled eagerly down to the dockside, breaking into a run toward the Gaiety.

"Devlin's back! He's in with Bessie! What on earth will happen now? What will he do?" The Gaiety girls were like a lot of twittering starlings as they struggled into negligees and crowded on to the corridor in order not to miss anything. Only Kate remained calm, a small secretive smile on her face. Carefully she brushed her pale blonde hair till it shone like silk, darkening her eyebrows and lashes and polishing her nails.

"She's *what?*" Devlin grasped Bessie so cruelly by the wrist that she screamed. "She *can't* have gone! She *knew* I was coming back for her! You turned her out, didn't you?" He let go of Bessie savagely, sending her sprawling into a chair, his eyes wild.

"You couldn't wait for the money and she refused

to work! So where did you send her? Where did she go?"

"With a sailor," Bessie gasped, her bosom heaving as she struggled for breath. "She left one night with a sailor and never came back. God's honest truth."

Devlin stood immovable, his face frozen.

"You're lying," he said at last through clenched teeth. "You're lying and I'll find out the truth if I have to break your goddamned stupid neck to do it!"

He moved toward her and Bessie shrank back against the padding of her chair.

"She was drunk. Wild, I've never seen her like it before. She went off with a sailor and left by the back stairs. We haven't seen sight nor sign of her since."

"I don't believe you!" His face was white, his jaw so tight the muscles twitched convulsively.

"It's true!" Bessie's cry was desperate. "You shouldn't have done what you did. Jemmy Cadogan told us all about it!"

"But I *had* to!"

He'd told her he would be away a few weeks and he'd been away nearly four months. Dear God, surely she could have waited four months for him? He would have waited a lifetime for her.

Devlin slammed his fist so hard into the back of Bessie's sofa that the china bird on her chiffonier tottered and crashed into a score of pieces onto the floor.

Neither of the women dared speak. At last Devlin regained control of his breathing and when he turned to face them his face wore a masklike quality that Bessie found even more frightening than his anger.

"There's the money I promised you." He slammed a fistful of notes onto the delicate *secrétaire*. "And send Bert to the hotel to collect my cases. There's some finery for the girls. And you can have this as well!"

A small jewelry box was thrown contemptuously on top of the notes.

"Give it to the next sailor to be taken in by a whore!" and he crashed from the room, the Gaiety's walls vibrating as the doors crashed behind him.

Devlin drank hard and long. He'd been taken for a fool. It had happened to hundreds before him and would no doubt happen to hundreds again. But not to him. From now on Devlin O'Conner would never be taken in by a woman. He would use them, enjoy them, and leave them. Just as Christina had done to him.

A sailor! A whiskey hit the back of his throat. Not even a captain. Just a common sailor that no one had seen before or since. And the little slut had gone off with him without a moment's hesitation. So much for her avowal of love. Another whiskey followed in quick succession. He laughed mirthlessly. He should be celebrating, not drowning his sorrows. He was free, wasn't he? If it hadn't been the unknown sailor it would have been someone else. Marriage would have made no difference to her. He would have been the laughing stock of every seaport in the world. "Devlin O'Conner? Yes. Heard his wife's a great little mover in bed. No need to be careful. He's too blind to her charms to see her for what she is!" He finished the bottle and wiped his mouth with the back of his hand. He'd had a lucky escape. From now on the only thing he would care about was money and more money. Life on board the *Mauretania* had given him a taste for it.

From behind the red velvet curtains of Bessie's parlor Kate saw him approach, stumbling slightly with the effect of drink. She ran her tongue around her lips in anticipation. Christina was gone and she remained. All she had to do now was make quite sure no one else spoke to him. She slipped away from the window and went downstairs.

"Nice to see you again," she said, running her hand up his arm and across the back of his neck. "I missed you." Her voice was husky, almost purring.

Her heavy breasts brushed against him, her familiar perfume permeating his alcoholic haze. She raised her lips to his, kissing him open-mouthed, pressing against him.

"A bottle of whiskey," he said to the girl behind the bar, his arm tightening around Kate's waist.

She rubbed her leg against his. "Forget the usual conversation with Bessie tonight. Let's go upstairs now. It's been a long time."

His hand traveled slowly upward, cupping her breast.

"Too damned right," he said slurringly, and with the whiskey bottle in one hand and fondling Kate with the other, he made his way up the familiar staircase to Kate's room.

His lovemaking held a savagery that only Kate could have enjoyed. Afterwards, as he lay in drunken sleep, she slipped from the bed and deftly searched his pockets.

The return half of his sailing ticket was dated for the next day and with it was one single ticket to New York. Christina's ticket. Kate dressed hurriedly and returned to the bar, asking Bert for two more bottles of whiskey for Devlin.

As dawn broke, Kate woke Devlin in the most arousing way she knew and then handed him a full glass of the best whiskey the Gaiety served.

"She didn't deserve you," she said, brushing his chest lightly with her lips. "The day after you left she started working again even though Bessie told her she needn't. *And* she demanded that Bessie give her the money you'd left for her keep."

Devlin, still not sober from the previous evening's drinking, downed the whiskey and poured himself another one.

"She was a lying little slut too. When she came back from Wales she told the other girls they weren't missing a thing. That she'd rather have that Negro from the *Icelandic* any day. Not that they believed her of course. I saw to that. Just that she wasn't as straight as she seemed and the Negro gave her what she wanted. Mucky little cow."

Devlin's glass was almost empty and Kate obligingly refilled it, running her hand caressingly down between his thighs.

"Why don't you take me back with you to America? I'd like to see Christina's face when that stud of a sailor finally tires of her and she comes crawling back here for a job. I 'spect she thinks you'll still have her back. She always said she could twist you round her little finger. Used to call you her little dog. Serve her right if she finds out you took me with you instead."

Devlin no longer bothered with a glass. He drank the liquor straight from the bottle. To have laughed at him! To have made fun of the days they had spent in Wales. Days that he had looked upon as sacred! And to have been referred to by all the Gaiety girls as her little dog! If he ever laid hands on her again he would choke the life out of her.

In a murderous red mist he broke the seal on the second bottle and Kate watched him with a satisfied smile on her face. She wasn't going to ask again if she could accompany him back to New York. She was simply going to go. When he finally lost consciousness she went through his case, selecting a red suit with a fox fur collar intended for Christina, dressed herself with care and, leaving Devlin sprawled out on the bed, walked triumphantly to Bessie's bedroom and knocked on the door.

Bessie did not take kindly to being awoken just as she had fallen asleep, but the sight of Kate in the exquisitely cut ankle length suit, her blonde hair framed by fur and with a matching muff casually in one hand, had her instantly awake.

"Where the hell are you going?"

Kate smiled triumphantly. "I'm leaving. I'm going back to America with Devlin."

Bessie dragged a satin negligee over her shoulders.

"What about his wife?"

"She's no problem," Kate said, an infuriating smile on her face.

Bessie eyed the little jewelry box on her *secrétaire* and said nothing. Whatever the present was it was obvious Devlin was not going to give it to Kate. It was impossible to tell what Kate was thinking. The pale, almost opaque eyes gave nothing away.

Bessie had the uncomfortable feeling that somehow, somewhere she had missed something. Kate had been scheming for a long time to take Devlin away from Christina and now she had succeeded, but for the life of her Bessie couldn't see how Kate was responsible. Christina had gone on her own accord. There had been no fight. No arguments. Nothing. All the girls were adamant on that point. In fact Kate had made every effort to be nice to Christina in her last few days at the Gaiety. The only possible reason for Christina's behavior was news of Devlin's marriage. A marriage that didn't seem to be altering his way of life in the slightest. It didn't weigh up and Bessie's suspicions deepened.

"Where's Devlin now? I'd like a word with him."

"Sleeping the drink off. He's left instructions for Bert to have a cab round in an hour's time. We have to catch the eight o'clock train if we don't want to miss the boat."

"And you wouldn't want to miss the boat, would you Kate?" Bessie said, viciously. "I wish you well of him, but he'll never love you like he did Christina!"

Kate's pale eyes leapt into life as she leaned forward and slapped Bessie hard across the cheek.

"Stupid old bag," she said angrily, retreating hastily as Bessie threw a salvo of perfume bottles and powder-pots at her head.

Bessie had no more illusions about Kate, and she was determined to dispel any that Devlin might have.

Thanks to Kate it was impossible. He was too drunk to even understand what she was saying. Despairingly

she watched as Bert half hauled him into the waiting
cab, a triumphant Kate at his side.

Kate smiled to herself. Men were quite easy to
handle with just a little common sense and a lot of
deceit. And she had plenty of the latter. More than
enough to outwit Christina Haworth and Bessie Mulholland and anyone else who stood in her way.

Chapter 17

Mrs. Reed's wardrobe aboard the *Corinthia* was small
but opulent. Small because she used it only for the
parties that preceded the sailing of the ship and opulent because even amongst artistes' and diamond glittering politicians' daughters, the captain's wife had to
shine.

Christina shone. With Mrs. Reed's tortoiseshell-
backed hairbrush she had tamed the wildness of her
hair till it gleamed like jet. Fixing it with combs high
on top of her head—the defiant waves soft and un-
dulating—so that it seemed the merest touch would
make the whole beauty of her hair cascade once again
around her shoulders. The formal hairstyle did nothing
to lessen Christina's blatant sexuality. Instead it
heightened it. Her borrowed dress was the palest
lemon, a cloud of chiffon over a foundation of exquisite taffeta. The finest silk stockings imaginable
sheathed her long legs and Mrs. Reed's delicate evening shoes, dyed the exact color of her dress, fit to
perfection.

Christina stared at her reflection in the mirror. The color of her dress accentuated the satin gleam of her olive skin, and the extraordinary amber of her eyes.

Around her throat she fastened a band of matching velvet with a jeweled butterfly at the center. There was no similarity between the vision in the mirror and the Christina Haworth who had danced half naked in the Gaiety's bar. For a moment a wave of longing swept over her. She wanted Devlin to see her like this. Beautiful and desirable and a lady at last. Painfully she shrugged the thought away. He had made his choice. Let him live with it. There were plenty more fish in the sea, and blinking back bitter tears, Christina turned and walked with easy grace, her head as high as that of any duchess, toward Captain Reed's cabin.

It took Caleb Reed a good two minutes to regain his composure. He had known she was a beauty. Anyone with half an eye could see that. But she had something else. An inner radiance that outshone even that of the famous Lana de Palmer. He bowed graciously and offered Christina his arm.

"If you will accompany me into dinner, m'am, I shall be greatly honored."

"The pleasure, sir," Christina said with an impish grin, "is all mine."

The purser had been informed that an extra place would be set at the captain's table. He had been as assiduous as usual in checking the passenger list and singling out those he deemed worthy to dine that evening with Captain Reed.

Miss Fleery and her mother sat at the coveted dinner table. Mr. Fleery, though not accompanying his wife and daughter, was chairman of the largest tin plate company in America, and as the purser rightly assumed he was a millionaire several times over, it secured his womenfolk their envied position.

Miss Fleery smiled shyly at Christina with gentle eyes and her mother, though slightly shocked at such self-assurance in so young a girl and at the absence of any chaperone, decided that as she was sitting at the captain's table she needed no other proof of social acceptability and asked kindly if she had enjoyed her stay in Europe and seen any places of interest.

Christina replied with only the slightest Northern intonation, that in fact England was her home and Captain Reed breathed a sigh of relief. Her demeanor was perfect. The array of knives and forks would have foxed anyone unused to them, and on sitting at table he had cursed himself for a fool on not seeing to it that Christina had had a preparatory lesson in their use. He needn't have worried. She ate a little more slowly than the other guests, and though it was obvious to no one but himself, he watched carefully. From the hors d'oeuvres to the French ice cream, Christina's table manners were faultless.

He found his heart beating rapidly as Mrs. Fleery asked Christina where her home was and Christina answered that though it was a very *interesting* house, she doubted if Mrs. Fleery had ever heard of it.

"You are being coy, Miss Haworth," Mrs. Fleery chided. "Are you afraid to disclose the whereabouts for fear of sightseers? I understand that England's great houses are often flooded with them and must be a considerable inconvenience to their owners."

Christina replied that her previous address *had* been subject to the sudden influx of visitors and Captain Reed had hastily turned the conversation before his heartburn began to inconvenience him, drawing Christina's attention toward the openly admiring young man on his left.

The young Earl of Claire was mesmerized. Her evasive answers to Mrs. Fleery's prying questions and the captain's obvious discomfiture only served to convince him that Miss Haworth was traveling under a nom de plume. If she was daughter of any member of the English aristocracy he would have met her at hunt balls and house parties. Besides, she would hardly be a plain "Miss," a point the American, Mrs. Fleery, had overlooked. No, Miss Haworth was not from England. The sun-kissed skin and cloud of black hair was either Spanish or Italian.

"Is this your first trip to America, Miss Haworth?" His voice lingered on her name, his eyes seeking to hold hers. Miss Haworth was not overcome by an earldom.

She smiled, murmured yes, and turned her attention to Captain Reed and Mr. Humphrey Hoover, who were discussing Mr. Hoover's priceless racehorse safely stowed away in a specially made stable mid-ships.

Marcus, Earl of Claire, was not used to being so easily dismissed when he set himself out to charm. His dark gray eyes and black lashes usually had a devastating effect on the young women he chose to favor with an extra long glance. A man who could call half of Southern England his own was entitled to expect simpering adoration when he showed interest. Miss Haworth was showing him no interest at all. She seemed far more entranced by Humphrey Hoover's anecdotes about his horse. Captain Reed, seeing the effect Christina had so easily produced on one of Europe's most eligible bachelors, leant back and lit a cigar, well content. Old Hoover was looking like a man besotted and every male head in the dining saloon was turning as discreetly as possible in Christina's direction.

The young businessmen who had been drinking their whiskey so desultorily only an hour ago had squared their shoulders and had the light of battle in their eyes. In another half hour dinner would be over, the orchestra would strike up in the ballroom and competition for Christina's hand would be fierce. He could feel a ripple round the room, an excitement that had been lacking on his previous voyage.

"I thought you said there was no talent on board,"

young Wellesly Wallace, son of a Detroit merchant and philanthropist, said to his companion, "I'd get your eyesight seen to if I were you."

"But I watched them *all* come aboard, Wells. Swear to God I did. There was only the one with the brace on her teeth, and the one with a face like a horse, and the other girl at the captain's table. All the others were over forty."

"She's not over forty!" Wellesly Wallace said, noting the rise and fall of Christina's breasts beneath the light covering of chiffon.

"And a fat chance you stand," Matthew Charles, his English friend said. "The fellow with the moustache and the moonstruck eyes is Claire. *Earl* of Claire."

"So what? My father probably has twice as much cash as that English earl. Half of them are bankrupted by inheritance tax. Say, she smiled at me. Didn't you see? She *definitely* smiled at me!"

"The trouble with you Americans is you're always so pathetically optimistic," Matthew Charles said.

"So are you," Wellesly said, with his usual disrespect. "In the head. There's only one dame on this ship worth a light. You wait till the band begins to play. Then I'll show you the supremacy of American manhood!"

"I hear the Sultan of Gurapore is traveling on the *Lusitania*," Mrs. Elwyn Reinstadt said to her husband over the vanilla éclairs.

"Mebbe he is, but he ain't seein' a sight like I'm seein'," her husband said, and not for the first time Mrs. Reinsadt wished Elwyn had just a *little* more culture.

The Earl of Claire discreetly asked if he might be allowed to squire Miss Haworth into the ballroom as she was without an escort. An imperceptible twitch of Caleb Reed's eyebrows indicated to Christina that she should accept and she did so graciously, but distantly. She had considered herself lucky beyond her wildest dreams when Devlin had fallen in love with her. *Professed* to have fallen in love with her, she mentally corrected herself. From now on, earls, millionaires and steel barons would think themselves lucky if *she,* Christina Haworth from the Liverpool docks, bestowed the slightest favor on them.

The walk through the public rooms from the dining saloon to the ballroom gave Christina a curious sense of *déjà vu*. It was as if she were a child again exploring the magnificent interiors of the newly-built *Mauretania*. There was the same sense of heady luxury. Draperies of palest blue velvet, exquisite carpets, glittering chandeliers, gilded carving on anything and everything. Only then she had been a barefoot child and now she was dressed in chiffon and taffeta, with her arm held lightly in that of an earl of the realm.

The ballroom was a galaxy of lights and music. Potted palms and bamboo screens were discreetly arranged so that couples could take rest and refreshment in relative privacy only inches away from the dancers. The earl, having had the honor of escorting Christina into the ballroom, claimed first dance, and as Christina slipped easily and lightly into his arms, Marcus caught his breath. She moved like an angel. Gone was the gracious languor she had displayed at the dinner table. The orchestra was playing ragtime and the earl, who fancied himself something of a leader amongst his own set for his dexterity on the dance floor, found that his partner was more than equal to his fancy footwork. The more he tried to outpace her, the more she laughed, her lemon-slippered feet moving with sheer abandon across the perfectly smooth floor.

The music ended and Christina thanked him, the generous mouth still parted in a smile, but she refused to be detained for the next dance. The young earl, aware of the many scores of interested eyes upon them, conceded defeat and walked her back to the captain with what he hoped was a proprietary air.

"Mr. Wellesly Wallace," Captain Reed said, introducing Christina to the young American who was heir to millions and who he had heard only hours ago expressing disappointment in the voyage. There was no sign of disappointment on his face now.

"I am pleased to meet you, Miss Haworth. May I have this dance?"

Without waiting for a reply he whisked her away from beneath the nose of the infuriated earl and out onto the dance floor.

"Colonel Belmont tells me you're an actress traveling under a nom de plume."

Christina laughed.

"You're not?"

Her perfume was faint and intangible, seeming to come from her hair itself.

"I'm not traveling under a *nom de plume*."

"But you are on the new nickelodeon screens?"

"No."

"You certainly should be. I know a lot of influential people making one reelers. How about letting me arrange it for you?" He grinned hopefully. "What do you think?"

Christina grinned back.

"I like your style, Mr. Wallace, but I have no desire to be anymore of an actress than I already am."

"Shame. How about just letting me be your protector until we reach New York? Not everyone is like me. Some of these guys," he nodded in the direction of the frustrated earl, "are simply on the make. Now with *me*, Miss Haworth, your reputation would be as safe as the Bank of England's."

"My reputation," Christina said gravely, "can come to no harm Mr. Wallace, I assure you."

"Wellesly," he said, his arm tightening around her waist. "Son of Gerard Wallace, a multimillionaire. Not that I'm trying to impress you. It's just one of those throwaway lines that come in handy in life."

"I'm sure it does," Christina said, laughing at his engaging frankness.

The music swirled to a close.

"You're not going to leave me before we're properly acquainted, are you?" His grip on her waist tightened. The question was answered for him by a firm tap on the shoulder by Humphrey Hoover.

"My dance, son," he said, leaving the heir to millions empty-handed.

"Of course, that's not her *real* name," Captain Reed heard a tightly-corseted lady saying to her companion. "I have it on very good authority that she's a member of the Portuguese royal family," the republican American by her side said bluntly.

"The deposed king was a *personal* friend of mine," the elderly lady said, her chins quivering.

The murmur spread.

"She's a personal friend of the king."

"What king?"

"England of course. What other goddamn king is there?"

"Some Portuguese Princess," Mr. James Vaughan said to his wife. "Beautiful creature. I expect the publicity that traveling on the *Mauretania* inevitably attracts would be distasteful to her."

His wife, a generous-hearted woman, nodded sympathetically.

"I always *did* think the Cunarders just the *tiniest* little bit ostentatious. All playboys and chorus girls. The Goldenberg Line is *much* more refined."

"Much," her husband agreed. "As I've always said, Annie. Only the best for you."

She clasped his hand affectionately. "What a pity," she said dreamily, "that our own dear Prince of Wales isn't of a marriageable age yet. They'd make such a *striking* couple."

Captain Reed blanched, and was sincerely glad that the young man in question was *not* of a marriageable age *or* traveling on his ship. Otherwise there was a distinct possibility he would find himself ending a distinguished career in the Tower of London.

"How romantic," another lady exclaimed, as Christina drifted past in the arms of the Earl of Claire once more. "An exiled princess."

The dance ended, and Christina was surrounded by a bevy of young men, all eager for her hand.

"I would like," said Mr. Hardy Glynn (of the famous New York store) to the captain, "to be introduced to the young lady in lemon."

Mr. Hardy Glynn was a regular passenger, and Captain Reed had heard it rumored by his steward that he had been thinking of changing his allegiance to one of the other major shipping companies.

"My pleasure, Mr. Glynn," Captain Reed said, and watched with contentment that gentleman's eyes glazed as he held Christina in his arms, her body pressed lightly against his as they danced to the strains of a romantic waltz.

Everything was just as he had planned. Christina had brought glamor back to the *Corinthia*. He rocked back on his heels, his hands clasped behind his back with satisfaction.

"Wonderful girl," he said to himself, watching her beguile the hardened president of the Glynn Department Store. "Marvelous girl."

"I thought you said she was a drunken little slut," his nephew's voice said discreetly at his ear.

"Rubbish." Captain Reed ignored his first officer. "Only got to see the way she handled that young earl to see she wasn't a slut. The girl's got class. I could tell that right away."

"So could Victor Jackson," First Officer Pegham murmured with a grin and moved away sharply before he incurred his uncle's wrath.

A princess indeed! The rumor had already reached the ears of the crew and the stewards were beaming with more sincerity than usual as they evasively answered the passengers' queries as to the true identity of the beautiful young woman traveling alone so mysteriously.

The girl had cheek and spirit, and it was good to see the likes of Mr. Humphrey Hoover and Mr. Hardy Glynn taken in by a slip of a girl young enough to be their daughter. Besides, Willy Harrison had told them her father had been Captain Haworth, who had sailed the *Umbria* and the *Orion* in his day. As far as the crew were concerned she was one of them.

"You look tired. Shall I escort you back to your cabin?" Marcus, Earl of Claire, asked gently.

"Yes, please." Christina felt suddenly fatigued. It was past twelve but for her that hour was early. It was something else, something she couldn't define.

Here she was, her dream come true, and suddenly all she felt was an indescribable sadness. She would gladly have forfeited all the richness of her surroundings and the wealth and title of her companion for a brief moment in Devlin's arms.

When in the darkened corridor outside her cabin Marcus drew her closely toward him, speaking her name with his lips buried in her hair, Christina's arms slid round his neck, her mouth aching for love. She kissed him with a desperate urgency which inflamed him with a desire so intense he felt himself tremble. But Christina remained unmoved, his passionate kisses awakening no response in her. With a small cry of despair she pushed herself away from him and fumbled with the key to her cabin.

"Christina, please! *Christina!*"

The cabin door closed, leaving the young earl half mad with unfulfilled desire, while on the other side Christina pressed her hands to her face as scalding tears fell without restraint.

Chapter 18

The next morning Caleb summoned Christina to his cabin and approved her black velvet day suit, with its long narrow skirt emphasizing her slender hips and the pointed sleeves of the jacket drawing attention to perfectly manicured, almond-shaped nails. Her hair was waved loosely into an elegant *chignon*, and a broad brimmed hat, with a curling ostrich feather, half shaded her eyes, giving the same tantalizing effect as a veil.

"You behaved superbly last night. The steward said you only spent the briefest minutes with young Claire alone and that when he returned to the upper deck he looked distinctly crestfallen."

It had been one of Captain Reed's fears that Christina would take advantage of her new position and pursue her previous profession with his illustrious passengers. He had been proved wrong and he was delighted.

"That's just the way I want it," he said with satisfaction. "Flirtation. Shipboard romance. But nothing to bring the name of the Goldenberg Shipping Company and its president into disrepute."

"I wouldn't dream of it," Christina said drily, wondering what paragon of virtue the president of the line was.

"Good. Hamilton tells me your father was Captain Haworth?"

Christina nodded.

"Fine man. He was my first mate years ago when I captained the *Orion*. Glad I've been able to do something for his girl." And, feeling magnanimous, the captain dismissed her with a fatherly nod; there was another idea slowly forming in the back of his mind.

If Christina sailed *every* voyage on the *Corinthia* and it was known that she did so, a lot of the passengers who traveled regularly on business to Europe from America and vice versa would very likely reserve cabins well in advance. Men like Mr. Hardy Glynn and Humphrey Hoover. Of course, he would have to think up a respectable reason for Christina's continued presence on board, but it was a minor problem compared to the advantage of being able to show Mr. Goldenberg an increase in first class reservations

Wellesly Wallace beat the earl in reaching Christina's side as she emerged on the promenade deck.

"It certainly is a brisk day, Miss Haworth."

"Please call me Christina. I've never been referred to as Miss Haworth."

Young Wellesly raised his eyebrows. "Never? I *knew* you were traveling under a nom de plume. Guess it's Countess or Duchess or something like that. Don't worry. I won't let on to anyone. Civil of you to allow me to call you by your first name. We Americans are pretty informal, but the English are still all John Bull and stiff upper lip. Hear you're from Europe yourself."

"In a way."

"Portugal? Spain?"

Wellesly had heard the rumors of Christina's Portuguese pedigree and had had a long discussion with Matthew Charles the previous night as to whether it could possibly be true. Matthew had been adamant that there wasn't a member of the Portuguese royal family of Christina's age or sex. Young Wellesly remained unconvinced.

"Spain," Christina said, dispelling his illusions.

Frantically he tried to remember who ruled Spain and if Christina could possibly be its future queen. He failed. He'd have to ask Matthew.

"I hear you've never been to New York before?"

"No. This visit wasn't actually *planned*." Christina felt an uncontrollable urge to giggle.

Wellesly, not understanding the joke but enjoying the obvious pleasure his company was giving her, grinned.

"Mighty fine city. Beats London hands down. Everything there is so *old!* It's about time they refurbished the place. New York is spanking new. No other city like it in the world! Perhaps I could show you round the city."

Christina shook her head. "I shan't be staying in New York for any length of time."

Wellesly's face fell. "That's too bad. I really would have liked to have shown you the Brooklyn Bridge and the Statue of Liberty. There's nothing like it in Europe!"

"It was a present from the French," Christina said impishly, continuing to avoid the Earl of Claire's desperate eyes. "What are the words scribbled on the pedestal? I've forgotten."

Young Wellesly came into his own. He doffed his hat, spread wide his arms and orated loudly, " 'Give me your tired, your poor . . .' "

"You can have Miss Pucy if you like," Matthew Charles said obligingly.

Wellesly rammed his hat back on his head and said with as much dignity as he could muster, "This is a *private* conversation."

"Sorry. Thought you were addressing the huddled masses yearning to be free. Good morning, Miss Haworth."

"I was just telling *Christina* all about New York. Why don't you go to the smoking room and I'll meet you there? *Later.*"

Matthew struggled not to smile. Wellesly was so easy to tease it really wasn't fair.

With a slight inclination of his head toward Christina he made his way to the main lounge.

Marcus then wrenched Christina away from Wellesly Wallace, and tormentedly told her that he was head-over-heels in love with her and that he could make her the happiest woman in the world if only she would spend a little time alone with him.

Christina, who had no illusions about the earl's intentions, and who doubted that he was in any way more gifted in that department than the score of other young men that she had known, declined. She permitted the anguished earl only the slightest intimacies. An occasional kiss, the apparently accidental brushing of her breasts against him as they rose from the dinner table, the slight pressure of her body against his as they danced. Devlin may not want her but other men did. Men of wealth and breeding. She found a curious sense of satisfaction in being able to tease the handsome young earl until he was nearly out of his mind and then dismiss him, her own emotions still dormant.

The Earl of Claire wasn't the only man on board to be ensnared by Miss Haworth's undoubted charms.

Colonel Belmont even proposed marriage, though he blustered so much in doing it that it took Christina quite a while to understand just what it was he was suggesting to her. She declined his offer with such kindness that the colonel was left more in love than ever.

Mr. Humphrey Hoover promised to name his best yearling after her, and honored her by allowing her to visit his priceless racehorse, Kelly. Seeing girl and horse together Mr. Hoover decided there were certain similarities. All favorable. The same sleekness and innate good breeding. The same long graceful legs and proudly held head.

Wellesly Wallace was her most constant escort and Christina enjoyed his company more than that of any of the other eligible bachelors who sought her hand.

"Christina," he said as he kissed her on the moonlit deck while the Earl of Claire searched frustratedly for them. "If you aren't the most beautiful woman in the whole wide world. You're a real doll, d'ya know that? Won't you change your mind and stay in New York?"

Christina would not.

Mr. Hardy Glynn went so far as to inquire of Captain Reed if Miss Haworth was a regular traveler on the *Corinthia* and Captain Reed seized his chance, saying that indeed she was. She would patronize no other ship. Mr. Glynn reviewed his decision to book his next voyage to Europe on a Cunarder and made arrangements to retain his same cabin on his next trip to Europe in October.

Captain Reed rubbed his hands with glee. He no longer had the slightest doubt as to the wisdom of keeping Christina on board ship. All he had to do was have his decision ratified by Theobald Goldenberg. And Goldenberg was going to be pleased with him. Caleb could feel it in his bones.

It was with more than usual elation that he approached the entrance to New York Bay. Christina remained in her cabin until all the first class passengers had departed, their valets carrying scores of suitcases to waiting limousines and horse-drawn cabs.

As the second class passengers also disembarked, and the hopeful immigrants were taken by barge to Ellis Island, Captain Reed sent a steward to ask Christina to join him on the bridge.

"Aren't you going to see the sights?"

Christina looked around her at the Hudson, jammed with sea traffic, at the magnificent liners berthed alongside the *Corinthia* at their Manhattan piers. Round the wharves were the familiar sounds and smells of dockland. Brownstone houses that were a mixture of brothels and boarding houses, shops being restocked and refueled. She had no intention of going ashore. Any one of the ships around her could be

Devlin's. At any street corner she could bump into him. All of a sudden it seemed to Christina that the world was a very small place.

"I'll stay aboard until we return to England."

Captain Reed shook his mane of white hair. "I don't want you to do that. I want you to come with me."

"But why? I'm quite happy on board ship. I won't get in anyone's way."

"We have some visiting to do," Captain Reed said, smoothing his beard with his hand. "Important visiting."

"Who? Your wife?"

Caleb laughed. "I hadn't thought of that but I don't see why not. Later. First of all, we're going to see Mr. Theobald Goldenberg, President of the Goldenberg Shipping Company. I've already telegraphed him and he is expecting us."

"But what *for?*" Christina asked with sudden alarm. "I thought you were pleased with the way I behaved on board."

"I was. That's why I want to see Mr. Goldenberg."

There was no new-fangled limousine for the captain. A horse-drawn carriage was summoned by First Officer Pegham, and as it made its way through the bustling, overcrowded streets Captain Reed said, "How would you feel about traveling aboard the *Corinthia* regularly?"

Christina's eyes were his answer.

He laughed. "I thought as much. I'm going to tell Mr. Goldenberg the effect you had on the passengers, and I think he will agree with me that you could be a great asset to the company in enhancing the image of shipboard romance."

"This is the man you were worried about in case I brought his name into disrepute?" Christina asked.

Caleb nodded. "Mr. Goldenberg owns his own railway and steel company as well as his shipping line. He's very influential and very respected. On no account should the impression be given that your background is—er—dubious. I shall tell him you are a lady of breeding bereft of family and without adequate financial means. That shipboard life suits you and that you have a certain—er—talent. The man has eyes in his head so he'll see that for himself. Here we are.''

Adjusting the cuffs of his uniform Captain Reed helped Christina from the cab outside the soaring building that housed the Goldenberg shipping empire.

An elevator whisked them to floors high above ground level. A secretary with starched collar and cuffs ushered the captain into the great man's presence, while Christina was left waiting on a spindly-legged chair in an outer office.

Silently Theobald Goldenberg heard the captain out. The theory was good but he knew a man like Caleb Reed could never have found a suitable girl. He'd give her a glance, pay her off and get looking for a girl with class to carry out Reed's ideas.

"Well, what do you think?" Captain Reed asked nervously.

Theobald Goldenberg stuck his cigar between his teeth, swung his feet onto the top of his gigantic desk, and said, "Send her in."

Christina had expected to see a tall thin man with cadaverous cheeks and puritanical eyes. Instead she saw a broadly built, muscular man with deeply-tanned skin and a mane of thick, grey, almost white hair springing back from his forehead so that he looked like an aging and powerful lion.

If Christina was surprised, Theobald Goldenberg was amazed.

Their eyes held.

"It's a great idea," Theobald Geldenberg said to his captain without even looking at him. "Leave Miss Haworth here and get back to your ship. Mary—" he said to the secretary who ushered the captain away from the holy of holies, "telegraph Mrs. Goldenberg and tell her there's an epidemic going about. Tell her to move herself and the children out to Rhode Island by tonight. And no more telephone calls. I don't want to be disturbed. Understand?"

"Perfectly, Mr. Goldenberg."

She withdrew, leaving Theobald Goldenberg and Christina Haworth alone in the vast room. It said much of her years of training that she didn't even raise an eyebrow as she heard her distinguished employer lock the doors from the inside and then, a little later, heard the sound of delighted female laughter.

Chapter 19

Christina stood immobile as Theobald Goldenberg walked past her, locked the door, slid the key into his desk drawer and then slowly moved toward her, putting his strong hands on her shoulders.

"You," he said, "are one hell of a woman."

"And you are one hell of a man," Christina said, and she meant it.

From the first minute she had walked through the door and their eyes had met she had been aware of a current of physical attraction between them so strong that words were unnecessary.

Theobald Goldenberg, President of the Goldenberg Shipping Company, a man whose reputation Captain Reed had been so anxious to preserve, was going to make her his mistress and Christina wanted him to. It was crazy. He was fifty if he was a day. She had just spent five days being wooed by handsome young men in their twenties and not one of them had aroused her.

Now, silently facing the craggy features of the President of Goldenberg Shipping, Christina felt a deep physical longing, a desire that demanded to be satisfied. It wasn't love and Christina wasn't fool enough to believe it was. But it was better than the crucifying deadness she had felt since leaving Liverpool.

Theobald Goldenberg was slowly and purposefully taking off her black velvet jacket. This was stupid; insane. He'd had mistresses before but not for the last ten years. A man of fifty was entitled to think he no longer had to prove himself in that field.

Beneath the light chiffon and lace of her blouse he could see the firm outline of her breasts.

Damn society. He knew he had thoughts like a man twenty years his junior. Now he knew he felt like one.

His eyes never leaving hers, he undid the top two pearl buttons of her blouse. She remained motionless, excitement rising in her like a fever. Slowly Theobald Goldenberg's eyes traveled down to the exposed base of her throat. Slowly he bent his leonine head and kissed the racing pulse that beat there.

Christina raised her own hands, undoing the rest of the buttons and Theobald Goldenberg was permitted to see a sight he had never seen before in his life. A beautiful young woman who wore no constraining stays or corsets. No undergarments at all.

With a hoarse blasphemy that was wholly admiration, he took her breasts in his hands, kissing the rigid nipples while Christina felt herself shiver with desire.

He drew her down on to the deep pile of the carpet, kissing her mouth, her lips parting willingly beneath his. Blunt capable fingers moved over her shoulders, her neck, her breasts. She moved beneath him, hungry for his lovemaking. Neither of them had any time for preliminaries.

Mr. Goldenberg's secretary was a very genteel girl. Hearing the groans and cries of mutual ecstasy, she covered her typewriter carefully and left for home. Mr. Goldenberg, she was sure, would wish it.

"Honey," Theobald Goldenberg said later that evening as they dined in the most expensive restaurant New York City had to offer, "I want you to go out and buy yourself anything you want. Furs, jewels, evening·dresses. You'll need an entire wardrobe for the *Corinthia* and you'll need only the best. Understand?"

"Yes, Theo." Christina held her glass out with a pleasurable smile as he re-filled it with champagne.

"And remember what I told you. Stick to the rules. Flirtation only. When it comes to anything else that's my preserve."

"Don't worry." Christina covered his hand with hers. "I won't let anyone else poach on it."

"That's my girl. Now tell me the truth. What the hell were you doing aboard the *Corinthia?* Reed gave me the usual flannel but I didn't believe a word of it. What really happened?"

"I was a whore."

Theobald threw his head back and laughed so loudly that the waiter behind spilled a drink on his tray.

"Jesus Christ! Only you would come clean like that! So—you were a whore. Why? You don't look like any whore I've ever seen."

Christina shrugged. "My father died, and I had to live with my uncle. I had no other home or family."

"And you had the same effect on him as you had on me?"

"Yes, only it wasn't mutual. I'd already been approached by Bessie Mulholland, the madam of the Gaiety brothel, to work for her. She promised to look after me and I liked her. So I went. I didn't regret it either."

Theobald Goldenberg, who valued honesty above all other virtues, nodded. "What then? Why the *Corinthia?*"

Christina paused and then said in a different tone of voice, "I met a sailor. We were going to be married."

"And . . ." Theobald's eyes narrowed as he saw

the sudden taut lines of suffering around Christina's mouth.

"He worked for Anglo-American. He sailed back to New York with his cargo and with the intention of borrowing enough money to buy a ship of his own."

"And you couldn't wait for him to return so you stowed away to follow him?"

"No." Christina's voice trembled. "He found a backer for his ship by marrying the daughter of the man with the money. His father-in-law backed him. He never returned to Liverpool. A sailor he had met in New York docked a few weeks later and told us the news."

"I see." Theobald's face was grim. "That still doesn't explain about the *Corinthia.*"

Christina gave him a bleak smile. "It's simple. I got drunk with one of Bessie's sailors and asked to be taken aboard. When I woke up we were at sea and Captain Reed refused point blank to lose any sailing time by returning me to shore."

"And he saw what I saw and had the only brilliant idea he's ever had," Theobald Goldenberg said with a grin. "You've been honest with me. Let me be honest with you. I'm a married man and even bringing you here for dinner is likely to cause more trouble than you could ever imagine. There is no question of my leaving my wife and there never will be. Not because I love her. That was finished years ago. But simply because she's my wife. I have two kids that are nothing but a pain in the arse. And I want you. Whenever that ship of mine docks in New York Bay there'll be a limousine waiting to bring you straight to me. And I don't want you messing around, understand?"

"Yes, *sir.*" Christina saluted him smartly and Theobald laughed.

"We've wasted enough time over this crummy meal already. Let's get back to my apartment. Hell. My doctor would have heart failure if he knew what I was doing. He's always telling me to remember my age and giving me pills. From now on I'll tell him he's giving people the wrong medication. What they really need is a good woman!" And as he slipped her jacket around her shoulders his hand slid, unseen by the rest of the diners, across Christina's bottom. "He tells me to take three tablets at night with water. Think you can equal that?"

"Easily," Christina said mischievously. "But let's substitute champagne for water!"

For two days while the *Corinthia* was loaded with supplies and cargo and refueled, Christina only left Theo's apartment to buy herself anything her heart desired.

Mr. Goldenberg was always at his desk at nine A.M. sharp, and never left it, except for business meetings which were always conducted in the Goldenberg Shipping Company building. For two days his desk was deserted, his office empty. It was unprecedented. Rumor spread that Mr. Goldenberg was confined to his bed. A rumor that for once was true.

On the Wednesday evening he made his first appearance at the customary farewell party as the *Corinthia* prepared to leave her North River pier for her voyage back to Europe.

He had made what could only be described as a miraculous recovery and was looking fitter and stronger than ever. Mr. Goldenberg's doctor, the whisper went round, was one of quite *exceptional* talents.

The champagne flowed, streamers filled the air, horns hooted and Theo kissed Christina a last passionate goodbye in the finest stateroom the *Corinthia* possessed. From now on, he had informed Captain Reed, it was to be Christina's. As a single young lady traveling alone, Christina's opportunity for flirtation with passengers would draw too much undesirable attention. Far better, Theo had decided, if she were to be a widow. The name was wrong, too. From now on she would be Mrs. Christina de Villiers, widow. A lady with a preference for shipboard life and who, with her innate good taste, had chosen the *Corinthia* for her present home. Traveling the Atlantic time after time in an effort to forget the grief of her loss.

Captain Reed had basked in the president's praise for his quick thinking and brilliant idea and remained happily unaware of the relationship that existed between Christina and his employer. He would, he assured Mr. Goldenberg, take the utmost care of her, and Theo had replied that he goddamn better or there would be hell to pay.

Captain Reed, only too thankful that Christina had behaved herself with the propriety necessary in the presence of such an eminent figure as Mr. Goldenberg, had fervently assured him again and as the ship blew a long blast on the horn, the president of the line disembarked and the *Corinthia* began to slide downstream to the harbor, lit from stem to stern like a floating palace.

Christina leaned over the deck rail as the lights of New York receded. Only minutes ago she'd been all sparkle as the party had reached its height. Now she felt a sudden loss as she left behind the only man with whom she now had any empathy. A darker thought came unbidden into her mind. One that she had refused to acknowledge in the last two days. Somewhere out there in the huge city of brownstone houses and soaring office blocks, Devlin O'Conner would be making love to his new bride.

"Champagne, Madam?"

Christina turned, a brilliant smile on her face. "Of course—thank you," she said, and with her chiffon scarf trailing in the breeze behind her, her sequined evening dress shimmering with every movement she made, she smiled winningly in the direction of Mr. Louis Rothenheim, one of the two millionaires Captain Reed had carefully pointed out to her.

Mr. Rothenheim mentally adjusted his opinion that

life, apart from money, was a bore, and bowed gracefully over her hand as Captain Reed introduced them.

"A canapé, Mrs. de Villiers?" he asked as Captain
Reed discreetly left them alone; with a provocative
touch on Mr. Rothenheim's arm, Mrs. de Villiers allowed herself to be escorted to the lavish buffet table.

She was wrong in thinking that Devlin was making
love. Either to his bride or anyone else.

When he had fought off the pounding pain in his
head and slaked his thirst with pint after pint of water
he had been appalled to find Kate happily sharing his
cabin.

"What the hell," he had asked, struggling to regain
his senses, "are you doing here?"

"You asked me, remember?" Kate lied, winding
her arms around his neck. "I told you all about Christina and . . ."

Devlin remembered only too well what she had said
about Christina. He felt suddenly sick, thrusting Kate
abruptly away from him. Laughing at him and calling
him her little dog! Savagely he splashed his face and
neck with ice-cold water. No wonder he had got
drunk—and this was the result of it. Kate in his cabin
and at his invitation. He cursed himself for a fool.

"I'm going on deck for some fresh air," he said,
scarcely looking at her.

Kate suppressed her disappointment. She had known
enough men suffering from hangovers to be able to
accept Devlin's behavior as being perfectly natural.
She admired her reflection in the glass and then
changed into yet another of the exquisite dresses Devlin had bought for Christina, twirling around with one
hand on her hip. The whiskey that the steward had so
obligingly brought earlier when Devlin was still unconscious remained unopened. Laughing to herself
she poured a generous measure into a cut glass tumbler
and then divested herself of her new clothes, drowning

her body in sweet-smelling Ashes of Roses perfume, waiting expectantly for Devlin's return.

The fierce breeze on deck blew away all the cobwebs in Devlin's mind. In drunken stupidity he had asked Kate to accompany him and he might as well make the best of it. He doubted if even she would have been brazen enough to have asked Bessie for the money he had left for her keep and then returned to work the very next night. He wanted to banish Christina from his mind, just as he had every other girl he had met. And he intended doing it in the only way he knew how.

When he returned to the cabin Kate was not disappointed. He ripped his clothes off as if he had not seen a woman for years, and took her body, time after time, in bouts of frenzied but loveless lovemaking.

Because of his apparent ceaseless need of her, Kate's confidence grew, only to be dashed to pieces on the last night before they reached New York when he cried out at the height of his passion: *"Christina! Christina!"*

From then on Kate knew the battle was not yet over. Despite everything she had said Devlin still desired Christina, and the hatred Kate had always felt for her grew daily, as she became aware that though Devlin always treated her with civility and demanded her sexually just as much as ever, he never, even in their most intimate moments, showed her the slightest sign of affection or tenderness.

When the *Mauretania* docked only hundreds of feet from the *Corinthia*'s pier, his first act was to deposit Kate at his rooming house and set off to see Duane.

"Well, where's the bride?" Duane asked genially, glad to have Devlin back again and eager for the work at Halifax to be completed.

"There isn't one," Devlin replied shortly and Duane, aware of his friend's barely controlled fury, said only, "The work's coming along at Halifax, but I'm glad to have you back. That man you left is capable enough but he doesn't get the same work out of the foremen that you did. When are you leaving?''

"Tomorrow.''

"Good.'' Duane threw his arm across Devlin's shoulders. "How about a night on the town tonight? Just the two of us.''

"Great, except I've got one little problem.''

"What's that?''

"A woman. She sailed on Chri . . . On the spare ticket I took.''

"You don't seem too pleased about it.''

"I'm not,'' Devlin said bluntly. "But I've known her a long time and she's always treated me well. I can't just dump her in a strange city halfway across the world from home.''

"She'll make out.''

"She'd better. But until she does I feel responsible for her. I'm taking her with me up to Halifax. Maybe she can get herself a job there, and then I won't have to worry about her any more.''

"Just as long as she doesn't interfere with work on the *Ninevah*.''

"Don't worry,'' Devlin said bitterly, "I'll never put a woman before work again.''

Duane, dying to ask what had happened to the woman for whom Devlin had left the *Ninevah*, restrained himself and poured two glasses of bourbon.

"To the *Ninevah*,'' he said, raising his glass. "We should have her afloat by the spring.''

"You'll have her afloat,'' Devlin said grimly, downing his drink and returning to South Street to inform Kate that they were leaving in the morning for Halifax.

Life at Halifax was not what Kate had imagined when she had boarded the *Mauretania* with Devlin. There was no luxury to her life now. Not even that that she had known at the Gaiety. The weather was colder than any she had ever thought possible; Devlin's rooms were among those of the other working men and she hardly saw him. When he did come home it was only to snatch a few hours' sleep, and the name he constantly called out in a tortured voice was always that of Christina.

Kate took her own revenge. One thing Halifax didn't lack was men. As Devlin spent twenty out of every twenty-four hours on board the *Ninevah*, Kate entertained more and more of his workmen on the large double bed that Devlin so rarely occupied.

For the first time in his life, though ignorant of the fact, Devlin was being laughed at. The men were forced to respect his knowledge of ships and the miraculous change he was bringing about on the *Ninevah* but it was common knowledge that he wasn't man enough to satisfy the woman who lived with him. Kate did what she had accused Christina of doing. She belittled Devlin's sexual prowess to the men who knew him. Only the arms of Stanislav Mikolij saved her. Without his arrival her activities would inevitably have reached Devlin's ears. But with the arrival of Stanislav, Kate found herself needing the others less and less. And Mikolij was not a man to brag of his adventures with the boss's woman. He was a massively-built Pole who drank alone and spoke to no one. Except Kate. The sight of his gigantic shoulders and huge thighs had aroused Kate the moment she first saw him. Stanislav knew an available woman when he saw one, and within twenty-four hours of arriving in Halifax was enjoying Kate in Devlin's bed.

Stanislav Mikolij proved himself a rare man. He alone was able to satisfy Kate's insatiable sexual appetite. Gradually, the other men were dropped and with Stanislav as a lover, Kate found herself in a state very nearly approaching that of happiness. Only the fascination that Devlin unwittingly exerted on her prevented it. Her passion for him was changing. She began to hate him for not loving her, and she hated Christina for preventing it. It was a hatred bordering on insanity. When Stanislav asked her if she would leave with him when work on the *Ninevah* had finished, Kate had refused. If she left with Stanislav, Devlin might find Christina again and it had become the crusade of Kate's life that he would never do so.

For Kate the spirit of hate was far stronger than that of love. If she could not have Devlin, no one else would. Where Devlin went she would follow. He would never escape from her. Never.

Scarcely aware of her existence, let alone of the intensity of her feelings, Devlin continued to sweat day after day on the *Ninevah*. By April her resurrection was complete, and on a glorious spring morning with white clouds scudding across the rain-washed sky, Devlin proudly walked the length and breadth of her with a satisfied Duane Yates at his side.

"She sure is one hell of a ship," Duane said admiringly.

"She ought to be. She's practically rebuilt. Twin screws. Eight watertight bulkheads. Four decks. Cabins for three hundred first class and four hundred second class passengers, and room for over a thousand steerage passengers. Two four-cylinder quadruple expansion engines . . ."

"Spare me," Duane said, raising a hand laughingly. "The engines are your province. If you say they go, they go. That's all that matters to me. What do you think of the decor?"

"She looks like the Ritz."

Duane was suitably gratified.

"There's nothing you can tell me about what people want when they travel. Give 'em ostentation. And what you've done here is a bloody miracle. If you've done it once you'll be able to do it again. Another few years and we'll have a fleet of ships to rival the Goldenberg Line!"

"You think so?"

"Think so? I know it!" Duane threw his astrakhan hat high into the air. "Just look around you. We've made it! The Conyates Shipping Company is in business!"

Chapter 20

"You can't leave me!" Kate's eyes were glazed with an expression that unnerved even Devlin. "You brought me all the way from England to this God-forsaken hole. You *asked* me to come! You can't leave me now!"

Devlin strove to control his anger.

"The *Ninevah* is ready to sail and I'm captaining her. You know enough about the sea, Kate, to know you can't come with me."

"But you'd have taken *her!*" Kate spat, trembling with rage. "You'd have taken your precious Christina, wouldn't you? She treated you like dirt and yet you still want her! I've heard you! Crying her name in your sleep! The rules of the sea wouldn't have mattered where *she* was concerned, would they?"

Tight-lipped, Devlin reached for his kit, exerting all his self-control to restrain himself from slapping her across the face.

She threw herself after him, clinging to his arm.

"Take me with you! You can't leave me like this. You can't! I've been good to you, haven't I? I haven't looked at another man. I've been left alone for hour after hour in a strange land and with no other woman to keep me company. *She* would never have done as much for you. She took your money and laughed at you. But I've taken nothing! *Please!*" Tears coursed down her face.

Devlin felt suddenly tired. She was right. She had

214

done nothing to deserve such treatment. Her being with him was due to his own stupidity. He had hoped she would have found Halifax boring and left of her own accord. But she hadn't. She had stayed in the meanly furnished cabin waiting day after lonely day while he worked on the ship. To abandon her now was unthinkable.

"Get your things," he said curtly, moving away from her grasp.

Kate moved like lightning. With her back safely toward him her small pearly teeth showed a triumphant smile and her eyes were alight with success.

"Ready?"

She turned, her expression once more subdued and obedient, linking her arm proprietarily in his as they left for the docks.

Stanislav Mikolij watched them approach the *Ninevah* through narrowed eyes. For the past four hours he had been working deep in the hold, storing the bales and boxes that formed the *Ninevah*'s cargo to Southampton. Kate had refused to leave Halifax with him and it had not occurred to him that she would be accompanying Captain O'Conner aboard the ship.

To take the captain's woman behind his back was one thing. To feel that he, too, was being made a fool of was another. He'd see the woman. Talk to her. The captain didn't love her. Nor she him. There was something else between them. Something he couldn't understand. The expression in her eyes whenever she spoke of O'Conner had been fanatical—the eyes of a madwoman. No, there was no love there. She would be better off with him. He would speak to her. Reason with her. For she would seek him out. He knew that beyond a doubt. Her need of him was too great to be restrained just because she was on board the captain's ship.

The crew, most of whom had enjoyed Kate's body before Stanislav had arrived, gave each other meaningful glances as she boarded the ship with her baggage. A woman aboard was always trouble, and this one more trouble than most. A sense of unease spread among them. Devlin, quick to pick up the vibrations amongst his crew, put it down to traditional superstition about maiden voyages.

The locks were opened and water began to pour into the drydock. Devlin's sudden sweep of weariness vanished. The crew was on board, and leaving Kate in his cabin he strode onto the bridge, filled with an excitement so intense he felt physically sick.

Kate, who had never before had the privilege of being aboard the *Ninevah*, took her opportunity and stroked the red damask walls and deep sofas lovingly. Duane Yates's taste had an awful lot in common with that of Bessie Mulholland, and the oriental rugs and shaded light fitments made Kate feel immediately at home.

By noon Kate had finished her exploration of the *Ninevah*'s interior and, disobeying Devlin's instructions, wandered up on deck.

She walked desultorily back to Devlin's cabin and searched for something to drink. Finding an unopened bottle of bourbon, she poured herself a half tumblerful and lay down on the bunk, running the long nail of her forefinger meditatively around the rim.

If Christina Haworth could see her now. She laughed out loud, enjoying the searing warmth of the liquor.

The sailor she had gone off with had been on the New York run. Perhaps if she asked a few questions in the right places she could find out what had happened to her. To what depths a penniless Christina had been reduced to. She knew enough of brothels to know that Christina would never find another like Bessie Mulholland's, and even in Bessie's establishment she had been treated like a piece of bone china. Kate took another swallow of the bourbon. Little cow. She wouldn't be holding her head quite so high after a few nights of taking all and sundry. But most of all, Kate wanted to know Christina's whereabouts so that she could prevent any chance meeting between her and Devlin. "Bastard," she said under her breath, reaching for the bottle and topping up her glass. He hadn't wanted her to come with him and she hated him for it. She wanted to hurt him in the only way possible: By seeing to it that he never met Christina again and never knew the truth about Christina's reasons for behaving so wildly and for her sudden disappearance.

"The drydock is now filled," the chief engineer said to Devlin.

"Great." Devlin's face was exultant. "All systems go."

"Easy off," a voice shouted, and then another, minutes later, "Hard away." Seconds later there came a faint, throbbing sensation vibrating through the *Ninevah*. The official launch of the ship was to be done by Duane in New York, and it was to be covered by as many reporters as he could summon. For the moment the *Ninevah* was his entirely. With tugs in place the *Ninevah* moved slowly seaward. Every man on board felt dizzy with elation. Only Kate remained oblivious of the momentous event, too deep in her thoughts of revenge to be even aware of the ship's motion.

Devlin checked the time. Duane had asked that he bring the *Ninevah* into New York under cover of darkness and as quietly as possible. All the pomp and ceremony was to be reserved for the next day. Kate, waiting expectantly for Devlin's return, was disappointed. The hours dragged by and still he remained on the bridge.

Half drunk, she staggered to her feet, determined to face him on the bridge.

The roll of the ship was making her feel ill. Perhaps she would have been wiser to have left the bourbon alone.

"Sorry, miss. No one is allowed on the bridge but the captain and chief engineer."

"Get lost," Kate said, pushing him out of her way. His hand closed over hers.

"My orders are that no one is to approach the bridge."

"If I want to approach the bloody bridge, I'll approach it," Kate said, her voice rising. "Who the hell do you think you are?"

"Look, I don't want any trouble." The sailor was beginning to feel out of his depths.

Stanislav approached and said threateningly, "Let go of her."

Kate dragged her hand from the restraining grip and half reeled against the giant Pole.

"This pig says I can't go on the bridge."

"He's right." Stanislav's enormous hands steadied her, then without another word he led her away to a deserted corner of the lower deck.

"The captain doesn't want you," he said simply. "Let's both leave ship in New York. I'll be a good man to you."

She leaned against his chest and for the first time in her life shed genuine tears.

"I can't," she said helplessly. "I've got to stay with him. I've got to prevent him finding *her*."

"Her?"

Kate wrung her hands together fiercely. "He would have loved me if it hadn't been for her. I'll kill him rather than let her have him!"

Stanislav did not understand her frenzy but he did know how to ease it. He imprisoned her in his arms, kissing her deeply, pulling her dress open and sucking on her nipples, kneading the huge breasts in his roughened hands.

Kate's eyes glazed as she clung to him. "Make love to me now, Stanislav! Now!" Her voice was a pleading moan.

Stanislav Mikolij smiled to himself. "It's me you

want, not Captain O'Conner. He only loves his ship. It's me you want, isn't it? Me. Stanislav."

"Oh yes, yes, please!" She strained her body upward, desperately seeking his. Stanislav put his big hand across her mouth to stop her cries of pleasure drawing attention to the darkened saloon. She would leave the captain and go with him. She couldn't do without him now. The knowledge intensified his own desire and he drove deep and hard into her while Kate gasped in a frenzy of ever-increasing lust as spasm after rapturous spasm contorted her body.

It was past midnight when Devlin returned to the cabin. From the depths of the specially-made double bunk Kate watched him as he splashed his face and chest with ice-cold water and then drank a mug of steaming coffee, oblivious of her.

Her fingers moved lightly over her naked stomach. She could still feel the pressure of Stanislav's hands on her, between her legs she felt a nostalgic twinge of pleasure. She smiled, stroking her self gently. Devlin would make love to her tonight, while she was still damp from the lovemaking of one of his crew. The thought gave her a feeling of satisfaction as she stroked herself with increasing rhythm. He would kill her if he knew, but he would never know. Her smile deepened and she opened her arms wide, her heavy breasts swinging against the sheet, the nipples standing out darkly.

"You've been a long time. I've been lonely," she said huskily.

And Devlin, the steady purr of the engines carrying him on a wave of exultation, reached out for her as he hadn't done for weeks while Kate delighted in the knowledge that his seed was mixing with that of one of his lowest deck hands.

Quietly, accompanied only by the tugs, the *Ninevah* entered New York harbor and berthed at her pier. From the waiting black limousine Duane Yates stepped into the freezing night air. The gang plank was lowered and Devlin met him, escorting him to the same saloon that only hours before Stanislav and Kate had used to make love.

"Did she run smooth?" Duane asked, his face alight with boyish enthusiasm.

"Like a dream."

"Great. Everything's all laid on for tomorrow. Every paper in town will be represented and you should see the passenger list!" Duane's grey eyes shone. "It rivals any of the Cunard or Goldenberg Line's. You name 'em. I've got 'em. Actresses, literary lions, even a statesmen en route to the Court of Saint James!"

"How in God's name did you manage that?" Devlin asked incredulously.

"Easy. Masses of publicity and free tickets."

"Free tickets! We're not a bloody charity. We're in this to make money. We'll be running at a loss to start with anyway . . ."

Duane grinned and laid a hand restrainingly on his arm. "You captain the ship and leave the finance to me. I know what I'm doing. The society columns will have a field day and when the rest of New York and Philadelphia and Boston see the names traveling on the *Ninevah* you can bet your bottom dollar they'll want to be on the bandwagon too."

Devlin's brief anger subsided. Duane was right. What did it matter if they ran at a loss to begin with as long as they attracted the right sort of customers for the future.

Duane snapped his fingers and his personal valet, who had boarded with him, hurried deferentially forward with a tray carrying champagne and two glasses.

Duane uncorked the bottle himself, and as the champagne fizzed and he filled the glasses, both men faced each other with beaming smiles.

"God bless this ship and all her company," Duane said in the traditional manner, raising his glass high.

"Amen to that," Devlin said sincerely.

"Till the morning," Duane said, draining his glass, his eyes bright and his cheeks flushed. "We won't get much sleep tonight but who the hell needs it?" And with his fur-collared coat nonchalantly across his shoulders and his hat at a rakish angle on his blond hair, he left the *Ninevah*, already picturing his photograph in the next day's tabloids.

Devlin stretched, realized the most sleep he would get would be three hours and decided he couldn't afford to waste a minute of it. Kate was asleep, a small secretive smile on her face. She was an encumbrance he should be ridding himself of, not encouraging by making love to her as he had only a few hours ago. Her need of him seemed as great as ever. Yet he didn't love her and never would. He closed his heart and mind against the memory of the woman he had loved and who had not been so faithful. He must sleep.

But there was no escape. As his consciousness slipped away into sleep she was there, in his dreams. Merry eyes full of laughter, her wide generous mouth curving in a smile, her mass of black, waist-length hair curling and waving as he knotted his hands deep within its softness. "Christina . . ." At the pain and longing in his voice Kate only smiled to herself in the dark. He would never find her. Never have her. She closed her eyes and slept.

At first light Devlin was on deck, supervising the *Ninevah*'s crew as they made sure she was ready to greet the press and her distinguished passengers. Bunting was tacked into place, hundreds of champagne glasses were washed and polished and delicacies for the magnificent buffet were being freshly made in the newly-installed galley.

Duane was first on board, a giggling entourage of young girls in his wake.

"Shine, darn you, shine," he said to the watery sun rising in the sky.

"She'll shine," Devlin said with a confident grin. "Who are the girls?"

Duane shrugged. "Chorus girls from the *Dominion*. They're not traveling. They're strictly for show."

On the pier a collection of reporters was beginning to gather, and Devlin could see cameras being set up. Duane had certainly pulled out all the stops. As the first load of pigskin and initialed suitcases began to be loaded on board, Devlin made a last careful inspection of his ship. By now Kate was putting the finishing touches to her face. The dress she wore had been bought with Christina in mind. Devlin paused. On Kate it looked flashy and yet it had cost him a fortune. He wondered whether he should ask her to change, and decided against it. He couldn't think of anything that would make Kate look any different.

On the wharves, sweating longshoremen labored to unload a nearby ship, piling bales, bags and boxes colorfully on the cobbles. Horse-drawn cabs and a few motor driven vehicles were edging closer to the *Ninevah*'s pier. The reporters had already been ushered aboard and were now in with the purser, drinking champagne and examining the *Ninevah*'s illustrious passenger list.

The sun rose and warmed, and the *Ninevah*'s three funnels shone under their many coats of bright new paint. Kate was happy. Even Duane Yates had condescended to speak to her, his hair brilliantined and gleaming under his hat, his waxed moustache making him look older than his twenty-three years and more like the sophisticated tycoon he wished to be seen as.

She had never met a gentleman before. Not on his own ground. The dandies at the Gaiety could hardly count, and there was something about Devlin's partner that disconcerted Kate. She had known hundreds of men and all of them had been excited by her body. Duane Yates was not, and Kate wondered what it would take to excite the expensively dressed rich young man of New York's high society. She had broached the subject of Duane's girlfriends to Devlin, but he had been uncommunicative. He didn't know anything about Duane's private life. It was a subject that was never discussed, and apart from his brief glances of beautiful girls waiting in the back of Duane's limousine, Devlin had never seen him with a woman. Even if he had known the details Kate wanted to hear, he wouldn't have told her. Duane's private life was his own. As was his.

Suddenly, among the sailors reloading the ship at the next pier to the *Ninevah*, Kate caught a glimpse of a stoker from the *Corinthia*. For a minute panic gripped her. The *Corinthia* had been the ship on which she was sure Christina had inadvertently sailed. She scanned the glittering liners at their Manhattan piers, searching for the familiar name but failed to find it. Reporters and photographers forgotten, she ran across to the starboard side of the ship and felt a slight feeling of relief as no *Corinthia* greeted her gaze.

She searched the crowded dockside for another glimpse of the stoker. He was there, smoking a pipe and gazing up at the *Ninevah* with interest and admiration. Kate pushed her way through the crowds toward him and grabbed his arm.

He blinked, staring down at her in surprise.

Kate struggled for breath and then smiled, brushing close against him.

"You remember me, don't you? Kate, from the Gaiety in Liverpool?"

He grinned, showing blackened teeth. "You bet I do. What are you doing this side of the water?"

"I'm on her." Kate nodded in the direction of the *Ninevah*.

"Are you now. I hear O'Conner is captaining her. Lucky bastard."

"I wondered if you'd seen my friend, Christina Haworth from the Gaiety. I believe she landed in New York some months back. I wondered if you knew where she was. I'd like to see her again. Have a chat."

"Seems like you Gaiety girls do all right for yourselves. First her, now you."

"What do you mean? First her, now me?" Kate asked sharply.

"Her sailing the *Corinthia*, you the *Ninevah*."

Kate's nails dug into his arm so hard that he winced.

"She sailed on her over here, but where is she now? That's what I want to know."

"England probably. The *Corinthia* set sail a few days ago. I left after the last trip. I'm going whaling again."

"But where's Christina Haworth?"

"I've told you. Aboard the *Corinthia*."

"You mean they took her back to Liverpool?"

He shook his head. "She's living on board. Great joke it is. Captain Reed took it into his head she'd be an asset on board and dolled her up in his wife's finery. Traveling as a widow she is now. A Mrs. de Villiers. All the crew know and love it."

"She's sailing on the *Corinthia* every trip?" Kate's voice was little more than a whisper, her eyes as hard as pebbles.

"Yes. That's what I've been telling you. One of the crew she is now, even though she travels first class and has her own state room."

All she could think of was the fact that the *Corinthia* with Christina on board was traveling the regular run from New York to Liverpool and that the *Ninevah* with Devlin on board was traveling from New York to Southampton. Eventually the news of Christina's whereabouts would reach Devlin's ears. It couldn't fail to.

From out of the crowd Stanislav grabbed hold of her.

"Let's go . . ."

"No." She shook herself free.

"We can start a new life in America. I'll give up the sea. I'm a strong man. I can easily find work. We'll have fine sons . . ."

"No." Her eyes stared through him.

"I hope you find your friend," the stoker said uncomfortably. "She's a great girl. One of the best. Give her my love."

"I'll give her more than that," Kate said, white-mouthed, as she marched back toward the *Ninevah*'s gangplank.

Stanislav stared after her, shrugged and picked up his kit. He wasn't a man to plead. He turned in the direction of South Street, his huge shoulders hunched, his heart heavy.

Chapter *21*

As Christina danced round and round the chandelier-lit ballroom a tall, elegant-looking man watched her with amusement.

She had Rothenheim eating out of her hand and there hadn't been a murmur of jealousy from any of the female passengers. The Duke of Marne swirled his brandy round in his glass and then sipped it. Mrs. de Villiers. Widow. She couldn't be a day over twenty. The waltz came to a close, and despite Mr. Rothenheim's presence Mrs. de Villiers was besieged with requests for her hand for the next dance.

The Duke grinned to himself. Rothenheim was only five years his senior. Forty-five years to his forty, but mentally the Duke of Marne put Mr. Louis Rothenheim in his dotage. The fellow took himself too seriously.

He was traveling alone. A fact that would have astonished his contemporaries, for the wealthy and mature duke had a reputation for fast living. In his twenties he had been a privileged member of the Marlborough House set, which was a firm favorite of the pleasure-loving King Edward VII. He had been known as a wild young blood who raced, gambled and womanized his way with style and panache from Paris to Biarritz to Cannes. His mistresses were all beautiful, the coquettes who vied for his favor, notorious. The scenes in some of the private supper rooms attended by Marne and the younger members of the aristocracy would have made a hardened sailor blush.

He was worldly and had everything that good breeding and wealth could buy, but the Duke had found that in the last few years the women and champagne had lost their sparkle. Boredom was creeping in. His palate was becoming distinctly jaded.

The turning point had been Bertie's death. With that irreplaceable monarch no longer adding his own zest for life to the interminable round of house parties and weekends, the Duke had found them increasingly tedious. The women even more so. The one he was watching now would be incapable of bringing tedium to any gathering.

Mrs. de Villiers was English, undoubtedly wealthy or she wouldn't be traveling first class, and in the most sought after stateroom, and accepted by everyone on board as being a leader of English high society. The Duke, who had a lifetime's experience of that society, knew better and the knowledge intrigued him. Her voice lacked the high-pitched staccato of the English upper classes. Instead it was soft, well modulated and full of laughter. The Duke found it exceedingly soothing and a welcome change from those of the women in his own set. No. Whatever the Americans aboard might think, Mrs. de Villiers was not a member of the select few who spent the first week in August at Cowes for the yachting, jaunted up north for the grouse shooting, visited a European spa to recuperate from the excesses of overeating and, finally, journeyed on to the Riviera for the rest of the summer.

A steward refilled his glass, and as he raised it to his lips Christina's eyes caught his. She was in the arms of young Gerardson, and by the expression on his face it seemed unlikely that the beautiful widow would remain a widow for long. Her eyes were alight with mischief as if she had been reading his thoughts. The Duke raised his glass to her and for a brief second it was as if they were united in a silent conspiracy unknown to those around them.

"Who had Mr. de Villiers been?" wondered the Duke. Probably some old fuddy-duddy she had worn into the grave within a matter of months. At least, the Duke mused as his eyes followed her round the ballroom, Mr. de Villiers had died a happy man.

"If I could escort you into supper, ma'am," Mr. Louis Rothenheim asked almost brusquely, raging inside at the insolence of the young English puppy who had robbed him of Christina's charms.

"Not yet, thank you, Louis. I must have a word with the Countess of Dethley. She's chairbound, you know, and tends to get forgotten once the dancing starts."

"She has a companion . . ." Mr. Rothenheim protested.

Christina squeezed his hand. "A paid companion is not always enough, Louis. Thank you for the dance. Perhaps I shall see you later?" and to Louis Rothenheim's incredulity, she left his side and crossed the crowded room, to disappear behind potted palms where the elderly Countess of Dethley watched the gaiety from the confines of her wheelchair.

The Duke of Marne watched her progress too. There weren't many women who would decline the attentions of a multi-millionaire to spend time keeping an elderly and often querulous lady company, yet Mrs. de Villiers did it nightly. And it wasn't only the Countess. She had taken the trouble to befriend Mrs. Windsmoor-Cooper's plain and pathetically shy daughter, and the Duke was sure that it was thanks to Mrs. de Villiers that the ungainly Miss Windsmoor-Cooper was now dressed in something more suitable for her height and figure than the babyish pastel dresses she had worn on the first two evenings at sea. In a rich red dress of heavy velvet she looked quite elegant and sophisticated. A young American banker who had immediately sought out Mrs. de Villiers as companion had been gently and unobtrusively guided by her in the direction of Miss Windsmoor-Cooper, and tonight, as the young couple danced together, Miss Windsmoor-Cooper looked almost radiant. A changed girl from the one who had embarked at New York.

Mrs. de Villiers had also, on discovering that Mrs. Marchant was suffering severely from sea sickness, not only taken the trouble to visit and commiserate with that unfortunate lady, but had taken her a remedy she had made up herself, which had worked miracles.

"You're doing a good job," Captain Reed said to her with satisfaction. "Return bookings are up twenty-five per cent *and* that isn't all. Mrs. Marchant writes a social column under a pseudonym for one of the London magazines. She's so pleased with her trip she's going to make a point of recommending the Goldenberg Line to all discerning travelers!"

Always, away from the bright lights, the music and the company of other passengers, Christina's gaiety faded away, to be replaced by aching emptiness.

"What's the matter?" Captain Reed asked paternally, seeing the light fade from her eyes and the sad expression around her mouth.

Christina forced a smile. "Nothing. Is it necessary for me to continue on to Cherbourg or could I spend a few days in Liverpool? I've friends to see."

Captain Reed frowned. "I understand your concern about your friends but don't forget you are a lady of wealth and breeding now. You can't be seen in your old haunts or the word will get around."

"I'll be careful," Christina promised. "I just want to see Bessie and explain things to her. She was very good to me and she doesn't deserve to be left in the dark."

Reluctantly Caleb agreed, and with a lighter heart Christina returned to the music-filled ballroom.

The Duke had wandered out on deck for a smoke and had seen Mrs. de Villiers approach the captain. A very different Mrs. de Villiers from the sparkling vital girl of a few minutes ago. She looked wan and indescribably sad. He dropped the butt of his cigar into the ocean and strolled back to the ballroom, taking a seat at the entrance, half hidden by a statue of Aphrodite.

His eyes sharpened as she approached. Her sadness hadn't been a trick of the moonlight, it was still there, but as she neared the ballroom he could see her square her shoulders, hold her head higher and widen her lips in a gay smile. It reminded him of when he had had the privilege of watching Sarah Bernhardt prepare herself to go on stage in Theodora. The sparkling vivacity of the gay young widow was nothing more than an act. Mr. Rothenheim claimed her almost immediately and she laughed coquettishly up at him. The Duke frowned and lit another cigar. There was an air of desperation in her determined gaiety. There were three more days before they reached Liverpool. The Duke of Marne resolved to abandon his position as voyeur and go out of his way to deepen his acquaintance with Mrs. de Villiers.

Christina enjoyed the Duke's company. He didn't try to make any overtures to her. There was none of the pawing and fondling that made Mr. Rothenheim and his like such a nuisance. He was a great raconteur, and had her in fits of giggles as he described some of the less dignified goings-on that he had enjoyed as a friend of the late King.

"Go on, you don't say," she said as he told her a particularly racy story about the King and Mrs. Keppel, and the Duke of Marne hid a smile. For once, Mrs. de Villiers had lost her careful accent, and he wondered again what her background was. Certainly not true-blue British. She looked almost like a gypsy at times, and he toyed with the idea of inviting her to Anersley, his country seat in Yorkshire.

"Perhaps if you have the time while you are in England you would like to spend a weekend at Anersley?" he asked as he waltzed her round and round the glittering ballroom, aware that he was becoming increasingly intrigued by her, that his cool detachment was gradually being eroded.

Christina had no need to ask who or what Anersley was. From his anecdotes she knew it was the Duke's main residence, and that he had often entertained the king there.

"That's very kind of you," Christina said sincerely, "but I already have arrangements for my few days in England. I'm visiting friends."

"Then Anersley's loss in their gain," the Duke replied gallantly. "Perhaps another time."

"Yes. Captain Reed tells me you are traveling again to New York in a few months' time. I look forward to seeing you then."

"And I you," the Duke said, feeling an unexpected sense of disappointment that he wouldn't have the pleasure of entertaining her.

When he did return, his staff found him listless and bed tempered, and they were quite relieved when he announced that he would be returning to America sooner than he had anticipated and demanded that his personal secretary secure a stateroom aboard the *Corinthia* at the earliest opportunity.

Christina waited until all the first class passengers had disembarked at Liverpool and then, dressed in a blue walking suit trimmed with red fox, she made her way alone down the gangplank.

She had been away less than a month. It seemed like a lifetime. She ignored the cabbie who was waiting hopefully to give her a lift to the Station Hotel and made her way over the familiar cobbles of the dockside. In the distance she could see the warren of streets that included Gorman Street and the house belonging to Ernest Miller. Despite the warmth of her *couture* suit and its fox fur trim, she shivered. Further up, she caught a glimpse of the green of tangled grass in the cemetery. Strange that once it had been the first place she had run to. Happy and secure in the knowledge that Josh would be there waiting for her. Josh, who she had believed would never let her down. The breeze ruffled the fur against her cheeks and she continued, ignoring the curious stares as she made straight for the Gaiety.

"Jesus Christ!" Sheba said blasphemously, a Japanese kimono tied loosely around her Junoesque figure. "Look what the cat's dragged in!"

Christina grinned, feeling near to tears as Sheba proceeded to hug her fiercely.

"Where the hell did you get that rig out? I thought you'd gone off with a sailor, not a bloody millionaire!"

"It's a long story. Is Bessie in?"

"As always. Everyone else is asleep. There's been some changes while you've been gone. Merry's still in Southampton with Josh, or was the last we heard. God, you should have heard the row his wife kicked up. Molly got married and is living miles out the other side of town in the country. Her fella's a farm laborer. Belle's left and opened a tea shop in Bootle. We've got four new girls. Dixie, the American; Louella, who has to be seen to be believed; and two Yorkshire girls. They're all right till they open their mouths. Straight off Ilkly Moor they are."

"Why four new girls if only three have left? Is Bessie expanding the business?"

Sheba looked suddenly uncomfortable. "Kate left as well," she said, knocking on Bessie's door. "I don't know why the hell you left like you did, but make the explanation good for Bessie. She hit the roof." And as Bessie called bad-temperedly for her to enter, Sheba gave her a wink.

With a sudden feeling of apprehension Christina opened the door and entered Bessie's boudoir.

Bessie, who never appreciated being disturbed until it was past noon, was struggling into a marabou-edged satin negligee and saying crossly, "What do you want? No one disturbs me, young lady, as you . . ." then she raised her eyes from the ribbon fastenings and saw Christina. Abruptly she sat down on the bed. Slowly her eyes traveled from Christina's leather-shod feet up the length of the perfectly fitting ankle-length suit, to the unmistakable fox of the collar and to her fine kid gloves.

"So you weren't a fool after all," she said at last. "Who was he? Some rich dandy who got his kicks dressing up like a Jack Tar?"

"No." Christina removed her gloves and laid them on a table cluttered with china birds. "He was a sailor all right. From the *Corinthia*."

Dazedly, Bessie rose to her feet and crossed to her cupboard and the inevitable bottle of spirits.

"I think I need a drink before I can face all this." She filled up two glasses. "Why didn't you tell me you were leaving?"

"Because I didn't know."

Bessie's eyebrows flew up. "It's me you're talking to, remember? Bessie Mulholland. I don't want any flannel."

Christina sat down and nursed her drink. "I'm not giving you any, Bessie. It's the truth. I was upset that night after . . ." She paused. ". . . after the news about Devlin . . ." She took a deep breath to steady her voice. "I got drunk, and you know I never did drink much. I wasn't used to it. The sailor I was with was from the *Corinthia*, and I knew it was the sort of liner Devlin would be captaining. I just wanted to go aboard."

"So you did?"

"Yes. Victor Jackson was as drunk as I was. When I came to we were miles out in the Irish Sea and on our way to New York."

"If that don't beat the band. I couldn't believe you'd just sneak off in the night without a word of goodbye. Poor old Molly was nearly demented with worry, and all you were doing was entertaining the entire crew of the *Corinthia!*"

"No." Christina suppressed a smile. Trust Bessie to think she'd had a captive clientele and made the most of it.

"I traveled most respectably under the patronage of Captain Caleb Reed."

"Oh, yes," Bessie laughed. "And did Captain Reed's 'patronage' extend to buying you that little outfit?"

This time Christina did smile. "No. A certain American gentleman was responsible for this."

"And you're going back to him?"

"Yes."

Bessie put her glass down. "Well, I'll miss you, Christina. The kindest thing you can say about the rest of the girls, Marigold and Sheba apart, is that they're pea-brained."

Christina could feel her pulse begin to race as she steeled herself to ask the question she had vowed she would not ask.

"Does . . ." she hesitated. It was too hard to say his name. "Does he still come here?"

There was no need for Bessie to ask who she meant. The twisting fingers and tormented expression in her eyes was enough.

Bessie poured another two drinks. "Just the once. He brought you a present," she said, nodding her head in the direction of the still unwrapped jewelry box on her *secretaire*.

Christina felt the blood drumming in her ears. "Did he say anything about his . . ." She struggled for composure. ". . . his wife."

"Not a thing. Whoever she is, she doesn't seem to be cramping his style. When he left he took Kate with him."

Bessie had been deliberately cruel. There was no use in prolonging Christina's agony.

Christina felt the room swim around her and heard Bessie asking: "Are you all right, dear? Do you want to see what it was he bought you?"

"No . . ." Christina felt she was suffocating. She had to get out into the fresh air. She should never have come. Never have asked. With her hands pressed hard against her mouth she rose unsteadily to her feet.

"You can't go while you're in that state," Bessie said anxiously. "Sit down. Have another drink."

"No." The word was barely a whisper. She turned her anguished face from Bessie. "Goodbye, Bessie."

Outside in the street she began to weep. She had thought all her tears for Devlin had been shed, that there was no further hurt or betrayal she could suffer at his hands. She had been wrong. Forsaking her for a marriage of convenience had not been enough. He had taken Kate with him to satisfy the physical desires his wife could not. She hugged her arms across her breasts as she walked blindly back toward the *Corinthia*.

Lust was all Devlin O'Conner was capable of, not love. If she had loved him body and soul in that fleeting precious week in Wales all Devlin had done was slake his lust on her. If she hadn't gone with him no doubt he would have asked one of the other girls. The talk of marriage and love had been nothing but a mockery. Her heart breaking, she stumbled down the *Corinthia*'s companionway to her cabin, opened the door and then, throwing herself on her bed, breathed with harsh, shuddering gasps.

Chapter 22

Captain Reed, seeing that Christina had reboarded almost immediately and that she was in a state of distress, hesitated. His instinct was to go and comfort her, but crying females made him feel uncomfortable. *Best leave her alone,* he thought, as he captained the *Corinthia* across to Cherbourg. Her friends had obviously not taken kindly to Christina's new position in life and fancy clothes.

By the time the new Cherbourg passengers, mainly steerage, had embarked and they had picked up the first and second class passengers from Liverpool and the *Corinthia* had eased out to sea again, Christina had emerged from her stateroom; she was slightly paler than normal, but to all outward appearances she was her usual gay self.

"We've got another duke on board. Doubt if you'll enjoy his company as much as Marne's. He's a lecherous old devil and he'll need careful handling. There's some sweet-scented, brilliantined dandy by the name of Fletch Jerome who they tell me appears in the moving pictures. The press showed a lot of interest in him. There's the usual sprinkling of American businessmen. A steel magnate, and a Wall Street banker of international repute. The heavily bearded gentleman in Stateroom B-6 has just written a novel that is considered very racy, and his journey to New York is to supervise the adaptation of one of his plays. Rupert Pennington is the heir to the Pennington fortune, all built on wool, but I doubt if young Pennington would recognize a sheep if he fell over one.''

He sighed. ''We've missed out on a couple of Russian princes.'' He flicked a newspaper distastefully with his hand. ''They're sailing from Southampton. As are most people of note.''

''Then why don't we change our port of call? Southampton is nearer London and we'd get far more passengers.''

''Because Liverpool has *always* been our port,'' Captain Reed said irritably.

''Then maybe it's about time we changed it. My presence on board may liven up the dinner table but it isn't enough to persuade anyone to travel from Liverpool instead of Southampton, and for the sort of clientele you're trying to attract Southampton is by far the most convenient point of embarkation.''

''And what do you know of our clientele?'' Captain Reed asked, half amused and half annoyed.

''I know the vast majority are traveling from the States to Europe to recuperate at a spa or on the Riviera.'' She grinned. ''Liverpool doesn't fall into either of those categories. I know we rely on buyers traveling to the fashion shows of London and Paris. Docking at Liverpool means a much longer train journey to London than Southampton. I know that four out of five of our passengers are Americans and that what they want is to reach England's capital city as soon as possible. That's why Southampton is by far the most sensible port.''

''You're right, you little minx. I'll put it to Goldenberg when we reach New York.'' He leaned on the deck rail. ''Competition wasn't so fierce when I first took to sea. Now, if we are to maintain competitive schedules, we have to steam at very nearly full power for the greater part of the voyage. There are new lines opening every day, though I doubt if any of them, the Goldenberg Line included, will ever rival Cunard, White Star and Inman.''

"We could," Christina said thoughtfully, "if we had something *different* to offer."

Caleb laughed. "You get any bright ideas on *that* score, tell President Goldenberg straight away. His new ship has already passed the drawing-board stage."

"Is Mr. Goldenberg launching another ship?" Christina asked with interest.

"Yes. She's not named yet. But she'll be the pride of the fleet when she's finished. Whoever captains her will be a lucky man."

He looked sad.

"Would you like to captain her?" Christina asked gently.

He patted her hand. "Bless you child. Of course I would. But my sailing days will end on the *Corinthia*. The new ship will go to a younger man. One with what Goldenberg calls 'dash and vigor.' "

That evening at dinner Christina dexterously avoided the attentions of the Duke, whose hands tended to stray somewhat under the table, and flirted with Mr. Fletch Jerome, who asked if she would like a part in his new moving picture and said he would willingly audition her then and there if she would only accompany him to his cabin.

The next day Christina, determined to inspect the *Corinthia* with a practiced eye from stem to stern including steerage, searched her wardrobe for an inconspicuous looking outfit. It was a difficult task to find one. Theo's taste was for the lavish and spectacular. Sequined evening dresses hung rail upon rail. Day suits in rich jeweled colors sported fur at neck and wrist. Bead-fringed dresses swung against *soutache* embroidered ones. Peacock-feathered hats and elegant little toques vied with stoles and muffs of finest sable. A chinchilla coat hung temptingly within her reach. Finally Christina found the dark green dress first lent to her by Captain Reed, which belonged to his wife.

Closing her cabin door behind her, she walked along

the thickly carpeted corridor toward the stairs leading down to the decks below.

She was surprised to find that the new innovation of electric light fittings was not extended to the second class dining saloon and reception rooms, and she wondered why. It would have greatly increased comfort and at very little extra cost.

"What are you doin'?" a steward asked saucily. "Slumming it?"

"Seeing how the other half lives," Christina said with a grin. "Do me a favor and show me the inside of one of the cabins."

"I'll show you something a darn sight more interesting than the inside of a cabin if you've got five minutes," he said cheekily.

"The inside of the cabin will do. Any more lip from you and I'll give you a thick ear," Christina said good-naturedly.

"Not a patch on up top, is it?" the steward asked chattily as he opened the door for her. "And if you really want to make your heart bleed you should see *my* bunk. If you'd a shred of Christian charity you'd ask me to share your stateroom. I wouldn't 'alf keep you warm on a cold night!"

"Clear off," Christina said, with a friendly grin, and continued her inspection of the decks while the steward heaved an exaggerated sigh of disappointment.

She was a one and no mistake. He'd had hopes, as had the rest of the crew, that she would have been obliging with her favors. He'd been disappointed, and if rumor was anything to be believed, so had the passengers. Victor Jackson had steadfastly refused to say where he had found her, but wherever it had been, she was a lady all right. He watched her long graceful stride, her slender hips swaying beneath the soft fabric of her skirt, and fantasized happily.

Christina found the second class deck spartan and cheerless. There were none of the patent fans that were fitted into the first class staterooms, admitting fresh air but excluding the sea. No hot running water. And the only baths and lavatories were communal, and not within easy reach of the cabins.

Thoughtfully she descended the next lot of stairs to the steerage. Second class had been quiet. Steerage was like being back in Liverpool. Shawled women chatted nonstop, cramming every inch of space on the bunks. The men stood around in the small area of deck space reserved for them, smoking pipes and spitting lustily over the side. Children scrambled everywhere. Babies cried. Food was being cooked on a makeshift stove. Lacking any refinement at all, it seemed to Christina that the steerage passengers were enjoying themselves hugely.

For the rest of the voyage Christina carried out her part of the bargain she had struck with Theo, charming and flirting with his illustrious first class passengers, but in her free moments she sought the company of steerage, sharing with them their elation as word spread they were approaching their destination: America, the land of all their dreams.

As at Liverpool, the reporters hastily scanned the purser's passenger list and waylaid all the notables, artistically arranging Fletch Jerome against the deck rails with a lifebelt around his neck.

Christina watched with interest as the pilot boat followed the Coastguard cutter, noting with amusement that the seamen who boarded the *Corinthia* to guide her through the Narrows and into New York Bay looked more like suited businessmen than sailors. With Captain Reed's permission she stood unobtrusively by their side as they piloted the ship through the upper bay.

This time Christina enjoyed every moment of the sight of the West Side of Manhattan and the Hudson opening away before her, with the brownstone houses high above, as the *Corinthia* docked in the long line of piers protruding like giant fingers into the murky waters.

The thin, mouselike figure of the Goldenberg representative personally escorted Christina down the gang plank and into the waiting open-topped Rolls-Royce, and the chauffeur sped through the city streets to where Theo Goldenberg waited impatiently.

"Honey," he said as she entered the bedroom of his apartment, "it's been too long a time."

It was a long time before Theobald Goldenberg spoke again. When he did it was to say: "I thought I'd dreamt it before. Now I know it's for real."

Theo made her feel like a woman again, making her body respond with a passion that was at the very core of her nature. None of her flirtations and light kisses on the moonlit decks of the *Corinthia* had stirred her in the slightest.

It was twelve hours before they dressed and sat down to a candle-lit dinner of lobster and champagne.

"Captain Reed tells me you are launching a new ship soon," Christina said, enjoying the languor Theo's lovemaking had induced.

"That's right."

"Will she be like the *Corinthia?*"

"Three funnels, twin screws, turbine engines, only bigger and a lot more fancier."

"Because you want to rival the major shipping companies?"

"I *am* a major shipping company," Theo growled and pinched her knee underneath the table, letting his hand linger beneath the warmth of her legs.

"If you were, you would make your English port of call Southampton, not Liverpool."

Theo's eyes sharpened. "Why?"

Christina told him.

He nodded. "Any other ideas?"

"Plenty." She laid down her knife and fork. "You'll never rival a ship like the *Mauretania* by trying to imitate her decor. It isn't possible. But you could be different."

"How so?" Theo was rapidly beginning to appreciate Christina's sharp brains as much as her beauty.

"What are you naming the new ship?"

"It isn't decided. Which is probably a good thing as you're going to go right ahead and tell me what I *am* going to name her!"

"Call her the *Swan*. Everything else at sea ends in *ia*. And do her out in white instead of that Victorian damask and gilt. Have lots of mirrors and potted palms. Have the wood pale oak instead of mahogany and cream silk walls instead of heavy red damask. Be daring. Make the *Swan* different from any of the other ships on the Atlantic route."

Theo stared at her. "You know what a risk I'd be taking, don't you?"

"I know what taste is," Christina said with confidence, "and I can bring it to the *Swan;* first class, second class *and* steerage."

Theo lit a cigar. "I must be losing my marbles, but I'm going to let you have a free hand with her. Because something tells me you're right." He blew a cloud of fragrant smoke into the air. "And it felt right to take you the first time I set eyes on you. I know I'm never going to regret it. Let's get back to bed. I'll take you to see the ship's designer in the morning. Right now there's more pressing business."

To Captain Reed's surprise President Goldenberg informed him that Christina would not be sailing for a while, as she was helping with the refitting of the new Goldenberg ship. Caleb Reed had shaken his head in admiration. She hadn't wasted her chances there!

In the fall she was back aboard the *Corinthia*, elated at the success of her decor on the *Swan*. The ship would not be ready to be launched until the spring, but the carpenters and painters were following Christina's instructions to the letter, and she had Theo's promise that she could travel with the *Swan* on her maiden voyage. At the moment Theo was busy securing the best possible crew for her. None of his existing captains fit Theo's idea of what the captain of the *Swan* should be. He wanted someone young, yet with experience. Someone with dash yet able to take responsibility for hundreds of lives in a crisis. On his desk he read the memo from his personal secretary and leafed through the attached documents: The Conyates Shipping Company. A grand title for a fleet of one ship.

He read the history of the *Ninevah*'s captain carefully. Devlin O'Conner sounded just the type of man he needed on the Goldenberg Line, but he was a partner of the Conyates Shipping Company. It wouldn't be easy to persuade him to give up his partnership and join him at Goldenberg. Still, it would be worth the try.

Christina spent the winter in New York in Theo's penthouse suite. She had been reluctant to do so.

"Surely you should spend Christmas with your family," she had said, a frown creasing her forehead.

"The kids have gone to Europe skiing." Theo pulled her closer to him on the sofa, enjoying the warmth and scent of the pinelogs that burned fiercely in the grate.

"But your wife."

Mrs. Goldenberg was a subject never mentioned. Apart from knowing that Theo had despatched her smartly to Rhode Island the first day he had met her, she knew nothing else about her. Wherever Mrs. Goldenberg was now, it certainly wasn't in Theo's sumptuous New York apartment.

Theo's leonine features hardened. God knows, he'd stopped loving Mildred years ago, but he'd always shown her respect, and behaved discreetly. When the rumors first filtered through to him he had been frankly disbelieving, but Grainger had worked for him a long time and the man had been genuinely embarrassed. Theo had decided to investigate the goings-on at his home on Rhode Island more thoroughly. There were times when he wished he hadn't.

Mildred Goldenberg was in her early fifties, a plump faded figure beside that of her husband. She had long ago stopped trying to please him. She had given him two children and her health, despite what Theobald's doctors said to the contrary, was delicate. Another baby would surely have killed her. Besides, she detested all that grunting and groaning, the heaviness and sweat of Theobald's body on hers, the vulgarity of the whole proceedings that Theobald seemed to enjoy with such relish. Her fastidiousness had finally communicated itself to her husband. She had come from the best of New York families. Her pedigree as a wife was impeccable. Outwardly, the Goldenbergs were a successful, happily married couple. Privately, they lived separate lives. Mildred spent endless days gossiping with friends, discussing dress patterns and changes in fashion.

There were the children to consider, too. Neither Theobald Junior or little Daphne seemed to have any rapport with their vigorous and outgoing father. For a comfortable twenty years Mildred devoted herself to their interests and then they no longer seemed to need her. They went off to stay with friends. Enjoyed trips abroad without her. It was all very depressing. Until her sudden departure from New York to Rhode Island.

Mildred, terrified of every germ, real or imaginary, had needed no urging to leave the confines of the city when Theobald had told her an epidemic had broken out. The Rhode Island home was ready and waiting for her when she arrived. The permanent staff had aired her bed and put fresh flowers in all the rooms. There was, the butler told her, a new neighbor. A Miss Maude Lorenzo. On the second day after Mildred's arrival Miss Lorenzo paid a call. Mildred liked her immediately. She was much younger than herself, with soft blonde hair and gentle eyes and a voice soothing to Mildred's shattered nerves. A pleasant contrast to Theo's loud laughter and voluble swearing.

On closer acquaintance Mildred realized that her new young friend didn't have quite the same financial resources as she did, and found great pleasure in surprising her with little but expensive gifts.

Maude's gentle fingers were expert in smoothing away the tension in Mildred's forehead when she was beset by one of her innumerable headaches. For the first time in her life Mildred had found someone who really understood her delicate health and the suffering that went with it.

"Theo never did," she complained. "He always used to say a good walk was all I needed."

Maude murmured sympathetically, her fingers stroking Mildred's brow. "Men are so callous."

For the first time Mildred heard her own sentiments expressed and she agreed fervently.

Maude's skillful fingers moved from Mildred's forehead to the base of her neck, massaging gently. Mildred sighed with pleasure.

"They have no understanding," Maude said sympathetically. "None at all. Only one woman can truly love and understand another."

"You're so right my dear, so right." Mildred's headache had nearly disappeared and she felt more relaxed than she could ever remember.

It was easier for Maude to massage Mildred's head and shoulders in the privacy of Mildred's bedroom than in the drawing room where there were so many unwarranted interruptions.

Within two weeks, guided by the persuasive and skillful Maude, Mildred Goldenberg had found a pleasure in life previously denied her. That of sex.

The massages had increased in intimacy and Maude, having taken a bath in Mildred's bathroom, had inadvertently exposed herself to Mildred and, overcome with shyness, had asked Mildred if she thought her body was attractive.

Mildred had thought it the most beautiful thing in the world.

As to when the two women had become lovers, Grainger, the butler, did not know. But by the end of the first month he was more than sure that they were. His loyalty was wholly Theobald's. He found not the slightest pleasure in having to inform him that his wife was acting indiscreetly—and with another woman.

Another man Theo could have stomached. Would even have welcomed. At least it would have shown him that Mildred had some warmth in her veins. But this! It was beyond his comprehension.

For Mildred's sake, for the sake of his children and also because, despite his human weaknesses, Theo had an ingrained respect for marriage, he had told Christina right at the outset that he would never divorce his wife. Now he felt completely free to do so.

"Honey," he cupped her chin in his hand. "Give me the best Christmas present in the world. I'm getting a divorce—tell me you'll marry me."

Christina stared at him in amazement. "But your wife . . ."

"Forget about her. I'm getting a divorce whether you marry me or not. What's your answer?"

Their eyes held in the firelit room, and Theo could see all the conflicting emotions chasing each other through Christina's amber eyes. The last one was one of sadness. Theo knew her answer.

'Why?"

Savagely he drove his fist into one of the cushions. 'We make love like it's never been made before. You're faithful to me. I knew that beyond a doubt. Even though you've had dukes and earls and multimillionaires hanging around you. So why not?"

Christina struggled to understand her own emotions. She liked Theo. She admired and respected him, but though he sparked off and satisfied the passionate side of her nature, she did not love him as she had loved Devlin.

The memories that she kept so firmly hidden rushed to the surface, showing on her face.

"It's him, isn't it?" Theo said angrily. "The bastard who left you in Liverpool? You're still in love with him, aren't you?"

Her face was white and she could feel herself tremble.

"I'm sorry, Theo. Truly I am."

He pulled her toward him, his brief anger subsiding, comforting her tenderly.

"If I ever get hold of that son of a bitch I'll hang him from the nearest yardarm," he said grimly, rocking her in his arms, wondering if it wasn't about time he got Reed to have a word with the young captain of the *Ninevah*.

Chapter 23

"I see the Duke of Marne is aboard again," Captain Reed said with a twinkle in his eye. "You'll be a duchess yet if you're not careful!"

"Silly," Christina said affectionately. "He just likes my company, that's all. No trying to lure me to his stateroom with iced champagne like the American congressman in Suite A-4."

"Do you realize it's a year now since you stowed

away?'' Caleb asked, staring out over the heaving waves.

'' 'Stowed away' is a very polite way of putting it,'' Christina said with a grin. ''Carried away would be more accurate.''

Caleb shook his head in fond reminiscence. ''God, what a little wildcat you were. Eyes flashing, your hair looking as if it had never seen a brush in its life, and cursing and swearing to be returned to Liverpool.''

''I think you're exaggerating the cursing and swearing,'' Christina said primly. ''I was simply annoyed.''

Caleb laughed. ''I'll say you were and I can't blame you! Still, it's all been for the best. I shall miss you when you leave the *Corinthia* for the *Swan*.''

Christina patted his arm. ''If the schedules are kept the ships should cross mid-ocean. I'll make sure the *Swan*'s captain gives three blasts every time we do.''

''*When* they get a captain,'' Caleb corrected.

''Mr. Goldenberg has been holding out to get the young captain of the *Ninevah*. Seems he isn't as grateful for the chance of captaining the *Swan* as Mr. Goldenberg thinks he should. Leastways he hasn't agreed to meet and talk to Mr. Goldenberg about it, and all the other applicants have been turned down. Mr. Goldenberg will have to come to a decision soon. The ship is ready to be launched and crewed, and it's the captain's privilege to hand-pick his officers. As it happens, we'll be in Southampton the same time as the *Ninevah* this trip and I've got strict instructions to make contact with her captain to make sure he understands what Mr. Goldenberg is offering. Fancy turning down the chance of a ship like the *Swan!*'' Caleb sighed. ''It seems almost unbelievable.''

''What sort of ship is the *Ninevah?*''

''Small compared to the Cunarders and White Stars. Apparently she was resurrected from a battered hulk and it was her captain who achieved the miracle. He's young, which is certainly what Mr. Goldenberg wants, and knows his job. For my own sake I hope I can get

him to agree. Otherwise I can see Mr. Goldenberg
pensioning me off.''

"Nonsense," Christina said stoutly. "You're the
most experienced and respected captain in the fleet."

"And the oldest. There's not many of us old Cape
Horners left now, though I believe the *Ninevah*'s captain sailed three-masted barks and whalers too as a
boy."

"Then he sounds just the man for the *Swan*. I'm
looking forward to meeting him."

On the promenade deck below the bridge she caught
a glimpse of the Duke of Marne braving the sea air.
He waved his ebony-topped cane at her and she waved
back.

"Away with you," Caleb said affectionately. "Keep
him happy. He's becoming as permanent a figure on
board the *Corinthia* as yourself. His suite is reserved
for the next two months!"

Christina adjusted the sable scarf around her throat
and, enjoying the fresh breeze on her face, made her
way down to the promenade deck and the duke.

"Watch out for the American," the duke said, nodding in the direction of the congressman. "At home
he's an outspoken crusader against vice. Away from
it he's a notorious lecher. Prudes always are."

"So I've already discovered."

The Duke smiled. "I don't know how you do it.
Don't you ever find yourself in compromising situa-
tions?"

"All the time," Christina agreed cheerfully, "but
I always get out of them."

The Duke laughed and they continued their stroll,
acknowledging the greetings of their fellow first class
passengers who sat in deck chairs, half hidden by rugs
and blankets, determined to enjoy the experience of
the Atlantic, even if it *was* colder and rougher than
the publicity brochures had made out.

The Duke of Marne was seldom at a loss for words,

and he was not a man to act hastily. What he was about to say he had thought about long and hard.

"I suppose you get lots of proposals of marriage, Christina?"

They had long ago reached the intimacy of Christian names, though Christina preferred to refer to him affectionately as "Duke" rather than "Frederick," which didn't suit him in the least.

"It has happened," Christina agreed, not liking to say that there hadn't been a trip when it hadn't.

"Millionaires, state governors, copper-mine owners. Yet you never accept any of them. Why?"

"I've never loved any of them."

"Ah, love." The Duke leaned over the deck rail, gazing at the scudding foam far below, pondering on the great force that was love when one was as young as Christina.

"Your husband must have been a very fine man."

Christina leaned her elbows on the brass rails and cupped her chin in her hands. She owed Theo the loyalty of playing the part he had assigned to her, but it was becoming increasingly difficult. The initial heady intoxication of wearing beautiful evening dresses and fine furs, of being courted by rich men, old and young alike, was now nothing but a rather boring way of passing the time. The sea was her only compensation. To be at sea. To enjoy the sight of the endless waves and the limitless horizon. Here and *only* here did her spirit feel free. But the Duke had become her closest friend, and as such he deserved honesty.

"I never had a husband."

The Duke's face didn't change expression by so much as a flicker.

"Would you consider me as one?"

"You wouldn't ask that if you knew anything about me. I'm not what I seem."

"Very few of us are," the Duke said drily.

Christina grinned. "My father was a sailor. My

mother a Spanish gypsy. They loved each other but they were never married. I don't think that they would fit into the Marne family tree very well."

"With the Marnes it was rather the other way round. They married but never loved each other."

They laughed and then the Duke said, "You still haven't given me your answer."

Christina shook her head, her eyes clouded. "A man to whom I owe everything and who I care for very deeply asked me in America and I refused. I don't want marriage, Duke. I did once, but not any longer."

Abruptly she turned and walked away from him. He remained at the deck rail. Whoever the man had been, the duke thought, he had hurt her very deeply.

At dinner that evening the conversation was all about the new White Star liner, the *Titanic*.

"She's colossal," the First Officer said. "If she stood vertical she'd be higher than the Washington Monument."

"The biggest ship in the world," little Adam Rooney said in awe. He was only fourteen and quite overcome by the privilege of dining at the captain's table. His father, a State Governor with all the self-assurance of a Harvard background, dragged his attention from the beautiful woman on the captain's right hand and said, "That's right son. There's never been a ship like her before. I reckon you'll be sailing empty from now on, Captain Reed."

Captain Reed smiled. "I doubt it, Mr. Rooney. Goldenberg ships may be smaller, but for comfort and cuisine they are unbeatable, and our new vessel, the *Swan*, is years ahead of her time in interior decor. His eyes met those of Christina. "Her launching will cause quite a furor in the press I can tell you."

Little Adam Rooney wasn't interested in the *Swan*. "Is it true the *Titanic* is unsinkable?"

"Most ships are these days," his father said genially. "Isn't that so, captain? Watertight bulkheads and all that. There's no more danger left in crossing the Atlantic these days than there is in crossing the street."

Captain Reed, whose job it was to instill confidence in his passengers as to the safety of the ship on which they were traveling, agreed, but privately retained doubts. He was too old a sailor to believe that anything at sea was unsinkable.

"We're coming back on her," Mr. Rooney said proudly. "Couldn't miss a chance like that. She sails on the tenth of April so it's only a week later than we would have been sailing anyway. Sorry about that Captain Reed, but I'm sure you understand. Junior here would never forgive me if I did otherwise."

"I understand you too are deserting the *Corinthia* on that particular trip?" Captain Reed said, turning to the Duke of Marne.

The Duke nodded. "Just for the maiden voyage. As Mr. Rooney says, it's a once in a lifetime experience not to be missed."

Mr. Rooney's eyes were back on Christina. She wore a black fringed dress decorated with jet and black pearls, her hair wound loosely on the top of her head in deep waves, a stray curling tendril touching her cheek. He had to fight an overwhelming temptation to reach across and stroke it gently back into place. He willed her eyes to rise and meet his, but they remained firmly lowered as she toyed with her salmon mousse.

The *Titanic* was to sail on the anniversary of her mother's birthday, and though the Duke had not said so, she had a stateroom booked and adjoining his. Theobald had been insistent that she take the first possible opportunity of sailing aboard his rival's newest and biggest liner. He wanted full details about her. The furnishings, the food, the service, the amount of roll she had in heavy seas. The *Swan* was due to be launched in early June, and Theobald wanted to have all his publicity material ready with one hundred reasons why travelers should prefer the *Swan* to the gigantic *Titanic*. He was hoping that her enormous size would make her unwieldy, especially when it came to docking in New York's notoriously heavily silted bay. Christina was to look out for and magnify the slightest defect.

"Big," Theobald had said, jabbing his cigar at his public relations men, "isn't necessarily better. We have to get that point over, and over hard!"

Returning on the *Titanic* meant that she would have nearly three weeks on shore. The duke had again asked her to visit Anersley but she had refused. Instead she wanted to look for Merry and Josh. Her life was too full of acquaintances and too empty of friends for her to lose contact with two of the people she cared about most. There was Theo and Caleb and the duke. Apart from them she had no one. The *Corinthia* never docked in Liverpool now, and the Gaiety seemed light years away.

Christina sighed. Merry was living happily with Josh. Molly was now a proud mother. For a second she envisaged a red-haired baby boy gurgling with pleasure as he tottered on fat little legs toward her outstretched arms. She moved abruptly, banishing the thought, adjusting the emerald ring that had been Theo's last present to her. Why did such idiotic fancies invade her mind? Devlin O'Conner had been nothing but a shallow womanizer, and she had been more than well rid of him. Why, if she wanted to now, she could be a duchess! Her sons would be the elite of English society, not barefoot ragamuffins living on a schooner or tramp steamer.

Only—an insistent voice whispered to her—Devlin had sold himself for a liner, not a tramp steamer. In all that time she had never tried to find out what liner. The knowledge would only have been an added pain.

"Fool," she said, giving herself a mental shake. Why should Devlin O'Conner still invade her private thoughts? She was over him long ago. Instead she remembered Theo greeting her the last time she had berthed in New York; his divorce was under way and he no longer gave a damn for convention. He had ordered his private yacht dressed stem to stern with fluttering pennants to meet the *Corinthia* out in the bay, and as the yacht had swung alongside the *Corinthia*'s passengers had crowded the deck rails, watching as he seized a rope ladder and climbed the fifty feet to the deck with a cigar rammed firmly in his mouth and a straw boater on his head. On hearing that the enterprising gentleman was none other than *the* Mr. Goldenberg of the Goldenberg Line, a huge cheer had gone up and Theo had grinned, tossed the butt of his cigar over the side into the murky waters, and headed straight for Christina's stateroom.

"If you change your mind I shall send my chauffeur to you immediately," the Duke said as they bade each other goodbyes at Southampton. "Change it now, Christina. Come to Anersley with me."

"No." She smiled. "It's only three weeks and then we'll have the *Titanic* to enjoy together."

"We could have the three weeks to enjoy together, too. If you saw Anersley perhaps you would change your mind about other things."

She shook her head. "I want to look up old friends."

The duke sighed, acknowledging defeat. He wanted her, yet a sixth sense had told him it would be unwise to make any physical advances to her. The relationship he had built up with her had taken time and patience and he didn't want to jeopardize it. Perhaps on board the *Titanic* things would be different.

Christina dug her hands deeper into the black and white fox muff and, with the matching hat tilted provocatively over one eye, waved him goodbye.

The duke waved back, wondering if any of his friends would believe him if he told them he was irrevocably in love with a girl he had never kissed and who regarded him only as a friend. He had been regarded as a lot of things by countless women but "friend" had never been one of them. His skill and experience as a lover told him he could have her for his mistress whenever he wanted, but if he did it would end there. And Frederick, Duke of Marne, wanted more. Over the last few months he had become more and more convinced that he wanted Christina, bastard and gypsy though she cheerfully admitted she was, as his wife.

Christina booked in at the South Western Hotel, ignoring the curious stares and raised eyebrows that a woman on her own inevitably caused. The aura of wealth that surrounded her, the initialed luggage, the exquisite fur hat and muff saw to it that no questions were asked. Deferentially a page boy carried her cases to her room and an hour later Christina, bathed and dressed, descended, moving through the lounge with an unconscious grace that turned every head.

Josh was a boilermaker. A young boy of about eight, overawed by the perfumed vision before him, could only be persuaded to speak when Christina reverted to her Northern dialect and said, "Please luv, what pub do the boilermakers 'ang out in?"

A large piece of silver pushed into his hand went some way to enabling him to recover his speech.

"There's the Lamb and Flag and the Old Oak. And the Duke of York."

"Thank you." She had been bending down to him, and now she stood up.

"But *you* can't go in them. They're not for the likes of you!"

"Don't worry." Christina patted his grubby cheek with an exquisitely gloved hand. "I've been in far worse places."

The inmates of the Lamb and Flag gazed mesmerized as a vision in white fox fur hat stepped over the filthy threshold and into their male domain.

"Josh Lucas. Does anyone know him please?"

Shock at such an invasion rendered them dumb, then, gathering his wits, the barman said, "Sorry madam. Better try the police. Reckon they'll catch him for you.''

Undeterred, Christina made her way to the Duke of York, while the Lamb and Flag's occupants agreed by common consensus that the lady was obviously not quite right in her head to be wandering in and out of pubs on her own.

She met the same reaction in the Duke of York, with the exception of one brave laborer who asked if he'd do instead. Christina had pertly replied that she'd tell him in another two years when he was old enough to shave, and left amidst a roar of laughing approval.

"Third time lucky," she thought, entering the dark and smoky interior of the Old Oak. "Josh Lucas?" the barman said. "Big fella from up north?"

"That's right." Christina's heart rose.

"Lives in the row of cottages round the back. Number thirteen or fourteen."

"Thank you." Christina took a note out of her bag and gave it to him.

The barman eyed it apprehensively. "I hope he isn't in trouble. He always seemed like a good man to me. A bit on the quiet side, but an honest worker. I don't think it's him you want."

Christina felt a sudden wave of nervous hostility from the listening men. She understood immediately. Here she came, sweeping into a workingmen's pub in her kid gloves, Worth suit and fur hat and muff. They probably thought she was taking justice into her own hands and looking for him because he had stolen her silver. She laughed and to everyone's amazement seated herself on a bar stool.

"He's a friend," she said chattily. "How about a pint of bitter?"

There was a moment's stunned silence and then the barman grinned and pulled on the pump handle.

"By bloody hell," he said. "Where did you spring from?"

"Up north, same as Josh Lucas."

"He's got a wife now, love," someone called out from one of the crowded tables.

"I know, and she's my mate," Christina called back, and lifted the foaming pint glass in her hand. "Cheers!" she said, raising it to her lips and drinking it down without a break till the glass was drained. She hadn't been one of Bessie's girls for nothing.

The men watched her open mouthed. "By bloody hell," the barman said again, while the men thronged round her, all eager to show her personally to the Lucas's cottage.

In the end over a dozen of them left the Old Oak with her, while the barman watched the fox fur hat bob gaily down the street and dazedly picked up the foam-flecked pint glass to wash it.

"By bloody hell," he said to himself again. "I wouldn't have believed it if I hadn't seen it!"

The strange procession rounded the corner of tiny cottages, so like the ones in Liverpool that Christina felt her heart suddenly constrict. Then she saw number thirteen. Frilly net curtains veiled the windows. Spring flowers filled the tiny front garden, herbs crammed into a roughly made window box, the scarlet of tulips lining the miniature path that led from the street to the front door. The doorstep was scoured and white stoned, and the door and windows had been painted a gay blue. Trudging round her the army of men whistled and shouted so that curtain after curtain twitched back to see what was happening and long before Christina reached the gate of number thirteen Merry had thrown open the door and was running down the path to meet her. The men ringed them in an applauding throng, as Merry, in clogs and starched, flowered apron, wrapped her arms around her friend. Christina's eyes were bright with tears and the men quietened down, slightly abashed.

"Come on in, luv. What are you doin' with this mob?"

"Met 'em in the Oak."

"She can't 'alf down a pint of beer!" one of them shouted as Merry's front door closed in their faces.

Christina looked around her. The tiny room glittered with care and cleanliness. The large table had a spotless white cloth on it, laid for tea. There was a wooden breadboard, a large loaf still warm from the oven, a hunk of cheese and a big teapot with roses on the side.

"*Josh! Josh!*" Merry was calling up the stairs. "Do come down and see who's here! You'll never believe it. Oh, Christina! I'm so glad you've come. It's grand to see you, really grand—" she broke off, coughing harshly.

Christina's radiant smile vanished. She had been too near Merry to have seen her clearly before. Too busy kissing and hugging her. Now with an ice-cold shock she saw that Merry had lost weight, her shoulder blades gaunt under the patterned apron. As she coughed into her handkerchief Christina saw the tiny flecks of blood that Merry deftly hid and then Josh was in the room, big and blundering, knocking the table so that the teapot rocked precariously.

She was lost in a bearlike embrace, her hat falling onto the floor. Finally he held her at arm's length and they looked at each other. Josh smiled sheepishly.

"You look smashing, luv."

"Look at this hat!" Merry picked it up and placed it on her short curls, prancing gaily round the tiny room. "Seems to me like you've a lot to tell us, so you might as well do it over some bread and cheese and a cup of tea."

She began to cough again and Josh's exuberant expression turned to one of consternation. He put his arm around her shaking shoulders while Merry coughed chokingly. To Christina it seemed to go on forever.

Then at last, white faced, Merry raised her head, smiling gallantly.

"Stupid old cough," she said dismissively. "Nothing that a bit of Northern air wouldn't cure."

Christina's eyes met Josh's. At what she saw there she wanted to cry out in protest.

"Now then," Merry was saying with her old gaiety. "Where did the fur and feathers come from? Father Christmas?"

It was dark by the time Christina had finished telling them about Caleb and Theo and the Duke. Josh and Merry sat on their shabby sofa, hand in hand, listening enthralled. There was no need for Christina to ask if they were happy together. Whenever Josh looked at the little figure by his side his eyes were full of such devotion that Christina felt a pang. Of jealousy or of loneliness she didn't know. She only knew that she was happy for them. But at increasing intervals as the evening wore on Merry was wracked by paroxysms of coughing.

"So you're staying with the gentry at the South Western," Josh said. "You *could* have stayed here. But I expect you wouldn't feel comfortable. Not after living so fine, like."

"I'd *love* to stay here," Christina said eagerly. "I could sleep on the sofa. I wouldn't be any trouble."

"Do you *really* want to stay?" Merry's eyes shone.

"Course I do. The South Western isn't a patch on this place. No homemade bread there!"

"You'd have to go a long way to find homemade bread like my Merry's," Josh said proudly. Merry squeezed his hand and blushed.

And so it was that their neighbors were privileged to see two amazing sights in one day. The second being Josh Lucas carrying pigskin cases on his giant shoulders, down the street and into his little cottage. The Lucas's had a visitor, and whoever she was she was someone to talk about.

"Never seen the like of it," was the general opinion, and it was one that didn't change as Christina entered with gusto into the local life of the street, becoming the toast of the Old Oak much as she had the *Corinthia*. In the cottage she took all the work off Merry's frail shoulders, making her rest and summoning the best doctor in town to have a look at her.

"He's a friend," she lied glibly to them. "Ever such a nice man and a doctor as well. Might as well let him have a listen to that cough."

"She's seen the doctors," Josh said when Merry was out of the room.

Christina nodded. "I know, but this one is a specialist. He ought to be able to help."

He couldn't. It could be months or it could be weeks. Whichever it was there was nothing he could do.

When at last Christina could speak she said almost inaudibly to Josh, "You knew already, didn't you?"

He nodded. Upstairs in the bedroom Merry slept. Josh's eyes were bright with tears.

Merry died on the 29th of March, and Christina and Josh were the only mourners. The whole street would have come but Josh had wanted it like that. Just him and Christina—and Merry.

He had wept unashamedly at the graveside, looking stiff and uncomfortable in his Sunday suit, his clumsy hands turning his hat round and round, refusing to leave until the last shovelful of earth had been scattered.

"What will you do now?" she asked as they entered the cottage, the brightness and glitter seeming to have vanished overnight. Without Merry it was only a shell. Just another cottage, nothing more.

"I don't know." He sat down heavily on the sofa, his head in his hands. "I can't stay here. Not without her."

There was a long silence as the shadows outside lengthened and deepened into twilight.

"Maybe I'll try America. I've heard there's opportunity in America."

"I think America would suit you, Josh." She took his hand, holding it tightly. "Let me pay for your passage . . ."

He shook his head. "No lass. I'd rather work my way there. I'll get a job on one of the ships. I'll manage."

"But you hate the sea. It always makes you sick."

"Nothing can make me sicker than I am," he said simply. "I loved her and now she's gone."

He began to cry like a child and Christina, blinded by her own tears, fumbled to put the kettle on the range and make them some tea.

That night she moved back into the hotel. Not that she cared a damn what people might think, but they were Josh's neighbors and he had to live amongst them. He might change his mind and stay on in Southampton. If he did it wouldn't help if the gossip mongers spread a tale of how he had another woman stay the night with him only hours after burying his wife.

In utter weariness she entered her bedroom at the South Western and slowly eased off her elbow-length kid gloves and threw them on the bed. Then she kicked off her shoes and walked into the bathroom, turning both bath taps full on and undoing the tiny buttons of her jacket as steam gushed into the air.

There was a knock on the bedroom door. Listlessly she opened it to a page boy who handed her a cablegram. She opened it and there, her first thought being that Theo had been taken ill. It was from Caleb and read simply, MR. GOLDENBERG WANTS YOU TO SEE CAPTAIN OF NINEVAH AND REPORT BACK TO HIM OPINION IN CONFIDENCE STOP MEETING ARRANGED NINE O'CLOCK ABOARD NINEVAH FRIDAY THE FOURTH STOP CALEB.

She looked at her wristwatch. It was already after eight. "There's no reply," she said to the page boy, giving him a tip, "but please ask for a cab to collect me at eight forty-five."

"Yes ma'am," he grinned at her, but for the first time received no answering grin back. She looked as if she'd been crying. What she needed was cheering up. Having become an expert at reading confidential cablegrams from awkward angles, the page boy jangled Christina's generous tip in his pocket and hoped that the *Ninevah*'s captain would be the fellow to do it.

Chapter 24

The cab smelled stale and musty and reeked of old cigar butts and cracked leather. Christina dug her hands into her muff and wrapped the soft long folds of her walking suit so that it did not trail in the debris littering the cab floor.

Christina's head throbbed. The last thing she wanted was to assess any future captain for the *Swan*. She wanted to submerge her grief in sleep. She wondered how Theo had explained her visit to the *Ninevah*'s captain. Did he know his future lay in her hands? Did he care? Or did he simply think he was extending courtesy to one of Theobald Goldenberg's associates? Already her ability in design was becoming known in the shipping industry. Those that had been privileged enough to see aboard the *Swan* had been unanimous in their verdict that the interior design was revolutionary. And Theo had made sure that all the credit had been accorded to Christina.

The cab bumped unevenly over the rough cobbles, and through a murky pane of glass Christina could see the light of the setting sun flashing in the portholes of tugs and shining in swathes of yellow and orange over the dark water. The sails of a schooner glowed in the last flush of rose and she could see sailors busy loading stores aboard as the ship bucked on the evening tide.

"Here we are, missus," the cabbie shouted to her.

Christina tipped him handsomely and in the growing darkness picked her way carefully between hawsers and crates toward the *Ninevah*'s lowered gangplank.

She stepped across the brass threshold into warmth and light—and silence. There was no movement from the ship. In the distance she could hear the thud and rattle of anchor chains. Then silence again. Curiously she walked to the companion-way, noting with interest the plush, rococo elegance of the decor. The *Ninevah*, though smaller, had been fitted out in the grand manner of the Cunarders. A young petty officer strode smartly to meet her.

"Welcome aboard the *Ninevah*, Mrs. de Villiers. The captain's compliments, and he is awaiting you in his cabin."

Christina smiled, and the petty officer felt his heart tighten in his chest. He'd heard about her of course, but he had expected the cool, brittle beauty of a wealthy English gentlewoman. Instead he was faced with lustrous dark eyes, silken lashes and flawless olive-toned skin. Jet black hair gleamed in a smooth chignon and though she looked tired, her smile was warm and wide, without any of the usual reserve to be found in women of her class.

A seaman approaching them from the opposite direction gazed at her with open admiration and was rewarded with the same guileless smile.

"The old man's in luck tonight," she heard him say to a companion, when he thought her safely out of earshot.

With a great mental effort Christina pushed the previous events of the day to the back of her mind and concentrated on the job in hand. She knew the *Ninevah*'s captain was only in his early thirties. Theo had told her so. The expression "the old man" was one used about any captain, regardless of age. Nevertheless, she felt a sudden trepidation in meeting him. Theo had turned down dozens of eager applicants for the job of captaining the *Swan*. All of them men with vast sailing experience. Some of them, men who had captained Goldenberg liners for over fifteen years. Theo had a short list of one or two likely names. Sadly Captain Reed was not amongst them. But he refused to make a decision until he had done everything in his power to persuade the *Ninevah*'s captain to change his allegiance from Conyates to Goldenberg.

Christina knew that was one of the reasons for the meeting tonight. Not only was she to assess the *Ninevah*'s captain's suitability, but she also had to do everything in her power to persuade him to meet Theo on his return to New York and to consider seriously where his future best lay. That it lay with the Goldenberg line went without saying.

The narrow corridor was lit softly by two lamps in gilt brackets on either side of the captain's carved oak door. The carpet beneath her feet was thick, and the same wine red as the walls. There was no sound of life aboard the *Ninevah*. The seaman she had passed had long since disappeared with his friend. There was no sign of luggage or cargo being loaded. No sign of refueling or restocking. The *Ninevah* lay in slumbrous silence as the petty officer knocked deferentially on the door and opened it.

Christina stepped inside. The cabin was even bigger than Caleb's aboard the *Corinthia*. A table gleaming with white napery and silver shone beneath the soft light of a lamp. A bottle of champagne was cooling in a lavishly engraved ice-bucket. Fine china plates held a delicious selection of hors d'oeuvres. Beyond the giant mahogany desk with its litter of papers, bookshelves ranged the wall and Christina felt a surge of pleasure at the sight of so many leather-bound volumes. Theo, as always, had been right. The *Ninevah*'s captain was definitely a man of distinctive tastes.

His back was toward her and in shadow, out of the

warm circle of light above the table. He was pouring himself a brandy and did not turn at her entrance. Christina, unused to such discourtesy, studied the broad back in its brass bound uniform with interest. Perhaps he resented her being thrust upon him in this way, and she couldn't blame him. Time in port was precious and not to be spent on fripperies. A bronzed hand replaced the cut-glass decanter on the desk and he turned toward her.

The lamp swung over Christina's head, casting a halo of gold above her dark hair. He felt his resolution weaken as desire flooded through him; then he was master of himself, stepping forward as she gasped in disbelief at the pelt of curling red hair. She felt the room spin around her in a dizzying vortex of light and color. The blood thundered in her ears and it felt as though a band of iron was squeezing tightly around her chest; she had to fight for breath and consciousness.

Devlin smiled and swirled the brandy in his glass. "Not quite the reception you expected is it, *Mrs*. de Villiers?" He emphasized the name with contempt.

Christina felt as if she were drowning; her body began trembling uncontrollably with shock, and yet she knew she must not give him the pleasure of having taken her so unawares. If it killed her she would be as indifferent, as contemptuous as he was himself.

"You knew it was me?" she asked, her voice seeming to come from light years away.

"Yes." The lines round his mouth deepened as they had when he had laughed down at her. Only now the blue eyes were as hard as flint.

"I've known who you were for the last six months. Harlot of the high seas, isn't that what they call you?"

Beneath the muff Christina's nails dug deep into her palms.

"Then your arranging to meet me here is in as bad taste as your last remark. Goodbye."

She swung on her heel, sending a wine glass crashing to the floor, sweeping to the door on a dignified exit while she could still master her warring emotions.

The brass door handle turned and the door remained closed.

Devlin laughed. "I didn't go to all this trouble," he indicated the elegantly set table with a casual wave of his hand, "to have my prisoner escape so easily."

Christina's eyes flashed. "I'm not your prisoner, Devlin O'Conner! Not your *anything!*"

He rolled the bowl of the brandy glass between strong hands and gazed at her insolently.

"That's just where you're wrong, *Mrs.* de Villiers. You're anything to any man. The captain's brat. A harlot. A whore."

He stepped so close there was only a foot between them. She could feel his breath on her cheek, smell the maleness of him. In one movement she could be in his arms, feeling the curves of her body fitting against the hardness of his. Feel the touch of his skin beneath her fingers. The curling hair springing against the palm of her hand as she whispered words of love, changing the indifference in his eyes, replacing that frightening cold contempt with love and desire.

She drew her hand back and slapped it with all the force she was capable of against his cheek.

He grasped her wrist, his eyes at last blazing to life with anger.

"There's champagne. Only the best, of course. All the things you give your body for so freely aboard the *Corinthia*. Why should I be any different?"

His grip on her wrist was so cruel that she winced.

"You didn't think I invited the notorious Mrs. de Villiers aboard the *Ninevah* for any other purpose, did you?"

With one swift movement he tore the muff from her other hand and tossed it violently across the cabin. Then his mouth came down on hers, hard and unyielding as she struggled vainly in his grasp.

It was not what he had intended. From the day he

had discovered Christina's whereabouts he had anticipated his revenge on her, but it was to have been a humiliation of words. Not for anything would he lower himself to touch so much as one strand of her hair again.

It had been early morning in New York. The sun had been pale and cold, and on the *Ninevah*'s deck Devlin had shivered in the damp as the crew prepared for yet another voyage. Stewards were piling baggage. The engines were throbbing soothingly behind the bulkheads. The buildings of Manhattan rose starkly against the skyline, a magnificent backdrop to the tangle of barges, steamers, chimneys, wharves and bridges, and the four red smokestacks of the Goldenberg liner moored at the next pier.

The Packard touring car swept along the wharf in luxurious arrogance.

"Who's that?" Devlin had asked his first officer, as a thick-set man with pugnacious features and a magnificent head of white wavy hair stepped from the chauffeur-driven car, a cigar rammed firmly between his teeth.

"Mr. Goldenberg," the first officer said reverently.

Devlin's well-shaped eyebrows rose fractionally. He had been at sea long enough to know that the owners of shipping companies seldom stepped aboard their own vessels.

And then he had seen her. She was wearing a dress of apricot-colored linen. It was cut simply and magnificently, showing off the contours of her body and breathing wealth all at the same time. Her thick black hair waved beneath a large picture hat which was secured against the breeze from the Hudson with a covering of whispy veiling tied lightly beneath her chin. A kid-gloved hand rested in that of the aggressive bulldog featured owner of the Goldenberg line, as confidently and affectionately as that of a child.

"And the woman?" Devlin's voice was tight.

"Mrs. de Villiers. She has a permanent stateroom

aboard the *Corinthia*. I believe she lost her husband very tragically, sir.'' The first officer attempted to enlighten his captain further. "A pity she isn't sailing aboard the *Ninevah.''*

"A great pity,'' Devlin said grimly, and swung on his heel as he made his way to his cabin. She had gone straight from the Gaiety to the *Corinthia*. There had been no time interval in which she could have been married and widowed. Mrs. de Villiers was a charlatan and Devlin knew quite well why Goldenberg allowed her the freedom of his ship. She was whoring across the Atlantic just as she had whored in Liverpool. No wonder so many male passengers returned time and time again on the *Corinthia*, only instead of Bessie Mulholland as protector, Christina now had Theobald Goldenberg and Devlin knew what Christina had done to gain *that* envied position.

. At the thought of her in Goldenberg's bed he swore blasphemously, his temper not helped by the sight of Kate petulantly fingering the paperweight on his desk.

"It's time you left ship,'' he said curtly. "We sail in an hour.''

"Can't I sail too?'' Kate asked sulkily.

Devlin looked at her with distaste. The desire she had once aroused in him had faded entirely. For a while he had felt responsible for her and then sorry for her. Now he felt nothing at all. He just wanted her off his back, but nothing he said or did would persuade Kate to move out of their rooms in South Street. She clung to him like a leech, alternately hurling abuse at him and then pleading with him to make love to her. An act that had once given him carnal pleasure now revolted him. Familiarity had bred contempt. Without Bessie's stern eye over her she neglected the tiresome task of washing and tried to drown any stale smell of sweat with generous applications of cheap perfume. Dirty undergarments lay for days on the floor till Devlin kicked them away with disgust.

Duane had told him to boot her out but Devlin had

helplessly said he couldn't without more cause. If only she would take up with another man, then he could. Until then he still felt some sort of responsibility for her. Duane had called him a fool and Devlin had agreed with him.

It was a tepid word to the one he would have used if he had known that Kate was profitably accommodating a growing number of sailors and asking each and every one of them if they knew of the whereabouts of Stanislav.

"There's a woman aboard the *Corinthia* every trip. Jerry told me."

Jerry was the first officer, and Devlin eyed her keenly. If he could catch her just once . . .

"She hostesses the captain's table and Jerry says she's the best attraction the *Corinthia* has. Why couldn't I do that?"

For a moment Devlin hesitated. Kate had been one of the most popular girls at the Gaiety, her tiny waist and abnormally large breasts excited men on sight. He had seen the effect she had had on the members of his own crew. But he wasn't turning the *Ninevah* into a brothel, and there was no way Kate could pass as the lady Christina was passing as.

Damn her to hell, Devlin thought savagely. She had looked as beautiful as ever as she had approached the gangplank on the arm of the middle-aged shipping owner. Clean and fresh and vital. She was just as much of a whore as Kate but she could transcend all social barriers. She had looked every inch a lady as she walked the few yards from the Packard to the ship. A mischievous one, but a lady. He had seen the impish glint in her eyes as she had turned to Goldenberg and whispered in his ear, and heard Goldenberg's deep-throated laugh as he kissed her goodbye.

"Bitch," Devlin said as he poured himself a full tumbler of brandy. "*Bitch. Bitch. Bitch!*"

Kate, thinking he was talking about her, gazed at his back through narrow eyes. She would kill him for not loving her. Not now when she was totally unprepared but when he returned. Then she would kill him and finally be free of him. He would never have Christina. Never have another woman again. It was such a simple solution that Kate couldn't imagine why she hadn't thought of it before.

She laughed, trailing her hand lightly across his unresponsive shoulders, and then to Devlin's relief she left the ship.

From then on Devlin had often asked careless questions of his first officer as to whether Mrs. de Villiers was still a permanent passenger aboard the *Corinthia*.

The first officer, who prided himself on keeping his ear to the ground, had informed him that rumor had it she was going to be the second Mrs. Goldenberg. The head of the Goldenberg Shipping Line was getting a divorce and without its being contested by his wife. It was also rumored that Mrs. de Villiers was about to end her widowhood and marry the Duke of Marne. Or young Wellesly Wallace, the son of a Detroit philanthropist; or a Russian prince.

When Devlin first received a letter from Theobald Goldenberg, proposing that they meet and discuss the captaincy of his newest vessel, the *Swan*, Devlin had screwed the paper into a tight ball and thrown it into the nearest wastepaper basket; but on receiving a cable suggesting he meet with Mrs. de Villiers, who had supervised the interior decor of the *Swan*, he had cabled back his agreement and then remained in his cabin, sitting motionless until the twilight turned to night.

The moment before he turned round had been one of the hardest in his life. He had smelled her hair, fresh and clean, and been filled with an overpowering desire to plead with her to leave Goldenberg and join him aboard the *Ninevah* and had turned toward her, still irrationally expecting to see the same Christina he had left in Liverpool. Thick black hair hanging waist long, olive skin gleaming without the aid of paint of powder, a cheap cotton blouse and skirt enhancing her firm young body and her feet as bare as when she had been a child. For a second, seeing her face Madonna-like beneath the lamp, he had instinctively moved toward her, filled with love and yearning, and then he had seen the exquisitely cut traveling suit, the fox fur of her muff, the perfectly shod feet. All because she was a whore and a harlot, incapable of being faithful to any man—even a man who had loved her as he had—and a savage bitterness had filled him till he could no longer control it.

At last she managed to wrench her head away from his, biting at him like a wildcat as she struggled to get her hands free.

Her teeth sank into his ear lobe and he yelled with pain, letting her go.

Gasping for breath she rushed to the door and turned the door knob in vain. She beat her fists on the wood, crying out for help as Devlin's hands sank into her shoulders and he dragged her, kicking and screaming, away.

"This is *my* ship," he panted. "No one will come to your aid, not even if I murder you!"

He hurled her violently onto the floor, and as she scrambled to her feet he made no effort to stop her. Instead he was taking his jacket off, throwing it over the back of a chair, undoing his shirt with rapid determination.

"*Help! Help!*" Christina rained her fists against the wood, her voice breaking with sobs.

"You're wasting your breath. Are you ready for me now Christina? You were always ready for me before. Remember?" His voice was harsh.

She turned, shrinking back against the door, the lamplight flickering over the naked muscles of his chest, his hands lowering slowly to unbuckle his belt as he approached her with the familiar arrogant swagger of his hips.

"You're ready for anyone, aren't you Christina?

Rich man, poor man, beggar man, thief. They're all the same to you, aren't they?'' His trousers followed his shirt and jacket, the buckle tinkling against the chair seat as it fell. He stood naked, his hands on his hips.

"What's the matter? Am I so different from all the other hundreds you've laid on your back for? Just because I'm the one to be taken in and fooled by you?''

"I don't know what you mean,'' her voice was a whisper. The golden red hair curling low on his neck, the strong hands bronzed by the sun, the familiar mat of tight pubic hair were all achingly familiar, all Devlin. But his eyes, his voice, were those of a stranger.

"You know what I mean all right,'' he said, moving toward her grimly. "I thought you were different. Even paid money so that you'd never have to whore again.'' He laughed harshly. "God what a fool you must have thought me! Well, I'm no fool now, Christina Haworth. You're a harlot and that's just how I'm going to treat you. Seventy pounds you had off me and I'm going to have my money's worth. Every penny of it.''

His eyes terrified her. She didn't understand what he meant and she didn't understand the insane cold fury that possessed him.

"No,'' she backed away. "No . . .''

"Oh yes,'' Devlin said softly, and raising both hands he gripped the neck of her jacket and the blouse beneath and tore them open. For a few seconds Christina had been like a rabbit cornered by a fox. Incapable of coherent thought or movement. Now she beat her clenched fists against his head as he wrenched at the band of her skirt, tearing it away as if it were no more than a covering of tissue paper, ripping the rest of her blouse and jacket from her shoulders.

She could see long scratch marks bleeding where she had raked his chest with her nails; then he picked her up in his arms, and the more she struggled the more her breasts rubbed against his chest. He threw

her down on the wide bunk and before she could even
roll to one side his weight was on top of her.

"This is what you want, isn't it?" he said crudely.
"This is bigger and better than all those old men you
whore for aboard the *Corinthia*. Those doddering
dukes and earls don't do it like this, do they Christina?" And he entered her with such savagery that she
screamed in pain.

Devlin drove himself into her, trying to expiate all
the agony, all the longing, all the humiliation she had
caused him. He wanted to hurt her till she begged for
mercy. He hated her for what she had done to him.
Hated her, he told himself again and again as he felt
the familiar softness of her beneath his hands. An intangible perfume filled the air as her hair cascaded
from its pins.

Christina arched her body vainly, trying to rid herself of him, her face wet with tears. Devlin gripped a
handful of her hair and pinned her head back as he
rode her, gazing at her with what he intended to be
contempt. His body would not obey his mind.

"Christina." Desire filled his eyes and her name on
his lips was a moan.

Involuntarily Christina's body began to move in
rhythm to his. Her nails dug deep into his flesh.

He lowered his head and this time kissed her deeply,
his tongue searching hungrily for hers. Her arms
curved round his shoulders, and at last she ran her
fingers once more through the thick gold hair as his
arms tightened around her. He lifted his mouth from
hers, burying it against her throat, her breasts, whispering her name as they moved together in a blind
frenzy and Christina was only partially conscious of
her own cries and of Devlin's name on her lips.

For what seemed like an eternity they clung together, gasping for breath, Christina's legs wound
around the base of his back. It had never been like
this with anyone else. Not before she had met him.
Not since. Compatible as she and Theo were, their

lovemaking never reached the mindless intensity it did
with Devlin. Yet Theo loved her and treated her with
respect. Devlin had called her a harlot and treated her
as one, and she had not had enough physical control
to prove herself otherwise.

Over his shoulder, in the open wardrobe, Christina
saw one of Kate's unmistakable black dresses swing
tauntingly. It took her some seconds to understand.
To remember why she had come aboard and what had
happened before she had been lost to the world in his
arms, uncaring of her pride, uncaring of anything. The
cabin steadied around her, took shape, and still the
black dress remained on its hanger and she could smell
the sickly sweet perfume that was Kate's. Her pride,
so easily forgotten, reasserted itself as her eyes still
stared at the taffeta dress in hypnotized revulsion. Her
body had momentarily given her away but she would
not give Devlin O'Conner the satisfaction of knowing
how easily and deeply he could stir her senses.

If the wardrobe door had been closed and if Devlin
had spoken what was in his heart, they would have
been united forever in an unbreakable bond. The moment came and passed and the gulf between them
deepened.

She uncoiled her legs, took a deep breath and said
icily, "I think I prefer the performances of the doddering dukes and earls. At least they have finesse."

For five or six seconds Devlin didn't move. His
head remained buried in her hair. When he finally
lifted it, his eyes were masked. He rolled off her and
reached for his clothes. "Then it gives me the greatest
pleasure in returning you to them. In fact I can say
quite truthfully that they are more than welcome to
you." And buckling his belt he unlocked the door and
left her.

Lying naked in the bed Christina was overcome by
a surge of utter desolation. Then, her body bruised
and aching from his lovemaking, she attempted to
dress herself in her torn clothing. The jacket was split

both front and back; the skirt torn from waist to hem. There was no way she could return to the hotel in them, even under cover of darkness.

With loathing she took the black dress from its hanger. Kate's dress. It was the final degradation. Sick at heart she slipped it over her head and, unseen by anybody, left the darkened ship and walked in the freezing night along the endless wharves and back to her hotel.

Chapter 25

From the darkness of the wheelhouse Devlin watched her go, his hands clenched so tightly that the veins stood out in ugly knots. The skeleton crew that remained aboard the *Ninevah* while the rest enjoyed the pleasures of the bars and brothels gave their captain a wide berth.

It had been impossible not to hear Christina's screams. Uneasily the seamen had eyed each other and continued with their tasks. He was a good captain and it was none of their affair. . . .

The first officer was there when Devlin strode into the wheelhouse like a man demented. He was naked to the waist, blood oozing darkly from long scratch marks on his chest.

"*Bitch!*" he said savagely, driving his fist hard on to the wheel. "Dirty whoring little *bitch!*" And then, to the first officer's horror, he saw that his captain's cheeks were wet with tears. Hardly daring to breathe he edged softly away into the darkness, terrified of the consequences if O'Conner should know he had had an audience.

Christina ignored the startled glances she attracted as she reentered the hotel in an entirely different outfit from the one in which she had left. And a much cheaper one. The hall porter eyed the shine of grease on the black taffeta dress with distaste and decided the hotel manager had made a grave mistake in accommodating Mrs. de Villiers.

Shivering with cold, Christina went straight to her room, running a hot bath and removing Kate's dress, throwing it into the corner with revulsion. She would ring for the chambermaid and order it to be burned. Clouds of steam filled the bathroom and as she stepped into the pine-scented water she caught sight of herself in the large gilt mirror on the wall. Even through the steam the bruises on her body showed clearly. She sank into the blissful comfort of the fragrant water and closed her eyes.

She could hardly remember what he had said to her, and what she could remember made no sense. The only thing she had been aware of had been his hatred, the savagery with which he had taken possession of her body and then, briefly, the desire in his eyes. Surely she had seen the same desire and love in his eyes that she had seen in Wales? Surely he had called her name out in an agony of passion as she had cried his? Or had she been so overcome by her own desperate desire that she had imagined it? Her head throbbed painfully as she slowly toweled herself dry. The bruises on her shoulders and breasts were turning a swollen blue, and between her thighs were the marks of his fingers. She drew on her negligee and sat at the dressing table, writing on two separate pieces of paper. Then she rang for the night porter and handed them to him.

"I would appreciate it if you would send these two messages for me by cable. The first is to the Duke of Marne, the second to Mr. Theobald Goldenberg. I have written their addresses on the top of each message."

"They won't go now until the morning," the porter said, eyeing the cleavage between Christina's breasts where her negligee fell open.

"I want them sent immediately. They are very urgent." She handed him a pound note.

The porter took it gratefully, and wondered how best he could prolong the conversation. As she had moved to hand him the money he had caught sight of the rapidly deepening bruises.

"Thank you." Without her usual smile she closed the door in his face and, physically and emotionally exhausted, crawled into the big, high bed with its spotless but cold sheets. Too much had happened in one day. Her mind was a kaleidoscope of Merry's pathetically small coffin; Josh twisting his hat round and round in his clumsy hands; Devlin calling her a harlot and a whore and then making love to her; and last but not least the shameful knowledge that under any circumstances her body responded to his with a will of its own.

He had deserted her, deserted his wife. It was Kate's dress that had hung in the intimacy of his wardrobe, not the clothes of a well-brought-up Pennsylvania girl. Christina had the charity to feel sorry for her before sheer exhaustion released her from her thoughts.

Theobald Goldenberg read the brief message in his office overlooking Central Park. He screwed it up savagely and jabbed his finger on the bell on his desk.

"Send Murray into me. Immediately!" he barked at his secretary.

His secretary, recognizing all the signs of a first class row, nodded eager assent, not daring to tell Mr. Goldenberg that his assistant was about to leave for an important meeting in Chicago. A chauffeur-driven car raced through the New York streets like a fire engine, its horn blaring its way through every intersection, equally regardless of pedestrians, horse-drawn cabs and other motorized vehicles. Murray was already on the train when Mr. Goldenberg's frantic secretary literally yanked him out of it. The train steamed out of the station, with his briefcase and papers still aboard.

"What the hell . . ."

"Get back to the office! *Quick!*"

One look at her frightened face was enough to convince Murray that if he wanted his future to prosper with the Goldenberg Shipping Company he had better do as she said.

He ran all the way from the elevator to Theobald Goldenberg's office. Then, pausing fractionally to smooth down his hair and steady his breath, he knocked and walked in.

"Where the hell have you been?" Theobald shouted, slamming the telephone receiver back on its rest with such force that Murray thought it had probably been disconnected for good.

"I want Reed as captain on the *Swan* and we move Johnson over to the *Corinthia* and get the new guy for his job."

"But Captain Reed isn't even on the shortlist . . ." Murray protested nervously. "I thought you wanted a much younger man . . ."

"The captain of a ship is no job for a fool! Reed's our most experienced captain and from now on the *Swan*'s his show. Understand?"

Murray motioned that he understood.

"And get me the file on the Conyates Shipping Company."

Murray, who had been personally responsible for bringing to his employer's attention the excellent record of one-half of the Conyates Company, looked puzzled.

"What are you going to offer O'Conner now? Nothing else but the *Swan* would tempt him."

"*Offer him?*" Theo yelled, ramming his forefinger

into his employee's chest. "I'm offering him nothing. I'm gonna break the bastard. I'm gonna see to it that Conyates goes bust! I'm gonna make sure that bastard never captains another ship. And then do you know what I'm gonna do?"

By now he had his petrified assistant pinned back against the wall.

"I'm gonna lynch him from the nearest yardarm. I'm gonna whip him till he's pulp . . . !"

Feverishly Murray scrabbled for the doorknob behind him.

"I'm gonna skin him alive! I'm gonna nail that bastard so he goes down for life! I'm gonna . . ."

Beneath Murray's sweating fingers the door opened and he fled. As he wiped his dripping brow in the outer office he listened dazedly with Theo's secretary to the sound of a brass paperweight smashing against the wall.

The Duke of Marne received his message in an entirely different manner. For some seconds he remained sitting on the terrace where he had been when the cable arrived, tapping it gently against his fingers, smiling to himself. Then he rose to his feet and called for his butler.

"Send Mason to the South Western Hotel, Southampton, to collect Mrs. de Villiers and order a suite of rooms to be prepared for her. And Holmes . . ." The butler waited deferentially. "Put an announcement in the *Times:* 'The Duke of Marne is pleased to announce his forthcoming marriage to Mrs. Christina de Villiers, widow, on the—' " He paused reflectively. "What do you think would be a good day to be married?" he asked his disbelieving henchman.

Holmes, who had been with the duke for fifteen years, gathered his scattered wits and answered gravely, "Your grace sails on the *Titanic* on April 10. Perhaps late May or early June."

"Haven't the time to wait till June," the duke said cheerfully. "Make it for May 10."

"If you would be so good as to give me the name of Mrs. de Villiers's parents for the announcement?" Holmes asked.

"Can't do that. Don't know them," and whistling like a small boy, the duke strode away, his walking cane swinging jauntily.

Holmes staggered toward the table and a decanter. For the first time in his long years of impeccable service, he helped himself liberally to the duke's whiskey.

The announcement in the *Times* and the knowledge that the mysterious Mrs. de Villiers, future Duchess of Marne, was already residing at Anersley caused a furor of curiosity amongst the duke's social contemporaries. Obviously there would be several large dinners at Anersley at which they would be able to assess the woman who had hooked Marne. Tiaras were cleaned. New ball gowns ordered. All to no avail. The duke had no intention of marring his precious days with Christina by undertaking the lavish entertainment expected of him. If it amused Christina he was quite willing to issue invitations to Anersley from the Court of King George V down.

To his housekeeper's annoyance, he personally supervised the preparation of Christina's rooms, adjusting the many vases of beautifully arranged flowers: moving a rose a little higher here, a carnation a little lower there. The Marne jewelry was duly brought from the vaults and cleaned in preparation for its new wearer. Rooms that hadn't seen the light of day for years were opened and spring cleaned, and all for a totally unknown woman! From kitchen maid to the elderly Countess of Cheale, everyone wanted to know only one thing. Who was she and where had she come from? No one knew, and no one got the chance to learn, for from the moment Christina arrived in the chauffeur-driven Darracq the gates of Anersley closed against the world. It was most frustrating and only served to increase speculation. An American heiress? A Russian princess? No rumor was too wild and everyone wanted to be the first to find out who and what the deceased Mr. de Villiers had been. No one succeeded. Everyone drew a blank.

Christina made the long journey from Southampton to Yorkshire in great comfort but the duke was shocked by her appearance when she finally arrived at Anersley. There were dark shadows beneath her eyes and her smile was wan as he helped her personally from the motorcar, taking her hand and kissing it.

Christina looked beyond him to the great facade of Anersley. Ivy, ages old, crept along the front face, curling round mullioned windows; the light from the setting sun cast a golden shadow over the weathered Yorkshire stone.

Anersley. Princesses had married into the family that owned it and married out of it. It had been built originally by a favorite courtier of Henry VIII and extended by his son under Elizabeth. The second of a long line of Marnes clever enough both to run with the hare and ride with the hounds. Staunchly Anglican, Anersley had supported the Hanoverian claim to the throne, and prospered. Their contemporaries, romantically rushing off to royal pretenders, were not so fortunate. Through all the vicissitudes of the years Anersley had remained unscathed—a spectator to royal marriages and royal disgraces. Sons were sent off to war, with some returning and some not returning. Births, marriages, deaths. Anersley's history was so full of them not even the archivist was sure of them all. The endless rows of portraits in the long gallery were testimony to the many generations of Marnes who had made Anersley their home and refuge.

"Do you like it?" he asked in sudden anxiety, as Christina stood on the carefully raked gravel and gazed up at the great edifice that was to be her home.

She kept her hand in his. "It's bigger than I expected, Duke. Vast. Even bigger than Mr. Darcy's home."

"Darcy?" The duke looked down at her, perplexed.

"*Pride and Prejudice*," Christina said, her smile holding a hint of its usual warmth. "I read it as a child and never forgot it."

"You can read it again if you want. Or anything else you like. Anersley's library is my pride. I don't think I have any prejudices."

He was rewarded by seeing her smile deepen as he led her into the great hall where a log fire burned in the grate. A couple of spaniels roused themselves from its warmth and barked welcomingly, sniffing around Christina as she fondled their ears.

"Harvester and Cherry Brandy," the duke said as the dogs gave their seal of approval to their master's guest by licking her hand. "I bought them as gun dogs when I used to hunt."

"How horrible." Christina shivered with distaste.

"I agree with you . . . Now."

He took her into the cosily-lit room that was his study. With the door safely closed against the prying eyes of his domestic staff, the duke gently removed her peacock-feathered hat and drew her into the circle of his arms.

"My life has changed. You have changed it, Christina. It's only fair to tell you that you're not getting the bargain you may think. I may have a title and I may have money but my reputation leaves an awful lot to be desired. I've spent twenty years of my life in completely meaningless activities. Hunting, shooting, gambling, embarking on one love affair after another. Do you still want to marry me?"

He could hear the fire crackle, the flames sending flickering shadows around the paneled room as he waited for her answer.

She raised her face to his and he traced the lovely lines of her cheekbones with his finger.

"I don't love you, Duke, but you know that, don't you?"

"Yes," he said gently. "I know. But I also know that you're fond of me and that love can grow. And I have enough love for the two of us, Christina. I want you to marry me more than I've wanted anything else in my life."

With a little sigh she entered his arms, her head on his chest. He stroked her hair tenderly.

"What happened in Southampton, Christina?"

She kept her face buried in his frilled shirt front, so that he could not see the tears in her eyes.

"I saw Devlin again."

"Devlin?" The duke frowned down at her. He had never known the name of the man who had brought her such unhappiness.

"It was horrible. Hideous. I never want to see him again, Duke. I want to feel safe."

His arms tightened around her. "Is Devlin the man you love?"

She nodded her head, tears blinding her. "But he doesn't love me. He hates me and I don't know why."

"Hush, my darling." The duke rocked her as if she were a child. "With me you will forget him. I will love and care for you until the end of my life. Do you believe me?"

She raised her tear-streaked face to him. "Yes, Duke. And I'll be good to you. I promise."

"You will be more than that, *ma chère amie*. One day you will love me." And he bent his head to hers, kissing her long and lovingly and then with increasing passion as Christina sought to forget the painful memories of her encounter with Devlin while giving herself freely and generously to the man who would soon be her husband.

In the next few days Christina captivated the duke's household staff and pleased him by saying fervently that she had no desire to socialize. She wanted only to be with him and to go walking through Anersley's woods with the dogs yapping at her heels. Or to be sitting on the terrace in the spring sunshine, overlooking Anersley's lawns and flower gardens stretching down to an endless vista of pasture and trees.

The duke was increasingly confident that in time she would love him as deeply as he loved her. Their uninhibited lovemaking delighted him. Her small signs of affection delighted him even more: her hand slipping into his on their endless walks; her head resting on his shoulder as they sat in the library in the firelight.

Christina had gasped with pleasure on first seeing so many shelves of leather-bound volumes. All the old favorites from her childhood were there. *The Three Musketeers, Pride and Prejudice, Robinson Crusoe.* Christina told the amused duke of how her father had read to her in the tiny cabin of the *Lucky Star* and of how Josh had always referred to Crusoe as "that poor geezer." It was enough to make him regret not holding any formal dinner parties. They wouldn't remain formal for long. Not with Christina's exuberant conversation.

By the time they returned southward to London, en route to Southampton and the *Titanic*, Christina had regained her natural vitality, enjoying the full week of operas, ballets and plays. One evening as they left the Café Royal after a lavish dinner in the Domino Room, a primrose seller came up to them, a knitted shawl around her shoulders, her feet bare on the cold stones as Christina's had once been. The duke had insisted on buying up her whole tray of tired looking flowers, leaving the girl staring down at the note in her hand with amazement.

Christina had said nothing, simply squeezed his arm the tighter, the walnut-sized ruby on her third finger glittering in the moonlight, grateful that she had found such a man to love her.

Duane Yates tapped a gold pen thoughtfully against his teeth as he read the offer from Goldenberg Shipping. Why the hell should Goldenberg want to pay so much cash for the *Ninevah?* It didn't make sense. The

Goldenberg Line was launching a new 20,000 ton liner within weeks. The *Ninevah* was peanuts compared to a liner that size. Disregarding the fact that it was still only ten in the morning, he poured himself a tumbler of bourbon and sipped it meditatively.

Competition in the shipping industry was growing fiercer month by month. White Star and Cunard were the leaders and conducted their private battle royal. Lower down in the batting order were the Goldenberg Line and the Conyates Shipping Company. Good publicity had seen to it that the *Ninevah* always sailed with her first class cabins fully occupied. Duane played heavily on the fact that the company was young and American, and a single photograph of the six-foot-three red-haired captain was enough to make scores of prospective lady passengers murmur discreetly to their husbands that they had heard the food aboard the new Conyates ship was far superior to that offered by the Goldenberg Line.

They must have been more successful in luring away Goldenberg customers than they had realized. But not from the *Corinthia*. The *Corinthia* was becoming fabled for its number of regular passengers and the beauty of the woman who had become virtual hostess aboard. Duane had liked the idea of a beautiful woman to grace the captain's table at dinner every evening. Too often the attractions of the women aboard ship was a hit and miss affair, and though he never sailed himself he alway read the passenger list with scrupulous attention. The wealthy women aboard the *Ninevah* seemed either to be old maids or in their dotage and the strong fascination that romance at sea had for travelers was not lost on Duane. He had suggested that they imitate the *Corinthia* and install a young woman aboard to liven up the staider passengers.

Devlin had sworn blasphemously, but Duane had pointed out that if they emulated Goldenberg and chose a woman not only with great beauty but with

wit and gaiety and class they couldn't fail to add to
the attractions of the *Ninevah*.

"Wit and class my arse! Goldenberg has a whore
on his ship and *that's* why so many men sail time and
time again on her."

Duane had not brought up the subject again. He
needed Devlin too badly to risk losing him and he was
beginning to become increasingly wary of Devlin's
volatile temper.

He frowned at the thought of what his partner's
reaction would be if he knew that Goldenberg had
offered to buy them out. The *Ninevah* was more than
just a business enterprise to Devlin. He would never
agree to sell to a rival company or anyone else for that
matter. Yet Goldenberg's offer was so high as to be
ridiculous. Duane, always cautious where money was
concerned, wondered why.

For years the Cunard Line, with the *Mauretania*
and the *Lusitania*, had the fastest and largest ships on
the Atlantic run. White Star had decided to tip the
scales and embarked on a bold new program of ship
building. Three liners, larger and far more luxurious
than the Cunarders, were all set to steal the blue ribbon. The *Olympic* was already an overwhelming success, turning Duane green with envy whenever he
read about her or saw her. The second mammoth
steamer had already finished her trial runs and was to
sail on her maiden voyage on the tenth of the month.

The photographs on his desk showed not so much
a ship but a floating deluxe hotel. At over forty-six
thousand tons she was described as a wonder of the
world, and anyone who was anybody had booked
cabins aboard. To Duane it seemed the best time in
the world to sell the *Ninevah* and turn his business
interests elsewhere. The *Titanic* was heralding in a
new era of travel and ships like the *Ninevah* and the
Corinthia would no longer be anywhere in the pecking
order. Yet Goldenberg had offered a fortune for a ship
that already had seen over twelve years of sailing. And

in the same week that the *Titanic* was to sail. What did Goldenberg know that he didn't? The man was no fool. He wouldn't have offered such a sum of money for the *Ninevah* without good reason. Duane decided to find out what it was, and in the meantime he rang for his stenographer and dictated a letter to Mr. Theobald Goldenberg thanking him for his offer and telling him he would give it careful consideration. He also told the stenographer that he especially wished no mention of the letter be made to his partner when he next paid a visit to the building. The stenographer agreed. As she typed out the letter she felt a glow of righteous indignation. It was quite obvious that Mr. Yates was not being entirely straight in his dealing with Mr. O'Conner. If Mr. Yates was negotiating, however obscurely, to sell the Conyates Company, surely his partner should be the first to know? If *she* were the one to tell him perhaps he would take notice of her instead of looking straight through her as if she didn't exist. But then Mr. Yates would be very angry with her and when the smooth-talking, suavely-dressed Mr. Yates was angry he terrified her.

Once she had been summoned to accompany him to a meeting in another part of the city. He was already late when they left and the streets had been congested.

"For God's sake, put your foot down, man!" he had said savagely to the chauffeur.

A small dog ran across the road and the chauffeur had swerved, mounting the sidewalk in order to avoid it. Ladies screamed. A horse whinnied in fright. They were surrounded by a melee of shouting pedestrians as the chauffuer struggled to reverse the car back on to the street again. By the time he had done so several precious minutes had been lost, and Duane's eyes glittered with a cold fury that had petrified her.

He ordered the chauffeur into the passenger seat and took the wheel himself; and then, to her disbelief, he turned the car round and roared down the street in the opposite direction.

The dog was inspecting the rubbish in the gutter. As she screamed Duane turned the wheel hard, accelerating as the dog disappeared beneath the front tires, not even bothering to glance behind him as he left the bloodied body in the dust. Then he smiled, handed the wheel back to the chauffeur and continued to his late meeting as if nothing had happened.

She shivered when she thought about it. That poor little dog. She could still see its eyes in the fraction of a second before the car hit it, when it had looked up in surprise at the automated monster bearing down on it. No. She would not like to anger Mr. Yates. Better to keep quiet and say nothing. She sealed the letter to Mr. Theobald Goldenberg and turned her attention to her filing.

Many times Christina had watched women board the *Corinthia* with several maids, over a hundred trunks and stacks of jewel-cases. Now to her amusement she was one of them. The duke had been insistent that she travel in a style that even exceeded Theo's lavishness. The scores of richly jeweled evening dresses and couture suits and furs she had accepted graciously, but she refused adamantly to be encumbered by a maid. The duke apologized for the fact that he could not be such a free spirit and would be taking his valet with him.

Christina giggled and squeezed his hand. The sight of the docks and the four magnificent, huge funnels of the *Titanic* that towered above the roofs of the shipping offices, which could be seen clearly from the dining room of their hotel, had banished any last trace of the sadness she had taken with her when she traveled to Anersley.

With a rapt expression she watched the procession of stokers and stewards wending their way to the ship, leaving her breakfast until it had gone cold and another had to be ordered. In promising to marry the duke she had forfeited the sea. At least as a permanent home. But she still intended studying the great ship with professional interest and passing on all her observations to Theo.

She jumped, turning suddenly as a voice that could have been his said, "Come on, honey. You'll only feel worse if you don't eat."

A well-built American in his early fifties was coaxing a dark-haired girl to at least partake of some toast. She shook her head wanly and Christina caught the gleam of a shiny new wedding ring on her finger.

"I'm sorry, Milton. I can't." Her voice trembled on the edge of tears.

Her husband leaned across and clasped her hand in his. "Never mind, sweetheart. It's only five days and we'll be in New York. There's nothing to worry about. That ship's so big it's gonna be like sailing on Lake Ontario."

She smiled valiantly, but Christina saw the fear in her eyes. She had seen it before in the eyes of women who had taken to their bunks immediately on leaving port, remaining there until the ship had reached New York Bay.

"Poor child," she said, turning back to the duke. "She's terrified."

"Child, indeed," the duke said, amused. "I doubt if she's a year younger than you are."

Christina didn't contradict him. He was probably right but only insofar as physical age went. In experience she was a generation older than the innocent-faced, fragile girl behind her.

"Are you ready to go aboard?" the duke asked as Christina gazed at the ship in an agony of impatience.

"Oh yes! I can't wait to be at sea again!"

"Then I shall have to sell Anersley and buy you a ship," the duke said dryly.

Christina laughed. "Anersley is beautiful and I'd hate you to sell it. Your family have had it for years."

"A good five hundred or so," he agreed gravely.

"Then I promise you I'll love it just as much as you do."

"I only love it now because you will be under its roof," the duke said, kissing her hand. "My home is where you are, Christina. If it has to be at sea then so be it. Thank God the English are a nation of sailors!"

An hour later, with her kid-gloved hand tucked securely in his, her long sable scarf wound round her neck—and her figure, beneath the exquisitely-cut Paris-made day suit, turning all heads—Christina stepped aboard the *Titanic*.

Chapter 26

The young sailor knew from the contemptuous way Kate rolled away from him that he had not been man enough to satisfy her. His body glistened with sweat and his limbs ached from exhaustion. He had carried on for as long as he could but it had made no difference. Despite Kate's frantic cries of "Faster! Faster! Don't stop *now* you bastard" his semen had spurted into her and within seconds he was as limp as a rag doll. Kate had cursed, straining against him to no avail, and then, vicious with frustration, she had belittled his manhood with every word in her vocabulary.

The door slammed behind him and Kate threw her bottles and jars of perfume and creams in a crashing volley against the woodwork.

Her body burned with an inner fire that was unquenchable. The sailor had been the third in as many hours and still she had not found the release she so avidly sought. There was only Devlin and Stanislav who were capable of assuaging it, and she was going to kill Devlin. She knew that he would never touch her again and the only way she could be free of him was to destroy him.

Without bothering to wash away the semen from between her thighs she dressed, repowdered and rouged her face and dabbed perfume liberally on her neck and breasts. Then she walked down South Street, asking in every pub and rooming house for the whereabouts of Stanislav Mikolij.

Stanislav had been holed up in the bottom end of South Street for over three weeks. He had been paid off after his trip to Brazil and the sight of the *Ninevah* at her Manhattan pier had filled him with brooding contemplation. He had wanted the English woman. He had seen Kate sulkily leave as the *Ninevah* had sailed and followed her at a distance back to the rooms she shared with Devlin. Then he had bought himself a cheap bottle of bourbon and retired to his own sleazy room to think. Captain O'Conner would be away for nearly three weeks. The English woman would not want to be without a man for so long. She had expected to remain on board with him. One glimpse of her narrow face between the long fall of straight blonde hair had been enough to convince him that she had been cruelly disappointed. If he went to her now she would have him.

Over the past few days he had heard from many sources that she was looking for the captain. He had smiled slowly to himself and waited a little longer. He knew of the men who entered the rooming house at all hours of the day and night and knew with the certainty of a great brown bear that none of them could do what he, Stanislav, could do. The more men she had the more desperate her searching for him had become.

He was sitting on the stoop of his rooming house, a bottle by his side, when a fellow Pole walked idly by and said, "The English woman is at Chertsky's asking for you."

Stanislav had nodded silent acknowledgment, finished his bottle of liquor and then slowly walked down the darkening sidewalk toward Chertsky's. His head was set low on his massive shoulders, his barrel chest a mass of thick black hair beneath his open shirt. He drank alone and made no friends. Slow thinking, slow moving, his powerful body had earned him respect among the hardened New York seamen.

Kate's questions in the bar had been abortive. The men knew where Mikolij lodged but none was prepared to tell her. A weather-beaten schooner captain had kept her glass full of rum, his hands taking increasing liberties as Kate had tried to drown her disappointment in the warmth of the liquor. His hands moved rhythmically over her buttocks, his fingers forcing their way exploratively between her thighs, hampered by the taffeta folds of her dress. She could see him swell and harden and finished the last drink in one swallow, circling his waist with her arm, steering him out onto the sidewalk. He was young and strong. Perhaps this time . . .

"Go back to your friends, mister," Stanislav said softly.

The captain, who enjoyed a good fight, stepped forward menacingly, saw the great hulk that was Mikolij and decided to postpone his enjoyment in favor of another drink with his friends.

"*Stanislav!*" She was in his arms, clinging to him, shedding genuine tears of joy as the giant Pole half carried her back to his room. When their mutual frenzy subsided dawn was breaking over the bay and the hooting of steamboat whistles sounded forlornly in the distance.

"We stay together now," Stanislav said. It was the most he had spoken to her since their reunion. "You do not return to the captain." It was a statement of fact, not a question.

"No." Kate wound her legs between his, running her fingers over the black mat of his chest. Then she said softly, "I shall kill the captain."

Stanislav's face bore no surprise. To kill was as natural as eating or making love. He too wanted the captain dead. The captain had exerted too strong a fascination on his woman. It was better that he should die. He could kill him for her with his hands but the woman needed to kill him herself. He had a hunting knife. It would be an easy task. And if there were difficulties then he, Stanislav, would only be yards away in the darkness to silence the red-haired Irishman for good.

Devlin had none of the usual courtesies for the first class passengers as they settled themselves aboard the *Ninevah*. The crew eyed each other meaningfully and got on with their tasks with extra zealousness.

Female hearts beat faster as Devlin strode around his ship, magnificent in captain's uniform, the gold braiding the perfect complement to his sun-bronzed skin. Devlin was unaware of the young women aboard. He criticized his chief engineer, raged at the firemen and trimmers and had sharp words with the cook. The men shrugged and speculated as to the change that had taken place in their commanding officer over the last few weeks.

Eventually there came the thud and rattle of anchor chains and the throbbing of engines. The pilot boats led the *Ninevah* out toward the Narrows and there were feminine gasps of pleasure as the gap between ship and dock widened.

"Look, there's the Battery!" a brown-haired girl called out excitedly. "And see how high Brooklyn Bridge is from below!"

Her fond parents smiled indulgently, confident that their only child was the prettiest female aboard. The famous Loretta Bankfield had looked years older in the flesh than she did on the silver screen. At *least* twenty-five. Nevertheless it was quite exciting to be sharing the adjoining staterooms to an artiste of such renown.

Loretta Bankfield had been aware of only one thing since boarding the *Ninevah*. The sexual attraction of her captain. Eyes the blue of cornflowers on a summer's day had passed over her as indifferently as if she were the mouselike creature in the next stateroom. She left her maid to do her unpacking and leaned against the deck rails, looking up at the bridge as Devlin took command of his ship. He moved like an angry animal. Beneath the immaculate uniform his muscles were as tense as those of a tiger about to spring on its prey. A dangerous man by anybody's standards, and Loretta Bankfield mused on the pleasure of taming such a creature.

The smoke of the city faded into the distance as the *Ninevah* slid downstream, past Governor's Island, through the Narrows and out into the bay. The air was vibrant, the sky vast; the sea foamed at the *Ninevah*'s prow. On any other occasion Devlin would have been exultant to be out on the Atlantic again, free of the city. Instead his jaw was clenched tightly, his eyes seeing not the glory of the endless ocean, but only Christina with her hair spread like a billowing cloud around her, her body answering unreservedly to his— and her mocking words that in one cruel moment had destroyed all he thought he had recaptured.

"Once a harlot, always a harlot." It was a phrase often used by seagoing men and it was one he bitterly agreed with. There had been a brief moment when he had been so lost in desire for her that he had been more than capable of forgiving her for the way she had run out on him in Liverpool. She had crushed the thought before it could be uttered. Just as well that she had done so. He would only have made himself a bigger fool than ever.

Loretta Bankfield discarded dress after dress and

then decided on a flimsy chiffon that showed the out-line of her breasts tantalizingly. Her maid sprayed her with expensive French perfume, made a last minute adjustment to her coiffure and Loretta made her way from her boudoir on *A* Deck to the resplendent dining room on *B* Deck. A discreet word with the purser had seen to it that she would dine at the captain's table.

Devlin knew a willing woman when he saw one. An unwilling one was a rarity he scarcely encountered. Loretta Bankfield was more than aware of her own sexual charms, and she gave Devlin the full benefit of them as they shared dinner with an elderly copper-mine owner and his fussily-dressed wife, and the pain-fully shy auburn-haired Miss Mary Donovan and her far too talkative mother.

Devlin was not in the habit of bedding the women who traveled aboard his ship. It was against his own personal code of ethics. Tonight, he decided, ethics could go to hell. He needed to prove to himself that he could enjoy another woman as much as he had Christina. It was a matter of pride, and Loretta Bank-field had all the sparkle and polish of an international artiste. She was an experienced, sexually attractive woman and he could see the dark shape of her nipples press against the coffee-color chiffon of her dress as she smiled provocatively across the table at him.

Dinner that night ended early. There was no linger-ing over cigars with the elderly copper-mine owner, and when he suggested accompanying Miss Bankfield in a stroll on the deck she had agreed gracefully, press-ing herself promisingly against him as they climbed the stairs of the companionway.

It had been so easy Loretta could hardly believe her luck. She had intended asking him discreetly back to her stateroom for a nightcap of cognac but he had purposefully steered her toward his own cabin. The holy of holies, Loretta thought with an excited giggle. He had kicked the door closed with his heel and before she even had time to catch her breath had taken her in his arms and was kissing her deeply, picking her up and carrying her over to the large brass-headed bunk. Propriety necessitated that she give at least a token struggle, but his tongue was searching for hers, his lips so hard and sweet that Loretta discarded any thought of wasting time on foolish protests.

All her previous lovers had been either rich businessmen who had helped to further her career or young men with white skins and delicate brooding dark good looks that transferred themselves to the moving pictures so successfully.

She had never seen a man with such a magnificent body as the *Ninevah*'s captain when he had stripped himself naked. The broad shoulders and strong chest, the lean hips . . . Her eyes were riveted by his arrogant maleness.

Loretta, she said to herself, *this sure is your lucky night.* And then, chiffon dress discarded, prepared herself for the performance of her life. She wanted to be in his bed every night until they reached Southampton and the only way to do it was to make him as crazy for her as she was for him.

Her body was satin soft, willing and uninhibited, responding with eagerness and wildness to his. Her obvious pleasure and mindless cries assured Devlin that for at least one of them their encounter had been worthwhile. For himself it had been a failure. Just physical gratification and nothing more. Languidly Loretta had opened her eyes, kissing his back as he had reached for his clothes. She elicited no response. Courteously the *Ninevah*'s captain escorted her back to her stateroom.

"Tomorrow?" she asked hopefully. She, the great artiste who never asked for anything.

Devlin had been noncommittal, kissing the back of her hand and bidding her good night with a coolness that had driven her wild.

The next evening the captain treated her as distantly as though they had shared no other intimacy closer than that of shaking hands and the great Loretta Bankfield found herself fobbed off with the first officer as companion.

Mary Donovan had been equally smitten by their captain, but shyness made her lower her eyes whenever he looked in her direction. She was a pretty little thing. Modest and quiet. The very antithesis of Christina. Devlin had not intended to make love to her. Their meeting on the darkened deck had been quite accidental. Mary Donovan had already wished her mother good night and had spent several sleepless hours in bed before slipping on her dressing gown and wandering up to the moonlit deck to watch the beauty of the night sky in solitary contentment. Devlin was returning to his cabin after checking with the lookout that all was well and leaving his first officer in charge of the bridge. He literally fell over her as she emerged from the head of the stairs. She gave a frightened cry as she fell against him.

"It's all right. It's only me," Devlin said comfortingly.

Beneath the thin dressing gown he could feel her body tremble. He felt a strange reluctance to release her. Miss Donovan turned her trusting face up to his and sighed with bliss and reassurance. Devlin stared down at her for a few minutes in silence. Perhaps he had been seeking to forget with the wrong sort of woman. Mary Donovan remained shielded from the chill Atlantic air by his body, loath to return to the warmth of her cabin. She smiled very shyly up at him and very gently Devlin lowered his lips to hers.

He didn't make love to her until the night before they docked at Southampton and when he did so it was with a tenderness that would have amazed Loretta Bankfield or Kate Kennedy. Her flesh burned under the experienced caressing hands, yielding with innocent pleasure as he coaxed her along to the point of no return.

This, Devlin had said to himself, would surely be

different. In the back of his mind he had already proposed marriage to the auburn-haired Mary Donovan. She was everything Christina was not. Modest and timid and faithful.

The only drawback was that making love to her was no different from making love to a hundred other girls. Only Christina was different.

His proposal of marriage was left unspoken. Fighting back tears Miss Donovan bade him goodbye at Southampton and wondered how she could return to leading a chaste life after experiencing the pleasure of Captain O'Conner's hard body.

When the *Ninevah* slid out into the Solent Channel Devlin was no longer the angry figure he had been the last time the ship had left Southampton. Instead he was thoughtful, his usual high spirits strangely subdued. His crew, who had watched his behavior over the last couple of weeks with increasing interest, debated as to whether their buccaneering captain was heading for a total breakdown.

He wasn't. He was coming to terms with himself— swallowing his pride and beginning to know that if he was ever to gain physical and spiritual peace he had to be reunited with Christina.

Time had helped him to see the episode between them in a clearer light. True, she had said cruel things to him, but hadn't he humiliated her first? Calling her a whore and a harlot and ripping the clothes from her back. He remembered her screams of pain and felt a wave of shame. He had behaved like a bastard toward her and yet she had still wanted him. Her body had shown him that. Taunting him with words had been her only defense. He had to believe that. To believe anything else was too unbearable. He would seek out the *Corinthia* and ask her forgiveness. Anything if it would enable him to hold her in his arms again, feel the suppleness of her body against his, see the warm curve of her lips and the mischievous sparkle in her eyes.

Christina . . . The sea wind seemed to whisper her name to him as the *Ninevah* ploughed out into the grey waters of the Channel. He felt his spirits lift. She had left him once but she would never leave him again.

"Full steam ahead," he called down the telephone to his chief engineer. "Let's make this the shortest crossing yet."

As the *Ninevah* slid seven days later into New York Bay, Devlin saw with an almost nervous excitement that the *Corinthia* was berthed at her Manhattan pier. He discharged all the formalities of landing in the shortest time possible, and leaving his first officer in charge, he headed determinedly toward the liner of a rival shipping company. Caleb Reed barred his way at the top of the gangplank.

"I'd like to speak with Mrs. de Villiers," Devlin said, flashing white teeth in a broad smile and holding out his hand to the venerable captain.

"She's not aboard, and I'll have to ask you to leave this ship or be forcibly escorted back to the pier."

Devlin's smile faded. A captain was always welcome aboard another ship. Reed was behaving oddly but his overriding concern was Christina's whereabouts.

"Then perhaps you could tell me where I could find her," Devlin asked with civility.

"With the greatest of pleasure," Caleb said, his fist longing to smack itself against the jaw of the arrogant young buck opposite him. "With her future husband, the Duke of Marne."

Devlin's mouth tightened and Caleb laughed shortly "You'll not be able to maltreat her again and get away with it. Nor will you this time. Mr. Goldenberg is out for your hide and from what he's told me, if I were a younger man, I'd thrash you myself."

Abruptly Devlin turned on his heel. So she had told Goldenberg, and Goldenberg was out for his skin. He bet she hadn't told Goldenberg how she had reacted to his rape. How her nails had clawed into his back not in defense but in passion. He went into the nearest bar and asked for a bottle and a glass. And what was this about marrying an English duke? He thought Goldenberg was the prospective husband. The liquor hit the back of his throat with fiery warmth. He had sailed into New York to see Christina and he was bloody well determined to do so. No Goldenberg or English duke was going to stop him.

The sky was darkening over the waterfront as he stepped out onto the sidewalk. Almost immediately two pairs of strong arms grabbed him from behind and drew him, kicking and struggling, into a narrow alleyway.

"From Goldenberg," one of the roughly-dressed men said, as he hit Devlin full in the face with all the force of his clenched fist, while the other still retained a grip on Devlin's arms.

He raised his fist for another blow, but Devlin had knocked his captor off-balance and they had fallen to the floor in a tangled heap, hitting wildly at each other. It took a few seconds for his companion to make out which of the panting bodies was Devlin and when he did so he began to kick him viciously as the two men rolled over and over on the cobbles. Devlin regained his balance and knocked his attacker's front teeth down his throat, dislocating his jaw with one powerful blow. Moaning in pain the man reeled out of the contest. Now that the fight was on fairer terms his companion seemed to have lost the heart for it, especially after Devlin's fist connected with his nose and a spout of blood gushed down his face and over his chest. Another blow from Devlin and both of them took to their heels, leaving Devlin panting and swearing, lifting his captain's cap from the ignominy of the dirty alleyway and dusting it off on his sleeve.

Reed hadn't been joking when he said Goldenberg was out for revenge. The sooner he saw Christina, asked for her forgiveness and seduced her in such a way that she forgot all about Goldenberg and her English duke and the brutal way he had treated her aboard the *Ninevah*, the better.

Mikolij had watched the *Ninevah* dock from a waterfront bar and then had gone back to his rooming house, taking the deadly hunting knife from its sheath and polishing it lovingly.

"He's back?" Kate's eyes glittered like pale marble.

"He's back—and asking for the woman on the *Corinthia*."

"Give me it." Kate took the knife caressingly. She had known he would return to Christina eventually. But not for long. She stroked the blade with her fingers. He would never have her. She had vowed it and Stanislav had told her she was right.

Wearing one of the black taffeta dresses she always affected and with a black woolen shawl tied tightly around her head to disguise the distinctive blondness of her hair, she followed Stanislav out into the South Street night. Drunks reeled mindlessly against the walls of the brownstone houses, prostitutes loitered hopefully, firemen and trimmers hurried backward and forward between the docked ships and the bars.

Stanislav carried the knife sheathed and within his shirt. His slow mind had not yet thought out just where and how they would attack the captain. He had not been able to follow him and had no idea where he was.

The captain had either to board the ship or leave her. That much was obvious, and as they stood in the shadows of the waiting cargo the captain would not be aware of them until he passed only inches away. There was no one to see them as they walked silently across to the *Ninevah* and stood, hands clasped, their backs against the steel-bound crates.

The ship was quiet. A handful of lights indicated the presence of a skeleton crew but no one walked the decks. Mikolij had taught her how to drive the knife down into the captain's chest so that he would die without so much as a cry for help. Kate had been disappointed. She had wanted to savor the moment. To have Devlin beg her for mercy.

Footsteps approached and Devlin loomed out of the darkness toward them. They shrank back against the stacked boxes. Nearer and nearer. It seemed impossible to Kate that they should remain unseen and she didn't *want* to remain unseen. She wanted him to see her. To see the expression in his eyes.

"*Now!*" Mikolij whispered as Devlin drew near them.

With both hands gripping the hilt of the knife Kate sprang.

His instincts already sharpened by his encounter with Theo's hired thugs, Devlin's reaction was swift. He side-stepped quickly, the knife glancing down over his cheekbone, scoring the skin. The black-skirted figure cried out in frustration and raised the knife yet again. Devlin caught her wrists and then, as he shouted to his ship for help, Mikolij felled him with one blow.

Only seconds behind Devlin were members of his crew returning from a tour of the city's bars. On hearing their captain cry out they burst into a run and Mikolij hesitated. Kate was bending over Devlin's inert body, the knife raised high ready to plunge.

Mikolij grabbed her arm, pulling her away, running for the warren of waterfront alleyways.

One of the trimmers yelled, "After 'em lads," while two firemen and a greaser lifted Devlin's still unconscious body and carried him aboard his ship.

When he recovered consciousness he was in his own cabin, the ship's surgeon bandaging up the knife wound on his face.

For the moment memory eluded him, and then he remembered the feminine cry, the slender feel of her wrists in his hands. Christina. He moved over the edge of his bunk and vomited into the bowl that the doctor had so thoughtfully provided.

Chapter **27**

Maurice, the duke's valet, accompanied them deferentially, appalled at the future duchess's lack of a maid. Her behavior, too . . .

Instead of retiring gracefully to her luxurious stateroom and resting, she was busy asking the purser questions, not about the social standing of her fellow travelers but about bulkheads and waterproof compartments.

The purser smiled indulgently at the radiant young woman with her arm in Marne's. Mrs. de Villiers. Widow and future duchess. Soothingly he assured her that yes, the *Titanic* has sixteen watertight compartments and was absolutely unsinkable, wondering who had put the nonsense of bulkheads into such a pretty little head. He had handed her a list of names of her fellow passengers, pointing out with pride that there were a dozen millionaires aboard including, of course, her future husband.

Christina had dug the duke sharply in the ribs when the purser had turned his attention to more of his illustrious passengers.

"You never told me you were a millionaire!" she said indignantly.

"I hardly thought it necessary, *ma chère amie*. I thought Anersley and the ring on your finger would speak for themselves." His voice was amused.

Christina laughed delightedly. "Does that mean that *I'm* a millionairess?"

"Only by proxy," the duke replied gravely. "What other rubbish did the purser give you? Is that the ship's routine?"

"Yes." Christina read the printed details with interest. "The bars open at half past eight in the morning—I couldn't face a drink so early in the day, could you?"

"Not personally, but my housekeeper tells me you *are* rather partial to champagne and orange juice for breakfast."

"That's different. That's in bed—not in the bar! And they close at half past eleven at night. On the *Corinthia* you can get a drink any time in the twenty-four hours. Lights are to be extinguished at eleven o'clock at night in the saloon and the Smoke Room closes at midnight." She frowned. "Whoever drew this up must be a rigid puritan. Midnight is *early!*"

"It is for you, my love," the duke agreed indulgently.

"We can hire deck chairs at four shillings each for the voyage. Oh look! You can send a Marconigram to America for eight shillings and fourpence for ten words and sixpence for every other word! Can I send one to Theo?" And then, without waiting for a reply, "No, I'd better not. Anything I have to say about the ship had better be private. The operator will probably show the captain my message."

The duke eyed her curiously. "Are you still going to give Goldenberg a report on the ship?"

"Of course. That's why I'm aboard!"

"It's only why you *originally* decided to sail on her. You're aboard now because you're soon to be my wife."

Christina squeezed his arm affectionately. "I know, and I'm not likely to forget. Not with this weighing my hand down all the time!"

The duke lit a cigar thoughtfully. "Why did you choose to marry me, Christina, and not Goldenberg?"

Christina's radiance vanished like a summer breeze.

He cursed himself and patted her hand. "I'm sorry. I shouldn't have asked."

"Yes you should. You have every right to know."

She leaned on the deck rail, not seeing him or the bustling activity on the dockside. She was lost in a private dark world of her own. One in which however much he loved her, he could never enter.

"It was because if I had married Theo I would have lived the rest of my life in the shipping world—and I would have seen Devlin again."

"I see." The duke puffed fragrant clouds of cigar smoke into the air, his heart aching for her.

"Living with you at Anersley I can forget all about that part of my life. Put the past behind me and start afresh with no chance encounters to bring back painful memories."

The duke put his arm around her shoulders and said huskily, "*Ma chère amie*. The past shall never hurt you again. I swear it."

Eyes bright with tears she turned to him, raising her face upwards for his kiss, grateful for his love for her and determined to repay it in every way she could.

Not only were the *Titanic*'s decks thronged with prospective travelers, but numerous guests and sightseers crowded into the public rooms, oohing and aahing at the splendor they found. The duke, inadvertently pushed again as the children raced past him, grimaced.

"Peace and quiet and some light liquid refreshment are called for. As it would seem it can only be obtained for the moment in my own stateroom, that's where I'm going."

He held his hand out to her. She laughed and shook her head.

"Not yet. There's too much to see."

"Then see it, *ma chère amie*." He kissed her lightly on the cheek and strolled away through the crowds.

Christina watched him go—an elegant, sophisticated man in a cream linen suit and wide panama hat, the touch of gray at his temples only serving to make him look even more the aristocrat that he was as he swung his Malacca cane and approached the grand entrance leading down to his first class stateroom.

The purser would have been amazed if he had known the extent of the facts and figures in Mrs. de Villiers's pretty little head as she began her tour of inspection on the topmost deck, the Boat Deck. The *Titanic* was the largest liner in the world—over two thousand people would be sailing on her, though only a mere three hundred and twenty-two were first class passengers. If he had known Mrs. de Villiers's interest in second class passengers and steerage and of her intentions to visit their quarters he would have blanched.

No steerage passenger was allowed into second class accommodation or deck space. No second class passenger into first class accommodation or deck space. The rules for first class passengers were non-existent, as it was taken for granted that no first class passenger would *want* to visit second class or steerage!

Christina emerged from the entrance of the first class stairway, her attention immediately caught by the open door of the gymnasium. *There* was an idea that could be easily incorporated into the Goldenberg vessels. She walked in, eyeing with professional interest the brightly-blocked linoleum floor and comfortable wicker chairs.

Christina then strolled the length of the Boat Deck before descending to the main Promenade Deck, well satisfied with what she had seen. The gymnasium was a brilliant and simple idea, but something nagged at her and she couldn't think what it was. Some fault she had seen and not recognized.

The duke was relaxing on a wicker lounger, a whiskey and soda in his hand. The *Titanic*'s whistle blew as a signal for all guests to depart and Christina dragged the reluctant duke to the deck rails to join in the excitement as the gangway was withdrawn and the ship prepared to sail. Those on board shouted last minute messages to friends on the quayside and friends and relations shouted loud farewells as the *Titanic* slipped majestically away from her moorings.

"Now if that had been New York," a deep timbred voice said from behind them, "there would have been steamers whistling the whole length of the Hudson and a fleet of ferryboats with flags flying to escort us out to sea."

They turned to see the genial face of the man who had been seated behind them in the hotel dining room at breakfast.

"And it would have been midnight," Christina said knowledgeably. "With streamers floating everywhere and champagne flowing."

The man grinned. "I see you're no stranger to New York, ma'am." He held out his hand. "Milton Barnard. I believe my stateroom is just a short way from yours."

The duke, an expert at sizing up his fellow men, liked what he saw in the rugged features of the American, judged him to be nearer sixty than fifty, and shook his hand, introducing himself and Christina.

"Sure wish Isobel was here to join in all the fun. She's feeling awfully sick already. She isn't much of a traveler and we've only had a short break since leaving Vienna."

"A beautiful city," the duke said. "Have you been touring Europe?"

"Yep—and getting myself married at the same time. Isobel is Austrian. A countess. Is that higher or lower than a duke?"

The duke laughed and Christina said before he could reply, "We're just about to *be* married."

Milton eyed the huge ring on her finger and slapped the duke's back in congratulations.

"Well, if that don't beat all."

The duke, unused to such familiarity, but realizing it was rapidly going to become a feature of his life with Christina, asked Milton if he and Isobel would care to join them at dinner that evening.

"Love to, Your Lordship," Milton said expansively, "but I reckon Isobel's going to be confined to bed till we reach New York."

Christina, who knew how rough the crossing ahead of them could be, said: "Would it be all right if I came in to see her later on? I have some medication for seasickness that is better than anything she will get from the ship's doctor."

"That's mighty kind of you," he said sincerely. "Isobel would appreciate that. She hasn't had another woman to talk to since leaving Austria. She's shy and only nineteen; she needs some young company like yourself. I'd best be getting back to her. She'll be getting lonesome. We'll look forward to seeing you later."

"I like him," Christina said to the duke as they returned to their own staterooms.

"I thought you might," the duke said, well aware of the striking similarity between Mr. Milton Barnard and Theobald Goldenberg. He felt a twinge of jealousy at the thought that Goldenberg had been Christina's lover and then suppressed it. Christina would never deceive him. She was too forthrightly honest. No other woman of his acquaintance would have told him about her past life as Christina had done, knowing it could wreck the chance of becoming his wife and mistress of Anersley. Christina hadn't thought twice. True, he had needed nearly a full bottle of brandy when she told him about the Gaiety and Bessie Mulholland, but to his own amazement it had not made the slightest bit of difference. Her love of life, generosity, vivid beauty and spontaneous affection were all his and he could not face the thought of life without them.

"Would you mind," Christina asked hesitantly, "if

I just slipped down to the Orlop Deck. I didn't have time earlier on.''

Orlop, Upper, Middle and Lower Decks were all the same to the duke, He smiled affectionate agreement and she was off, running down flight after flight of stairs to the bowels of the ship.

"You can't come down here love," a fireman said, wiping the smoke from his eyes as he took a breather in the corridor. "It's all boiler rooms and engine rooms down here."

"I know. That's what I wanted to look at."

As if we were blinkin' monkeys in a zoo, the fireman thought to himself. *Bloody idle rich.*

Out loud he said, "Sorry, madam. This deck is only for crew." A group of trimmers emerged, laughing and swearing. They stopped short at the sight of Christina.

"Lady wanted to look round," their colleague said expressively. "I've just explained to her it ain't possible."

"*Josh!*" Christina pushed the fireman to one side and to everyone's amazement ran open-armed to the coal-begrimed figure, the bare muscles of his chest gleaming with sweat.

"What on earth are you doing here? Why didn't you tell me you were sailing the *Titanic* . . .''

Josh, blushing to the roots his hair, took her to one side and while his mates watched with interest said in a low voice, "I told you I was going to America, lass."

"But you *can't* leave the ship in New York," Christina protested, and then, aware of the listening ears, "It's not *allowed*, Josh. You have to complete the voyage and sail back on the ship."

"Aye, mebbe you do, but no one will miss me and it isn't as if I'll be wanting to sail aboard another ship. In fact," Josh said with something of his old vigor, "I'm never going to sail again. I've had enough already."

Christina giggled. "Let me have a word with the captain. I'm sure I can sort something out and have you transferred to the passenger list. I'm going to marry the Duke of Marne and he's a millionaire. He can fix anything."

Josh's eyes widened. "So you really will be a lady at last?"

"Not just a lady. A duchess."

"I'm right glad for you," Josh said generously. "But don't go bothering him about me. I'm fine where I am. I'm used to hard work and we'll be in America by Wednesday. Reckon I can last out till then."

"But the sea. It gets ever so rough and you know how sick you get."

Josh nodded grimly. They were only just passing the Isle of Wight but already Josh was finding the roll of the ship decidedly uncomfortable.

"T'aint nowt you can do about it lass. You'd best get back on top where you belong. Else you'll be getting me into trouble."

Realizing the truth of what he said, Christina reluctantly agreed, but only on making Josh promise that he would meet her once they had docked in New York.

Hurrying back to a world far removed from the one Josh inhabited, Christina suddenly remembered what it was that had nagged at her on her tour of the Boat Deck.

She took out her notebook and hastily scrawled: "not enough lifeboats," then gaily surprised the patiently waiting duke with the news that her childhood friend was aboard as a trimmer and was it possible for the duke to help him start a new life in America?

The duke wiped a smudge of coal dust from her nose and took her into his arms, asking if there were any other firemen, greasers or deck hands she would like provisions made for. Christina told him not to be silly, kissed him affectionately and wondered whether to wear her white or yellow ball gown for dinner that evening. She finally decided on the white, as Milton knocked on the duke's stateroom door, saying his wife was sicker than ever and asking if Christina could possibly visit her and dose her with the medicine she had spoken of.

The duke, rapidly becoming accustomed to Milton's lack of formality, assured him that Christina would attend his wife as soon as possible.

Some minutes later, flicking an imaginary speck of dust from his jacket sleeve, he knocked on the adjoining door and entered.

Christina was surveying herself critically in a full-length mirror. Her white satin ball gown was decorated with exquisite lace and had a demitrain sweeping behind in a confection of ruffles. A single white rose nestled in the gleaming waves of her upswept hair.

"Do you think this is a little too grand?" she asked anxiously. "It looks as if I'm about to be presented at Court."

"Among Astors, Guggenheims and Rothschilds nothing is too grand. You look magnificent." He took her hand and kissed it. "Our American friend has asked if you would send your medication along to his wife. Apparently her *mal de mer* is increasing."

"Oh dear!" Christina's face was anxious. "She looked desperately ill at Southampton. I'll go along and see her now."

The duke gently caught her arm and pulled her against him. "Ring for a bellboy and he'll take the medicine to her. Dinner is waiting and I still haven't seen the glories up above yet."

She wound her arms around his neck. "Then you must enjoy them alone tonight, Duke. I can't possibly dance the night away knowing that poor girl is sick. She needs sympathy and reassurance just as much as she needs the medicine."

The duke sighed, knowing the battle was already lost. He had to be satisfied with a soft kiss, a gay smile and the expression of relief on Milton's face when Christina knocked on his stateroom door and announced she would keep Isobel company for the evening.

"That is certainly a fine woman," Milton said admiringly as they walked down the thickly carpeted corridor toward the stairs. "Say, this ship beats even Austrian palaces for grandeur!"

Down on the Saloon Deck they approached the dining room through an annex covered in Aubusson tapestries, and the duke nodded in recognition toward a vision in pale lemon and pearls.

"Who's that?" Milton asked as they sat themselves at a table in the big white Jacobean room.

"The Countess of Rothes," the duke replied. "One of the pleasanter members of the English aristocracy."

"You don't talk like any English duke I've ever met before," Milton said frankly. "Are you sure you're the genuine article? You can confide in me. I like a man for what he is, not *who* he is."

"I take that as a compliment," the duke said, a muscle twitching at the side of his mouth. "But I assure you that for better or worse I'm the genuine article."

"You mean your people came over with William the Conqueror?"

"So much so that they referred to him intimately as William the Bastard."

Milton laughed. "You're really my kind of guy. I stayed at the Ritz earlier this year but didn't seem to fit in very well. English reserve, I suppose."

The duke agreed that it probably was.

"Austria was the same. All formality and etiquette. Not that Isobel's like that, but then, though she has the breeding, her family hasn't a dime, which helped. Guess they were glad to get her off their hands. Leastways, they made no objection to her marrying me. Not when they realized that I had so much money.

Pretty sharp, those foreigners. They relieved me of plenty of it before I left but I guess it was worth it. I don't mind telling you, Duke, that I'm just crazy about that little girl. Can't wait to get her to New York. Milton Barnard marrying an Austrian countess. My ex-wife is going to choke on her alimony."

"You've been married before?" the duke asked unnecessarily as his attention was caught by the sight of Mr. Bruce Ismay, the Chairman of the White Star Line.

"And it was a real disaster. It was like living with Torquemada. That's the reason I went to the trouble of marrying again. I want my money sewn up tight. I don't want her laying claim to the lot of it. Now the bulk of it will be Isobel's which suits me fine. It's time she had more in life than being cooped up in a decaying palace with an aunt old enough to be my grandmother."

The consommé temporarily silenced him and the duke was able to take stock of his fellow travelers. They made an impressive sight. Captain Smith reminded the duke of Caleb Reed. He was a typical British sea captain. Strong in command but gentle in manner, shaggy white eyebrows giving him a grandfatherly appearance.

The women were beautiful, even by the duke's standards, but none had Christina's gaiety and unique spirit. He recognized the distinguished figure of Sir Cosmo Duff Gordon and wished he had Christina by his side in order to arouse envy in the breast of a fellow aristocrat. He also hoped that Milton's young bride recovered quickly so that he could enjoy displaying his own bride-to-be on his arm. If he had seen Isobel he would have known the prospect was hopeless.

She lay white-faced in the vast bed, smiling wanly at Christina, who had introduced herself with the minimum of fuss. She had taken the medicine like a dutiful child and Christina had been relieved to discover that though Austrian, Isobel's slowly spoken English was flawless, betraying only the slightest accent.

"Thank you very much. You are very kind." She lay her dark head back on the pillows, exhausted by the act of drinking.

Christina patted her hand. "Only five days and then you'll be able to enjoy your honeymoon properly."

Isobel's eyes were anxious. "I hope so for Milton's sake. He's been so good to me . . ."

Her forehead was damp with sweat and Christina soaked a flannel in cold water and pressed it against her brow.

At ten o'clock a concerned Milton returned to the stateroom to relieve Christina, immediately sensing the friendship that had sprung up between the two girls.

He clasped Christina's hand tightly.

"I am grateful to you, Mrs. de Villiers. Anything I can ever do. Anything at all."

"Just keep the duke company while I sit with Isobel," Christina said, laughing. But later, when the duke came in to say good night to her, her face was serious.

"Isobel is really very ill," she said as she unpinned her hair, letting it cascade over her bare shoulders.

The Duke of Marne watched her, entranced, glad that she had dispensed with the services of a maid. She turned her back to him so that he could unhook her dress and then stepped out of it, as free of corsetry as she had been when she worked at the Gaiety.

"She'll be all right," the duke said reassuringly, and before she could slip into the froth of lace and satin that served as a negligee he took her in his arms, kissing her deeply.

Christina responded warmly, hoping that this time she would be carried beyond herself by his skilled and gentle lovemaking. It didn't happen. Afterwards, lying in the darkness, she damned Devlin O'Conner to hell. If it hadn't been for him she would never have known the madness that love could induce. She would have been content with her feeling of deep affection for the duke, not yearning for that which could never be again. It seemed as if there was a devil inside her, binding her to Devlin, exercising control of her body over her mind. She knew that only by forgetting him could she regain happiness and peace of mind as the duke's wife and mistress of Anersley.

Sleep was impossible. She slipped a fur coat over her nakedness and with high-heeled mules on her feet, walked through the now nearly silent ship to the main stairway, climbing until she reached the splendid isolation of the Boat Deck. In the distance she could hear the faint sound of laughter coming from a party in a private suite.

She hugged the coat close to her body. The night was black, and so clear that the brilliance of the stars took her breath away. The *Titanic* steamed with throbbing engines through a sea that was as calm and smooth as glittering glass. With a chill not caused by the cold she realized that this voyage and the return would be amongst the last she would ever make. Her future life would be on dry land, yet the sea was in her blood. She wanted only to be part of a ship, part of the sea and the sky.

Yet if she traveled the oceans she would hear about Devlin, see him. The prospect of the pain and the constant reopening of old wounds was too much to bear. At Anersley she would be loved and protected. No woman could ask for more. Shivering, she made her way down to her first class stateroom and the luxury of her giant-sized bed.

The next day they called at Queenstown for extra passengers and mail and then the coast of Ireland faded slowly over the horizon as the *Titanic* steamed out into the Atlantic.

Isobel felt even weaker and Christina stayed with her while the duke resigned himself to the fact that she was going to play nurse for as long as Isobel needed her. He proceeded to enjoy the experience of sailing on the largest liner ever built with as much enthusiasm as he could muster without her presence.

"There's Thomas Andrews, the *Titanic*'s architect aboard," the duke said in an effort to tempt her up to the glitter of the Café Parisienne. "And the band is as good as that at the Ritz. Not just old fashioned waltzes. The bandmaster is a young man and they play ragtime. Come on, Christina. I've never known you when you didn't want to dance."

She grinned ruefully. "If you could see Isobel you'd understand my concern. I'm more and more convinced that her sickness is far more serious than an attack of *mal de mer*. I've told Milton and, as Isobel is refusing to see the ship's doctor, he's promised he will take her to a specialist the minute we dock in New York."

"But that's three *days* away and I want to show you off. Even the Countess of Rothes can't hold a candle to you."

"You have the rest of your life to show me off," Christina said affectionately.

He tilted her chin upwards with his finger. "The rest of my life," he said, a smile on his lips but his eyes deadly serious, "will not be enough," and reluctantly he had left her and joined Milton and Mr. Ben Guggenheim in the smoking room.

Isobel was vainly plotting the *Titanic*'s progress on a map provided on the back of the passenger list.

"At least we're more than halfway there," she said weakly on Saturday. She had closed her eyes wearily, and once satisfied that she was asleep Christina had gone in search of Milton.

He was in the squash courts, taking advantage of the services of a professional coach.

"Isobel really should see the doctor," Christina said. "She's as weak as a kitten. She hasn't eaten anything since Thursday night."

"But she's not been sick?"

"No . . . I wish she had. That I could have understood, even though the voyage has been so smooth."

Milton sighed. "I've tried, but she can be a stubborn little thing when she wants to be. We'll be in New York by Wednesday. I imagine she'll pick up when we're back on dry land."

"I only hope you're right, Milton. But I doubt it. Are you sure Isobel wasn't ill *before* you left Vienna?"

"No. A little peaky but I guess that was from all the commotion of the marriage. Her only living relations are an elderly aunt and a doddering old uncle. They wanted her to marry me all right, but they wanted their pound of flesh too, and their attitude upset Isobel. She said I shouldn't have given them a dime." He laughed. "She's been brought up in such genteel poverty that she hasn't really grasped the kind of money I have." He flung a towel round the back of his neck. "Forty years ago I hadn't two cents to rub together. Now I own more Manhattan real estate than any other man in New York City. Railroads, steel, you name it, I have a part of it." He leaned forward. "I'll tell you something in confidence, Christina. Last year I had a nasty shock. A heart attack. Nothing serious—look at me now, chasing that young squash coach till he doesn't know if he's coming or going, but I don't mind telling you that at the time it scared the hell out of me. Not the dying part—the thought of all my hard-earned money going to my ex-wife and to a younger brother who's never lifted a finger. Whatever I put in my will they would have contested but I figured even they couldn't contest it if I left it to a wife! So there it was in the back of my mind, marrying again, and then I saw her and I said, 'that's the one, Milton.' Young, sweet-natured, and a countess." He smiled beatifically. "I'm a happy man. They won't get their hands on my millions now and when I die it'll be with a smile on my face!"

On Sunday the weather was so cold, though the sea was calm, that only the hardiest ventured on deck. Christina, undeterred by any weather, had stood watching the wake of white foam as the giant propeller blades sliced through the slumberous Atlantic rollers. It was two thirty in the afternoon and Isobel had fallen into a restless sleep. Her need of Christina was increasing every day and the amount of time Christina could spend away from her was growing less and less.

The absence of the two girls amongst the other first class passengers aroused little curiosity, though Lady Cosmo Duff Gordon would have liked to see the girl who had finally enslaved the eligible Duke of Marne. *Mal de mer* was a very common complaint, and though few people were suffering it on this particular voyage, they all had sympathy for Isobel and expressed open admiration at the way the duke's fiancée was so unselfishly keeping her company.

"We could be in New York by Tuesday evening at the speed we are traveling," Christina had said to her cheerfully. "Three hundred and eighty-six miles Thursday noon to Friday. Five hundred and nineteen miles Friday to Saturday, and five hundred and forty-six miles from Saturday to today. She must be making twenty-two knots."

"Is that fast?" Isobel asked hopefully.

"*Very* fast for a ship this size. We'll knock hours off the journey."

The cold had increased and Christina said to the duke as Maurice helped him change for dinner, "I can't imagine why Captain Smith is still going ahead at full speed. It's so cold it must mean there are icebergs further south than usual."

The duke grinned and said to Maurice, "Did you know the future duchess is an expert sea-woman? She could probably sail this ship just as well as the captain!"

Christina giggled. "I'd love to have the chance," and then, more seriously, "You may laugh at me but

I still think he's making a mistake blinding on at this rate. Caleb always said a man could never be too careful on the Atlantic run."

"But Caleb never captained a giant like the *Titanic*. Don't worry my sweet, Captain Smith knows what he's about."

Milton and the duke hastily sought sanctuary in the private smoking room after dinner as the sound of second class passengers singing Sunday evening hymns assailed them. Christina had finished her notes and had gained Isobel's interest as she explained what they were and what they were for. A stewardess brought them in coffee and biscuits at ten o'clock and then Christina read to Isobel for a short while from a Thomas Hardy novel. Seeing Isobel's eyes slowly close, Christina laid the book down, wished her good night and went back to her own stateroom. She was tired as she hurried down to *E* Deck, asking the crew if there was any chance of her speaking to Josh Lucas, trimmer, but the men had looked at her as if she were mad.

She glanced at her wristwatch. Ten forty-five. The duke would be down soon to kiss her good night and tell her of the happenings in the Palm Court and Café Parisienne. She grinned suddenly to herself. Milton had said naively to her shortly after they had first met, "How come that guy doesn't allow you to call him by his Christian name when you're about to be married?" and Christina had told him, much to his relief, that as Frederick was his Christian name and didn't suit him in the least, she always referred to him simply as "Duke."

"Do you reckon I can call him that as well? 'Your Lordship' doesn't sound none too friendly, but I wouldn't like to cause offense."

"You wouldn't be causing offense at all," Christina had said and had gently informed the man who loved her that from now on "Duke" was his nickname as well as his title.

She climbed into bed, too tired even to read. Another forty-eight hours and they would be in New York. She would see Theo for the last time, give him her overflowing notebook and turn her back on America and the shipping world for good.

Eleven thirty-five P.M. The duke and Milton were making a late night of it.

She closed her eyes, lulled by the familiar rhythm of the engines and then there came a faint grinding jar from somewhere deep within the ship. The mattress beneath her shuddered from the vibration. The engine ceased to throb. Christina opened her eyes, startled. The time was 11:40.

Chapter 28

She lay there eyes open, puzzled. The engines remained silent; the great ship was drifting silently. There was no sign of unusual activity. No bells were being rung. She picked up her book and tried to read.

Ten minutes later her stateroom door opened and the duke came in, his cheeks flushed with the cold, saying elatedly, "I've brought you a souvenir."

"A what?" She sat up in bed, perplexed.

He laughed, showing her a chunk of ice. "We were in the smoking room when we grazed an iceberg. It must have been a hundred foot at least. The decks are littered with the stuff. Milton put some in his highball!"

She was wide awake now. "Is that why the engines have stopped?"

"I expect so. The iceberg probably scratched the paintwork."

Christina swung her legs out of the bed. "The captain wouldn't have stopped the ship in mid-Atlantic for a reason like that. I heard the bump. The iceberg must have holed her."

"Nonsense," the duke said placatingly, putting the ice on the marble washstand. "We saw the iceberg slide away into the night and there was no damage."

She kissed him affectionately and reached for her clothes. "How would a landlubber like you know if there was any danger or not? A transatlantic liner doesn't suddenly cut engines for no reason."

He smiled ruefully, abandoning his idea of making love to her. "All right. You'd better come up top and see for yourself. Only wear something warm. It's freezing."

As they entered the corridor an anxious-looking woman in a dressing gown had stopped a steward.

"Why have we stopped?"

"Nothing to worry about, madam. We'll soon be under steam again."

"I told you so," the duke said, taking her arm and escorting her up on deck.

They crossed to the deck rail and stared down at the glittering black ocean. It was so still and calm that Christina's sense of unease increased. The duke felt her shiver.

"What's the matter, my darling. Cold?"

She shook her head. "No. I just don't like the Atlantic when it's so still. It makes me nervous."

He laughed. "You won't find anyone else agreeing with you there. Everyone says its the most comfortable crossing they've ever had. The only one suffering from seasickness is Isobel."

"I still prefer it when it runs to form with mountainous waves and strong winds. This calm is unnatural."

She strained her eyes into the distance. There was no moon. Only stars hanging brilliantly in the otherwise all-encompassing darkness. There was no sign of the offending iceberg and no sign of damage, but still the *Titanic* continued to drift powerless.

"Convinced?" the duke asked, taking her hand and leading her away. "The best place on a night as cold as this is in bed. With company."

Christina snuggled against his arm and allowed him to lead her away. He was a skilled and considerate lover, and affection and gratitude made her respond unreservedly. Yet try as she might she could never reach the height of mindless ecstasy that she had with Devlin. The duke was everything she could wish for, but he didn't send her senses singing or set her blood on fire as one glance or touch from Devlin did. And he knew it, too. She squeezed his arm, determined that this time would be different.

Milton was emerging from his stateroom, a frown furrowing his brow. "Say, the steward has just been round telling us all to put on life jackets and go up on deck."

"Whatever for? We've just been on deck and there's not a thing to see."

"Have you ever thought that half a ship is below the water line?" Christina asked him indulgently. "Come on. If the captain wants us to put on life jackets we'd better do so. Is Isobel dressed?"

"No, she's too sick to dress."

Steward bells began to ring and Christina said, "She'll be better off in warm clothes if we have to assemble on deck."

"But surely it won't come to that," Milton protested. "They won't send a sick girl on deck just as a precaution. This is the *Titanic*, not a row boat!"

"On deck, please, sir," a steward said as he made

his way down the corridor, knocking deferentially on the stateroom doors, telling the bewildered occupants to don life jackets and make their way to the Boat Deck.

"Why have we stopped?" an earnest looking man in spectacles and dressing gown asked.

"I don't know, sir, but I don't suppose it's much."

"Then why must my wife leave her cabin?" Milton asked pugnaciously. "She's too sick to move."

"Captain's orders, sir."

Other stewards were now quietly and efficiently helping the more elderly passengers into the cumbersome life jackets and coaxing them on deck.

"This is really *too* ridiculous," a woman protested in a high-pitched voice. "I insist that my maid bring my jewelry box. I shall complain to your superiors when we reach New York."

"*If* we reach New York," said the steward, who had the thankless task of seeing her to safety.

The woman was too busy enjoying the sound of her own voice to hear him, but Christina did.

She turned her attention back to Milton and the duke. "I think we'd better get to a lifeboat station as quickly as possible. Captain Smith wouldn't cause all this disruption for nothing."

"Reckon you're right," Milton said worriedly. "Though how the hell I'm going to persuade Isobel I don't know."

"Let me do the persuading."

Christina entered the Barnards' stateroom with a smile and a brisk, no-nonsense approach that would have done credit to a nurse. While Isobel protested tearfully she helped her into a thick ankle-length tweed skirt, insisting she wear at least two jumpers and then placing a fur coat around her shoulders.

"It won't be for long," she said encouragingly. "Just until the captain can tell how bad the damage is."

"Then why can't I stay here? I feel dreadful. The night air will kill me."

"Rubbish!" Christina said brusquely, opening a drawer and finding a pair of elbow-length kid gloves. "Put these on. You can sit in the foyer. It should be warm and sheltered in there."

Milton gratefully took his wife and led her with other complaining passengers up onto the next deck.

Christina gave a hasty look round the stateroom before closing the door. On the bureau lay Isobel's purse containing photographs of her dead parents. Instinctively Christina picked it up and slipped it into her skirt pocket. The jewelry so casually left behind was replaceable. The photographs weren't.

"Better get your fur," the duke said as she stepped back out into the now busy corridor. Hurriedly she crossed to her own cabin and unhooked one of the several furs in her wardrobe. She hesitated for a brief moment. Normally the coats and dresses swung gently with the rhythm of the ship. Now they hung perfectly still.

"That's right, miss," a steward said with a friendly grin. "It's a bit nippy up top. Got everything you want? I'm locking all the doors. Don't want anyone taking advantage, do we? A dozen millionaires and all their cabins open to the world! What a pity I'm an honest man!" and he turned the key smartly in the lock.

The duke was doing his best to persuade an irascible old lady to leave the warmth of her stateroom for the glacial night air. The steward with him was rapidly losing his temper.

"Madam, I *insist*," he said for the fifth time.

"I'm not leaving my bed at this time of night," she retorted fiercely. "I've never heard such rubbish."

"I'm sorry madam, but you must leave your stateroom immediately. Captain's orders."

"Then he's a fool. And so are you," she turned on

the duke rudely. "Have you both been drinking? Strong spirits are of the devil. I shall report you both to Captain Smith for being drunk and disorderly and disturbing my sleep."

"I am not a member of the crew, madam," the duke said in amusement, "and I assure you I have not been drinking. The ship has struck an iceberg and Captain Smith thinks it best that we report to our boat stations until the damage can be rectified."

"Stuff and nonsense!"

Only the duke's foot prevented the door being slammed in his face.

"The Astors and the Guggenheims are on deck, and Lady Cosmo Duff Gordon and the Countess of Rothes," Christina said, smiling winningly.

The mention of so many illustrious names made the old lady hesitate.

"Perhaps I could help you with your life jacket? I'm sure the steward is needed elsewhere."

Seeing that Christina was unmistakably one of the first class passengers, the old lady allowed her to slip past the steward and the duke and into the cabin.

Christina pursued her advantage, saying merrily, "Even Mrs. Astor is wearing a life jacket. She looks quite chic. Let me help you into yours."

"Thanks," the steward said gratefully as his cantankerous opponent allowed Christina to slip the offending article over her head. "I'm needed in steerage. If you could escort the lady to the deck I'd be grateful. The captain has ordered all women and children into the boats so the damage must be worse than we'd thought. You'd best get up on top as soon as you can."

"Children?" the old lady asked agonized. "I didn't pay for a first class stateroom to be annoyed by *children!*" Her double chin shook with indignation. "Doesn't the man know who I am? Has he no sense of propriety?"

The man hadn't. Sensing a kindred spirit he grinned at Christina who grinned back.

"I'd like to know what the Guggenheims think of all this nonsense," Christina's charge said to the duke as he hurried her down the corridor.

Christina wasn't listening to her. She was frowning as they climbed the stairs. They looked normal enough but they gave her the curious sense of being off-balance. As if they were tilting.

They emerged on *A* Deck and the old lady adamantly refused to go further. There were comfortable chairs in the reading room. If she had to put up with tomfoolery she would do it in comfort, not on a freezing cold deck. There were plenty more ladies of the same mind, and Christina and the duke reluctantly left her to voice her complaints to anyone around who would listen.

In the foyer on the Boat Deck Milton and Isobel were clearly visible amongst their strangely-dressed companions. Most of the men still wore pajamas beneath their heavy overcoats, some of them only dressing gowns and slippers. Many of the women were still in evening dress, small jackets and stoles clutched tightly across their shoulders—poor protection against the glacial night air. Isobel was buried in her fur, clinging pathetically to a grim-faced Milton.

"This is worse than we thought," he said as Christina and the duke joined them. "The captain has ordered the crew to prepare the lifeboats."

As the men stripped off the canvas covers and cleared away the lines to the davits, a sense of unease and confusion was growing among the groups of passengers who only a few minutes ago had been joking and making light of their predicament, treating it as an unexpected adventure. The expressions on the faces of the sweating crew members persuaded them it was no such thing.

The duke lit a cigar, blowing a large cloud of fragrant smoke skyward as he looked over the side of the ship to the freezing black sea some seventy feet beneath them.

"I don't fancy it myself," he said languidly.

Milton's frown deepened. "Do you reckon that they're actually going to *lower* those things?"

"They appear to have every intention of doing so," the duke replied, watching intently. "My taste for shipboard life is rapidly diminishing."

So was Milton's. For once he looked his sixty years.

Isobel's large eyes filled with tears. "I'm frightened. I want to go back to my cabin. *Please* Milton."

"In a minute, honey," Milton said protectively. "Let's find out what's happening first."

He strode abruptly across to the waiting men, noticing with growing anxiety that they were busy putting lanterns and packets of biscuits into the boats.

"Excuse me, officer," he said in a voice accustomed to being taken note of. "Is the situation really serious or are you simply taking precautions?"

The second officer was about to offer bland reassurance when he recognized the steely glint of the eyes and the determined thrust of the jaw. Milton Barnard, the million dollar railroad king, was not a man to be easily fooled. Neither was he the type of man to cause a panic.

"We're taking water fast, sir."

"You mean she's sinking?"

"Yes, sir. Rescue ships are on their way."

"*Rescue* ships? For the *Titanic?*" Milton asked incredulously.

"Yes, sir. Please don't tell the ladies. We don't want them worrying. You'll soon be aboard another ship. Now if you'll excuse me sir." He resumed feverishly fitting in the davits' cranks as his men uncoiled the line.

Milton stared beyond him to the Atlantic's glassily calm surface. High up above the stars shone brilliantly in the biting cold. New York seemed a long way off.

"Goddamn it," he swore beneath his breath. "Even a blind man could have seen a 'berg on a night like this!"

Knowing that Isobel was watching him, Milton fixed a confident smile on his face before walking back to her.

"It's nothing, honey. But we have to get in the boat for a short while."

"In the *dark?*" Isobel asked, aghast.

Milton kissed her hairline where the soft curls clung like a child's. "I promise you when we reach New York you need never see another ship in your life."

Above her head his eyes met those of the duke. The grim expression in them did not match the light-heartedness of his voice. The duke raised his eyebrows. So it *was* serious. He sighed. Like Isobel, he much preferred a warm bed to the dangers of a small rowboat in the vast darkness of the Atlantic.

Christina intercepted the look and drew her own conclusion. Her first thought was for Josh. He would be as bewildered as any of the passengers yet there was no way she could find him. If the ship was in trouble then he would be at his post with the rest of the firemen and trimmers.

The duke slipped his arm around her shoulders, squeezing her tightly as the *Titanic*'s four huge funnels blew off steam with a roar that made Isobel cry out in fear.

"Nothing to worry about, sweetheart," Milton said comfortingly. "It's just what trains do when they stand idle. It doesn't mean anything's wrong."

"We've lost a propeller," a distinguished-looking gentleman said to them authoritatively. "This will mean a trip back to the shipyard when she returns to Southampton I shouldn't wonder."

The deck was filling now. The groups who had preferred the warmth of the foyer were being coaxed on to the Boat Deck by their stewards. Christina recognized Mrs. Astor, who looked as immaculate as ever, and another well-known beauty whose hair was cascading down her back with only a girlish ribbon holding it in place.

"Oh God, I'm so cold," Isobel said, shivering convulsively, her face pinched and white.

Milton looked at her with growing concern. "I'll go back for another fur and your muff," he said.

"Oh no!" Isobel clung to him pitifully. "Don't leave me, Milton. I'm frightened!"

"I'll have to leave you if I'm to get you another coat."

She began to cry, drawing indulgent glances from the gentleman standing nearby.

"I'll go for it," Christina said to her, moving away.

The duke hastily transferred his attention from the davit and held her hand restrainingly. "I think it would be better if you stayed here. I don't want you getting lost at a moment like this. You're too precious."

She smiled impishly. "You're forgetting that I'm as much a sailor as the crew, Duke. I won't get lost."

Before he could argue, she slipped quickly away, threading between the confused knots of passengers toward the entrance to the stairs.

Milton grinned. "That little baggage is going to give you a good run for your money when she becomes a duchess. What did she mean, saying she's as much a sailor as the crew?"

"She comes from an old naval family," the duke said airily. "The sea is in her blood."

Christina had forgotten that the stewards had locked the cabin doors. Frustratedly she twisted and turned the knob but to no avail. There was no one else about. The last of the first class stragglers had been ushered on deck. Kicking the door for good measure she turned to hurry back toward the deck; as she did so there came a loud bellowing cry, and a panic-stricken youth raced down the corridor toward her.

"They've locked the gates! Get someone to open

*them for God's sake. There's hundreds of people
down there and the water's pouring in!"*

Christina stared at him, horrified. "What do you
mean, they've locked the gates?"

He rushed past her, yelling: *"Third class! They
won't let them through!"*

She broke into a run, seeing him seize a sailor by
the scruff of his neck as he burst out onto the deck.

"Great God, man!" he shouted, *"open the gates
and let the third class through. There's women and
children down there in water up to their waists!"*

At that moment there came a loud whooshing noise
and a distress rocket raced skyward, exploding into a
shower of brilliant light.

"Thank goodness you're back," the duke said
grimly. "Don't go off again like that. They've already
lowered some boats level with the Promenade Deck
and sent the Astors and Ryersons down there to
board. This boat will be free of the davit in a few
minutes and I want you and Isobel in it."

She shook her head, gasping for breath.

"I'm going down to steerage. The barriers are still
up and even if they take them down there's no one to
lead those people to safety."

"There're plenty of stewards," the duke said, seizing her arm before she could make a dash for it.

"For first class, yes," Christina said, her eyes flashing angrily. "But there won't be in steerage. They're
five decks down. How are they going to find their way
up here. *And* there's water rushing in!"

"All the more reason for you to get in a boat!"

It was the nearest they had ever come to a quarrel.
Christina looked at him and said, "There're sixteen
lifeboats on this ship. I know because I counted them
the day I boarded. And according to the passenger list
there're over two thousand passengers, not counting
crew."

"Then you're definitely getting in this boat!"

"No," she shook her head firmly. "I know the layout of the liner. I can be as much help as any of the crew. I'm going down to steerage and I'm going to bring those people up top before the last of the boats go and they're trapped."

She turned on her heel and forced her way through the frightened crowd milling on the deck.

"Christina! Christina!" the duke's voice was lost in the clamor. Not until he had vaulted a barrier and entered the third class lounge on *C* Deck did he catch up with her.

He grabbed her arm, pulling her out of the way of a demented crowd of youths, the bottoms of their trouser legs saturated with water.

"What are you doing?" she gasped, the breath hurting her chest.

"Coming with you." He grabbed her hand and together they broke into a frantic run as she dragged him after her toward the stairs leading down to *E* Deck.

The vast length of *E* Deck's main alleyway was a shoving, pushing mass of hysterical women, struggling with babies and toddlers. The men were clinging to their possessions, cardboard boxes grasped firmly, rusty trunks and packing cases high on their shoulders. Beneath the low ceilings and naked light bulbs they jostled against each other, pathetic in their bewilderment.

"You were right," the duke said grimly, "but how the hell do we bring any order to this chaos?"

Christina braced herself on the stairs, shouting out over the sea of heads, "Take no notice of the barriers! Smash them if you have to! But get up on deck—the ship is sinking!"

"The rest of you follow me," Christina commanded the blank faces that gazed at her uncomprehendingly.

"They don't understand you," the duke said, picking up a crying child and setting it on his shoulders to enable his mother to get a firmer hold on her baby and small boy. Christina recognized the look on the immigrants' faces. Not only did most of them not understand English but those that did were intimidated by her furs and the duke's aura of wealth.

Eyes blazing she thrust one hip forward, arms akimbo, and shouted, "Come orn now, girls! Let's be 'avin' yer before it's too bloody late!''

Several women pushed forward through the crowd and Christina shouted again. "That's the way! Follow me and to 'ell with the bleedin' barriers!"

Reassured by an accent they recognized, they followed her like the children of Hamelin following the Pied Piper, a mass of women and children and crying babies, hurrying up the stairs and through the third class lounge on *C* Deck and across the open-well deck. There were screams from the rear as water spurted from beneath a closed door, swirling round their ankles, black with oil from the boilers.

"Your boats are not on this deck," a burly seaman said, standing aggressively behind the barrier that marked off their quarters from the rest of the ship.

"Open this barrier immediately!" The duke's voice was like ice amidst the cries of the women.

"Sorry, sir. This area is second class."

"This ship is sinking and either you open this barrier or I'll smash both it and you!"

The duke's face was white with anger and Christina could see a muscle twitching convulsively at his jaw.

"I've got my orders . . ."

The duke swung the still crying child off his shoulders and into Christina's arms and smashed the lock with his bare fist while the seaman fled, terrified.

"Come on! There can't be much time left," he shouted to Christina who was staring at his bloodied hand. "Which is the quickest way?"

There came the sound of tables and chairs crashing into walls as the ship tilted even more sharply and the surging water rose.

Christina began to run. Down past the second class library and into first class quarters. Along the long corridor past the surgeon's office. The duke shouted out to keep them together as they hurtled past the maids' and valets' private saloon and—finally—up the grand staircase to the Boat Deck.

As they spilled out on deck, the duke guessed there were at least fifty still with them. Fifty people who, if it hadn't been for Christina, would still be milling about in the death trap on *E* Deck.

The Boat Deck was crowded, and if it hadn't been for the duke's powerful shoulders and authoritative voice none of the shawled women would have stood a chance of reaching any of the few boats that were left.

"There are women and children back here!" he shouted over the voices of men clamoring to be allowed into the boats with their wives.

"Then let them through!" The second officer fired a gun in the air as a group of crazed men and women tried to rush the lifeboat. "Anyone getting aboard without my permission will be shot. Is that understood? Now for God's sake make way and let the children through! . . . That's right"—the officer called encouragement as the first of the steerage passengers struggled through to the front of the crowd—"pass the babies over your heads, men."

With a sigh of relief Christina saw her charges, including the child and mother the duke had carried tearfully reunited, climb tremulously aboard the lifeboat.

She looked in vain for the ships that must surely be coming to their assistance. The Atlantic was as dark and as empty as it had been before.

The davits creaked, the pulleys squealed, and the boat was swung free of the ship.

"In you get," the duke said, swinging her up into his arms.

"No! We must go back! There are still hundreds of people down below!"

"I know and I'm going back for them. You're getting in this boat while there's still one to take you!"

The lifeboat was swinging perilously down the side

of the ship while the officer stood with his pistol pointing at the surging mass of men that ringed him. Christina struggled vainly as the duke's arms tightened
round her.

"You're going to do something you've never done
before, *ma chère amie*. You're going to do as you are
told!"

His mouth came down on hers, hard and sweet, and
then he swung her over the deck rails, dropping her
down into the boat already halfway to the sea.

The breath knocked from her body, Christina saw
his face recede into the darkness; at the last moment
she saw him raise his hand to his mouth and blow her
a kiss. He was smiling.

Chapter 29

The lifeboat had scarcely hit the water before the duke
was fighting his way back through the hysterical mob
and to the grand stairway. At the entrance, wearing
a strange selection of underwear, overcoats and dressing gowns, the band was grouped, steadfastly playing
ragtime as if nothing was happening.

The duke broke into a run, racing through the sinking ship as crockery and glass crashed in a growing
crescendo; the tilt of the deck was steepening even
more precariously. In second class a group of terrified
girls were pleading to be let through a still-erect barrier
while a member of the crew insistently directed them
through their own quarters.

The duke wasted no time on words. He lifted the man bodily to one side, silencing his protestations with the back of his hand, helping the weeping girls through and then, as they stood bewildered, grabbing their hands and running with them back up top.

The duke's grip on their wrists tightened; the third girl began clutching at his coat as they raced ahead of the water, finally climbing the companionway onto the Boat Deck with hammering chests.

It was no use going to the point where he had seen Christina to safety. There were no boats there. He dragged them, crying and gasping for breath, away from the mass of people now crowding the stern, which was rising higher every minute as the bow plunged beneath the waves.

"We're going the wrong way!" one of the girls screamed, tugging away from the duke's hand. His fingers cut into her wrist. Ahead of him, water swirling around their waists, he could see a group of sailors struggling to float a collapsible. The angle of the deck and the freezing, rising water made their task almost impossible.

"If you can iron out a kink in the fore we can do it!" one of the sailors panted, as the duke joined in with the rest of the men, tugging till his damaged hand was sodden with blood.

The deck jarred, tipping perilously, and the sea gurgled up the companionway as the collapsible finally floated free.

One of the girls made a jump for it, landing safely, and an officer and the duke literally threw the other two girls aboard as a stoker and trimmer seized the oars, pulling desperately to clear the ship before the suction dragged them down with her.

"Jump for it, man!" the officer yelled, but it was already too late. The collapsible was moving swiftly away to safety and a wall of water knocked the duke off his feet. Blindly he struggled. The wave receded and there was solid timber beneath him once again. The stern rose high, black with a mass of cowering survivors, delaying the inevitable moment of death for as long as possible. The lights still blazed and the band still played. At the entrance to the grand staircase the duke saw the unmistakable figure of Milton, puffing on a cigar and standing next to the cellist. Gathering his remaining strength the duke climbed the steep tilt of the deck and grasped his shoulder.

"Did Isobel get away?" he managed, as he struggled to control his breathing.

Milton nodded. "Yep. What about Christina?"

"Safe." His breathing was returning to normal.

"Looks like this is it," Milton said as a big wave swept along the Boat Deck and the screams in the stern grew louder. "Should we join the rush and climb higher?"

The duke shook his head. "Lemmings. There's no chance now. If I'm going to die I'm going to do it in style. Not cringing with a hundred others."

"My thoughts entirely," Milton agreed. "Have a cigar."

The duke divested himself of his overcoat, adjusted the immaculate lace frill on his shirt cuffs, straightened his bow tie and lit one of Milton's Havanas. Milton grinned and did likewise, slinging his astrakhan coat into the maelstrom of eddying water that surged around their knees. Then, splendidly clothed in full evening dress, cigars in hand, the Englishman and the American prepared to die with the dignity and panache they had both displayed in life.

The bridge dipped under the sea and a giant wave rolled aft along the boat deck. The bandmaster tapped his violin, the ragtime ended, and the strains of the hymn "Nearer My God To Thee" flowed across the deck and drifted into the night air. Milton's last thought—and it brought him satisfaction—was that his wealth would go to Isobel and not to his family; the duke's, that Christina was safe and had loved him before he died.

Then the sea foamed and swirled and engulfed them.

Josh had been off duty when the iceberg had struck, lying on his bunk and counting the hours until the ship reached New York. The door opened with a crash and one of his shipmates yelled, "Get down to the boilers! We've struck a 'berg!"

Josh jumped down, scrambling into his clothes; the seasoned sailor in the next bunk laughed, stretching, as if he had all the time in the world.

"This'll mean another trip back to Harland and Wolff for another lick of paint."

He sprang down to the floor, pulling his sweater over his head. "Come on, let's see what the old man is panicking about now."

He paused suddenly, head cocked, listening. No engines. He shrugged, slapping Josh on the back as they left the cabin.

"Dropped a propeller, I shouldn't wonder." He didn't wonder for long.

Cries of "Shut the dampers" and "Draw the fires" held a note of desperation that shook him out of his complacency and had him rushing down the iron-runged ladder toward the boilers.

Josh, half bewildered and half afraid, clambered down after him. He was no seaman and never had been. It was a miracle his bluff hadn't been called before now.

"She's taking water fast!" a voice called out to them as they ran into a wall of steam and then, through the stifling vapor, Josh could see men slaving over the pumps and water spouting in through a gash in one of the doors separating the boiler room from the other watertight compartments, only they weren't watertight any longer. Josh was in black, oily water up to his knees as he plunged in to help—and then up to his waist.

"Jesus bloody Christ!" his cabin mate yelled at an assistant engineer. "What the bloody hell happened?"

"A 'berg," a panting voice shouted back over the clamor. "Gashed her wide open."

"You mean there's water in the other boilers?"

"In the forepeak . . . Boiler Room 6 is already a write-off . . . It took the men all their time to get out . . . The mail room's flooded . . ."

"The whole lot's flooded," a fireman shouted. "This is the only boiler room the pumps are holding!"

"Shut your mouth," an engineer ordered shortly, "and get working."

Josh didn't need to be told twice. The sea was flooding in from the boiler doors and up through the footplates. Working at fever pitch he manned the pumps, his only thought that of Christina. There was no way he could get to her. No way he could see she was safe. His duty was down here with the rest of the crew.

The eddying sea was slick with grease from the machinery, which coated his sodden breeches and belly.

"Is she sinking?" he yelled across to his cabin mate, a barely distinguishable figure in the heavy steam.

"She ain't having a bloody birthday," came the answer as he struggled with the pump, fighting to keep ahead of the water.

"What about the passengers?"

"Never mind the bloody passengers," the engineer shouted at him. "Just keep these pumps going. Christ Almighty!" The lights went out and the men were in total darkness, the water swirling higher.

"Keep at it men," the second engineer commanded. "We'll have 'em on again in a minute."

"But I've got to know! I have a friend in first class . . ."

"Jesus Christ, what a time to name-drop," one of the men said with a laugh, breathing a sigh of relief as the lights flickered back on again.

"Don't worry about your friend, lad. If she does go down he'll be taken off in a lifeboat."

For what seemed like an eternity Josh sweated at the back-breaking work, boxing up the boilers and putting on dampers to stop the steam from rising, his workmates nothing but vague shapes moving about through the mist.

For a few brief minutes the men thought they were winning, and then the sea came roaring between the boilers at the forward end of the room, causing the whole bulkhead to collapse.

A churning, foaming torrent swept Josh off his feet, buffeting him against the escape ladder as his fingers desperately closed around it. The force of the water prevented his feet from making contact with the rungs and he climbed upwards by the power of his arm muscles, with the sea swirling round his chest and neck, foaming over his face. Another handhold, another rung, another gasp of air as he rose above the boiling surface. Christina. He had to get to Christina.

He had never been above his own deck. The maze of corridors and companionways and vast lounges were a mystery to him. Time after time he had to double back, blocked by water lapping hungrily from beneath closed doors. By the time he felt fresh air on his face and reached the Boat Deck the bow was already slipping beneath the waves; the lights were still burning below the water line, giving the hideous suck and slap of the waves a ghastly luminosity.

The lifeboat davits hung mockingly empty and the number of people running to seek sanctuary in the stern was so great he knew it would be impossible to find her. A steward gazed out into the darkness over the deck rail, a cigarette in his hand.

"The passengers." Josh shouted at him. "Did any of them get away?"

"Women and children." The steward didn't bother to turn his head.

"But there's still women aboard! I can hear them!"

"Steerage. Hundreds of them have just surged up top."

"First class." Josh dug his nails into the steward's arm. "Did the first class women get away?"

"Reckon so. Except for those that wouldn't leave their husbands." He nodded over his shoulder in the direction of an elderly woman sitting in a deckchair holding her husband's hand.

"What about everyone else? What about us?"

The steward laughed. "Not a hope in hell. Have you seen that?" He pointed to a barely discernible shape in the darkness. "No more than a dozen in that boat and she'll hold over forty."

"But surely she'll come back?"

"Does it look as if she's coming back? There's a highfallutin female member of our aristocracy in that boat. Reckon if you swam out to her all you'd get would be an oar crashed over your head." He continued to smoke, his voice not even angry. It was far too late for anger.

From below decks there came the crashing of china and the sound of loose furniture falling through open doorways and down the corridors as the bow slid lower toward the waiting sea. Some twenty yards away a member of the crew jumped high over the sinking rail and belly flopped into the water. He broke surface and began striking out in the freezing sea. Josh strained his eyes in the darkness but the man's head merged with the waves and he was lost to view.

Josh had no intention of waiting passively for death like the steward. It was no use waiting till the boat sank before trying to swim for it. He would only be dragged under by the suction of the ship. The bow dipped lower and lower, the stern swinging up until the *Titanic* was almost perpendicular. A mass of screaming bodies slithered relentlessly down and into the seething water. Others clung to the deck rails, the trailing ropes from the davits and to the winches and ventilators.

Josh turned his back on them, cursed the sea as he had always cursed it and dived in. The impact of the sub-zero water rendered him momentarily senseless. When he recovered consciousness he was spinning round and round in a whirlpool of water, his legs tangled in rope, the sea closing above his head. With a mighty effort he kicked himself free of the ensnaring rope and struck out for the surface. From behind him came a deafening roar as the engines broke free, tearing through the ship as though she were made of paper. He did not see the *Titanic*'s last few moments—he was too busy fighting for his life amongst a maelstrom of deckchairs and planking.

He struck out blindly, knowing only that he must get away from the sinking swimmers threatening to drag him under with them.

The cold knifed through him like a thousand spears and only his massive physique and strength saved him. After ten minutes strong swimming he saw dimly a half-empty lifeboat wallowing in the water.

"Oh don't capsize us!" a female voice cried as he threw his arm over the side and heaved himself aboard. No one offered to help him. There were sounds of crying as he lay like a beached fish in the bottom of the boat, vomiting sea water.

"Oh please, are you a sailor? Oh what shall we do?"

Josh shook himself back to full consciousness and gingerly sat up. The oars were lifeless and unmanned. A group of ashen-faced women huddled at one end of the boat. Screams still rang out over the darkened sea and Josh seized an oar.

"Grab the other oar and pull for all you're worth," he said harshly. "There are people drowning out there!"

Timidly a young girl did as he told her while the others protested weakly. There came the sound of splashing and a hand grasped upward. Josh leaned over, hauling a man in a water-logged fur coat into the boat.

"Take an oar," he commanded, but the man just lay whimpering and it was the girl who pulled manfully back toward the spot where the *Titanic* had sunk and where the heartrending cries filled the night.

"Over there," Josh called. "There's someone in the water over there." The face of his cabinmate grinned up at him.

"Best get away as quick as possible—otherwise we'll be swamped."

"Not till the boat's full," Josh said stubbornly.

"Don't be a bloody fool—row back into that mess and we'll all drown!"

"So would you if we hadn't!"

The argument was halted as more hands struck out toward them. The women, shaken from their numbed reverie, helped pull in some more members of the crew and a badly burned fireman.

"We're nearly full now. Let's pull away while we still have a chance."

"No!" Josh was resolute. He was no leader and had never tried to be but he knew right from wrong, and it was wrong to pull away in a boat that would hold even one more of the drowning. Some yards away to the left another lifeboat was rocking aimlessly, making no effort to return to those screaming for help. Over the water Josh could hear the sound of a violent argument as yet another strong swimmer reached them and was dragged aboard.

"That's it," the fireman said, his voice weak from pain. "There's two dozen of us now. Let's pull away while we have a chance."

"Just one more!" a voice shouted from the water. "Give me a hand, boys." A greaser clad only in underpants was lifted out of the sea. The lifeboat was now so deep in the water that the slightest movement rocked her dangerously.

"Pull away," Josh's mate said to him. "We've done our bit. One more and we'll all be under."

Josh pulled on the oar, accepting defeat. They were full now. He had done all he could. The screams for help continued and the women put their hands over their ears, sobbing uncontrollably. Then, above the noise of the drowning, Josh heard a voice shouting in anger. It was Christina's.

Christina's thoughts were in turmoil as the lifeboat hit the sea and the two crew members assigned to it pulled strongly on the oars. There was no sign of any rescue ships and no more lifeboats. The duke was facing certain death and he was facing it without her. And so was Josh. In agony she watched as the *Titanic*'s bow slipped beneath the sea, the water reaching and covering the glowing lights from the portholes, her bulk huge against the backdrop of stars.

"She's going down," the stoker who had taken control of the lifeboat said quietly, and the women around Christina began to cry.

Christina's eyes never flinched. With a face as still as if it had been carved from marble she watched the giant hull rise higher and higher as the sea rushed over the bow as it stood—for a few seconds—absolutely perpendicular to the water. There came a deafening roar as the engines tore free and then the *Titanic* began to slide slowly under the water until, with hardly a gasp, the waves closed over her and all that was left was a glassy sea littered with deckchairs and crates and floatable rubbish. And people. Hundreds of them screaming for help as the icy water engulfed them.

For a full minute no one in the boat was capable of speech or action and then the stoker gave the order to pull away.

"*No!*" Christina cried out. "There's room for another dozen!"

"Not in this boat, love," the stoker said grimly, pulling on the oars.

"You can't leave them! It's murder!"

The cries from the sea assailed them on all sides. The steward who was pulling on the other oar looked uncomfortable.

"She's right. We could pick up another half dozen."

"*No!*"

An imperious-looking lady clutching a jewel case and with a fur pulled tight around her shoulders said, "I *order* you not to return. There's quite enough people in this boat already. I'm most dreadfully cramped."

"We go back," Christina said, her voice like steel. "There's women and children drowning out there!"

The stoker hesitated and his mate said, "She's right. We don't have to go that far, just stand easy off and pick up those that are strong swimmers. There'll be no fear of our being capsized then."

He began to pull on his oar, swinging the lifeboat around. The stoker leaned on his oar, torn by indecision.

"For goodness' sake help him," Christina cried— and then, as the stoker seemed to fall into a stupor, she rose to her feet, picking her way along the women and reaching for the oar herself.

"Why should we lose our lives for them?" the upper-class accent of one of them asked hysterically. "It's foolishness. I demand that you pull away. I shall report you to the company. I shall . . ."

"Perhaps we should go back," a nervous woman sitting next to her said. "There's still some room left."

"Nonsense," said another. "There are plenty more lifeboats. I don't believe anyone is drowning. They are simply singing to keep up their spirits."

"Singing my eye," Christina said rudely, stepping past her and reaching for the oar that lay idle in the stoker's lap.

A heavily beringed hand grabbed at Christina's sleeve, pulling violently. Christina cried out, lost her balance and fell over the side. Her thick fur dragged her under. She fought to the surface and heard the confused shouts from the lifeboat and then she was sinking again, the freezing water paralyzing her limbs, her clothes weighing her down.

Once more she reached the surface, gasping great lungfuls of air, and then she submerged as she struggled out of her cumbersome coat. With the blood pounding in her ears, her lungs bursting, she struggled free of it, clawing her way upward, striking out for the boat. It was a good fifty yards away and pulling away from her. The cold was unendurable, it leadened her arms and legs, cut through her body in a pain so intense she could hardly breathe. Away to her right she saw the faint glimmer of another lifeboat, so deep in the water it was barely discernible.

"Help!" she cried, swimming out toward it, knowing that she would never reach it, that the sub-zero temperature of the sea would claim her first. "Help!"—and then, as the water closed over her head and her consciousness ebbed—"Devlin! Devlin! *Devlin!*"

"Don't be a bloody fool," his mate said as Josh sprang to his feet, sending the precarious boat rocking crazily.

"She's fallen overboard!"

The shouts of accusation and frigid replies of defense from the nearby lifeboat sounded clearly over the water.

"If she has you'll never find her!"

"The bastards are pulling away!"

"They'll pick her up," the fireman said reassuringly. "There's no room left here. Not even for one."

"I go along with that."

"So do I."

More than a dozen voices agreed vehemently that they were full to capacity. Josh strained his eyes into the darkness; faintly, he heard her cry for help and then he dived, striking out strongly, praying to God to guide him.

The sodden fur coat brushed past his face and then he saw her, a white hand still raised above the surface of the pitch black sea. He swam down, searching blindly, his hands closing round her, dragging her back to the surface, crying with relief.

"It's all right, lass. I've got you. It's all right."

The lifeboat drifted aimlessly where he had left it.

"She's dead, mate," a greaser said. "Let her go."

"Take her." Josh could hardly speak, his jaw was clenched together, his eyes blinded by salt water.

"There's no room," his cabin mate said as the rest of the boat's occupants approached hysteria at the thought of another passenger to weigh them down even further. Even now water slopped over the gunwhales at the slightest movement.

The man Josh had dragged aboard in a waterlogged fur grabbed the oar out of the stoker's hand and raised it threateningly over Josh's head.

"Take her," Josh repeated. "Give her my place."

"But she's dead . . ."

His cabin mate reached down and dragged at Christina's wrists.

"Thanks, pal." Josh managed a smile as he watched Christina being hauled aboard. Then he trod water as the men pulled once more on the oars, and his mate's pleas that they risk taking him as well were shouted down.

"Bye, lass," he said, the sea heaving and swelling around him. "God bless." Then he turned, striking out into the darkness.

Chapter 30

When Christina returned to consciousness it was to find herself huddled face down on wet wood. She stirred; a scream rose to her lips and escaped in a dull moan.

"There now. You're all right, dearie. Couldn't lift you up. We're packed like sardines in a tin."

Christina pulled herself up on her elbows and found herself wedged between two fat knees.

"Best keep still. There's not a mite of room. Any movement and we'll ship more water."

The voice and knees belonged to a middle-aged lady Christina vaguely recognized. She had been one of the group she had led to safety from *E* Deck. The woman laughed.

"Thought you were a goner we did. Here. . . ." She took off her shawl and wrapped it around Christina's shoulders. Christina took it gratefully; she was so cold that she burned with the pain. Her legs and feet were immersed in the water slopping around the bottom of the lifeboat.

"I thought you'd left me." She remembered the vicious tug on her sleeve that sent her toppling overboard and searched the faces around her for the fur-clad culprit.

"They wouldn't have been able to see you, dear. Not in the dark. It was one of our fellows who saved you."

Christina moved gingerly to a more comfortable position.

"Come on men. Move about steady and make room for her to sit," her champion said. "Poor girl's sat in water here. She might just as well be in the sea."

Five minutes of careful maneuvering enabled Christina to squeeze into a space next to the shivering woman.

"Your shawl. Take it back, you're freezing."

"That's true, but I ain't wet and you are. Keep it dearie."

She looked at Christina's face keenly. "Weren't you the lass that led us top?"

Christina nodded weakly, trying to marshal her thoughts together.

"Then you could have my dress as well if I could manage to take it off. Here Sid, give her your coat. The girl's a bloody heroine. If it wasn't for her you'd be a widower!"

"Where is he?" Christina asked through chattering teeth.

"Where's who?"

"The man who saved my life. I want to thank him."

There was an uncomfortable silence. Josh's cabin mate, tugging strongly on an oar, said at last, "Can't do that, lady. He's drowned."

"You mean he drowned saving me?" Christina asked horrified.

"In a manner of speaking." The oars squeaked and splashed in the water. "Wasn't room for more than the one. You can see that for yourself. Josh wouldn't take no for an answer, even though we all thought you were a goner. 'Take her' he says, and then off he goes, swimming into the darkness."

"He was a bleedin' hero," Sid said gruffly.

"Josh Lucas?" Christina gave a cry of pain as the seaman nodded.

"There now, dearie. No need to take on so. It was

what he wanted to do. Tears won't bring him back now."

Josh. Josh, who hated the sea. Who had refused her offer of a first class passage. Who had been her sole friend as a child and who, despite his brief happiness with Merry, had always loved her. Josh was dead and because of her. Christina pressed her head against the unknown woman's comforting arms and wept.

A long time later, through her grief, Christina heard the stoker shouting at the fur-coated gentleman sitting at the other oar.

"For God's sake, man, pull!"

"I can't. I'm too cold. My hands hurt."

The stoker swore and the fireman said feebly, "Here, let me."

"Not with those burns," the stoker said grimly.

Christina turned her head, seeing hideously damaged hands and becoming aware for the first time that the stoker and his burnt companion were the only crew members aboard.

"I'll row," she said quietly, and while everyone held their breath in case they capsized, she made her way carefully to the center of the boat.

The stoker swore. A woman at the oars would be worse than useless. Five minutes later he reversed his opinion. She pulled expertly and in rhythm with him.

"Reckon you've done this before," he said.

"Yes." The hard physical work helped keep her mind off Josh and the frantic hope that somewhere, in another boat, the duke had survived.

Slowly the night passed. The women alternately cried quietly and shouted out into the darkness whenever they glimpsed another lifeboat, wanting to know if their husbands were aboard. The answers were all negative.

"How long do you think it will be before we're picked up?" Christina asked the stoker, her efforts at the oar warming her slightly.

"Dunno. Shouldn't be long. There was plenty of

time to wireless for help before she went down. Just keep your eyes skinned.''

The first pale rays of dawn began to light the horizon but any relief was tempered by the change in the sea. The glassy calmness now became choppy, as a bitter breeze ruffled the surface. Waves slopped overboard, drenching shin and knee.

A second later the stoker rested on his oar, saying to Christina, "Can you see a light over there?"

Christina scanned the horizon intently. Far off she saw a faint light.

"Yes. And it's growing brighter."

"It isn't. Look. There's more. Rows of them. It's a steamer!" and then the weakened women gave a "hurrah" as the ship fired rockets into the air to announce its presence.

Christina tried to smile but could not. Josh was dead, the duke's fate unknown. And what of Milton and Isobel? The stoker lit a piece of paper, holding it aloft as the terrible blackness of the night gave way to a pearly dawn, the sky becoming tinged with deepening rose and gold as the steamer drew nearer and nearer.

"It's a Cunarder," Christina said as they bobbed toward the side of the hull. "The *Carpathia*."

"It's a bloody ship and that's all that matters," Sid said, full of high spirits.

Lines were dropped and the lifeboat made fast. In the growing light Christina could see other boats converging from a wide circle toward the *Carpathia* midst a sea littered with icebergs both big and small.

Ropes were dropped from the open gangway high in the ship's side and the stoker stood aside to let Christina be first up.

Christina climbed agilely, refusing all offers to be hurried down to the prepared lounges all ready for the rescued. She accepted a hot cup of coffee and a blanket and steadfastly remained at the deck rail as the stoker and the more fit followed her up the rope ladder; the other ladies and the fireman were hauled up.

Gratefully the women allowed themselves to be ushered away to scalding hot soup reviving brandy and rest in the dormitories converted from lounges, smoking room and library.

Christina stayed alone, watching with a mixture of fear and hope as boat after boat arrived. Some of them held men. It was possible the duke was alive. One of them even arrived with his Pekinese dog. Others boarded in the same immaculate condition in which they had left the *Titanic*'s Boat Deck—still in full evening dress, their poise undisturbed by the horror of the night. Others were not so unmoved. Christina barely recognized Mr. Bruce Ismay, the Chairman of White Star, who literally stumbled aboard; refusing food and drink, his eyes glazed as the ship's doctor led him away to the privacy of a cabin.

The hours passed. The boats arrived less frequently and still there was no sign of the duke and Milton—or Isobel. She was joined by other anxious women, all frantically asking after lost husbands and children.

Christina watched without interest as the elderly British aristocrat who had pulled her overboard was hauled, complaining loudly, up the side of the ship. On reaching the safety of the deck her eyes met Christina's. For a second they showed a flicker of fear and then she adjusted her many furs and walked haughtily past her, demanding to see the *Carpathia*'s captain and that a private stateroom be made available for her use immediately.

By 8:15 all the boats had arrived but one. It was some several hundred yards away, packed to capacity. Christina's eyes hurt with the effort of trying to distinguish a familiar face. Surely Isobel had been saved. She had been one of the first on the Boat Deck.

The people in the boat huddled together as the sea grew rougher. A woman next to Christina began to pray, a rosary running through her fingers as a wave crashed into the boat, nearly submerging it. Painfully, inch by inch, it neared the *Carpathia* and still Christina could see no sign of Isobel among the many women. And none of the duke.

The boat made fast and began to unload and Christina watched the arrivals with a terrible numbness. There was no Isobel. No Duke. No Milton.

Down below in the main lounge the survivors gathered for a brief service to give thanks for the living and pay their respects to the lost. Christina remained on deck, watching with deadened eyes as the *Carpathia* steamed over the place where the *Titanic* had sunk, where the whole area was now scattered with debris: deckchairs and rugs, chairs and life belts, cushions and planking.

The *Carpathia*'s crew began the arduous task of taking a roll call of survivors. The vast majority of them assembled in the saloon. A few, like Christina, remained on deck, too numb to respond to the kindly nagging. A steward asked her to go below and then, as she gazed blankly through him, gently removed the sodden purse from her dress pocket. Water had seeped in but the papers were still readable. He ticked the name of Mrs. Milton Barnard off his list and instructed a stewardess to help Mrs. Barnard change into dry clothes, as she seemed to be in a state of shock and unable to help herself.

A gregarious American woman lent the young widow some clothes, for by now the roll call was completed and the stewardess had told her that the young girl had lost her husband. After a warm brandy and the comfort of a borrowed bunk and thick blankets, Christina slept the sleep of exhaustion.

When she awoke her first action was to search the list of survivors. The duke was dead and so was Milton. She had known it in her heart all along. With a surge of joy she saw that Isobel had survived—and then, lower down, she saw her own name marked as one of the dead. She stared at it, a chill spreading through her body. Isobel's purse. The steward had

taken it and assumed she was Isobel. It was Isobel
who had died, not her.

She saw a face she vaguely recognized from the
Titanic and said, "This lady—Mrs. de Villiers—how
did she die? I saw her leave in a lifeboat myself."

"I believe that was the young lady who died of the
cold. The boat was so crowded that there was no
choice but to slip her overboard. Was she a friend of
yours?"

A commiserating hand patted her back.

Christina continued to stare at the dancing names
in front of her. Poor Isobel. Poor Milton. So sure that
when he died his wealth would be his young bride's
and that he had foiled his ex-wife and worthless
brother. And the duke. Smiling down at her. Happy
in the knowledge that she was safe, greeting his death
with the same careless nonchalance he had displayed
in life. And herself. Bereft of those who had loved
her. Merry. Josh. The duke. Even Theo was no longer
a part of her life. His world was too bound up with
that of Devlin's and she could not face a future where
he could be a constant reminder to her of what might
have been. To leave that world had been simple before. She would have been sheltered by the duke's
love and wealth. Now she would have nothing. She
would be Christina Haworth again. Penniless and
homeless.

"A coffee, Mrs. Barnard?" a bell boy asked deferentially.

Christina took the proffered cup and saucer and
sipped the hot liquid. Since the *Titanic* had sailed from
Southampton she had stayed in Isobel's stateroom,
only venturing out for short periods—and always
alone, making no contact with the other passengers.
There was no one to know that she wasn't Isobel, for
neither of them had been seen and Isobel had no relatives except for an elderly aunt and uncle who didn't
care tuppence for her and never emerged from the
depths of their Viennese schloss. She wondered what

Milton would say and knew immediately. He would have been behind her every inch of the way, rubbing his hands gleefully at the thought of outwitting those who waited like vultures for his wealth.

"Take it, honey. For God's sake take it and have a ball." The voice was so real that she turned, expecting to see him grinning at her shoulder.

The bellboy removed the empty cup from her hands. "Would you like to eat now, Mrs. Barnard?"

"Yes," Christina said, leaving Christina Haworth and Mrs. de Villiers behind her. "I think I would."

Devlin was in New York when the news of the sinking hit the streets. The newspaper headlines varied. The *Herald*'s read:

THE 'TITANIC' STRIKES ICE
AND CALLS FOR AID.
VESSELS RUSH TO HER SIDE.

The *Times* was more daring. The early editions reported that the *Titanic* was sinking and the last editions that she had sunk.

Devlin was as eager for news as the anxious friends and relatives who thronged the White Star offices. His interest was purely professional. It seemed hardly credible that a ship with the *Titanic*'s reputation could sink, and if it had, it could cause the *Ninevah*'s bookings to fall dramatically. Such a tragedy would make even the hardiest traveler nervous.

"Nothing to worry about," Duane said to him blandly over the telephone. "I have a copy of the *Evening Sun* here. The *Titanic* collided with an iceberg all right but it says that everyone has been saved. They're towing her into Halifax."

Devlin hoped he was right. He had three days ashore, and didn't want them spoiled by seeing the passenger list for his next sailing dwindling into insignificance.

He strolled into his favorite bar and was immediately joined by a pretty redhead. Kate was no longer an encumbrance. She had left him for Stanislaw Mikolij and Devlin had breathed a deep sigh of relief. The scar running through one eyebrow and down his cheek had done nothing to detract from his fierce good looks. It had only enhanced them. The surgeon who had stitched him up had said that another fraction of an inch and he would have lost the sight of his eye. Devlin had merely shrugged. He knew who had marked him for life, all right.

The captain of the *Dereta* joined them, putting his hat on the bar and asking for a double bourbon.

"Thinks look pretty bad for White Star," he said to Devlin. "The latest reports are pretty grim. There's a survivor list up now and crowds are storming the offices for information."

"She's definitely gone down?"

"The *Carpathia* picked up the lifeboats and is returning to the city with the survivors. There are only 675 of them, according to the list."

"Christ!" Devlin's hand faltered and he put his glass back on the bar. "How many was she carrying?"

"Over two thousand."

Even the redhead was subdued.

"Old Reed's been round there since news first started coming in. He should have sailed hours ago. Goldenberg will be pensioning him off at this rate."

"Why's Reed so concerned? Is his wife aboard?"

"No. Some young widow he's taken a fancy to."

Devlin's face drained of blood. "A Mrs. de Villiers?"

The *Dereta*'s captain shrugged. "Don't know her name. It will be on the list of those lost. Hey, finish your drink . . ."

Devlin had gone. The redhead gazed after him in annoyance and the *Dereta*'s captain shrugged. She was a pretty little thing.

"Want another?" he asked.

The redhead suppressed her disappointment. He wasn't as dashing as Captain O'Conner but he still had the magical four rings on his sleeve.

"A highball," she said and smiled coquettishly.

The sidewalk was filled with frantic crowds waiting for further news, hoping against hope that the wireless reports from the *Carpathia* were wrong—that there were more lifeboats still to be found—that their husbands, wives and children were not really among the dead.

Devlin shouldered his way through. The survivor list was pathetically short. Mrs. de Villiers was not on it. He saw Caleb Reed staring dazedly around,* and marched across to him.

"Was she aboard?" he demanded, feeling his blood run cold as the old captain raised his head. There was no need for him to reply. The answer was in his eyes.

Devlin's cry of anguish permeated even Caleb's grief. No one else took any notice. They were too immersed in their own losses.

He pushed blindly through them, not knowing where he was going. Not caring. She was dead. He had wished her dead a hundred times. Had wanted to choke the life out of her for her infidelity. Had wanted to ruin her for her crazed attack on him. Until that moment he had convinced himself that he hated and despised her. The tears streamed down the cheeks, and passers-by eyed him curiously as he strode down to the waterfront and stood on the edge of the wall, gazing out toward the Narrows and the open sea.

He could never hate her. No matter what she had done to him he was bound to her by a bond he had no way of understanding. Even death would not sever it. She would haunt him now as she had haunted him in life. The sloe-black eyes flashing with anger or alight with love. The elusive scent of her hair. The unconscious sensuousness of her every movement. Gulls screamed around his head and the wind from the sea stung the salt tears on his cheeks. He raised a hand, a finger following the line of the deep scar that marred his face. It was all he had left of her. Not a gesture of love. Only of violence. The knowledge did nothing to lessen his agony of spirit. The pain of loving her had nearly driven him mad. The pain of losing her was more than he could bear. He stood, fists clenched, massive shoulders hunched, staring unseeingly out over the darkening bay.

Chapter 31

Christina had steamed into New York Bay many times, but never to such scenes as met her on that Thursday as the *Carpathia* edged past the Statue of Liberty. The shoreline was black with silent, tearful spectators. The Battery was one huge respectful crowd.

She stood alone, not thronging the deck rails with her companions, who were all eager for a reunion with their loved ones. Would anyone be meeting the widowed Mrs. Milton Barnard? Would Milton's younger brother be there to greet his unseen sister-in-law? Christina had no way of knowing.

It was early evening, and the harbor was misting in the twilight; a stiff wind was blowing downriver. Tugs converged on the *Carpathia* from all angles, reporters were yelling frantic questions through megaphones. The *Carpathia* steamed on up the North River, ignoring them.

It had begun to rain, and as the green-indigo of the water between the ship and pier narrowed and narrowed Christina could see thousands of people standing on the waterfront, indifferent to their soaked heads and shoulders.

It was nine thirty before the *Carpathia* finally moored and the gangplank was lowered. Christina stood aside as those who had been saved with her hurried to reach dry land, stumbling in their haste as they were besieged by newsmen.

"Mrs. Barnard?" A harassed official had hold of her before she had even taken a step onto the crowded waterfront. "Your automobile is waiting. And a doctor and a nurse. This way if you please."

She was ushered like a queen to where a poor replica of Milton stood, a homburg on his head, an overcoat buttoned tightly to his chin.

"All suitable preparations have been made for your arrival." The small lips in the fleshy face pursed distastefully. "There is medical attention if you require it."

"I don't," Christina said, disliking him on sight. "Are you a relation of Milton?"

"I am—was—Milton's younger brother."

"I'm afraid I don't know your name. Milton never talked about his family."

The petty lips tightened even further. "That doesn't surprise me in the least." Then, realizing he was speaking ill of the dead and to the deceased's wife, added stiffly, "I am Cyril Barnard. My brother was reclusive. He lived very privately and did not discuss his ideas and plans with the rest of the family."

Christina suppressed a smile. "Reclusive" was the very last word anyone could have used about the ebullient Milton.

"His marriage came as a total surprise to us. He was, to say the least, approaching old age. It was an act I can only view as rash in the extreme."

There was no word of welcome or of grief for the

loss of his brother. If he had shown either Christina would have abandoned her reckless impersonation, formally handed over all Milton's wealth and disappeared out of Cyril Barnard's life forever. His open disapproval of her did not bother Christina one whit. But it would have destroyed the gentle Isobel. And his open indifference to Milton's death settled the matter. Milton had not wanted Cyril to receive one penny of his money and Christina did not blame him.

"No doubt you will wish to return to your own country at the earliest opportunity?" he said coldly, as the chauffeur settled blankets around their legs and the automobile carrying the unneeded doctor and nurse followed them through the rain-washed streets.

"No. I've every intention of staying in New York."

Cyril Barnard's knuckles whitened as he clenched them on the mohair traveling rug. He had expected to meet a young girl who was afraid and unsure of herself and hardly able to speak his language. Instead he was met with a quiet composure that threatened to thwart all his plans. He'd had the documents drawn up ready, anticipating that it would take very little coercion to persuade his young sister-in-law to sign over most of Milton's money, graciously allowing her enough with which to return to her own country in comfort. After all, she wouldn't want to trouble her head with stocks and shares and real estate. The money was tied up. Very little ready cash. As a personal favor he would see that she received several thousands in ready money . . . His prepared sentences seemed already ineffectual.

"My brother was not quite as wealthy as he may have led you to believe, Miss . . . Mrs. . . . ." He stuttered helplessly. What in God's name did he call her.

"Countess," Christina replied sweetly. "Milton was very proud of my title . . . He had no wish for me to discard it on becoming his wife."

Cyril spluttered. "This is a democratic country, Miss . . . Mrs. . . . ."

"Then *Mrs. Barnard* if it causes you embarrassment—Cyril."

Cyril choked and struggled to continue. "No doubt he told you he was a millionaire but that's only on paper. However, under the circumstances I see no reason why I shouldn't pull all the strings I can and free some ready money for your personal use. I have the papers ready at Greenwood."

Christina, assuming rightly that Greenwood was the Barnard's family residence said imperturbably, "No doubt you are right, Cyril. I shall have my accountants look into my late husband's affairs at the earliest opportunity. I couldn't possibly sign anything without his advice or the advice of my lawyer."

Cyril, seeing Milton's millions disappear forever out of his reach, twitched convulsively. The rest of the journey was conducted in stony silence. Christina felt Milton's presence and knew he was enjoying the confrontation between herself and his small-minded brother. And Cyril was wishing heartily that his young sister-in-law had gone down with the hundreds of others aboard the *Titanic*.

The staff at Greenwood were not as stony-hearted as Cyril. Their eyes were red from weeping and they greeted her with a kindness that touched Christina deeply. Christina, wanting to get in touch immediately with Theo, had asked the housekeeper if Mr. Barnard had a secretary. Her face tightened as she was told that he had but that Mr. Barnard's brother had dismissed the gentleman only the previous day. Christina knew very well why. No doubt he would have hampered Cyril's plan of gulling her into signing over Milton's money to him.

"Does Mr. Milton's younger brother reside here?" she asked the housekeeper after she had bathed and eaten and been escorted by a captivated maid to an enormous bedroom.

"No. He lives in Boston. We don't usually see much of him."

The maid began to brush Christina's long hair.

"I understand that my late husband did not get on too well with him?"

The housekeeper was shocked rigid for a moment and then chuckled. She had liked her new mistress on sight and if she wanted to know the truth of the situation, she—Ellen Roberts—would be only too happy to tell her.

"Hated the sight of each other."

The maid kept her eyes down and brushed the turbulent waves and curls assiduously. No one had ever spoken like this in front of her before. Life at Greenwood was going to be interesting in the future.

"Do you have my late husband's secretary's address?" Christina asked.

Triumphantly the housekeeper retrieved a piece of paper from her pocket. Christina took it and smiled.

"Thank you. That will be all. Perhaps I could be woken early in the morning. Before eight. My brother-in-law as well. No doubt he wishes to attend to his own business affairs in Boston at the earliest opportunity."

"Is there anything you particularly like for breakfast, madam? Mr. Barnard was partial to deviled kidneys."

Christina shuddered. "A lightly boiled egg, toast, a glass of champagne and fresh orange juice."

The maid bobbed a curtsey and the housekeeper inclined her head, grinning broadly. Champagne and orange juice, indeed, *and* orders to wake the pompous Cyril Barnard at an early hour. There was going to be no trampling over their new mistress, that was for sure. She had her brother-in-law weighed up and was more than capable of handling him.

By nine o'clock next morning Christina had assembled Milton's lawyer, his financial adviser and his secretary. The lawyer affirmed that Milton's money was hers entirely. That there were no other bequests. The financial adviser had agreed to stay on at Greenwood

and explain the intricacies of Milton's business affairs
to her. The reinstated secretary had made contact with
Theobald Goldenberg and arranged an appointment
for him to see Mrs. Milton Barnard who had traveled
on the *Titanic* with Christina de Villiers.

Amid a great deal of bluster and anger Cyril had
been despatched back to Boston, unable to compete
with the formidable line-up of professional advisers
smoking comfortably in his sister-in-law's presence.
A leading store had been telephoned and had already
delivered a vast selection of dresses, traveling suits
and furs for the clothesless Mrs. Barnard. Christina
had neither the time nor heart to shop for herself.
Neither the duke nor Milton nor, indeed, Josh, would
have wanted her to wear mourning.

Dressed in a blood-red suit trimmed with velvet of
a deeper tone and with a lavish chinchilla fur arming
her against the chill April air, Christina stepped into
the chauffeur-driven limousine. *Her* limousine. And
prepared to meet Theo.

He had kissed her, hugged her, blasphemed with
sheer joy at the sight of her and listened incredulously
as she told him of Milton and Isobel and of how she
had been mistaken for Isobel and carried on the de-
ception.

"But Christina, you're *known!* My secretary knows
you! Wellesly Wallace, Rothenheim, Hardy Glynn,
they all know you as Mrs. de Villiers!"

Christina finally disentanged herself from his arms
and perched on his desk, her legs swinging. "And *all*
of them were convinced I was traveling under a nom
de plume. A Portuguese princess seemed to be the
favorite bet. Why couldn't I have been an Austrian
countess?"

"Jesus, honey! It's too much of a risk. It's playing
with fire."

Christina's eyes lit up and he knew he had said the
wrong thing. The thought of playing with fire would

not deter Christina. It would be an added incentive.

He gazed at her, shaking his mane of white hair helplessly. "You realize you'll be the richest woman in New York State? Barnard made me look like a pauper."

"I *am* the richest woman in New York State," Christina corrected composedly, and Theo threw back his head and laughed, grabbing hold of her again, kissing her till she was breathless.

"What are you going to do with the money?" he asked. "You could buy the Russian crown jewels with the small change."

Christina grinned. "I'll tell you what I'm going to do with it, Theo. I'm going to become the lady I wanted to be as a child. And I'm going to live as I've always wanted. With bright lights and music and champagne and handsome young men vying for my attention."

"But you already had all that on board the *Corinthia*," Theo protested.

"Yes. But that was thanks to you. This time everything I buy will be out of my own money. And do you know the first thing I'm going to buy?"

Theo shook his leonine head, mesmerized.

"My own ship! You'd better look to your laurels, Theo. You've got a new rival!"

It wasn't long before New York society took the beautiful and vivacious widow to its heart. Theo grinned as day after day heavy newspapers thudded on to his desk, the society columns full of photographs of a laughing Christina throwing parties, attending parties, turning Greenwood into a name synonymous with fast, opulent living.

Caleb had sighed and kept his thoughts to himself. He owed her too much to mar her happiness by denouncing her. He was captain of the *Swan*, the pride of the Goldenberg fleet, and he knew it was only due to her intervention. Nevertheless, when chief officer Pegham, who had followed him to his new ship, showed him a photograph in a glossy magazine of Christina with a pet panther on a gold lead, her gold beaded dress making her look like a modern-day Cleopatra, he had shaken his head. Excess did not bring happiness. She had not been happy before. Caleb had known that. Beneath the gaiety had been a hurt that time had never healed.

When news broke that the Barnard millions were buying their way into shipping, Duane Yates had read it with interest. Christina's face vibrant and full of life seemed to leap from the page. He studied it for a long time, his eyes narrowing, his tongue running thoughtfully over his finely molded lips. He would like to meet his new rival. He would like to meet her very much indeed. There was to be a lavish celebration party for the launching of Mrs. Barnard's new ship, the *Vanity Fair*. Duane smiled. It was a hell of a name for a ship. He wondered where she had got it from. He picked up his telephone and instructed his secretary to do all she could to secure him an invitation to the exclusive party accompanying the *Vanity Fair*'s launching.

Devlin had hardened. He lived only for the *Ninevah* and even that was no longer the all-consuming passion it had been. The monotony of the ceaseless run from New York to Southampton and Cherbourg was beginning to tell. There was none of the physical danger and excitement in captaining a large liner that there was sailing a square rigger and wrestling with canvas and sail.

He had achieved what he had always wanted and slowly but surely it was growing stale. He found himself thinking longingly of Africa. Of the freedom of sailing a ship that blended with the elements.

Women came and went and made no impression on him. One day, marching stern-faced toward the bridge, he passed a passenger playing with his sons. The man was about his own age, with curly brown hair and a carefree face. The younger boy was still only a toddler, gurgling with pleasure as his father threw him high in the air. The other was a fine strapping boy of ten or eleven, his fine thatch of hair identical to his father's, his face bearing the same good nature. The man caught the toddler and ruffled the older boy's hair with an affectionate hand.

Devlin passed the happy family group feeling loneliness so intense it was a physical pain. Happiness like that could never be his. His endless succession of female conquests all bored him. Not one of them understood his love of the sea, his need of freedom. Only Christina had been a kindred spirit in those joyful days in Wales.

Down below on the luxury of *A* Deck, American socialites gossiped about the latest escapades of the incorrigible Mrs. Barnard. The men gazed at the pictures of Christina in dresses so daring they had taken New York by storm, and they lusted after her in vain. Only the captain was unaware of the new queen of New York's high society. He had no time for the cocktail parties and trivia that filled Duane's evenings. He would no more have read a gossip column than brilliantined his hair. To Devlin, Mrs. Milton Barnard was the name of a spoiled and pampered woman and nothing more. He had not the slightest interest in her.

Chapter 32

Christina ordered a 25,000 ton liner to be built, spending hours with the ship's architect, making suggestions here, alterations there. The liner would take over a year to build and then many more months to be fitted out. Christina could not wait that long before she was back at sea on a ship of her own. She wheedled Theo into parting with one of his older vessels, paying him a price she could easily afford and which was more than he would have got from any other bidder. She changed the ship's name to the *Vanity Fair* and had the interior done out like a sultan's palace. Mirrors everywhere, the pale wood and ivory silk walls that had revolutionized the *Swan* making the *Vanity Fair* equally light and airy. But there the similarity ended.

On board the *Vanity Fair* were velvet-covered couches in palest pink and peach. Besides the customary smoking room for the gentlemen Christina incorporated a sumptuous lounge for the ladies. Deep piles of cushions surrounded an azure-blue indoor pool. Palms, magnolia trees and orchids turned it into a Garden of Eden with tropical birds flitting hither and thither amongst the glossy foliage; the temperature, never below seventy degrees. Here champagne was served instead of coffee. Skilled masseuses gently massaged rich, aching muscles that had danced till dawn. Reclining like Egyptian princesses the ladies had their nails manicured and lacquered in the exotic silver or gold that their Bohemian hostess favored. For Christina sailed every voyage on her ship. Gone were the respectable, sedate after-dinner dances. Instead there were evenings of wild gypsy music.

The older, more staid members of society gave the *Vanity Fair* a wide berth, but the younger set fought for staterooms aboard her. The name of Mrs. Milton Barnard was on everybody's lips. Her past was a mystery that only enhanced her glamor. She drank champagne for breakfast. Had a panther for a pet. Wore real gold leaf on her nails. Bathed in milk. And danced in public with all the skill of Karsavina.

Duane had been unable to obtain an invitation to the *Vanity Fair*'s launching. His secretary, too terrified to break the news to him herself, had telephoned the office and spent a week in bed pleading a migraine, awaiting her employer's wrath to fade.

Duane abandoned his business deals and his parrying with Theobald Goldenberg for the *Ninevah* and booked himself a first class stateroom aboard the *Vanity Fair*.

Russian princes, English earls and famous artistes of the silver screen, with their dark brooding good looks, would have seen to it that he didn't come within speaking distance of his spellbinding hostess. But Christina, eyeing her passenger list with professional interest, saw the name "Duane Yates" and paused, ringing for the purser.

"Mr. Yates?" she asked questioningly, pointing a long slender finger at the typewritten name. "Is he the Mr. Yates that owns half of the Conyates Shipping Company?"

"Yes, madam."

"Introduce me to him this evening."

The young purser suppressed his surprise Mr. Yates was very small fish for his employer to be taking an interest in.

Duane had dressed with painstaking care, demanding that his valet re-iron his intricately lace-frilled shirt three times before he was satisfied with it.

He felt a surge of admiration when they were introduced. The pretty girls Devlin had seen waiting patiently in the back of Duane's limousines were nothing but the necessary appendages a man of his standing had to be seen with. Nevertheless the sight of the legendary Mrs. Milton Barnard aroused even *his* interest.

Her photographs hadn't done her justice. Baubles and beads had been temporarily discarded. She was dressed in a loose, flowing gown of exquisite flame-colored silk. The wide mobile mouth, the sloe-black eyes outlined with kohl and slanting tantalizingly gave her a look no other woman on the ship could hope to imitate. She was as rare and magical as one of the brilliantly plumed birds that darted across the surface of the warm waters of the pool.

"I understand we share the same business interests, Mr. Yates?"

He smiled smoothly, exerting all his charm, which could be considerable when he wished it to be.

"Shipping is one of my many interests. I have a liner. The *Ninevah*."

"Do you plan to extend your fleet?" Christina longed to ask questions about the *Ninevah*'s captain but could not bring herself to do so.

"No. In fact I'm thinking of selling out."

The drink trembled in Christina's hands. "Selling out? You mean you're buying a larger ship?"

"No. There's too much competition on the Atlantic run these days."

He indicated the glittering surroundings with his hand, saying gallantly, "No one could compete with the *Vanity Fair*."

Christina had spent five minutes trying to make sense of both Duane and the conversation. He was only in his mid-twenties, not the mature man with a daughter of marriageable age she had expected.

"Your father must be near retiring age," she said, trying to understand just whose daughter Devlin had married.

"My father retired years ago. Mississippi river boats were his business."

Christina forced a smile. "I always understood that the Conyates Company was *his* originally."

Duane brushed his sleek blond moustache with his forefinger and smiled. "No. Conyates is my baby and always has been."

"You and your captain's?"

Outwardly Christina was her usual self, the way she was with one of her first class passengers, showing a flattering interest in him. Inwardly she was in turmoil.

"Mine."

Christina drained her glass; an assiduous steward refilled it automatically. Her breath felt tight in her chest.

"I always thought that Conyates was a partnership?"

"Oh, I gave O'Conner shares in the company but he's not a businessman. As I said before, the company is mine."

"I see." Christina's mind raced. "And Mrs. O'Conner? Does she take much interest in the *Ninevah?*"

Music had begun to play and couples were taking to the floor.

"O'Conner isn't married. Would you give me the honor, Mrs. Barnard?"

He swung her out on to the floor, feeling her tremble in his arms and congratulating himself at the ease of what seemed a certain conquest.

Christina's head swam. Duane was talking again but Christina didn't hear him. Devlin wasn't married. There had never been an elderly shipping magnate trading the captaincy of his liner for the hand of his daughter. It had been a cruel lie of Devlin's. One to sever their relationship. He hadn't even had the guts to tell her himself he no longer loved her. Had never loved her. Had not meant the rash promises he had made aboard the *Adventurer*.

Duane was saying Goldenberg "has offered me a fair price for the *Ninevah* and I'm thinking of accepting it."

"Does Captain O'Conner know of your intention?" Christina hardly recognized her own voice.

Duane laughed. "Not yet. He'd try to throw a spanner in the works if he found out."

All that time believing Devlin had been married. Imagining him with his wife. Suffering through the long lonely hours of the nights in a torment of jealousy. And there had never been a wife. Only Kate.

"Perhaps I could equal Mr. Goldenberg's offer? I have a new liner being built but she won't be ready until the end of next year and unlike you, Mr. Yates, I have a great belief in the future of Atlantic shipping. My financial adviser is on board. Perhaps we could discuss the matter further?"

Duane was temporarily at a loss for words. It had never occurred to him that Mrs. Barnard would make him an offer for the *Ninevah*. She had enough money to buy the *Olympic* if she wanted to. He held her tight, whispering in her ear.

"I might ask for more than money, Mrs. Barnard. I might ask to see more of you. And I would insist that you call me Duane and give me the privilege of calling you Isobel."

Duane Yates. Devlin's partner and colleague. Her arm tightened around his neck.

"I think that could be very easily arranged. Would you like it put into the contract in writing?"

He laughed, and was too immersed in his own feelings to be aware of the unnatural brightness of Christina's dark eyes.

Devlin had deceived her and lied to her and now

she had the perfect chance for revenge. She would buy the *Ninevah* and Devlin O'Conner would no longer have a ship to command. It should have brought a feeling of great satisfaction. Instead she felt only an aching emptiness as Duane Yates and her financial adviser thrashed out the details, and in her perfumed and pastel private lounge Christina signed her name with a flourish to a document giving her complete control of the Conyates Shipping Company.

She had felt no anger at the knowledge that the smooth-talking Duane Yates had duped Devlin, taking advantage of his lack of interest in the legal side of their partnership and of his accepting on trust what he, Duane, had told him. It served him right, she told herself time and time again. He had lied to her and probably a hundred others. Now someone had lied to him. Devlin O'Conner's pigeons were coming home to roost.

Christina had thrown herself into the world of vast wealth with high-spirited zest, convinced that now, at last, she had found happiness. The columns of newsprint about her doings delighted her. She was feted as a star.

No one in New York or London was anyone until they had traveled aboard the *Vanity Fair*, and to be able to claim acquaintance with her owner and hostess was the highest accolade one could hope for. She was the envy of whole nations of women. Her childhood dream had been fulfilled and surpassed beyond her wildest imaginings and yet, as had happened on board the *Corinthia*, once the initial novelty was over Christina was aware of a restlessness that was still not satisfied, and of growing irritation with the ex-royalty and vast landowners who dined at her table night after night.

Her current lover was a Russian prince. He was blatantly handsome and incredibly dashing. He boarded the *Vanity Fair* with over a hundred trunks, two valets, two private secretaries and a small black boy dressed in a turban and a scarlet uniform with frogged gold fastenings and epaulettes.

The rumblings of discontent were growing louder day by day in Russia and after a few weeks Christina could well understand why. The small black boy was no older than eight, yet Vladimir expected him to be at his beck and call at any time of the day or night. The valets and secretaries were treated with contempt and obliged to bow deferentially and retreat backwards from his presence. None of this had been apparent to Christina in the first few weeks of their affair, and it was only by accident that she discovered the other side of her lover's nature.

The child, weak and hungry beyond endurance, for the prince never considered his servants' meals, had fallen asleep when the prince had requested his presence. In a fury Vladimir had taken his whip to him, lashing him about the head and shoulders, and at that precise moment Christina had walked into the stateroom. The child's cries, the raised arm of the prince, the whip slicing through the air brought back the memories of her beating at Ernest Miller's hands with vivid clarity. She dashed forward, wresting the whip out of Vladimir's hands, ordering the cowering boy to leave the cabin.

"He's a worthless good-for-nothing," the prince said, straightening his shirt sleeves imperturbably.

Christina's magnificent breasts heaved. "And is that how you usually treat him?"

"But of course. How else does one usually treat scum? The whip is the only thing peasants and inferiors understand."

He smiled, reaching out for her. The whip caught him full across the face.

"It's *you* who are the scum! To treat a child like that! From now on my ship is barred to you!"

Shaking with anger she had marched into her purser's office to order him to see that the prince left the ship at Southampton and was never allowed to re-book; the prince's small servant was to be given a bed in her dressing room until she had decided what to do with him.

"But there *is* no bed in your dressing room," the purser said helplessly.

"Then put one in there!"

The door slammed behind her. The worst of the incident had not been the knowledge that a man she had given her body to could behave in such a way, but his utter mystification as to her anger.

Apart from the almost universal indifference displayed to people not in their "set," Christina found the level of conversation increasingly tedious. Literature was a banned subject. It was not fashionable to show interest in intellectual pursuits. The main topics of conversation amongst the women were fashions, jewelry and the activities of the Royal Family.

Christina liked the Americans more, but even they were totally preoccupied with money and still more money, leaving her tapping a satin-pumped foot impatiently under the table.

And the hypocrisy of some of the women! They made the Gaiety girls paragons of virtue in comparison. At least *they* never pretended to be anything they weren't and Christina had never made any secret of her own transient love affairs. The upright leaders of English society, supposedly the epitome of stalwart family life, condemned vice at every turn, but carried on in private in a manner that shocked even Christina. She had been amazed when the purser had first revealed to her how often he had to change staterooms around so that a certain married gentleman could be within easy access of a certain married lady.

It had not taken her long to discover that husbands and wives already knew of their spouses' infidelities and condoned them as long as they were carried out discreetly. Ladies who fluttered shocked eyelashes at the mention of H. G. Wells's newest novel happily paraded the first class corridors in the early hours of the morning like so many promiscuous alley cats.

Christina had no time for their double standards. She began to prune her passenger list of hypocrites. The *Vanity Fair* was a ship made for lovers but not for adulterous associations. Within its first few crossings it became the focal point for a new section of society: young writers and musicians, poets and actresses. Literary lions who preferred the stimulating atmosphere of the *Vanity Fair* to the tedium of other vessels.

And with the prince in disgrace Duane Yates stepped smoothly into the role of Mrs. Barnard's most ardent admirer.

His attentions did not take him the vital step across her cabin threshold. Her experience with Vladimir had left her feeling soiled in a way none of her escapades at the Gaiety had. In haughty indignance the prince had disembarked at Southampton with his one hundred trunks and his nervous valets and secretaries. The small black boy had remained aboard the *Vanity Fair*, but he was no longer decked out in his ludicrous livery.

"What's your name?" Christina had asked him when his new clothes had been delivered to the ship from a Southampton store.

"Boy, your highness," he had answered, backing away toward the door.

"I know you're a boy," Christina said patiently. "and I'm *not* 'Your highness.' My name is Isobel. Can you say that?"

"Yes your highness, Isbelle . . ."

"Now what is your name?"

Thin shoulders shrugged helplessly. "His highnes. only called me 'boy.' I don't know that I have a name."

"What would you like to be called?"

"I don't know, your high . . . Isbelle."

"What about 'Charles'?"

He remained quiet, his eyes never leaving her face. She could call him anything she wanted. She was the kindest, most beautiful creature he had ever seen.

"No. That doesn't suit you. What about Edward?" She stared at him, her head slightly to one side. "No. That doesn't suit you either. You're too black for a white name. They sound ridiculous." She grinned suddenly. "What about Mamba?"

"I've never heard that name before," he said, wondering if he was in a dream and would shortly wake up to find himself back in the prince's entourage.

"A black mamba is a snake. *Not* that you're anything like a snake. But I do know people who let them sleep in baskets at the end of their beds," she said, giggling at the thought of Cassie.

The boy giggled too.

"That's better. From now on I shall look after you and you will have your own cabin to sleep in. You can't sleep in my dressing room forever."

Taking his hand she led him down to the deck below, trying to explain that the cabin she was showing him was his and his alone and instructing the purser to see to it that all members of the crew knew of Mamba's new status.

The purser did his best, but as he didn't know exactly *what* Mamba's status was he found it a trifle difficult. He wasn't crew and Mrs. Barnard was certainly not treating the boy as a servant. More as an adopted son. Which was very difficult, even for a lady with as little regard for convention as Mrs. Barnard. After all, the boy was as black as the ace of spades.

Duane managed, with difficulty, to overlook Mamba's almost constant presence at Christina's side and on the night before they steamed into New York Bay asked her to marry him. For a fleeting second the prospect of marrying Devlin's partner brought an ironic smile to her lips, then she kissed him gently and refused with an ease that came of long practice.

As Duane watched her disappear into an adoring

throng, the lips that always smiled in her presence thinned calculatingly. He was a man who always got what he wanted. No matter what the cost. His wooing of Christina wasn't over yet. He turned his mind to more immediate problems: how to deal with Devlin's fury when he told him he had sold the company and that the documents Devlin had signed believing they were equal partners were meaningless and would not stand up in a court of law.

The first thing he would have to do would be to buy himself some protection. Duane had seen enough glimpses of Devlin's anger to know Devlin would smash him into the ground given a chance. Only he wouldn't get the chance and he, Duane, would realize his assets and be a rich man. Richer than Croesus if he persuaded Isobel Barnard to marry him. He lit a cigar and continued planning and scheming as the *Vanity Fair* eased her way through the Narrows and into the bay.

Chapter 33

"Life on the *Vanity Fair* is no life for a child," Theo said to her, regarding Mamba with interest. His eyes were bright enough, and he showed none of his former cowed servility. A few weeks of Christina's company and exposure to her philosophy on life had given Mamba a self-respect and inner confidence he was never to lose.

"I lived on ship as a child," Christina protested,

her plumed peacock-feathered hat at a seductive angle.

"Not like the *Vanity Fair*," Theo pointed out, grinning. "Champagne morning, noon and night and parties that would shame Sodom and Gomorrah. How old is he? Eight? Nine?"

"He doesn't know." She frowned. "Do you really think I'm doing him a disservice keeping him with me on the *Vanity Fair?*"

"Yes, if you're treating him as an adopted foundling and not a servant."

"You know damn well I'm not treating him as a servant," Christina said crossly.

Mamba began to look alarmed. He had liked the fierce-looking man with the piercing eyes but if he was about to persuade Isbelle to abandon him he would kick him in the shins and sink his teeth so hard into his arm that he would bear the marks for life.

Christina pondered thoughtfully, then she adjusted her sweeping sables over a vivid blue suit braided with an emerald green the exact color of her peacock plumes.

"Mrs. Reed," she said. "She has a heart as big as Bessie Mulholland's. She'll look after him for me."

"I doubt the respectable Mrs. Reed would welcome being likened to the madam of a brothel," Theo said dryly, "but you can give her a try. There's no one else in New York likely to take him, no matter how much money you have."

Mrs. Reed listened to the tale of Mamba's treatment at the hands of the prince with horror. She was tenderhearted and childless. She was also unique. Mamba's color made not the slightest difference to her reaction. He was a child. Motherless and homeless. For, like Theo, she viewed the idea of Mamba being brought up aboard the *Vanity Fair* as undesirable in the extreme.

"Leave him with me," she said, taking the little boy's hand.

"Want to stay with Isbelle," Mamba said defiantly.

Christina laughed and kissed his cheek. "I shall see you every time I'm in New York. Here with Mrs. Reed you'll be well looked after and able to go to school."

Mrs. Reed smelled of lavender water and the lacy shawl around her shoulders was soft against his face as she drew him toward her. Her eyes were kind, her mouth gentle.

"All right," Mamba said reluctantly. "If it's what you want, Isbelle."

"It's what I want," Christina said firmly.

The two women kissed goodbye. Mrs. Reed couldn't condone the outrageous way Christina lived but her honesty and kindness had long since won her heart as it had her husband's. And with Mrs. Reed's immediate acceptance of Mamba, Christina's faith in human nature was partially restored.

"What the bloody hell do you mean?" Devlin's fist slammed down hard on Duane's desk as he leaned across it, the muscles standing out on his arms and neck.

Duane flinched, exercising iron control by remaining sitting and not taking to his heels.

"Mrs. Barnard made a ludicrously generous offer for Conyates and I've accepted."

"You've accepted?" Devlin lunged across the desk and Duane, panic-stricken, jabbed at his buzzer before he was grasped by the throat and half throttled.

"What gives *you* the goddamned right to do *anything* without my say so, Yates? This is a partnership, remember? *Con-Yates!"* Almost incoherent with rage, he spat the last two syllables into Duane's face.

"But I have final control," Duane whispered, hardly able to breathe for the vise-like grip around his throat. "I always have had. It's in the contract we drew up."

"The contract *you* drew up!" Devlin hurled him sprawling on to the floor.

The door burst open and two heavily built men rushed into the room intent on seizing Devlin's arms. They stood no chance. Fists smacked against jaws and within minutes they were as dazed and reeling as Duane himself.

"Tell them to get out!" Devlin said disgustedly to his erstwhile partner. "If I'd wanted to kill you, do you think a couple of your pathetic bullies would've stopped me?"

"Out," Duane said weakly, staggering to his feet. There was blood coming from a cut on his lip. *His* blood. He began to feel sick.

"I want that contract, Yates! I'm going to take you through every court in this land!"

Obligingly Duane threw it across the desk top. "Take it to the president himself. It won't make a damn bit of difference. The company was *mine*. You should have been a little sharper, Devlin. A little less in love with that ship. Then maybe you'd have taken the trouble to have had the contract looked at by a lawyer before you went off to Halifax."

Devlin stuffed the paper in his pocket and swung on his heel. Duane's confidence told him he didn't stand a chance in hell. He'd been conned. Conyates had been a very apt title.

"Where are you going?" Duane was regaining his equilibrium; he adjusted his tie and staggered back into his chair, grateful that Devlin's act of violence had not taken a severer tone.

"To see the Barnard woman. Perhaps she'll have a shred of honor left."

Duane laughed with an effort at bravery. "You'll get no change from Mrs. Barnard. She's a sharp cookie who knows what she wants and what she wants is the *Ninevah*. She won't give a damn that you were too much of a fool to look after your own interests properly."

Devlin paused, facing Duane. The cold fury in his eyes terrified Duane far more than his outbreak of explosive anger.

"No doubt you're right. But that's only the first thing I'm going to do. The second is to break you, Yates. Whatever money you have made on this deal is half mine and I'm going to get it. And then when I've got it I'm going to see to it that your reputation for double dealing is known the length and breadth of New York State. You won't find another business partner in a hurry. The only place for your money will be a bank!"

"Don't you think you're being a little rash?" Duane's composure was returning. "I never said I was doing you out of the money. Half of it is yours."

"Too bloody right it is!"

"Another few hours and you'll see the sense in what I've done. We can't compete any longer with the major shipping companies. It was a hare-brained scheme. We'd have gone bankrupt in another couple of years. Mrs. Barnard has done us a favor. We're both rich now. Rich. Isn't that what you always wanted, Devlin?"

"*No!*" Devlin said savagely, realizing for the first time that it wasn't. "What I've always wanted is my own ship!"

"Then buy one."

There was a timid knock on the door. "Come in."

"Mrs. Barnard for you," his secretary said, her eyes wide at the sight of the chairs and tables Devlin had overturned in his fight.

"Send her in." Duane leaned his head against his leatherbacked chair and said with an understatement he was unaware of, "This should be an interesting meeting for you."

She still wore her turquoise suit with its emerald braiding. The peacock plumed hat tilted provocatively over one sleek eyebrow, making her look like an exotic bird of paradise.

"Christina!" Devlin swayed on his feet, his face ashen, his eyes unbelieving.

She halted. She should have known she ran the risk of meeting him at the Conyates office. But hadn't that been what she had wanted? To see him again? To have the satisfaction of taking from him everything he had ever wanted?

"Christina!" The expression on his face transfixed her.

Then, in two giant strides, he had crossed the carpet between them, seizing hold of her, hugging her to his chest so that the brass buttons of his uniform scored her cheek, her hat plummeting to the floor.

"I thought you were dead, Brat!" There was a break in his voice that would only have been a sob.

She could do nothing. She was helpless, wanting only to remain within his steel-like embrace and to feel him next to her again.

Duane remained at his desk, gazing from one to the other with incredulity.

Devlin pushed her roughly away from him, drinking in the sight of her, oblivious of Duane, oblivious of everything.

"Your face?" she whispered, seeing for the first time the cruel white scar that curved down through his eyebrow and over his cheekbone.

Devlin steadied himself. He was a man in shock. His defenses were down at the unbelievable sight of her alive and warm and vital.

"Why did you do it, Brat?"

She stared at him uncomprehendingly and Devlin felt something break within him. A whole tide of repressed emotions freeing him. It hadn't been Christina. Her eyes told him it hadn't been her. He seized her again, kissing her with ferocious intensity.

Christina's mouth responded to his as it had always done, her lips trembling beneath the sweetness of his, her body pressing against him in an agony of longing.

When at last he released her Devlin said, "Forgive me, Brat, I should have known it wasn't you. But when you didn't wait for me in Liverpool . . ."

"I *couldn't* wait for you. Jemmy Cadogan came to the Gaiety and said you had married. I know now it wasn't true but I still don't understand . . ."

He didn't speak; his throat constricted and his mouth was dry with desire. He looked at her long and hard and then at last said simply, "Neither do I. Come with me, Brat. We have a lot of talking to do." And without even looking in Duane's direction he began to lead her toward the door.

Duane coughed, tapping his gold pen on the surface of his desk.

"I didn't know you'd had the pleasure of meeting Mrs. Barnard, Devlin?"

"Barnard?" Devlin turned, looking from Duane to Christina. "You're Mrs. Barnard?"

"Yes. But . . ."

He threw her hand away from his in a gesture of contempt. "I should have known," he said bitterly. "Mrs. de Villiers! Mrs. Barnard! Your whole life has been built on lies and deceit."

"Devlin, *please* . . ." She reached out to him but the old terrible expression was back on his face.

"You may not have done this," he touched the scar on his face, "but you did something far worse to me when you bought the *Ninevah*, and you knew it. Mr. Yates is looking for another business partner. I suggest you get together. You both have the same sort of ethics. You should suit each other perfectly."

The door slammed behind him and Christina raced after him, calling, *"Devlin! Devlin!"* She followed him as he strode away from her down the corridor toward the elevator. The office staff gazed after her, open mouthed. The elevator door closed behind him. Sobbing and gasping for breath she made her way to the flight of stairs, her long skirt and high heels hampering

her as she ran crazily downward. The reception hall
was empty. The sidewalk outside was deserted.

She leaned back against the stone of the building,
her heart hammering painfully, tears coursing down
her cheeks. What had happened? For a few seconds
it had been as before. The feel of his arms around her.
His mouth on hers. The expression in his eyes. He
had given her no chance to explain. None. She wiped
the tears away and with aching desolation made her
way back into the Conyates building and entered the
empty elevator. His face. Why should he think she
had done that to him? Was he a madman or was she
a madwomen?

By the time she returned to Duane's office she was
outwardly composed. She picked up her hat, uncaring
of Duane's open curiosity.

"I didn't know you knew him."

"There was no reason why you should."

"Or that you were the Christina de Villiers of the
Swan."

"I've been a lot of things in my life," she said
bleakly.

Duane wasn't fool enough to probe further. He
walked round the edge of the desk, setting the extrav-
agant hat gently back on her upswept curls.

"He isn't worth a tear, Isobel."

"Yes." Christina forced a brittle smile.

"Let me take you back to Greenwood. Tomorrow
night is the party to celebrate your acquisition of the
Ninevah. Why don't you make it a double celebration
and allow me to announce our engagement?"

She shook her head, allowing him to escort her back
to her chauffeur-driven limousine, making no protest
as he joined her in the rear seat.

He was kind and sympathetic, and at the moment
she needed all the kindness she could get.

"Let me see to all the final arrangements for tomorrow night," he said as the motor car sped out of
the city. "You'll need quiet and rest."

"Yes."

A party to end all parties was to be given by the legendary Austrian countess, known to American society as Mrs. Milton Barnard, the most beautiful, vivacious hostess and businesswoman ever to grace the city. A guest list of those attending was included and anxious telephone calls were made by the rich and wealthy who had so far not been invited to an event that promised to be the high spot of the season.

A photograph of a laughing Christina, swathed in furs and with diamonds at ears and throat, taunted Devlin from a front page as a newsboy thrust the paper into his hand.

People knocked into him, rushing about their business as he stared down at the familiar face and the columns of newsprint.

Austrian countess. Wealthiest woman in New York State. Legendary hostess of the high seas. Most beautiful businesswoman in America. The words leapt up at him from the page. He crumpled it savagely, tossing it into the gutter.

She had all of New York at her feet. She had taken his ship from him. She was a whore and a harlot and he was damned if he was going to stand by and let her bewitch a whole country as she had bewitched him.

He ignored the *Ninevah* laying idle at her pier. He would never step aboard her again. He went back to his room on South Street, bathed and drank some bourbon, left his glamorous captain's uniform discarded on his bed and changed into tight-fitting trousers with a broad buckled belt. He drank some more bourbon and the slipped on a casual shirt open at the neck and waist. Some more bourbon. He ran his fingers through his unruly hair and with grim determination stepped out onto the sidewalk and hailed a cab.

"Greenwood," he demanded.

"What Greenwood?" the cab driver asked suspiciously.

"*This* Greenwood." Devlin's finger jabbed at the evening paper on the front seat.

Devlin sat hunched and tense, his hands clasped tight between his knees. She'd known damned well he was the captain of the *Ninevah* and that was why she had bought out Conyates. With her money she could have bought any ship, anywhere. But she hadn't; she had bought the *Ninevah*.

He swore savagely. She wouldn't make a fool of him again. Tonight was going to be her last as the uncrowned queen of New York. By tomorrow everyone would know exactly who and what Mrs. Milton Barnard was. He almost choked at her effrontery. The shameless way she had responded to his fevered kisses in front of Yates, knowing damned well she had just taken away from him everything he had ever worked for. She *knew* what a ship of his own had meant to him.

He groaned, dropping his head into his hands, running his fingers wildly through his hair. The cab driver looked over his shoulder apprehensively, then pressed his foot hard on the accelerator, determined to be rid of his crazy passenger as soon as possible.

Devlin was a man in torment. He loved her. Hated her. He didn't know where the one emotion began and the other finished. He was intent on one thing only— to destroy her as she had destroyed him.

Chapter 34

Christina was strained and pale as her maid dressed her hair for the evening's festivities. For the first time in her life she needed rouge on her cheeks to bring some warmth into them. Unlike Devlin she was calm. She had decided what to do. The party had been arranged and must be endured, but tomorrow she would find Devlin and make him listen to her. Everything had been all right until Duane had introduced her as Mrs. Barnard. He had thought she was dead and he had cared! He had taken her hand, wanting to talk, and she had felt herself on the verge of happiness. Suddenly she was sure that Jemmy Cadogan's message had been garbled right from the start. And then Duane had opened his mouth and the moment had been lost.

There was a distant sound of flustered conversation and then a brief knock on her door. Ellen Roberts hurried in, her genial face creased with anxiety.

"The guests are already assembling in the ballroom but there's a gatecrasher *insisting* that he see you. He literally knocked poor Larson down and marched into the library saying that not even an army could evict him. And to tell you the truth, looking at him, I doubt if it could! He said to tell you he was Devlin O'Conner and that . . ."

The last vestige of blood left Christina's face.

"He's here? Downstairs?"

"Yes, madam. Fortunately he marched toward the

library and not to the west wing and the ballroom.
Goodness only knows what would have happened if
he had found his way in there. Poor Larson thinks his
jaw's dislocated and . . ."

Christina was on her feet, trembling visibly.

"I thought perhaps a telephone call to the law en-
forcement officers . . ." Ellen Roberts suggested helpfully.

"No! It's all right. I know Mr. O'Conner. I shall
go down and see him—and, Ellen?"

"Yes, madam?"

"Please see that we're not disturbed. I want you to
lock the library door after me, Ellen."

"Do what?" The housekeeper looked at her mistress aghast. "Lock you in with a madman. Why,
I'd never forgive myself if anything happened to
you . . ."

"Nothing will happen to me, Ellen." Christina's
voice was unsteady. "But I don't want Mr. O'Conner
to leave until I've finished talking to him."

"Well, it's my belief he should be locked up
all right, but on his own, not with a helpless female . . ."

Christina was already leaving the room, on her way
to the library.

The chauffeur was busy restraining the red-haired
Irishman from setting off on a rampage in the house.
He had been delegated the task of keeping the un-
wanted guest at bay because of his own strapping physique.

This quiet room with its walls of books and comfortable chairs was not the scene in which Devlin had
envisaged meeting Christina. He had imagined a vast
room bright with lights from a hundred chandeliers
and crowded with people. Somewhere he had gone
wrong. There was no indication that a party was taking
place, but it must be and he was determined to find
out where.

The young chauffeur bravely barred his way.

"There *is* a party tonight but guests will not be arriving until eleven o'clock at the earliest," he lied smoothly.

Devlin paused. He had no idea of New York's high society etiquette. It was feasible that he had misjudged the time. It didn't matter. The high and mighty were coming to Greenwood in another couple of hours and he would still be there when they did so.

Christina's hand closed around the glass knob of the door and pushed.

The lamps in the library were few and heavily shaded. The hallway outside was brilliantly lit. She stood in the doorway in splendid silhouette, a vision in a dress of pure gold thread, the décolletage daringly low, exposing satin smooth breasts. A king's ransom of emeralds crowned her gleaming hair and encircled her throat and wrist. Devlin caught his breath.

"You may go," Christina said to the chauffeur without looking at him.

The boy remembered that he was in charge of a madman and began to protest but Christina raised a slender hand a fraction and without another word he inclined his head and left them.

"Another of your little dogs?" Devlin asked maliciously.

Christina licked dry lips. "I don't know what you mean."

"Don't you? You have a very short memory. That was how you referred to me behind my back, wasn't it? The little dog you could do anything you wanted with?"

His eyes were demonical, an animal savagery barely held in check. He wanted to tear the jewels from her hair, rip the gold from her back but he dared not, for he knew that one feel of her beneath his fingers and his desire would overcome all hate. It would be a repetition of their meeting on the *Ninevah* and he would give her the pleasure of knowing his body still craved hers He was here to destroy her name and rob her of her wealth, not to be enslaved once again by the power she wielded over him.

"I never spoke of you to anyone. Except to say that I loved you." Her voice was low and trembling with emotion. It held an undoubtable ring of truth that diffused Devlin's rage into bewildered perplexity.

"You still ran out on me!" He could feel his anger slipping away from him and fought to hang on to it.

"I told you why in Duane's office. Sheba told me you had married the daughter of the man you had gone into partnership with."

"Duane isn't *old* enough to have a daughter." She was lying to him again, bluffing her way out as she had always done.

"I know that now. And I still don't understand. But when Sheba told me I believed her. I couldn't believe you would do a thing like that. Not after . . ." She gestured helplessly, facing him across great yards of carpet. "I think it made me crazy. I wanted to hurt you—to show you it didn't matter to me that you had married some respectable spinster from America." She was crying new, tears thickening her voice. "I went with a sailor from the *Corinthia* and was still aboard when she sailed. Caleb Reed took care of me."

"And became your lover!" He was damned if he was going to be won over by tears. He would *not* cradle her in his arms. Comfort her. He would *not*. It was like fighting a hurricane in the South Seas. It took every fraction of his strength and effort.

"No. Never. Not Caleb." She didn't care that she was crying. That he was as unmovable as stone. That his whole attitude and bearing showed he didn't believe her. She would tell him the truth. She could do no more.

"He introduced me to Theobald Goldenberg and I became Theobald's mistress. And I'm not ashamed of it." Even through her tears her voice was defiant. "He was good to me and I needed someone to love me."

"And so you conveniently found a man old enough

to be your father and with a few million thrown in for good measure?"

"I didn't love him as I'd loved you. I'll never love anyone like that."

"What about the hundreds of men who sailed the *Corinthia?*" Devlin asked sneeringly, wishing to hell she would stop crying, wishing that he could stop believing her.

"There weren't any. I never slept with anyone aboard the *Corinthia.*"

Their eyes held and he knew she was telling the truth.

"You went off with Kate," she said despairingly, "and that night on the *Ninevah* it was Kate's dress that hung in your cabin. You made love to me and it was Kate's dress that was in your wardrobe . . ." She covered her face with her hands, sobbing desperately, her last shred of control disappearing.

"And so you said what you did? Because you thought I was still with Kate?" His voice had changed. There was no trace of anger now.

She could only nod and at last he moved. Slowly and with certainty he crossed the dimly lit room, lowering his hands to her shaking shoulders, raising her to her feet.

"I *did* take Kate with me. God knows, I don't remember asking her. I was too blind drunk. I came back from New York with only one thought in mind, Christina. You. You and me. I brought a wedding ring with me. It's probably still on Bessie Mulholland's *secrétaire*. She told me you'd run off with a sailor and Kate told me . . ." He shrugged dismissively. "Never mind what Kate said. I tried o forget you, Brat, but I couldn't. That night on the *Ninevah*." He raised her tear-streaked face to his, his eyes tortured. "It was because I couldn't keep my hands off you. I hated you for leaving me but I still had to have you."

"And I you."

Her arms closed around his neck, his mouth coming

down hard and sweet on hers. It was over. The unhappiness; the misery; the agony of being apart. It was
all over.

Eternities later he raised his lips from hers and said,
"The Duke of Marne—the man you were to marry—
did you love him?"

Her eyes held his steadily. "At the end, yes. He
deserved my love much sooner and I couldn't give it
to him because of you."

"And Barnard?"

"He was an old man with a young bride. He was
so happy, Devlin. Taking Isobel back to America.
Delighting in the fact that by marrying her his young
brother would have no claim on his estate. We made
good friends in those few days on the *Titanic*."

Her voice held a pain that agonized him.

"They all died. Milton. Isobel. The duke. Josh. I
had Isobel's purse with me and they marked me off
on the survivor list as Mrs. Milton Barnard. From
then on it just escalated."

"You never thought of telling the truth?"

"Not after I'd met Cyril," Christina said frankly.

He drew her down beside him on a deep sofa. She
lay in his arms. At peace at last.

"And so you're the wealthiest woman in New
York?"

She nodded. A fire burned in the grate of an enormous fireplace.

"I love you Brat, but I don't love this." He fingered
the gold dress, his eyes flickering from the emeralds
to the lavishness of the shadowed room. "I'm glad
you bought the *Ninevah*. It made me see clearly for
the first time in months. I'd got what I wanted and I
was still dissatisfied and it wasn't only because I
hadn't got you. It was something else. The captaincy
of a transatlantic liner is a job for a man at the end of
his career. It's the next thing to a desk job. I want to
be at sea. *Really* at sea. A schooner off the African
coast. Trading from the mainland to Madeira and the

Canaries. Feeling at one with a ship again. Hearing the creak of timbers and fighting the elements with nothing but bare hands and wits. Not shouting orders down to an engine room and being polite to passengers who bore you to death. I hated it and I didn't realize it. Not until now.''

Her fingers touched his face lovingly. ''Then let's go. To Africa and the sun and a ship with sails.''

His arm tightened around her. ''You'll give up all this?''

She pretended to consider and then grinned mischievously.

''To tell you the truth I'm as bored as you are! I'll buy a schooner and leave all this behind!''

''No.'' His eyes held a steely glint there was no arguing with. ''Not a penny of Milton Barnard's money is going into my ship. *I'll* buy the schooner.''

She could feel his heart beating beneath her ear as she rested her head against the comforting strength of his chest. ''All right,'' she said. ''*You* buy the ship. I never want to see Greenwood again. I'll give it to Charlotte Reed. She and Mamba will be happy there. As happy as we will be sailing the seas together.''

Master of his own woman at last, Devlin lowered his head, their lips meeting and clinging, parting only to whisper words of love as his hands removed the golden dress, discarding it as if it were no more than a rag. Once again he caressed the soft swell of her breasts, her nipples rising hard beneath his palm; her body ached with love.

Their bodies glistened in the firelight as Devlin's shirt and breeches followed Christina's clothes into a careless pile. Once again she saw the beautiful sight of his hard sun-bronzed body, the muscular chest and strong thighs, the sweet feel of him as he pressed her close, his hands caressing, tormenting.

''Oh, please, my love. *Please*,'' she whispered. She had been so long without him. She could not bear to wait another moment; another second.

It was like flying. Like nothing else on earth she had ever known. They were one entity, sharing a bliss and a joy so deep it transcended every other physical and emotional experience life had to offer. Devlin and Christina. Christina and Devlin. One without the other was nothing. Only together were they whole.